Dear Reader,

This month I'm delighted to include another book by Kay Gregory, whose first *Scarlet* novel, *Marry Me Stranger* was such a hit with you all. You can also enjoy the second book in Liz Fielding's intriguing 'Beaumont Brides' trilogy.' Then we have another romance from talented author Maxine Barry. *Destinies* is a complete novel in itself, but we're sure you'll want to read *Resolutions* next month to find out 'what happens next!' And finally, we're very pleased to bring you another new author – Laura Bradley has produced an exciting and page-turning story.

Do let me know, won't you, what you think of the titles we've chosen for you this month? Do *you* enjoy linked books and books with a touch of mystery or do you like your romance uncluttered by other elements?

By the way, thank you if you've already written to me. I promise I *shall* answer your letter as soon as I can. Your comments will certainly help me plan our list over the coming months.

Till next month,

Sally Cooper

SALLY COOPER,
Editor – *Scarlet*

About the Author

Maxine Barry lives in a small Oxfordshire village on the edge of the Cotswolds, with her disabled parents and a grey cat called Keats.

She worked for five years as the Assistant College Secretary at Somerville College, Oxford, where she spent most of her free time in the extensive and famous college library, before turning to full-time writing.

Maxine is a skilled calligrapher, and numbers her other hobbies as reading, walking, nature watching and avoiding shopping! *Destinies* is Maxine's fourth title for *Scarlet*, and we're sure you'll want to read its sequel, *Resolutions*, next month.

Other *Scarlet* titles available this month:

THE SHERRABY BRIDES by Kay Gregory
WILD LADY by Liz Fielding
WICKED LIAISONS by Laura Bradley

MAXINE BARRY

DESTINIES

Enquiries to:
Robinson Publishing Ltd
7 Kensington Church Court
London W8 4SP

First published in the UK by Scarlet, 1997

A copy of the British Library Cataloguing in
Publication data is available from the British Library

ISBN 1–85487–722–4

Printed and bound in the EC

10 9 8 7 6 5 4 3 2 1

CHAPTER 1

Germany, 1939

The schloss belonged in a fairytale – a castle of dreams. Its steepled and turreted towers stood tall and proud in the midnight sky as they looked down over lush, meadowed moonlit valleys. But its dungeons were full of prisoners, some dying, some dead already, whilst others sobbed in the darkness, heard only by the Gestapo officers who were their interrogators. A castle of nightmares, then, rather than dreams.

But on this night, Friday the 13th, October 1939, the schloss was also playing host to a social extravaganza. For the guests, the only battle tonight was to be the best dressed, to have the most stunning *coiffure*, to dazzle with the best jewels. For the men, the arena was to be fought in front of Hitler's elite – to have the ear of Goebbels, to be watched with favour by Goering or even any of their leech-like underlings. And for this battle, the castle had been transformed. Floodlights lit up the moat, where swans swam under the windows, ready to pounce gracefully on any scraps thrown their way; brightly coloured

1

paper lanterns hung from the portcullis, whilst music (Mozart, naturally) filled the night air.

Inside the flower-bedecked rooms, the clink of expensive crystal goblets, full of the best wines, fought for supremacy with the bright and brittle laughter of women. Instead of gunpowder smoke, the scent of imported Cuban cigars and finely mixed French cigarettes dissipated in the carefully perfumed air.

Outside, flirting with the mountain breeze, a huge red flag rippled in the crisp October night. Against its stark white centre, a huge black swastika was proudly visible, proclaiming the doctrine of the Third Reich to any and all who might have business on the lonely mountainside, high above sea level.

Wolfgang Helmut Mueller stepped out of the big black car that had transported himself and his wife from their Berlin mansion and surveyed the scene with a brief and coldly satisfied smile, before turning to help his five months pregnant wife from the back of the car.

'Trust Olga to hold her party here,' Marlene Mueller commented bitchily. She took out a compact and checked her make-up. It was, as usual, flawless.

'The Goebbels will be here,' Wolfgang commented with suave satisfaction. 'She'll be desperate for her little soirée to outshine the Press Ball.'

'Of course. But I shall be the belle of *this* ball.'

And Wolfgang didn't doubt it. His wife was perfectly, Teutonically beautiful, with white-blonde hair, and eyes truly a cornflower blue. Her skin, now thirty-six years old, was still flawless and wrinkle-free. Her one regret was that her pregnancy was beginning to show, spoiling the line of her usually svelte and slender figure.

Accompanying her husband into the schloss, she sighed deeply. The Führer was keen on German womanhood adding to the blonde, blue-eyed populace, and Wolfgang had insisted on another son. If only Helmut had been more to his father's liking, Marlene thought bitterly, she might have been spared this . . . this . . . inconvenience, for a second time. She thought briefly of her four-year-old son, waiting for them back in Berlin. He'd cried again when he'd heard that she and Wolfgang would be going out. Maybe, she thought, Wolfgang was right. The boy was a pitiful disappointment . . .

Her head came up and her smile raced into place as they stepped into the hall, the sound of the orchestra filtering sweetly through from the ballroom. By her side, Wolfgang stood tall and straight, the male equivalent of his wife. At six feet two, with blond hair and blue eyes every bit as natural and remarkable as those of his wife, he knew that they were considered to be the racial ideal, in this, the sixth year of Hitler's reign.

Wolfgang was an aristocrat and, like most of his class, secretly despised the lower-class, ranting little tyrant, but even he had been forced to admit that Hitler had restored Germany's strength and pride in a remarkably short time. Now, his fatherland would have another chance to show the world that Germany was the true master of Europe.

They were announced at the top of a pink-marbled flight of stairs and envious eyes watched their triumphant descent. In the uniform of a Luftwaffe major,

Wolfgang looked like a conquering hero of old, his reputation not at all suffering from his sheer good luck in having met, and flown with, Baron von Richthofen, the notorious and much-feared 'Red Baron' of the Great War.

'Wolfgang! Over here.'

Wolfgang nodded briskly at the Colonel who beckoned him, and murmured a brief word to his wife, who inclined her head graciously. Accepting a glass of champagne from a circling waiter, she selected a lesser wife on which to sharpen her claws, and moved into the crowd, smiling like a shark.

Josef Goebbels, Hitler's Minister for Public Enlightenment and Propaganda, lost no time in seeking out Wolfgang, who was a walking propaganda dream. With no Red Baron this time around, Germany needed another aerial ace to worship and adore, and Goebbels had selected Mueller for the job. With a beautiful wife and a blond-haired, blue-eyed son as the ultimate accessories, he was a rousing example of German manhood.

Wolfgang stiffened as Goebbels homed in on him. He would never be foolish enough to forget that, just as Goebbels had 'made' him, he could as easily break him again.

'Wolfgang, glad to see you could make it,' Goebbels greeted him, imperiously clicking his fingers to a passing waiter and selecting a fresh glass of a superior Rhine wine. 'I wasn't sure your wife was feeling up to it.'

4

'She wouldn't have missed it, Herr Goebbels, for all the world.' It was, both men suspected, something of an understatement. Marlene heartily approved of her husband's growing fame and power, and would do anything to ensure it continued.

Goebbels smiled. 'You are hoping for a girl this time?' he asked, nodding towards Marlene.

'No, I want another son,' Wolfgang said shortly.

'Oh?' Goebbels said, eyes narrowing. 'You named your first born . . .?'

'Helmut, Herr Goebbels,' Wolfgang supplied reluctantly.

'He is not . . . satisfactory?' Goebbels went on, his voice as mild as milk, which immediately set off a klaxon of alarm bells in Wolfgang's brain.

'It's not that, Herr Goebbels. He is a fine boy, tall for his age, and already he can read and write. It's just that . . . I suppose I am slightly old-fashioned. I still believe a man cannot have too many sons.'

Goebbels laughed, well pleased with the reply. A son who was not healthy and perfect in every way had no place being born to one of the 'chosen' few. He began to talk of Poland.

Wolfgang felt an immediate sense of relief. It was not that he had lied about his son – his tutor was already raving about his intelligence. In fact, if he'd been asked to pinpoint the exact reasons for his disappointment in the boy, Wolfgang wouldn't have been able to do so. There was just something in the boy's eyes, the way he looked at you . . . He only knew

5

he would be happier once Marlene had presented him with another son. He had the name all picked out – Hans, after his father.

'It appears that Finland is going to oppose Moscow,' Wolfgang said, steering the conversation firmly away from the subject of his family.

Goebbels nodded solemnly. 'Indeed, yes . . . ah, Wagner. I must confess to a weakness for Wagner,' he sighed, as the orchestra began to play a stirring piece. 'Come, meet your Commander-in-Chief,' Goebbels then ordered and, under Marlene's approving eye, her husband was led away to talk over important matters with some of the country's highest leaders.

She turned her thoughts back to dominating the party, and approached the buffet table. Several dashing young SS officers waylaid her there, offering her the tastiest of delicacies arranged on the finest Dresden china. She accepted a little of the more prestigious offerings, but declined the delicious desserts.

Shaking off her fawning audience, she walked through the spacious rooms to the interior balcony that overlooked the ballroom. Everywhere there was the flash of jewels, and the swirl of sumptuous skirts. After surveying the scene for several minutes, Marlene was finally assured that her own necklace of sapphires and pink diamonds were the finest there.

Her eyes narrowed as they sought out her husband and found him dancing with Magda Goebbels. Good. Once Wolfgang was established as *the* darling of the Luftwaffe, she could begin to rest on her laurels. She laughed happily. Excitement was in the air tonight.

Germany was poised on the brink of a glorious and, this time, victorious war. She spied the leader of the *Bunde Deutscher Madel*, the League of German Girls, and graciously approached, preening under the young woman's almost worshipful glance. Marlene was becoming as famous and powerful – in her own way – as her husband; again she laughed happily. A pleasant night of backbiting and compliments stretched ahead.

It was past midnight when Wolfgang excused himself from the presence of the Italian Minister for Popular Culture, and trotted up a spiral staircase in search of a toilet. Opening the first door he came to, his eyes encountered only a dark room, decorated with Louis XVI bergères and an authentic Aubusson carpet. He was about to leave when a slight sound made him hesitate. A soft but unmistakable groan was quickly followed by a harsher one. There was a mirror on the far wall opposite him, reflecting a rounded settee and the couple lying on it.

The girl was no more than twenty, with long dark hair. The top of her dress was undone and, in the moonlight shining through the mullioned windows, Wolfgang could see that her nipples were shiny with saliva. The man on top of her was older, and wearing the uniform of a naval officer. The girl's legs looked milky white as she hooked them over his back, her bare heels drumming on his back.

Wolfgang's eyes narrowed. They were fools to do that here – if Goering happened to stumble on them, there'd be hell to pay.

The man fumbled with his trousers, and in the mirror, Wolfgang saw the man's penis, engorged and hard, spring free. Then, with a forward lunge, he plunged neatly between her spread legs. The girl convulsed, their bodies rising and falling with jerking rapidity. The girl's head flew back against the armrest, her face now full in the moonlight. Wolfgang felt his own loins tighten at the rapturous look on her face. Her mouth fell slighly open and she moaned in low, guttural delight.

Wolfgang left them to it. He was suddenly in a hurry to get home. He knew that Marlene was getting less and less amenable as her pregnancy wore on, but there was always the new maid.

People were already leaving as he stepped across the threshold; within seconds, Marlene appeared by his side. She was always perfectly in tune with his thoughts and wishes, and never publicly disagreed with anything he said. Together they graciously took their leave, of their hostess first, then of Goebbels and Goering. Wolfgang had, of course, made a favourable impression on the chief of the Luftwaffe.

From his upstairs window, the four-year-old boy watched the big black car pull inside the double, wrought-iron gates, his little heart beating harshly. He was supposed to be in bed; if he was caught looking out of the window, he knew he would be beaten. Quickly, he clambered back in, folding the bedclothes neatly around him, just in case his mother came in to say goodnight. She didn't come very often; when she

8

did, she scolded him about the mess he made of his blankets. Every time he woke up they were in disarray, silent testimony to the restless nights he spent, plagued by bad dreams that he could never remember when he woke up.

Downstairs, in the salon, Marlene kicked off her shoes and quickly kissed her husband on the cheek, wishing him goodnight, before he had the chance to suggest something amorous.

In his bed, Helmut heard his mother's footsteps approaching and prayed for her to come to him. He loved the touch of her cold mouth on his forehead, and the way it always made him want to hug her. He never did, of course – he knew it wrinkled his mummy's clothes, and she hated him to touch her pretty hair. But the footsteps went past his room without pausing, so there would be no kisses. Instead he felt the warm wet caress of his own tears slide down his cheeks, and he quickly, furtively, wiped them away. It sent his father into a rage whenever he saw him cry, and Helmut would do anything to avoid being beaten.

The night settled back into its quiet desolation, but Helmut was restless. Perhaps Nanny would make him a hot drink of chocolate if he went to her and told her he couldn't sleep? Of course he'd have to be very quiet. If his father found out . . . Torn between fear of his father and the tortures of the night, he lay in agonized indecision for a few minutes. Then, spurred on by the thought of Nanny, plump soft warmth and soothing, sherry-fumed breath, he pushed the blankets aside. His little feet were bare as he set them upon the floor and walked over to cautiously open the door.

Wolfgang stood by the small casement window and watched the girl undress. She'd shown no sign of surprise on opening the door to his discreet tap and finding him on the other side.

She had the rosy-cheeked complexion that he'd expect from a country girl. At only eighteen, she was already big-breasted, with a triangle of curly golden hair below her belly. For a second or two he just looked at her, and then neatly stripped himself, revealing a well-muscled, slim body and well-endowed manhood. The girl gasped in pleasing admiration.

As she eagerly walked over to him, Wolfgang smiled. Falling to her knees, her hands went unerringly to his member, her fingers closing around it with surprising strength. Wolfgang closed his eyes, his fine, patrician nostrils quivering as he breathed in quickly. 'Ah . . .' what was her name? Urma, was it? – 'Ah, Urma, you have good hands,' he muttered, his voice even more guttural than usual.

The maid smiled. If she pleased him enough, perhaps he would come to her regularly – at least whilst the Frau was pregnant. Leaning forward, she closed her eyes and opened her wide mouth, slowly circling her tongue around the length of his shaft, grazing her teeth around the thick stem with teasing, threatening nips. Wolfgang drew in his breath sharply, his hands resting on the top of her head to steady himself; his own head was thrown back, throat tendons taut with ecstasy.

Made bold by the favourable reaction, Urma pushed him back until he sprawled on the lumpy mattress. Positioning herself atop him, she skewered herself upon his shaft with a grunt of pleasure, and began to move up and down rhythmically. Wolfgang closed his eyes and pictured the more beautiful face of the girl from the schloss. Urma clenched her stomach muscles savagely, making him buck in helpless reaction. Stretching out his hands, he gripped the iron headboard, like a man stretched out on a torture rack. And torture it was – but of the exquisite kind. Sweat stood out on his forehead as his head began to thrash from side to side. He began to moan, uncaring that the noise carried clearly to the other servants through the thin walls, unaware that the sound of his voice had transfixed his young son, who now slowly walked to the door and, goaded by curiosity, began to open it.

Sweat began to trickle down Wolfgang's chest as Urma began to quicken the rhythm, her strong knees on either side of his thighs holding him in a firm vice. He felt his heels dig into the mattress, as his climax pushed his seed to fountain deeply and triumphantly inside her.

Helmut stared at his father's face, a huge knot feeling hard in his chest. He couldn't understand all the heaving and groaning. Why should his father want to fight with Urma? Just then Wolfgang turned his

11

head, his eyes piercing the gloom to transfix his son, who promptly began to shake.

'What the hell are you doing there?' Wolfgang roared. He felt ridiculously ashamed that the boy had been watching his performance.

'I c-c-couldn't sleep, Papa,' Helmut gulped, the hated stutter coming to plague him as he slowly backed away. He never stuttered, except in the presence of his father.

'You've been spying again,' Wolfgang accused him, pulling on his trousers and stalking across to the terrified boy. 'You're nothing but a prying brat!'

'N-no, P-papa. I just w-w-wanted a hot drink . . .'

Leaving the rest of his clothes behind, he hefted the boy under one arm; once back in his son's room, he flung the boy on to the floor, where he cowered under his father's shadow.

'Tears again!' Wolfgang spat, disgusted. 'How many times do I have to tell you, boy? Only girls and weaklings cry.'

Helmut sniffed, hoping to stem the tears, but even that small, pathetic sound served only to enrage his father more. Taking off his belt, Wolfgang roughly hauled the boy by the scruff of his neck and upended him over a chair. Yanking down the boy's pyjama bottoms, he brutally applied the belt to the naked skin. Helmut screamed, and quickly stifled the sound, knowing it would only earn him a longer beating. In the morning, Helmut knew, Nanny would apply home-made salve to the vicious red welts, but he'd still have to sit on a cushion for the next few days.

Eventually, Wolfgang's rage abated, and he turned and left the sobbing child without a word, slamming and locking the door behind him. Helmut knew what that meant – nothing to eat or drink for the next day and night.

With every step pulling at his aching and bruised skin, the child climbed back into bed, pressing his hot cheeks against the cool pillows. Why had he been beaten? It had something to do with the strange thing his father had been doing with Urma. He began to cry again, soft, despairing sounds. But with a maturity that went far beyond his years, little Helmut Mueller finally admitted to himself that nothing he could do would ever make his father love him, or be proud of him.

His father was glad that his mother was going to have another baby. But for Helmut it was sheer agony. It made him want to beat his fists against his mother's rounded belly, to shout and scream his outrage at the thought of someone taking his place. His mother barely noticed him now. If she had another baby to take care of . . . He'd hate the baby – he'd hate it. And he hated his father too. And he hated the whole wide world and everyone in it as well.

That Friday the 13th, little Helmut Mueller came of age.

CHAPTER 2

Kansas, USA: Four Years Later

The day was hot and arid, the kind that sucked you dry of both water and willpower. The sky stretched overhead, sunbaked to a hazy white, and only the merest whisper of a breeze rippled over the young green stems of corn. A rust-riddled beat-up truck spluttered and almost cut out as its driver turned from the highway onto the dirt track that led to the small ramshackle farming community called Burmanville.

Hank Harcourt cursed as the gears jarred. Ramming his foot down on the sponge-like clutch, and using sheer brute force to ram the gearstick home, he cursed again. His face was that of a sixty-year-old, though he was not yet forty. His hat, of indiscriminate pedigree, was floppy and sweatstained around the brim and he lifted it now, tossing it on to the torn passenger seat.

After several miles of rough road, he came to the outermost buildings of the town – if one street, a few stores, and a number of scattered ranches could be called a town. The place had a scorched, dusted look: all faded paintwork and warped wood. A big dun-coloured dog lay panting under a raised sidewalk; as he rattled his way through the potholes, Hank sketched a salute to his old friend Fred Galaway, who owned the only garage for miles.

At this time of day, there was hardly a soul to be seen. A rusty sign squeaked on its hinges, and Hank swatted some flies from his face, hardly noticing that he did so, the gesture having become automatic over the years.

A large van, battered and old, but new to the neighbourhood, had him slowing down. Like all those who lived in the vast cornfields of Kansas, where little ever happened, his curiosity was easily aroused. Hank watched as a stranger dragged a huge table into the general store. He was small in stature, and wore a navy blue suit that was already wrinkled, sweat-stained and dusty. Hank pulled the battered Buick alongside, but did not cut the engine.

'Howdy,' he said, his washed-out brown eyes surveying the stranger with mild friendliness mixed with a touch of contempt. He had the look of a city slicker about him. Somewhere in his late forties, his round, shining face sported a neatly cut black moustache.

'Howdy,' the response came back readily enough, but sounded a little self-conscious, as if the new owner of the Burmanville Stores and Grain Merchants felt uneasy about uttering the laconic, all-American word.

Yep, Hank thought, definitely a city slicker. He reached out his hand, a huge, red, calloused paw and introduced himself. 'Name's Hank Harcourt. I own the High Bluff, about ten miles up the road.'

The stranger's hand was white, and soft. 'Oscar Smith.'

Hank nodded to the van. 'Just movin' in, then?'

'That's right. Mr Jennings was right when he said there was plenty of room.'

Hank grinned. Old Clyde Jennings would have said his store was sat on a goldmine if he thought it would help him sell it. He'd been saying he was gonna move out to Chicago and foist himself on his eldest daughter for years, surprising the whole town out of its collective breeches when he actually upped and did it. Hank surveyed the new man with a keen eye. He looked like the sort who'd charge you for the air you breathed, if he could figure out a way to do it. 'When d'you open again?' he asked, thinking of the state of his stores. June was running low on flour and salt.

'Tomorrow,' Oscar Smith promised promptly.

Giving a laconic nod, Hank was about to go, and had actually slipped the truck back into gear, when a woman appeared from out of the store, dusting her hands free from years of accumulated dirt. 'Lord, Oscar, you should see the . . . Oh, I didn't know you had company.'

Hank found himself being assessed by a pair of bright green eyes as the woman drew level with the truck window. She looked to be in her mid-twenties;

16

under the orange patterned headscarf she wore, just a few stray wisps of bright red hair clung to her damp forehead. Her face was lightly freckled, and her large mouth was pulled into a welcoming smile. But the fulsome image was misleading. Hank soon found himself squirming under her blatantly sexual appraisal.

'This is my wife, Magda. Magda, Mr . . . er . . . Harcourt.' Oscar Smith made the introductions with a reluctance so obvious, it was comical.

'How do you do?' Magda asked, leaning forward to give Hank a glimpse of her impressive cleavage. Hank took her hand like he might take the tail end of a rattler, gave it a quick shake, and quickly dragged his paw back into the safety of the Buick. He was old enough to be her daddy! This one was gonna have the town in an uproar, right from the word go, Hank surmised, half-amused, half-indifferent. Just wait until the women took her measure. He'd soon find all his drinking buddies operating under a strict curfew.

'Won't you come in for a drink, Mr Harcourt?' Magda offered, but Hank hastily refused. A simple man, born of simple farming folk, Hank was a one-woman man. He'd gone to school with June and, when both were seventeen, they had married. They'd had seven kids, and seemed to be holding at that, and his inclination to wander on to pastures new was completely zero.

'I have t'git goin',' Hank muttered. 'I'll probably call in t'morra for a few things, though.'

17

'You do that, Mr Harcourt,' Oscar said, his round little face lighting up at the thought. 'We'll be open from 6 a.m. to 9.p.m. from now on in. Yes, sir.'

'Uh-huh,' Hank muttered, roughly coaxing the old Buick back into first, and pulling away. Once on the road again, he let out a sigh of relief. Just what Burmanville needed – a moneygrabbing storekeeper with a maneater for a wife. Hank was glad there were younger men in town who'd be more-than-eager victims for the green-eyed Magda. Young Jimmy Banks for one . . . Suddenly Hank frowned. No. He was wrong. Soon all the youngsters would be off abroad, to France, and all them sort of places, fighting the Nazis and the Japs.

Hank had been too young for the First World War, and an injured knee from a farming accident five years ago would keep him out of this one. He felt sorry for them Londoners, having their homes blitzed, and their kids blown to bits. But it all seemed like a whole world away from Kansas and the corn. And he bitterly resented the thought of his own sons, and the sons of his lifelong friends, marching away and maybe never coming back.

As he slowed down to pass the town's simple wooden church, with its rickety, picket-fenced cemetery, his eyes strayed, as they always did, to the middle of a row of three, where a wooden cross, bleached white by the sun, stood in a row of similar crosses. His mouth went dry, and he swallowed hard as he lifted his huge hand from the steering wheel and gave a little wave towards the cemetery. 'Hello,

18

Pammy,' he whispered, his eyes watering for a few moments.

A few more miles, and he was back on Harcourt land. Another mile, and he rattled his way past two tall gateposts. They had once had the name '*High Bluff Ranch*' painted in red on a squeaking board hung about them, but it had long since disappeared. The ranch house itself was made of wood and thick mud-brick. As he pulled up in front, he noticed Kier, his youngest son, sitting on the bottom step, industriously drawing something in the sand with a stick. Climbing stiffly out of the truck, he limped around to open the hood, letting the steam gush out before checking the valve, which was red hot. Walking to a water trough, he picked up an old tin can, kept there for just such a purpose, and gave the thirsty truck a good lick of water, careful to shut the hood again. The sun could boil his gasket within hours, if left unprotected.

'Hi, Pa,' Kier said, his face still creased in a frown of concentration. The boy was six, going on seven, and was tall for his age. His hair was the same earthy brown that Hank's had once been, and his brown eyes were still deep and dark, and undimmed by worry and gruelling hard labour. He had the fine looks of his mother – long thick lashes, a straight, manly forehead with thick eyebrows. Already Hank could see that when the boy had a few more years on him, he would be able to have the pick of the girls for miles around. Maybe even get himself a city gal from Kansas City.

'What you got there, son?'

'A storyboard, Pa.'

'A what?'

'A storyboard. Y'know – like in the movies. This picture is of a boy, sneakin' around the back of a shed. Inside is a dog – see? The dog's been stolen and . . .'

'Is that what it is?' Hank interrupted hastily, totally uninterested and watched, half-amused, half-exasperated, as the boy's chin jutted out. Kier had all the stubbornness of a mule. If only the boy would save all his determination for the farm, Hank thought uneasily. But all Kier could talk about was Hollywood, and all this talk of movies was beginning to worry him. It was all Jim Cleever's fault for starting up a picturehouse in the first place. Ever since the kid had first seen John Wayne's *Stagecoach*, Hank felt as if he'd lost him.

'Have you chopped the wood for your ma?'

'Yes, Pa.'

'Good. I suppose you'd better do your homework, or Miss Ritter will be complainin' again.'

'I already done it, Pa. She say's I'm doin' real good in English, and she's even gonna let me write a story for the school play. Can you believe it? Ain't that great, Pa?'

Hank shrugged off his doubts. The boy was not yet seven. At Kier's age, Hank had wanted to drive a locomotive from the Pacific to the Atlantic. But now, nearing his fortieth birthday, he had never even been out of the state. But . . .

'I don't want you writing no play. The school never did plays when I went there. When is it, anyway?'

20

Kier felt his stomach dip in disappointment. He looked down at the sand, his lower lip trembling. 'Don't know, Pa,' he lied. Miss Ritter had warned him that just because he could write the play, it didn't mean he could play the biggest lead. She had looked quite amused when he'd sombrely explained that he didn't want to be an actor, just make sure the play went right. When Miss Ritter had jokingly said that it seemed that they had a new Cecil B. De Mille in their midst, he'd heard, for the first time, the word 'director'.

'Hmm. Well, your mother'll know, I expec',' Hank said, limping past his son into the house. Walking on through, he found his wife hanging out the washing on the clothes line at the back, and Hank paused in the doorway to watch her. Like himself, she looked far older than her years. Her shoulders were stooped, and the hair that hung limply to her shoulders was already turning grey. Her belly protruded in mute testimony to all her years of childbearing, but it was in cruel contrast the rest of her, which was so skinny and fleshless that she seemed to be a collection of sticks. Yet she was humming as she hung up the washing, and when she turned and saw him, her face broke out into a ready and still dazzling smile. Hank did not envy Oscar Smith his pretty, dissatisfied young wife.

But her smile couldn't hide the pain so obvious in her eyes. Ever since Doc John had told him she had cancer, that dreaded word that was never spoken of in polite company, Hank had known both terror and despair. Doc John had gently told him that his June had only months left. Hank had no idea what he'd do without her. Even though he'd decided not to tell her, and even though she never talked about it, Hank knew that she knew. The gnawing pains in her belly had nothing to do with the 'change', as Doc John had maintained. The knowledge was there in her eyes, in the way she would stop to stare at her children, as if imprinting them on her memory. It was there in the way her hands would squeeze tightly around his as they lay in bed at night. He wasn't sure whether it was to give him comfort, or because, in the dark night-time hours, she felt more afraid than she did when the sun was shining and the corn buntings were singing.

'You look good,' Hank told the lie lovingly, characteristically clumsy in his compliments. June didn't mind. He meant them – every one, and that was all that mattered to her. She gave him another smile.

'Did you get the chickenwire?' she asked, picking up the empty wicker basket, which he quickly took away from her and carried into the house. She silently followed him, a soft smile on her lips. The basket weighed next to nothing, and she'd just spent hours on the hand-wash tub, then another hour painstakingly putting the clothes through the mangle. Not that she begrudged the hard work. She knew that her husband laboured all the hours of God's day, and would labour even harder now that Pete was goin' . . . Every day she prayed Pete would come back, but if he didn't, then at least she, Pammy and Pete would all be together. They could wait for Hank and the others together. She didn't have any clear idea of what Heaven would be like, but she'd been raised a solid Baptist all her life, so she knew, with a certainty that was as strong as rock, that it did exist, and that it waited for her and all her children. 'Pastor Shimmidy came by this mornin',' she said, putting the kettle over the fire that perpetually burned in the grate, and spooned coffee grains into a battered tin pot. 'He said Amy was a natural-born singer. Asked if we had thought about having her voice trained . . . y'know, professionally, and everything.'

Hank grunted, but his eyes were fond. Amy, Kier's elder sister by three years, was the apple of his eye. 'Can't afford it,' he said heavily, and June nodded complacently.

'I already told him that,' she said, then looked carefully away. 'Did Kier tell you his good news yet?'

'Good news?'

'About the school play.'

'Oh – that. It's a waste of time. I told the boy so.'

June added raw sugar to the mugs, then gasped as pain savagely lanced through her body. She grabbed the worktop hard. In moments she felt his hands on the tops of her arms, aware that his tears were sliding down the back of her neck to run, hot and straight, down the ridges of her spine. She collapsed into a chair, taking deep, agonizing breaths. Wordlessly, despairingly, Hank straightened and poured out the coffee, unable to look at her in case his big heart burst on the spot. When the worst was over she took the cup he offered her with hands that would not stop shaking, and took a sip.

When she'd collected herself, she leaned back in the chair. What she had to do next was too important to let a small thing like pain stop her. 'Kier is different from the rest, Hank,' she said quietly, knowing she must get a promise from him before it was too late. For her, and for Kier. 'I've read the stories he keeps writing – you haven't.'

Hank blushed. He was not that good a reader.

'He's not like Marty or Pete. He don't have the soil in his blood like you all do.'

Hank sighed. 'I reckon that's true enough.'

'We've got to give him room, Hank. You've got to let him have his dreams, and let him go after 'em, when the time comes. He's good at schoolin', and Miss Ritter says she's gonna steer him towards a scholarship. Maybe even Oxford . . . y'know, in England. Promise me, Hank?' June pleaded, her soft voice raw with the pain that still ate at her.

Hank could see it in her eyes, and he quickly nodded his big craggy head. He'd do anything for his June. 'All right, darlin'. I promise.' His hand groped blindly for hers on the table top, his fingers engulfing them.

Outside, Kier Harcourt began to draw a new scene for his play. He was still too young to know what tragedy meant. But he'd learn, soon enough.

CHAPTER 3

Atlanta, Georgia – One Year Later

The mansion belonged in a scene from *Gone With The Wind*. Riveree, a fourteen-bedroomed, white-columned, gleaming and elegant edifice, stood on a gently sloping hill, looking out over the willow-draped expanse of the Chattahoochee river, flowing north of Atlanta. Moss-draped trees shaded it, whilst bougain-villea bled purple, scarlet and pink blooms from every flower bed. Clarissa Somerville opened the french windows at the east wing, and stepped on to a terrace. Her hair was ivory blonde and pulled into an elegant chignon. Her eyes were slate-grey, her skin, at thirty-two, was still as creamy and pink as the magnolia blossoms that lined the great driveway. Her figure was exquisite, and she fitted in at Riveree like a human extension of the house.

'I'll have the tea out here please, Billie,' she informed the black maid in her usual lazy, southern drawl, and pulled out a wrought-iron garden chair as the maid left to do her bidding. Life should have been wonderful for Clarissa Somerville. She was rich, beautiful and the leading light of Atlanta society. But she was so vulnerable, she lived in a state of constant anxiety. For Clarissa Somerville was also in love. And not with her husband.

'Your tea, ma'am.' the maid said as she returned. 'Will the master be coming home soon, ma'am? Cook's worried about him over in them foreign parts.'

'No, Billie, he can't leave Switzerland for some time,' she explained patiently, yet again.

'Yes, ma'am,' Billie replied miserably, and left. Clarissa continued to stare out over the beautiful gardens, her mind on other things. On a shabby cabin outside Burford, to be exact. Clarissa knew she'd have to go to him soon. She'd held out as long as she could, and now she was so restless it felt like a physical pain. She wandered into her husband's study, hoping to find something there to keep her mind distracted.

On the wall was a portrait of her mother- and father-in-law, ninth-generation Somervilles. Clarissa had been born a Charleston Gough, and everyone had agreed what a good match their families had made. Duncan Somerville's mother had been urging him to marry and produce an heir for years, and Clarissa knew that she wouldn't find a better husband than the amenable Duncan. If it was actually Riveree that she had fallen in love with at first sight . . . Well. One couldn't have everything. She'd settled down to become a good wife and hostess. The parties she'd thrown were all spectacular successes and written up reverently in the Atlanta press. She'd even produced the much anticipated Somerville heir. True, the child had been a daughter, but a woman could inherit as easily as a boy. And again, everyone had been so pleased. After all, heiresses were very fashionable.

Thoughts of her precious daughter spurred Clarissa on to the upstairs nursery, where squeals of laughter greeted her.

Her five-year-old might be dressed in white lace and organdy, but she rode her rocking horse as if it were a bucking bronco. Old Jennie stood with hands either side of her, to catch her if she should fall. But Oriel would not fall. She was too far too tenacious. Clarissa's child might have her ivory hair, grace, and beauty, but she had a strength of indomitable will that couldn't have come from either Clarissa or her easy-going father. Her eyes were a lovely periwinkle blue, and Clarissa felt her heart swell as she watched her daughter play. She was so talented, wayward and brilliant. Clarissa had Oriel's future as carefully planned as one of her own parties. The best school, the Ladies Academy in Charleston, followed by a year at a Swiss finishing school. Then home for a dazzling débutante season, and then marriage. To the richest, the best, the finest. 'Hello, my angel.' Clarissa kissed her daughter, her voice thick with emotion.

'Look!' Oriel gurgled, riding the horse with fierce abandon.

'Very nice, darling,' Clarissa murmured. 'Your daddy would be proud.' Oriel missed her father, and Clarissa faithfully read her his letters. Clarissa had made no demur when Duncan had joined the diplomatic service. It pleased her to see him happy, and it meant she'd have Oriel to herself for a while.

'Whoa there, poppet. You'll wear poor Dobbin out,' Clarissa scolded mildly, ruffling her daughter's hair.

'Don't care!' Oriel said, chuckling with high good humour as the room whizzed past her, her tummy doing funny somersaults that tickled.

'I'm going out for lunch today, Jennie. Make sure she eats her greens.'

'I will, Miss Clarry,' Jennie said, both women ignoring the child's woeful wails.

Downstairs, Clarissa paused in the high-ceilinged hall to check her reflection in the cheval glass. Her cheeks were flushed. She knew why, of course. She always looked that way when she was about to visit Kyle. It was ridiculous. The boy was practically a peasant, the youngest son of Burford's garage mechanic, and seemed perpetually dirty. Sometimes she'd make him shower. And then again, sometimes she wouldn't. It depended on how desperate she was for him. He was young, almost fiercely resentful of her wealth, and could be crude, ill-mannered and downright brutal. He was also the most spectacularly handsome young man she'd ever seen in her life. And she was viciously in love with him. It terrified her. If anyone found out, she'd be ruined. Her family would be scandalized. Her husband disgraced. But she was helpless. She could no more live without Kyle than she could breathe.

She got into her imported Bugatti sports car, her heart racing. She drove on autopilot, the outskirts of

Decatur and Eastpoint, Atlanta's suburbs, giving way quickly to the dreaming countryside. She paid no attention to the beautifully blooming orchards of citrus fruit, and the ubiquitous cotton, in their neat rows, were so commonplace as to be beneath her notice. Her thighs trembled in delicious anticipation. She knew it was madness, but put her foot down on the accelerator anyway. After an hour of steady driving she turned off onto the backroads and at last, the deserted cabin came into sight. She parked the car under the shade of an ancient oak, her stomach churning. As a lover, Duncan had been adequate, nothing more, but Kyle . . . With hands that shook, she opened the car door, and set her Nona Roche shoes onto the rutted dirt track. Kyle must never know the power he had over her. He must never know how much he obsessed her. If he did . . . she would be powerless. So it was that Clarissa Somerville acted the rich, tough bitch. In their relationship, she was the dominant one. The demanding one. And she played her role so well, she knew that Kyle hated her as much as he loved her.

She walked straight in without knocking, and headed for his bedroom. It was his day off, but he wasn't expecting her. Kyle never knew when she'd suddenly show up, all but ravish him, then leave again, to go back to her fancy house, and her fancy friends.

The room was dark, but her eyes were drawn like magnets to the young man sleeping on the bed. His shirt was off, showing a lightly muscled chest. His skin was tanned light brown, the nipples a darker, beckoning aureole. His jeans were dusty and rumpled, his feet bare and dirty. Clarissa felt her heart begin to trip harder as she slowly walked to the bed. She gazed down at his peacefully sleeping face, which was so handsome it made her breath catch. Although his hair was raven black, his complexion was surprisingly fair. His eyes, when they were open, were of the deepest navy blue that turned black when he was in throes of passion. And Clarissa loved to watch those eyes turn black . . . He was only nineteen, and looked it. The difference in their ages terrified her. Soon she would be forty, and he would think her old and ugly . . . She dragged her agonizing thoughts away from that road. Instead, she drank him in. His cheekbones were high and very finely shaped, his mouth sensitive. His tongue was long . . .

He murmured something, turning on the old-fashioned, kingsized bed. Clarissa slipped off her shoes and stockings. She hesitated only a moment before slipping off her panties too. Doing a slight gyration, she removed her bra without removing her dress, and felt her nipples press turgidly against the silk, yearning for the feel of his moist, hot tongue. But she remained silent, wanting to prolong the agony of waiting. His body had a tensile strength that she found thrilling. She stirred restlessly, feeling her thighs sliding together, made slippery by the juices that dripped from her own ivory triangle. The noise, slight though it was, woke him. In an instant he was up on his elbows, alert, his senses attuned to danger. His eyes focused on her immediately, and a smile, an almost ugly, yet reluctantly hungry smile, settled across his mouth.

Clarissa swallowed hard. She liked this game, even as it terrified her. 'Hello, boy,' she said softly, the term deliberately derogatory. Her use of it was purely defensive. She had to make him think he meant nothing more than that to her. She had to keep the upper hand. Her life – in a very real sense – depended on it.

'Hi, bitch,' Kyle said, slowly sitting up and swinging his legs to the floor. Clarissa quickly moved to stand in front of him before he could rise, looking down at him with a mocking, challenging smile. Kyle's lips pulled back into a sneer as their eyes met, clashed, and fought. Then the sneer vanished as he slowly looked at her bulging nipples, clearly visible through the creamy silk, now almost directly on eye level with him. Noticing how her lovely face had become tight and tense, he slowly leaned forward, his eyes never leaving hers until the last second before he fastened his mouth on one silk-covered breast.

Clarissa cried out, her whole body rippling in tiny shocks. She felt his arm come around her waist, and her knees buckled as she was pulled roughly onto the bed. 'Kyle,' she moaned as his dirty hand thrust into the clean, gardenia-scented freshness of her hair, and dragged it free of its elegant chignon. His fingers twisted in her hair as he jerked her head back, at the same time twisting his body over hers so that she was half-sitting and half-lying on the bed and he was leaning over her.

Her eyes, a stormy, sea-grey, opened with startled pain, and he stared at her for a long agonizing second whilst they fought a silent, familiar battle. Then, after what seemed an age, he lowered his lips to her exposed throat. She gasped, then moaned, as he ripped her dress open, forcing her back against the mattress as he did so. She was breathing hard now as he stared down at her. Kyle watched her eyes, not his own hands, as he slowly caressed her breasts, brushing his thumb across her nipples, smiling grimly at the way she shuddered with every rough caress. He moaned softly, almost despairingly, as he acknowledged that he was as hooked as she was. They were like a mutual drug, each needing a fix, each denying it until it drove them crazy.

'Oh, Clarry,' he said despairingly, then, with infinite gentleness, he lowered his head and suckled on her breast, greedily pulling its peak deep into his mouth, his tongue pressed flat and hard against the nipple. Clarissa closed her eyes, her body quivering in reaction. 'I hate you,' Kyle said softly, leaving her breasts to kiss her stomach, slowing making his way to her navel.

'Why?' she groaned, her breath leaving her in a pained gasp as his tongue dipped into the indentation on her stomach and flickered against her flesh.

'Because you make me want you,' he muttered angrily, his voice thick and harsh. 'You're a bitch – a rich bitch, who looked, and wanted.'

Clarissa laughed, knowing by the way he paled that she had hurt him. Instinctively she went to touch him, but then gasped as his hands suddenly jerked open her thighs. 'Want this, bitch?' he snarled, and dipped his head quickly, his fingers opening the womanly lips he found there, clearing the way for his tongue, which he thrust deep inside her. Clarissa arched convulsively in shock, but he was ready for her, his hands clasping her hips to hold her ruthlessly still.

'Oh, Kyle!' Clarissa screamed, her head jerking from side to side on the pillows as she writhed helplessly. Kyle's tongue was hot on her clitoris as he pleasured her without mercy. It was payback time.

If they met on the street, she looked through him like he was garbage, and then she came here, to his house, like a bitch on heat wanting . . . wanting this, he thought savagely, lifting his mouth from between her scented thighs and then delving two fingers deep inside her. He stretched alongside her as he did so, taking her chin in his hand to stare into her glazed eyes as he stroked her with erotic, savage skill. She stretched her legs, helplessly clamping her thighs together, but he was too strong for her. Panting, with their faces only an inch away, he found her clitoris once more and began to stroke it in a circular motion that drove her wild.

'You bastard,' she moaned, her legs jerking helplessly as he ruthlessly pushed her to a climax. She jerked, moaned and then lay panting, breathing in great gulps of air. While she lay, reclaiming her breath, Kyle took off his jeans.

'That Bugatti of yours needs tunin'. Bring it in to Dad's garage tomorrow.'

'All right.' She watched the jeans come off, and then he turned to face her, showing her the bulge in the square white briefs. 'Come here,' she demanded, her arms out.

'I need a new car,' Kyle said flatly. As revenge, it wasn't much, but it was the best he could think of.

'I'll buy you one,' she promised, feverishly. 'Just come here!' She sat up as he came to the bed and stood beside her. Greedily, her hands reached for the briefs and dragged them down over his thighs. She gasped, as she always did, at the size of his manhood, and her hand closed greedily around it. It felt on fire – hard as iron, and soft as velvet.

'I'm gonna own that garage one day,' he said. 'That and dozens like it, all over the south.'

Clarissa smiled. 'You're a greedy little boy, Kyle. A lower-class, dirty, greedy . . .' Her words broke off as he pounced on her with a snarl, coming down on top of her, roughly grasping her wrists and pinning them above her head. Without entering her, he slowly gyrated his body, rubbing his penis against the side of her thigh. She whimpered. He smiled. 'Kyle! Oh, Kyle . . .'

He felt the power of the moment, like an aphrodisiac, bite deep into him, but he wasn't fooled. His power was only of the moment, whereas hers was total. If she should withdraw her custom from the garage, he'd be out of a job. A word from her in the Sheriff's ear would have him thrown in jail, on any charge she cared to make. And she knew it. He hated her. And wanted her. Oh yes, he wanted her. Slowly he positioned himself at the very tip of her opening, and with a slow push began to enter her, only to stop and withdraw, and then enter her again. Clarissa moaned and thrust her hips up, but he was too quick and drew away. He began again, tormenting her, tormenting himself. Sweat broke out on his forehead, but though she pleaded, cursed, threatened, begged, he did not thrust fully into her.

Only when they were both on the verge of insanity did he suddenly bury himself deep inside her, and her scream, pure and high, reverberated around the tiny cabin. Her nails dug into his back, drawing blood, but he hardly noticed. His mates at the garage had become used to the scratches on his back whenever he stripped off his shirt. He fielded their coarse suggestions and ribald teasing with satisfied goodwill. If he were to tell them who had put them there, they'd die of envy. But Kyle was not stupid.

He plunged into her with sure strokes that buried the entire length of him in her. The southern princess was skewered to a lumpy mattress, staring at a dirty, flaking ceiling, and ecstatically enjoying every moment of it. She moaned, her heels making indents in his buttocks as she clamped him savagely. But he took his own time, slowly building the rhythm, forcing her to one climax after another until they all seemed to roll into one long, torturous torment of ecstasy.

'Kyle!' she screamed, her elegant, perfectly made-up face contorted with pleasure, her lips bitten free of lipstick, her elegant, upper-class body bathed in his sweat and her own, smeared here and there with oil and dirt. 'Kyle! Ohhhhh . . .' she shuddered, bucking so hard they almost fell to the floor.

He felt his own climax coming, and convulsed, the warning alerting her just in time. Quickly her hands went to his face, holding him still. 'Look at me,' she commanded, her elegant southern drawl harsh and demanding. 'Look at me, you bastard,' she screamed, driven beyond endurance. 'I want to watch. I want to see it in your eyes. I want to see the exact moment when your mind blows out of your head.'

Kyle snarled and tried to shake his head free, but it was too late. His body was exploding, his climax destroying him. He screamed, his eyes turning obsidian, his young, flushed face suddenly innocent again, but racked with the pain of his explosive orgasm. 'Clarissa,' he moaned helplessly, shuddering his seed into her.

Clarissa laughed, her hands holding his face as she claimed her prize. Oh, how she loved him. 'Poor Kyle,' she said tenderly as his strong, dominating body collapsed weakly atop her, all his wonderful strength spent inside her.

Kyle's head dropped onto her shoulder as he took deep shuddering breaths. He was almost crying as her hands stroked his damp scalp in tender, semi-circles. After a few minutes she rolled him onto his back. His arms lay limp beside him, his body drained.

'You can check the oil in my car before I go,' she ordered.

Kyle closed his eyes briefly, then opened them again. 'One of these days,' he said, his voice totally devoid of all emotion, 'I'm going to kill you, Clarissa.'

Clarissa looked down at him, then smiled. 'Not if I kill you first,' she said. And ran her hand up his thigh. He frowned, a helpless, totally stunned look flashing across his eyes as his body leapt at her touch. Soon he could only moan helplessly, cries of agony, of pleasure, of despair.

Clarissa watched him, outwardly trimphant but secretly beaten. For she couldn't help but touch him, anymore than he could help but respond to her touch. 'Poor Kyle,' she said, again, lowering her lips to within a millimetre of his but not kissing him, her hand busily at work, her hawk-like eyes feeding on every fleeting expression in his darkening eyes. He moaned again, his back arching off the bed.

'Poor, poor, Kyle.'

And poor Clarissa.

CHAPTER 4

Germany, April 1945

Wolfgang Mueller's armoured car paused momentarily at the gates of Koblenzi concentration camp as two privates scurried to raise the barrier. He was leaving the hellhole for the last time – though no one, as yet, knew it. The rats were deserting the Nazi ship with a speed that had set the top brass reeling. The defection of Hess in the early years had been little more than a propaganda defeat, but now not even Goebbels's expert media manipulation could hide the galling truth. The war was all but over. And Wolfgang Mueller was about to disappear. He'd planned long and hard to secure his own future – now, all he needed was some final insurance. Which was why he was headed for Berlin, instead of south, to Lake Constance and the charming town of Meersburg, where his wife and sons waited for him.

Wolfgang could admit to himself that he was scared. He'd sent his adjutant, Lt Heinlich, ahead, with specific orders to retrieve all files relating to Wolfgang that were currently being kept in SS files. These were dangerous times . . .

The last horrific year was one that Wolfgang would never forget. Germany had lost the war. April 1st had seen the evacuation of the Hela Peninsula by German naval forces, and the 13th had seen Vienna fall to the Allies.

As the car began to approach the suburbs of Berlin, Wolfgang knew what must, inevitably, follow, and he planned to be long gone when it did. He had had all his cash turned into precious gems, and through his contacts, had already shipped most of his more precious heirlooms onto a neutral South American steamship that was currently on its way to the Mediterranean, where Monte Carlo awaited. Wolfgang was going to be very rich, very shortly, but he needed insurance badly. There was going to be a first-class witch-hunt by the surviving Jews and Wolfgang, as Commandant of Koblenzi, knew himself to be a prime target. If only he hadn't been wounded so badly that he'd had to stop flying. He'd hated the boredom that had been his life at the camp, and the loss of kudos had been hard to bear.

The car turned into Kantstrasse and quickly accelerated. Everywhere the streets seemed ominously deserted. He made a quick stop on Perlebergerstrasse to say a tearful farewell to his mistress, then was once again back in the car, turning on to Leipzigerstrasse where the secret records office of the SS were hidden underground. Wolfgang strode confidently into the building, his rings, forged orders and his naturally commanding bearing easily allowing him to dispense with the fanatical SS guards.

The underground bunker was a poorly lit rabbit warren, full of bustling, sharp-eyed but pale women. Wolfgang made his way immediately to the office of his old friend Karl Zimmelmann.

'Wolf, my friend. I didn't know you were due in town.'

'I'm not,' Wolfgang said, quickly coming to the point. 'I want to see the records for Koblenzi.'

Karl said nothing for several seconds, simply looking into his friend's eyes with a long, level stare. 'You want to destroy them?' he asked softly, and Wolfgang paused, then nodded. If Karl would not help him, he'd kill him here and now. He had planned on pointing the finger of blame for the missing records on Heinlich, anyway. A murder, added to treason, would hardly make any difference.

'Of course,' Karl said, not the slightest trace of censure in his voice. 'Follow me.'

As he followed him even further into the labyrinth, Wolfgang wondered if Karl's own escape route was as safe as his own. 'Here. You've got ten minutes.' Karl opened a thick steel door to reveal rows and rows of filing cabinets.

Wolfgang nodded. 'Thanks. Are you all right . . . financially?'

'Of course. This is for old times' sake.'

Wolfgang clapped him on the back. '*Ja*, old friend.'

The moment the door closed he set to work, burning all the Koblenzi records in a big tin waste-

40

bin. Wolfgang watched the evidence disappear in smoke, and his handsome lips curved up in a whimsical smile. Behind him the door opened, and Karl coughed. 'A few more minutes,' Wolfgang said, not turning around. 'My man Heinlich is at the Tauentzienstrasse bunker. Can I borrow a couple of your police?'

Karl nodded. 'You have him in mind for a scapegoat?'

Wolfgang nodded. 'After I've recovered the documentation from him,' he confirmed. The SS were not so foolish as to keep all records in one place, and the other site held lesser, but still damning, proof of his Nazi involvement.

'I'll call the Section Overseer and have Heinlich held.'

'Good.' Wolfgang paused, then held out his hand. 'Good luck, Karl.'

'You also, my friend.'

His car was parked neatly in front of the offices. The day was appropriately dank and a dismal grey rain began to fall. Once at the Tauentzienstrasse offices, he was met by Otto Von Schtrom, the section superviser, with bad news. 'The traitor Heinlich has fled, Commandant. A record clerk showed him into the Camp section, as per your written orders, but after the call from Herr Zimmelmann, we found he had disappeared.'

Wolfgang felt surprised rage explode in his head, and he swallowed hard, keeping his voice level with the greatest of effort. 'What is missing?'

The supervisor was obviously waiting for this question and checked a list, quickly reeling off information. Again Wolfgang was surprised. The weasel had taken not only damning evidence against himself, but against other top-ranking officials. 'I see,' he said grimly, slipping back into the car. 'You have a search party out looking for him?'

'*Ja*, Herr Commandant.'

Wolfgang nodded, but did not hold out much hope, curtly answered the supervisor's salute, and gave the driver his instructions. 'The Hauptbahnof – quickly.'

The driver nodded, heading the car towards the main railway station with a knowing smile. In the back, Wolfgang seethed. He had underestimated Heinlich, a thing he very rarely did.

Wolfgang alighted at the train station and commandeered a seat on a goods train carrying coal. The countryside they travelled through was ravaged, the cities bombed and bleak. He was nervous, jumping every time the train stopped. But as the countryside began to become more mountainous as it neared the Swiss border, so Wolfgang began to smile. If only he knew where his treacherous adjutant was . . .

Frederich Heinlich stood on the Seestrasse in Meersburg, his eyes scanning the lake for the fishing boat that was going to take him across to Switzerland. He patted the briefcase he held to his chest with a small, smug smile, then quickly turned away as a tall blonde woman with two little boys turned his way. He was not out of the woods yet. If he'd known his superior was only hours away, and getting closer, he'd have been feeling a lot less sure of himself.

Marlene Mueller found a seat that overlooked the lake and sat down. 'Come here, Helmut,' she called impatiently as her eldest son wandered to the railings, next to the funny little man with the briefcase.

'Yes, Mama,' he said, but made no move to go to her.

Marlene sighed, and pulled Hans onto the bench beside her. Helmut picked up a stone and threw it. White water-birds bobbed on the azure blue lake. He'd felt no great misery on leaving Berlin, and looked forward to the adventure with half-hearted enthusiasm.

Marlene would be glad when Wolfgang arrived. She felt nervous on her own, and prey to bitterness. Damn the Allies! She thought with bitterness of all the things they'd had to leave behind – the paintings and grand piano that were worth a small fortune, the chandeliers and carpets, the beautiful Austrian furniture.

'What's Monte Carlo like, Mama?' Helmut asked, suddenly materializing at her side and making her jump.

'Stop sneaking up on people,' she snapped.

Helmut had grown even taller for his age, showing all the signs of the striking good looks that would shortly be his. His blonde hair was turning a light copper, and his face was square and firm-jawed.

Helmut shrugged and turned away, looking craftily at the man whose gaze was scouring the water with painful intensity. Helmut was sure he'd seen the man before. He had an almost photographic memory, and he never forgot a face. Helmut suspected that he was some SS officer on the way to Switzerland, like his own father. The way he hugged the briefcase, as if expecting someone to snatch it, gave him away as nothing else could. He's a fool, Helmut thought, with swingeing disapproval. Why didn't he sit down in a café, have a drink, look normal?

As if aware of the close scrutiny, Frederich looked around, but relaxed on seeing only the boy. Helmut almost snapped his fingers. Why it's Lt . . . Lt . . . Heinz? No, Heinlich, his father's adjutant. But why hadn't father told them the man would be coming with them? He turned reluctantly when his mother called him, and silently followed her back to the hotel. Hans, his four-year-old brother, was busily sucking a lolly. He had not been offered a lolly, and when Marlene wasn't looking, he quickly flicked his finger against his brother's hand. Hans wailed as the red ice slipped and fell to the pavement. 'You did that on purpose,' Hans accused, his little fists swinging in Helmut's direction.

'Did not,' he lied.

'Just because Mama didn't buy you one.'

For a moment Helmut felt tears sting his eyes, and he gritted his teeth. 'That's because I'm too old to have a lolly,' he said defensively. 'You're just a kid. I'm nearly a grown-up.'

Marlene turned, arms akimbo. 'Come on, you two, or I'll tell your father you've been bad.' At that dire threat, both boys hurried to catch up with her.

It was nearly two hours later when Wolfgang joined them. She expressed no joy at his safe arrival, neither did she kiss him. For his part, Wolfgang strode straight over to Hans and hoisted him into the air. Hans gurgled wildly. 'The boat's already in the harbour,' he said briefly, setting the boy back down. 'Are the things packed?' Marlene nodded.

The captain of the small battered fishing boat was Swiss, of German descent, and nodded curtly to Wolfgang, who thanked him and immediately went to a small wheelhouse where he changed into civilian clothing. Heinlich, sat on the deck by some tarpaulin, froze at the sound of Mueller's voice. His face bleached white, and he dove under the tarpaulin on his belly, to lay there quivering. He'd paid the captain extra to keep quiet, and the fisherman had no idea of any connection between them, but would he mention to his illegal passenger the fact that he was not alone on this boatride to freedom?

For the first time in his life, Frederich Heinlich began to pray . . .

Within moments the little fishing vessel was pulling out of the harbour. Helmut stood at the rails, watching the German coastline slowly disappear. Wolfgang emerged dressed in a sober black suit and walked over to Marlene, who stood weeping quietly a little further along the rails. Helmut moved a few steps closer the better to hear them. 'Be quiet,' Wolfgang said, a thread of steel running through his voice. 'The crew will see.'

'I can't help it,' Marlene murmured.

Wolfgang swore under his breath. 'I know. But we'll soon get used to Monte Carlo. You'll see.'

Marlene wiped her eyes, and sniffed. 'I still think we should go to Bolivia.'

'We're not living in that godforsaken backwater. Don't worry. Our new identies are iron-clad. We're Americans, of German descent. Even our children have American names now. It's rather ironic, don't you think?'

Marlene shrugged, in no mood to see the joke. Her own name was now Mary, a name that she thought sounded utterly ugly. Hans was now Henry and Helmut had chosen the name Wayne, mainly, she suspected, to offend his father, who had said grimly that it was just the kind of name he would have expected Helmut to choose. 'I hope our things will arrive on time,' she said querulously. 'What if the ship is sunk?'

'It won't. The house is already rented, the papers are safely here . . .' He patted his breast pocket, where there were passports, insurance numbers, identity cards and every other certificate and documentation needed to start a new life. 'Before long, we'll be speaking French like natives, and English too. How are the boys' lessons progressing?'

Marlene shrugged. 'Helmut . . .'

'Wayne,' he corrected sharply.

'Wayne,' Marlene repeated dutifully, 'is almost word perfect already. His tutor says he has an excellent brain.'

'And Hans?'

'Henry – ' Marlene took pleasure in correcting him '– is coming along.' Then she sighed wearily. 'I hate it that they have to lose their heritage, their . . .'

'I know. But it can't be helped. And it's more imperative now than ever that they adapt quickly. That bastard Heinlich has disappeared with the documents I sent him to collect.'

Marlene gasped, turning ashen. 'Wolf . . .'

'It's all right. No one will connect Marcus D'Arville and family of Monte Carlo, with the Berlin Muellers, that I promise you. Besides, Heinlich will probably be shot as a traitor before he has gone a hundred miles.'

Under the tarpaulin, Heinlich began to sweat. He must stay hidden until the Muellers had disembarked on the other side. The captain knew a way to dodge the Swiss patrol boats, and already they were headed for a little cove, miles from the nearest Swiss town or border post. Now, Heinlich froze as he saw that his tie was lying outside the tarpaulin. His hands shook crazily as he lifted the tarpaulin a bare inch and began to pull it in.

With his peripheral vision, Helmut saw the movement and turned, bending down on his knees a scant yard away from the sweating man. For a second, startled brown eyes stared into grave blue ones. Too late, Heinlich recognized his superior's son. Helmut smiled. Slowly Heinlich let the canvas cover him, his heart beating so hard he felt sick. He felt smothered, gagging. He was surely going to die. He waited for Wolfgang's brat to call out to his father. But a minute passed, and nothing happened. Then Mueller's voice was closer. 'Well, Wayne, we'll soon be in Switzerland. I hear you've progressed well with your language studies.'

'Yes, Papa.' Wolfgang did not praise him, and Helmut did not expect him too. 'Didn't Lt Heinlich come to dinner once, Papa?' Helmut asked, knowing that Heinlich would be in a state of near hysteria by now, listening to every word they uttered.

'I think so. Why?'

'Wasn't he small, with beady rabbit-brown eyes and dark hair?' Helmut prompted, glorying in his knowledge, his first taste of power. It was so heady and sweet. He knew, in that instant, that he must have more of it – much more.

'That's right,' Wolfgang said sharply. 'Why?'

'Oh, nothing.' Helmut shrugged. 'I just heard you talking to Mother about him. Would you like to know where he is, Papa?' Under the tarpaulin, Heinlich stuffed his knuckled fist into his mouth and wet himself.

'Indeed I would,' Wolfgang said savagely. 'Have you seen him?'

Heinlich waited, his hot urine trickling down his leg, his raw knuckles bleeding equally warm blood over his wrist. Then, after what seemed an eternity, Helmut said softly, 'No, Papa.' Wolfgang nodded, then turned to smile lovingly at Hans, playing on the deck. Wolfgang slowly relaxed. He was free and clear at last, and that was all that mattered.

Helmut watched his father walk away, then glanced at the tarpaulin. Slowly he began to smile. He had just discovered the joy of power, and life was suddenly very, very sweet.

CHAPTER 5

Kansas, Nine Years Later

The throng of youngsters running from the white-washed wooden building whooped with delight. School was out for the summer! Kier Harcourt walked slowly down the dusty drive, his face thoughtful as he swung his bundle of books, his mind going back to the exams. Had he passed them all or not? He shrugged. He'd either passed or he hadn't. No use worryin' about it.

'Hey, Harcourt – you on fer tonight?' Kier looked up as Billy Johnson's freckled face overtook him.

'Yeah, I'm on.' Kier said. 'And I don't want none of you clowns messin' with my play. It's supposed to be a modern tragedy, but you guys'd turn it into a farce, quick as light'nin'!'

Billy grinned. 'OK, Cecil,' he held up his hands placatingly. Ever since the Cecil B. De Mille incident at the school play all those years ago, the nickname had stuck, despite Kier's valiant efforts to shake it off. But over the years, Kier's plays had become the highlight of the church fund-raising, taking in more money than all the bring-and-buy stalls, home-baked cake stands and raffles put together. The club Kier had set up, however, kept a little bit of the money back to finance group outings to the cinema. A club had to live, after all.

Kier was seventeen and already turning female heads. At five feet ten, his hair was a rich earthy brown, thick and always glossy in the harsh Kansas sun. His eyes were widely spaced, with thick black lashes, and were the exact same shade of colour as those belonging to a timber wolf. He walked like a wolf, too, with a loose-limbed stride that required the minimum of effort and gave the girls who constantly gazed at him the sensation of watching liquid movement. One girl called him 'Poetry in motion,' so now all the girls called him 'The Poet'. Kier chose to look on it as a reflection of his directing and playwriting abilities, rather than as a statement about his physical attributes.

At the end of the school road he retrieved a battered pushbike from under a scraggly tree and pedalled off, his mind still stubbornly on his exams. He'd worked like a demon for the past two years and, if he failed now, he just didn't know what he'd do. Of all the scholarship opportunities Miss Ritter had put his way, he'd elected the most ambitious, the most outrageous of them all. Oxford University, England – where no one from Burmanville had ever gone before.

With the bike still in motion, he hooked his leg over the handlebar like a trick-cyclist and drew to a well-controlled stop in front of the store, where he had a part-time job.

'Howdy, young Kier.' Oscar Smith looked up as he came through the door, then returned to his books, checking columns industriously, always paranoid that someone would somehow cheat him.

'Mr Smith. What d'ya want me to do first?'

'I've got some flour sacks from the cellar that need bringing up and put on the shelves in the back.'

'Yessir.' He opened the door to the cellar and walked down the rickety stairs. It was windowless, stale and muggy, and with a quick impatient movement he pulled his shirt, still buttoned, over his head. Reaching for a hefty sack, he began the laborious climb back up the steps. After half an hour he was bathed in sweat, but he was used to gruelling hard labour and barely noticed. At the rear of the shop he began stacking them on the shelves.

From her window, Magda Smith watched his progress and licked her lips. It was time. She'd watched her husband's young helper mature from a boy of twelve, to a near-man of seventeen. Like a patient spider, she'd counted the four inches he'd grown last year, and could measure almost to the exact millimetre the amount his chest and biceps had swelled. She'd watched with glee, the hairs begin to march determinedly across his firmly muscled chest. In the dead and dusty town, Magda had thought it was her birthday the day young Kier Harcourt had come to the store looking for work, five long years ago. It had been a long wait, but one well worth it.

Magda began to tremble. He was covered in a fine white film of flour. It was about time she gave herself a special treat. And special was a word that suited Kier Harcourt. And not just because of his looks either. There was an indefinable 'something' that clung to him – a kind of aura, a feeling that made her skin tingle. Every feminine intuition she had told her that here was a boy who was going places. She could feel it, taste it, smell it. Unlike Kier, she had no doubts that he'd passed his exams and would later be going on to Oxford and all that culture.

She came downstairs, her heart thumping. 'Oscar, can I spare you for a few minutes?' she asked, as Jake Gordon, the town's odd-job man, walked in and started scrummaging around in a big box of mismatched odd screws and nails.

'For what, dear?' Oscar kept an eagle eye on Jake.

'I need some furniture moved, hon.'

'What can I do for you, Jake?' Oscar asked, just as Kier came into the storeroom. He was sweating hard, and he rubbed his hand wearily across his forehead.

'Honey,' Magda wheedled, with perfect timing, 'I need someone to move the furniture.'

'You know I can't leave the store,' Oscar hissed impatiently, looking around and spying Kier. 'You finished with the flour, son?'

'Yessir.'

'Then help Mrs Smith move some furniture, huh?'

Kier nodded, following the exultant Magda up the stairs with all the innocence of a lamb going to the slaughter. Magda went first to the kitchen, turning around and watching the boy who stood nervously in the doorway. 'You must be thirsty after all the hard work, Kier,' she said softly, walking to the refrigerator and bringing out a pitcher of iced lemonade.

Kier gratefully accepted a glass, wiping the taste of flour from his mouth with three or four healthy gulps. Magda watched his strong Adam's apple bob in his throat, and took a long, slow breath. She had waited a long time for this and she was going to enjoy it to the full.

'So, you're the last one left at home now,' she said, slowly raising a hand to her throat and then fanning her face. 'My, isn't it hot?' She undid the first two buttons of her dress.

'Yes, ma'am.'

'I saw your pa the other day. He ain't lookin' too good.'

Kier shook his head. 'Amy was his favourite. Now she's moved to Wisconsin, he don't talk much. It's not the same without Ma. And he still misses Pammy. She died during the Depression. She got real sick, and we couldn't afford to pay the hospital.' Kier hadn't been born then, but he recited the facts grimly.

'Oh, that's an awful shame,' Magda said, her voice soft with genuine sympathy. 'Life's a bitch. Whether you enjoy it or not, it all boils down to money.' She looked at Kier, then smiled. 'You'll have money one day, Kier. I can tell.'

'Yeah?' he asked, his face coming suddenly alive. 'You really think so?'

'I do,' she said, perfectly seriously, and Kier felt himself flush with pleasure. 'And what'll you do with all that money, when you get it?'

Kier's eyes began to glow. 'First thing I'm gonna do is buy the mortgage back on the farm, and hire some hands for Pa.'

Magda reached out and rested her palm against his cheek. 'You're a sweet boy, Kier Harcourt.'

Kier blushed, very conscious of her hand on his cheek, making him shift nervously against the door jamb. He wasn't sure where he was glad or sorry when Magda moved away from him and walked onto the landing. His eyes fell to her rounded bottom, which swayed hypnotizingly as she walked and, try as he might, he couldn't tear his gaze away. Magda nodded to the spare bedroom. 'The furniture's in there.'

He gulped and nodded. 'Yes, ma'am.'

'Do you want to wash up a little first?' She walked into the tiny cubicle of the bathroom and ran some water into the basin. 'You must be feeling sticky.' She turned and walked to the door, her body brushing against his as she squeezed past. Kier walked to the sink, surprised to find that he was trembling. He drenched a flannel and wiped it over his chest. His nipples seemed bigger than usual, and rock-hard.

Through the crack of the door Magda watched, panting slightly. When he came back out, she had moved a few paces away. Quickly she led him to the spare bedroom. It was square, tiny, and crammed with useless junk.

'I'll soon have it all cleared, ma'am,' Kier promised.

He walked to a crate by the window and dragged it across the floor. 'Just put it out back, by the trash,' Magda called, deciding to let him do some work first, just in case Oscar asked what they'd been doing all afternoon. When he came back, Magda had taken off her dress. Spying him, she seemed to flush in embarrassment. 'Oh, Kier, don't mind me. It's just so hot, and I didn't want to make my dress all sweaty. ''Sides,' she smiled, 'this ol' underskirt covers as much of me as the dress did, doesn't it?'

'Yes, ma'am,' Kier said doubtfully. The underskirt was white and see-through and he could see the outline of her bra-less breasts perfectly. The palms of his hands began to itch.

'And if you don't tell anyone, nobody'll know.'

'No, ma'am.'

'This town talks because it has nothin' better to do.'

'Yes, ma'am,' Kier mumbled dutifully.

Magda quickly ran a dry cloth over the windows. She looked around for inspiration, spotted something and smiled to herself. Stretching up against the wall, she tried to dislodge a couple of leather bridles that were hung from two nails near the ceiling.

'Here, let me,' Kier offered, walking over to her. He reached up, his fingers clutching the leather, his bare chest brushing against the cold, white plaster of the wall. Then he froze. Magda's hand was on his back, her fingers tracing the indentation of his spine. 'You know, Kier,' she said softly 'you've grown a lot since you first started working here.'

56

'Yes, ma'am,' he gulped, his eyes staring at the wall not an inch away.

With insistent fingers she turned him around. 'Let me take a good look at you. Hum . . .' Her fingers ran over his chest, slowly and idly circling one nipple, as if she was doing it absentmindedly and not really realizing what she was doing. Kier's eyes widened as they looked into cat-like green ones. Excitement began to inject adrenalin into his veins.

'You're gonna be a real heartbreaker, aren't you, Kier Harcourt?' Magda cooed, her hands reaching up to play with the leather straps that Kier still held above his head, the brass rings holding fast to the nails.

'I don't want to break no hearts,' he muttered, his own heart thumping so loudly in his chest he was sure she must hear it. He was a little bit scared but totally fascinated. It was going to happen. He wasn't quite sure what 'it' was, but he knew men laughed about 'it' in the saloon, and slapped each other's back when talking about Maisie's brothel, over in Buffalo. Now it was going to happen to him.

'But you will break them,' Magda said, stepping closer to him. Her breasts brushed against his chest and her nipples felt like hard pebbles through the flimsy lace of her petticoat. Kier swallowed hard. 'Mrs Smith,' he said, half a plea for mercy, half a demand for more.

'Hmm?' Magda purred and, leaning forward, kissed him full on the mouth. Kier felt her tongue dart against his teeth and his loins hardened, straining painfully against his jeans. He moaned, his eyes widening and then slowly, languorously, closing as the kiss deepened. Magda slowly pulled away and then looked down at his erection. 'Kier Harcourt!' she said, her voice sounding shocked and scandalized. Kier went scarlet. He made a quick attempt at escape, but Magda was too quick.

'Oh, no, you don't.' She placed a hand against his chest. 'If my husband knew what you were doing he'd take a horsewhip to you.'

'Yes, ma'am,' Kier said humbly, all but hanging his head in shame.

In response, she stood on tiptoe and began to twine the bridle leather about his wrists in tight, complicated hoops. Dumbfounded, he remained passive. 'So we mustn't tell him. Must we?' she whispered, looking into his startled brown eyes and smiling.

He shook his head, totally confused. 'No ma'am.'

With his hands held above him by the leather thongs, Magda ran her hands up his arms, and then suddenly dipped her head to kiss his armpit. Kier jerked, totally unprepared. 'You like that, my little poet?' Magda whispered, surprising him with her knowledge of his nickname. Wordlessly he nodded.

'You must say yes, ma'am, Kier.'

'Yes, ma'am.'

Magda kissed his throat, moved on to the ridges of his collarbone, then slid down to fasten her mouth on the nipple above his thundering heart. Kier gasped, his hands pulling down automatically, but the leather reins held. Kier curled his fingers around the straps, his palms sweating, his fingers sliding against the dark leather, unable to get a firm grip.

'Did you like that, Kier?'

'Yes, ma'am,' he said hoarsely, running his tongue over painfully dry lips. Again she stood on tiptoe, this time so that her eyes could be on a level with his. Slowly she slid her hand down between their bodies. When her palm was resting flat against the hard bulge of his jeans she began to rub him – surprisingly hard. Kier closed his eyes and groaned, his legs growing weak. Magda was panting hard now. She loved virgins – their reactions were always so strong and pure. And Kier was the choicest she would ever have, she knew this instinctively. She watched his sensitive face twitch, exulting in the way small gasps feathered past his lips, smiling as his young, innocent body began to undulate against the wall in a helpless rhythm that she dictated.

'You like that, too – don't you, Kier?'

'Yes, ma'am,' he groaned.

She quickly dispatched with his jeans, all the time looking up at his face. He had become perfectly still.

Magda smiled. 'Oh, I'm not going to hurt you, my little poet,' she promised. 'I'm gonna to teach you everythin' you need to know fer when you go to Oxford and meet all them fancy English girls.'

Slowly she kissed his sternum, then sank to her knees to kiss his stomach, her tongue darting into his navel. 'You like that, Kier?' she asked, then moved lower.

'Oh, yes, ma'am,' he moaned, his young, sweat-slicked body jerking helplessly as she sucked on him, her mouth a hot and wet implement of torture. He saw lights flash against his eyes, as his arms strained against his leather bonds. Kier moaned, his throat stretched taut as he leaned his head back against the wall.

Magda, her mouth full, nevertheless managed to smile. He might think it was all over, but she knew different. She'd untie him, and then start all over again. Only this time she wouldn't waste his erection. If he thought this was something, and the way he was moaning and carryin' on, he obviously did, just wait until she introduced him to her vagina. Her inner muscles would squash and mash him into a frenzy. She'd hold him clamped in her with her long, strong legs, and make him work like he'd never had to work before. She could hear his moans now, could see his young face contorting in the fiercest of orgasms that would leave him crying like a baby.

Kier, unaware of the afternoon that still lay ahead, began to jerk spasmodically . . .

He arrived late at the old barn, where rehearsals were halfway over, looking totally washed out.

'Hey – here's Cecil,' Johnny Carter greeted him cheerfully. 'Thought you'd show up then?'

'Yeah. Come on, you mugs, let's see how you've been spending your time.' And as he listened to Johnny go through the script, his professionalism began to take over. Under his eagle eye, the play began to take iron-clad shape. He improvised, redirected and even rewrote where necessary. And as the summer drew on, the play became perfected. The three nights that it was to run came and went without incident, earning record money. In July he learned that he had passed all his exams and had won a Rhodes Scholarship to Waynefleet College, Oxford, beginning in three years' time. Miss Ritter threatened to heap extra studies on him that would set his head to busting.

He worked on the farm, he worked at the store, he worked at his studies and he worked beneath, on top of, and by the side of, Mrs Smith.

Three years later, Kier was more than ready for Oxford and all them fancy English girls.

CHAPTER 6

Switzerland, Two Years Later

In the Bernese Oberland, Oriel Somerville watched a train approach, and meandered out of the railway station into the warm summer sun. A lone buzzard circled high on the thermals in the clear, azure sky. The station was spotlessly clean, and flowers hung from baskets, frothing scarlet geraniums, periwinkles and white, cascading bellflowers. The whole wooden structure was set against a backdrop of snow-capped mountains, liberally forested in rich, verdant green.

'We're terribly late, you know,' a glum voice said in her ear. Oriel smiled, and turned to look at her best friend, Betty Wooster, an English Right Hon.

'What's the matter? Scared old Scarecrow will have you served up for lunch? With the proper sauce, of course.'

Betty grinned. 'And all the appropriate cutlery and . . .' the two girls began to chorus together, in a high-pitched German-accented voice, 'the apprrrrroprrrriate linen, corrrrrectly folded.' They burst into laughter at the end of their imitation of the school's etiquette teacher, causing the station master to smile indulgently. Every year the young girls came to Johan's Finishing School for Young Ladies, and every year they seemed the same. There were the English – in clothes that were too tight, too short or too ugly, with nasal voices that always bemoaned the lack of horses in Switzerland. Then there were the mixed Europeans, dressed in classic French clothes, with haircuts of sleek bobs, perfect makeup, precise French and a superior attitude that always offended the townspeople. Then there were the Americans, who were perpetually friendly, outspoken, and good-naturedly boastful.

The little blonde American, who was asking for a ticket to Interlaken Ost was the pick of this year's litter. At five feet five, she had long pale hair that most girls would kill for, wide-spaced blue eyes, an elfin chin and a heart-shaped face that had his grandsons moon-eyed and unworkable.

The girls boarded the train, and settled on the surprisingly comfortable wooden seats. 'Oh, hell,' Betty grumbled. 'Why are we always late?'

Oriel grinned and shook her head. 'Beat's me,' she said, her southern drawl reminding Betty of Scarlett O'Hara. Betty sighed. Betty, to put it bluntly, was fat. She had a short, unruly mop of nut-brown hair that curled around her head like out-of-control barbed wire. She was a brilliant mathematician, lousy language student, and was the school

63

victim. It was a constant source of amazement that the school darling, Oriel Somerville, should have chosen the beleaguered Betty for a friend in the first place. Betty, at first, had suspected some cruel joke on Oriel's part. But, after a month, the two were inseparable, Oriel's daring exploits getting the blissfully happy Betty into more trouble in the space of a year than she'd ever been in for the whole of her life.

'I say,' Betty said. 'You will be coming home with me for the summer hols, won't you? Daddy will be in London – he practically lives in the House of Lords nowadays, and Mummy has already swanned off to the Bahamas. So we'll have the shack to ourselves.' The shack, as Oriel knew, was a 73-roomed ancestral mansion deep in the heart of Bedfordshire.

'I expect so,' Oriel agreed. 'But I'll have to go home for a couple of weeks first.' As the train began to pull away from the station, Oriel gave the stooped old station master a cheerful wave, and settled back against the seat.

As the train began to climb, they passed waterfalls that ranged from foot-wide torrents, to mere inches of clear trickling water. Chalets lined the railway tracks with their deep roofs and brightly coloured walls. As they began to climb even higher, lush meadowland began to stretch as far as the eye could see. Wild purple orchids became commonplace, as did pink and white campions, moon-daisies, buttercups and blue gentians.

'I love this country,' Oriel said, craning her neck as a small herd of cows came into view, all wearing monstrously outsized cow bells.

'What time is it, Or?' Betty asked nervously, and without looking at her watch Oriel gave an unconcerned shrug.

'Too late.'

'Wonderful,' Betty grumbled. 'I wish I had nerves of steel like you.'

'The trick is just not to give a shit,' Oriel told her, the crude word falling so gracefully from her friend's pretty pink lips that Betty laughed. Betty sounded like a horse with hiccoughs when she laughed, but Oriel didn't mind. She was so uncomplicated. Oriel's thoughts wandered to her mother, back home in Atlanta, and she began to frown. She was not looking forward to going home.

The train, after a hair-raising climb, pulled into their station. 'We're in for it, I expect,' Betty said glumly.

'Oh, I expect so,' Oriel confirmed off-handedly, and took Betty's hand. 'The dastardly duo strikes again.'

'Awol,' Betty said with glum relish. 'Worth at least five hundred lines. Thou shalt not sneak off during nature walks.'

Oriel nodded. 'And written in French, I reckon.'

'Oh no!' Betty wailed. 'Not French!'

The girls' feet began to drag the closer they came to the whitewashed three-storey building that was school, home, and entertainment centre. They were instantly spotted by the headmistress who, with a hooked, imperious finger, beckoned them forward. The two girls looked at one another, sighed deeply and trudged forward.

Frau Reinhart watched them approach with a heart that was much warmer than either girl could ever have guessed. 'Miss Somerville. Miss Wooster. We've been expecting you.'

'We do our best,' Oriel said cheekily, and Betty bit her lip, keeping in her horse's laugh with a great deal of effort.

'I think, under the circumstances, Miss Somerville, you can leave the school a few weeks early.'

Oriel paled a little, but other than that made no sign that she was surprised. 'I don't suppose that will pose any undue difficulties, Miss Reinhart,' she mimicked the prim diction of the older woman with perfect precision.

Miss Reinhart nodded. 'Max will take you and your luggage to the train station. I've been speaking to your mother, and she expects you soon.' Miss Reinhart dismissed and watched them go. It would take a good man to bring the southern belle under control. Miss Reinhart rather envied her.

'What a bummer,' Betty said, who had picked up the turn of phrase from her American friend and was using it now more than any other.

'Oh, I don't know. A girl should get expelled from at least one school during her lifetime, don't you think?' Oriel asked cheerfully as, once back in their room, she began to pack.

'I don't suppose I'll ever manage it, though. Unless I can get booted out of St Cats,' Betty said miserably.

'What?'

'St Catherine's. It's a college at Oxford. I'm going to read Mathematics there. I told you that, didn't I?'

'I wish I could go to Oxford,' Oriel murmured thoughtfully. 'Daddy could easily afford to send me as a foreign student. Oh, I don't want to go home,' Oriel finally admitted in a wail, holding a lambswool sweater in pastel pink under her chin.

Betty looked at her curiously. 'What's so bad about home?'

Oriel shrugged. 'Nothing really. It's just . . . stifling down there. If you've never been to Georgia, you can't understand. And, what's worse, Daddy will be away all summer.'

'What business is he in?' Betty asked, and Oriel grunted.

'The Somervilles of Atlanta don't do anything as gauche as business.' Then she sighed. 'But that's not fair. During the war, Daddy worked here as a diplomat. Now there's an international committee being set up to track down the Nazis, and Dad's on it. He just can't sit by, like everyone else, and leave it to others to tackle evil. He believes it's his duty to track down war criminals. He has the time and the money and nothing else to do with it. So . . .'

Betty sighed. Her father spent his time sleeping in the House of Lords.

'Which means there'll be just me and Mummy,' Oriel concluded gloomily. 'And every time I go home I get the feelin' that I can't breathe. There are coffee mornings, and cocktail evenings, parties and luncheon at Gwenny's. Always the same good ol' boys, the same conversations, over and over. Ugh' – she gave a theatrical shudder – 'the thought gives me the willies.'

67

Betty sighed again. Families!

'The thing is, I'm not like my mother,' Oriel went on. 'She leads a double life the way you or I would wear a blouse. It fits her somehow. I'll bet she can't wait till Daddy leaves for Europe so she can start seein' that lover of hers again.'

She finished packing, unaware that Betty's mouth had fallen open. 'A lover?' Betty squawked. 'You mean . . . a real-life . . . lover? An actual man on the side? I can't imagine my mother actually doing . . . it . . . with a man. Any man!'

'Well, I can imagine my mother doing it all right with Kyle O'Sullivan, or O'Connor or . . . O something, anyway.'

'You mean you know who he is?' Betty squealed.

'Oh, yes,' Oriel confirmed airily. 'He runs a garage in Burford.'

'What's he look like?' Betty asked, fascinated. 'Is he all short and oily?'

Oriel snapped her suitcase catches, her face thoughtful. 'Well . . . much as I hate to say it,' she mused, 'he is rather gorgeous.' Her face twisted for a moment. Poor Daddy. 'Oh well, it can't be helped, I guess. At least she didn't try to seduce our butler,' she added savagely.

Betty's eyes became round saucers, and Oriel could stand no more. She began to howl with laughter, ducking when her friend lobbed a pillow at her. The subsequent pillow-fight ended when a knock on the door brought Max, telling her it was time to go to the station. The two girls looked at each other

68

miserably, hugged, and promised to see each other soon, the minute Betty could arrange for Oriel to visit.

Oriel missed Switzerland the moment she got home. The south seemed to her like an overripe fruit, too soft, too hot, too . . . everything. Georgia hadn't changed much, she thought grimly. Nevertheless, as she set eyes on Riveree's white magnificence, she felt a reluctant sense of homecoming. She could see her mother's slender figure, straight and relaxed in the portico's massive frame. Oriel took a deep breath and paid off the taxi driver.

Oriel and Clarissa stood silently for a while, studying each other. Then Clarissa smiled and held out her arms, and Oriel ran into them. Held in the warm arms she could smell the familiar Dior essence of her mother's perfume, and felt the familiar sensation of cool silk under her cheek. Mother and daughter pulled away and looked deep into each other's eyes.

'Are you mad at me?' Oriel wanted to know, and Clarissa smiled ruefully.

'Not if you've learned how to be a proper lady.'

Oriel groaned and pulled away, walking into the hall. 'Don't worry, Mama. I'll never be able to burp or fart again.'

'Oriel!' Clarissa snapped, and her daughter stopped stomping across the hall and turned around, at least looking contrite.

I'm sorry. I'll be good, I promise. I can arrange flowers, discuss a menu like I was a cordon bleu chef, and I know enough about makeup and clothes to start my own boutique. OK?'

Clarissa relaxed, noticing the natural elegance with which her daughter walked, and the classic, understated simplicity of the dress she was wearing. Her money had been well spent, after all. 'You must be totally exhausted. Why don't you pop upstairs, take a shower and then sleep until dinner? Hmm?'

'Sounds blissful,' Oriel agreed, and headed for the stairs at a fast skip.

Clarissa watched her, full of pride and love. She was still so young, like a graceful filly.

She turned as a voice in the alcove behind her said, 'Was that Oriel I heard just now?'

'Yes, she's just this second arrived,' she told her husband. 'She'll be down for dinner. The poor girl was shattered. I didn't have the heart to scold her about her behaviour.'

Duncan looked up the deserted stairs and smiled. 'It's good to have her back,' was all he said, then turned and disappeared back into his study.

Sighing, Clarissa followed him in. 'We'll have to start preparing for her season,' she said. 'I know you'll be in Luxemburg for most of the time, but that's no reason why she shouldn't be deb of the year.'

'As you say, my dear,' Duncan said, sitting down in an enormous black leather chair that seemed to swallow him up.

'What do you think of Billy Bob Walker? He'll be inheriting his daddy's diamond mines in South Africa soon. What do you think of him as a husband for Oriel?'

Duncan opened his mouth, and then closed it again. It would have been pointless to point out that Oriel was only seventeen. 'Whatever you think best,' he said mildly, but a small frown tugged at his pale brows. Clarissa nodded, not expecting any other kind of answer, and left the study. Her husband was immersed in his search for Wolfgang Mueller before his wife had even closed the door behind her.

Dinner was a remarkably relaxed affair. Oriel entertained her father with tales of Switzerland. After a while, Clarissa deftly turned the conversation to more relevant topics. 'There's a party tomorrow at the Randolf,' she named the most prestigious hotel in Atlanta. 'You will come?' She looked across at her daughter, who nodded and said, 'I suppose so.'

'You don't sound very enthusiastic, kitten,' Duncan mused.

Oriel smiled, then shrugged. 'Oh, it'll be nice to see the old gang again. Oh, before I forget, the Right Honourable Elizabeth Endora Wooster has asked me over to the ancestral pile of bricks this summer. Can I go?'

'Of course,' Duncan said.

'I don't think so,' Clarissa said at the same time. Oriel looked across at her mother and reached forward for her wine glass.

'Why not, Mummy?' she asked, with misleading mildness.

71

'Well, there's so much to do this summer,' Clarissa said, a little nonplussed by the sudden hardness in her daughter's voice. 'I thought we'd spend some time in Charleston, and look out a whole new summer wardrobe for you. Then there's the Gregson Ball in July, and the Yacht Club meet in August. We've got to visit Savannah for the hunt, and then . . .'

Oriel closed her eyes and sighed. 'Oh, hell,' she said so quietly that only her father, sat immediately on her right, heard her. Under the table he reached for her hand, and squeezed it gently.

The following night, at one o'clock in the morning, Oriel burst into her father's study. She was wearing a beautiful lime-green evening dress, but her face was flushed and she was breathing hard. Duncan put down the papers he'd been studying. 'What's the matter?' he asked, instantly alarmed.

'That . . . that . . . bastard, Billy Bob Walker,' she spat. She wiped the back of her hand viciously across her mouth. Rage leapt into Duncan's eyes. His hands closed into fists.

'What did he do?'

'Got fresh, that's what,' Oriel snapped, then looked at her father with narrowed eyes. 'When I told him to get lost he asked me what was wrong. Didn't I know that he and I were practically engaged?' Oriel paused, her small breasts rising and falling with the effort of keeping her rage under control. 'Engaged!' she repeated, stating the word as if it were something ugly. 'Now where did he get an idea like that? Do you know?' She shot the question accusingly at her father, who sighed deeply and walked around from behind the huge desk.

'From your mother, I expect,' he said heavily. 'As usual, she's taken things too fast.'

'Mother? What's she done now?' Oriel asked, her shoulders slumping as her righteous anger began to wither. 'I thought that moron Billy Bob was acting too damn self-confident.'

'Your mother seems to think he's perfect matrimonial material,' Duncan admitted, pouring two small measures of the finest Napoleon brandy into huge, bulbous glasses.

'Oh, no!' Oriel wailed. 'I don't believe it. Daddy, you've got to help me. I need an escape route!' She half-laughed, but in her eyes her father clearly saw a growing panic.

He nodded his head briskly. 'All right. Where do you want to escape to?'

The question took her by surprise for a moment, and then she began to smile. 'I want,' she said clearly, and slowly, 'to go to Oxford.'

'Oxford?' Duncan repeated, totally taken aback. He'd never heard her mention that university before.

'Oxford,' Oriel repeated firmly.

Duncan slowly began to smile, then raised his glass. Solemnly they clinked them together. 'To Oxford,' he said. 'And your mother can rant and rave as much as she likes.'

Clarissa did.

CHAPTER 7

Monte Carlo

The Principality of Monte Carlo lay shimmering in the bright summer sun. In the Port de Monaco a flotilla of craft bobbed on the gentle swell of the Mediterranean, their white hulls echoing those of the seagulls' wings that soared overhead. Masts thrust into the air, sails neatly furled, brass adornments gleaming like gold. High up on the hill stood the Royal Palace. Rumours were rife, concerning the possible marriage of Prince Rainier to the American film star Grace Kelly. Already the women were deluging the boutiques and salons for hair colourants of the exact same shade as that fêted actress. The cool, elegant, blonde look was in.

Wayne D'Arville walked slowly along the sea-front promenade, his azure blue eyes hardly noticing the lighthouse in the harbour, or the swaying of the exotic palm trees all around him. A tourist next to him turned to his wife and excitedly pointed out that they could actually see the Cap d'Antibes, and Wayne didn't bother to put him right. His lips curled into a superior sneer as the couple began to take photographs with a cheap Kodak. He hated Monte Carlo in the summer. The roads became chock-a-block and you couldn't move on the pavements. Ice-cream cones littered the enchanted streets, and the blue-canopied cafés became overrun. Still, it also mean that the casino trade became ever more frantic. He could just imagine the millions of francs now pouring into his father's place, the Droit de Seigneur Casino.

Wolfgang was excessively proud of it. It served the best wine and food, and did not pretend to be a country mansion, just the best casino in town, the famous Monte Carlo Casino, naturally, being exempted.

Wayne strode between the traffic with ease. Now, at the age of twenty, he was six feet four inches tall. His hair was the pale copper of autumn leaves. His eyes were big and blue, and his face had the square, intelligent look of his race. Girls stopped to look at him, their eyes speculative, and not just because of his spectacular looks. He walked quickly and with purpose, as if he were in a hurry to get somewhere, and he had the hard-eyed, firm-jawed look that told everybody that he'd get exactly what he wanted. But then, he'd known that the moment they had all moved into the house on the hill, in La Turbie. He wanted everything his father had. It had been his constant goal in life, and drove him to be the best. He'd studied so hard and so furiously that he'd earned a place at the Sorbonne. Not content to be only intellectually superior, Wayne had worked on his body, exercising it until it was a well-muscled machine. And yet, as he neared the casino, its familiar Gothic façade holding no beauty for him, he could feel a familiar weakness coming back. It annoyed him because he could not place the source of it. Unbelievably, he knew, he still felt the urge to try and please his father.

He could still remember the glow of satisfaction he'd felt when Wolfgang had looked proud of him for coming first in his Baccalaureate exams. Even his mother, an older, still elegant version of the Berlin hostess, had pinched his cheek with her white-gloved hand and smiled proudly into his eyes. He'd felt capable of walking on air. Until the following day, when Hans had won the amateur local water-skiing competition. For Hans there had been a night out at the Belle Epoque at the Hermitage Hotel. For Hans there had been a reporter come to interview him for the local paper, the *Nice Matin*, with his picture being spread across the centre pages. For Hans there had been champagne, although Wayne had not been allowed to drink it at his age. For Hans, Wayne thought as he pushed through the revolving doors that led into the lush interior of the casino, there was everything. At only fourteen, Hans ruled.

Wayne paused inside the casino and looked slowly around him, letting his bitterness settle back into its usual hidden place, lurking like a diseased rat in the corners of his mind.

The décor of the casino was overwhelmingly crimson. Overhead, chandeliers lit the green baize of the gaming tables, and deep mahogany furniture glowed in the artificial lighting. The rooms had no windows and no clocks. Most of the games were rigged, of course. But every now and then Wolfgang would allow someone to win big. It was marvellous publicity, and kept the steady stream of idiots coming in. With an ease born of long practice, Wayne began to scan the faces. He could spot local housewives, gambling the money for the Sunday roast on the hopes of earning enough to buy a Balmain original. Then there were the professionals, men dressed in rumpled suits, whole faces betrayed nothing at all. And, of course, the tourists in T-shirts. The slogans varied from year to year. This year, '*Draft Beer – not Students.*'

Slowly Wayne walked through the room, avoiding the tuxedo-clad waiters. The constant whirr of the fruit machines, relegated to the outer halls, provided the background music. The clacking spin of the roulette wheel, the roll of dice, the tap-tap of chips, all droned together to become one long, insignificant hum.

A waitress deliberately nudged him. 'Oh, pardon, monsieur,' the girl said, a slight blush staining her suntanned cheeks as her pert breasts rubbed against his arm. She liked everything about the casino owner's son, from the way he wore the Pierre Cardin grey silk trousers and matching shirt with perfect ease, to his pale-flame hair. She pouted at him playfully. Wayne smiled, his loins tightening momentarily before shrugging the lust away. He had other things on his mind at the moment. Giving her a cool smile, he left her and walked on through to the high-risk salon.

Here only the greatest of high-flyers and the richest of the rich were accommodated. This was becoming, he noticed, more and more the domain of Arabs. Wayne barely paused. The spectacle of the casino was as commonplace to him as buses were to bus conductors. Walking through, he entered a private, narrow white corridor and entered the manager's office. Édouard de Lepee glanced up, his narrow face tight and alert. On seeing Wayne he visibly relaxed and Wayne felt the familiar helpless rage assail him. Édouard de Lepee was his father's right-hand man, and he had not taken long to see the lie of the land. Hans, and not Wayne, was the unspoken heir to the D'Arville inheritance. Around Wolfgang, Édouard was fawning and sycophantic. Around Hans, he was careful, and avuncular. Around Wayne, he was nothing at all. Wayne felt his hands curl into impotent fists by his sides as Édouard finished some paperwork.

'Wayne,' he said curtly. 'What can I do for you?'

'I was looking for my brother,' Wayne said, none of his almost murderous thoughts showing on his face. One day, Wayne thought, he was going to take the greatest of pleasure in sacking this piffling little nobody and . . .

'Hans is on the beach. He's practising the high-dive for the school competition.'

Wayne nodded curtly, turned and left. One day, he thought savagely, I'll be master here. And Hans and all the rest will jump when I say. His teeth began to ache, and he realized he was biting down so hard that his gums were going numb. Once more on the street, he took several calming breaths. He hated the noise of the tourists. He hated the heat of the sun. He hated his brother, his father, and that dog de Lepee. He still hated the whole world.

He walked to a Maserati two-seater and opened the door. It was bottle-green in colour and sported custom-made wired wheels. He pulled the top down, able to breath more easily once he was on the Rue Terrazzani and headed out of the city. Hans, he knew, would be further up the coast, diving from the cliffs at Saint Michel. High-diving was his younger brother's latest accomplishment. He drove fast but well along the serpentine road that hugged the coastline, called Corniche du Littoral. He was not sure what he'd say to Hans when he found him. He was never sure what to say to Hans. The boy worshipped him, much to Wolfgang's displeasure, and Wayne was aware of a dangerous conflict of emotions at work within him concerning his younger brother, rival and enemy. He'd grown perversely fond of little Hans, and it worried him sometimes. He could not afford to get close to anyone.

He gunned the engine viciously as Saint Michel came into view. The rock was a good forty feet high and as he pulled the car onto the grass dunes by the silvery shore, he saw a bright red blob halfway up the cliff-face, and recognized the scarlet trunks belonging to his brother. Without thinking, he tooted the car horn in a friendly, spontaneous gesture. Over the distance he saw a pale hand wave eagerly in the air. He didn't wave back. Still Hans kept waving with puppy-like determination, and slowly, almost reluctantly, Wayne felt compelled to lift his arm and wave back. Angry with himself, he took off his shirt and shoes and began to walk along the beach, slowly entering the shade underneath the rock face as Hans climbed higher, way above him. He could hear the chattering voices of Hans's entourage at the top of the cliff, ready to applaud their school hero's latest daring effort.

Wayne had never been popular at school. His sole ambition was to be the best, which made him a teacher's pet, but earned him the scorn of his peers. Angry and hurt by their scorn, he had become cold and superior. Boys stupid enough to pick a fight with him had ended up with broken noses and in one case, cracked ribs. He'd earned the reputation of school bully, although that was not totally fair. So long as they left him alone, he left them alone.

Wayne dragged his thoughts away from their painful direction as he heard his brother's voice, high above. Out on the waves a single fishing boat cruised a hundred yards or so away, and Wayne watched the single fisherman with vague interest, his mind on other things.

Hans enjoyed being liked. He enjoyed running in the sun with his friends, he enjoyed kissing girls and playing chess with his father. In short, Hans simply loved life. As he perched on the rock face, looking down into the gentle swell of the blue sea he felt no fear. He thought of Wayne, tall, handsome, wonderful Wayne, waiting on the beach to watch him dive, and he grinned, his freckled face revealing a missing tooth. As he paused, his arms extended, Hans decided to do a backwards somersault. That would make Wayne proud of him. If all went well on Saturday, he'd have another cup to bring home for Papa to put in the darkened glass cabinet he'd had especially made for him.

Hans leapt, his heart sure of himself and of his place in the world. Below, out of his peripheral vision, a plummeting body yanked Wayne's eyes from his casual interest in the fishing vessel. There was just an instant when he realized there was something horribly wrong; that there was something odd in the fall and angle of the body that was not right, causing Hans to hit the water with a harsh slap, instead of a clean glide. After a few, frozen seconds it became obvious Hans was not about to resurface with a laughing comment and a cheery wave, as he usually did. Wayne's heart jerked in his chest and his mouth went dry. He stepped two paces forward, his body tense and quivering, ready to plunge into the surf . . . and then he stopped. He stood for long seconds, watching the sea, then saw his brother's pale hands flap limply above the waves. Wayne felt his innards churn. The sand under his bare feet seemed to burn his soles, but his eyes stayed fixed on those white hands, slapping weakly against the water. They looked like pale butterfly wings, insignificant and irrelevant in the mighty blue sea. Wayne felt sunk in the sand and unable to move.

★ ★ ★

Claude Rissaud straightened on the deck of his boat, his youthful face creased into a frown. '*Merde*,' he muttered, dragging his faded blue T-shirt off his head and levering off his deck shoes. Claude was only seventeen, but had been swimming since he could talk. Within moments his fit brown young body had hit the water like an arrow. Dimly Wayne heard the splash and dragged his eyes away from where his brother's hands had been. He could see another swimmer in the water now, pulling away from the rusty trawler with brisk, overarm strokes.

Within a few minutes Claude had reached the inert body of Hans Mueller, also called Henri D'Arville. Water trickled from the small face, and the boy's chin felt cold and clammy when Claude cupped his hand under it and began to haul the body towards the shore where he'd noticed the copper head of the man who'd stood on the beach and watched the boy drown. Rage filled Claude as he found the shale under his feet and stood up, dragging the body onto the sand. He collapsed onto his knees and stared down at the boy's face. His eyes were open, but the boy's chest didn't move. Quickly, Claude administered the kiss of life, remembering how it was done from a book he'd once read in a dentist's waiting room.

Nothing. He began desperately to thump on the boy's chest, but again there was no reaction. Claude began to shake with shock. He had never encountered death so closely before. Those open blue eyes, the small, lifeless body . . . He felt tears begin to smart in his eyes, and he took a deep shaking breath, rubbing the back of his hand against his nose.

A shadow fell over them, and Claude sat back on his heels, looking up into the man's face. He recognized him immediately, of course, just as he had instantly recognized the drowned boy as being the younger son of Marcus D'Arville. Claude gasped. The man who'd watched him drown had been the boy's own brother! For the first time doubt began to circulate in his brain. Had shock rendered Wayne D'Arville unable to go to his brother's aid? Was that why he had stood, frozen to the spot, when only yards away his own brother had lost his pitifully short life?

'Monsieur D'Arville . . . I'm so sorry,' Claude stuttered, rising shakily to his feet. He was horribly conscious of the older man's status and power, and felt dwarfed by Wayne's size. Would he blame him for not reaching Henri soon enough? 'I . . . I just couldn't get there in time,' Claude cried, his voice uneven and appalled. He began to shift uneasily under Wayne's steely blue gaze, and self-consciously rubbed the wet black hair from off his forehead. 'The dive went wrong, you see . . . I watched him. He couldn't straighten out and he hit the water on his back.' Claude gestured helplessly to the cliffs above them, and then stumbled into silence.

Wayne nodded. 'I couldn't see his dive from where I was.'

'No, of course not,' Claude muttered, ice beginning to shiver in his blood. 'You probably didn't see it all go wrong.'

'No,' Wayne repeated with soft, chilling emphasis. 'I didn't.'

Claude nodded vigorously. He was suddenly terrified, but was not sure why. There was something very still about the giant man standing in front of him – something menacing. 'It's a tragedy, monsieur,' he finally muttered, unable to stand the silence any longer.

Wayne looked down at Hans's face, and a small muscle began to beat at the side of his jaw. 'Yes,' Wayne said, his voice dead. 'It was a tragedy. I wish . . . I wish I'd never seen it happen.' His voice began to crack.

Claude let out his breath in a relieved woosh. He had been wrong, after all. For a few awful seconds he'd actually thought . . . 'In fact,' Wayne said, his voice suddenly hard and precise, 'there's no reason anyone should know I was even here. There's no point in upsetting the family even further.'

'Monsieur?' Claude said, puzzled.

'The kids on the cliff top did not see me arrive. And you did not see me here, either. Did you . . . Rissaud, isn't it?'

Claude went white. He knew he did, and he took a few steps back, as if Wayne were some poisonous cobra about to strike him. 'You did it on purpose,' he accused, his voice an appalled whisper. His young face wore a look of such disgusted horror that Wayne felt a white-hot fury erupt in his brain. In a flash his fist shot out and caught the young fisherman on the side of his face. Claude flew back in the air and landed in the surf. He lay there unmoving as Wayne walked a few more steps and stood towering over him.

'Your family own a fishing boat, yes?'

Claude said nothing.

'I believe things have not been going too well recently,' Wayne continued grimly. 'Tourism is ruining the lobster beds, and the catches are getting smaller and smaller. That's so, isn't it, Rissaud?' Claude nodded. The waves felt like ice water around his elbows, and his heart was hammering so loud he felt sick. The way the man talked, the way he acted, no one would know that his younger brother lay dead at his feet.

'You don't want the bank to call in any outstanding loans, do you, Rissaud?' Wayne asked. 'Or for your boat to mysteriously catch fire one of these dark nights?'

Claude turned away and vomited into the sand. Tears streamed down his face. He'd never known that such ugliness could exist in the world.

Wayne looked around quickly. There were no other boats on the water, and Hans had had the wind knocked out of him, preventing him from calling out his brother's name. No one need know he had ever been there. But the kids would be down soon, crying and screaming. Wayne looked down at Hans, an odd pride overriding his cold logic. Yes, his little brother deserved screams and tears. No one, Wayne thought with a cold certainty, will cry for me when I die.

'Pick him up,' Wayne said coldly. 'Take him to the road and flag down a car. And Rissaud,' Wayne said softly, 'unless you want to join him – ' he glanced at his brother's lifeless body for one last time '– keep your mouth shut.'

CHAPTER 8

Oxford

Kier sat in the lecture hall of St Bartholomew's Hall, affectionately known as the Bull Pit, staring at a stage that was small but adequate. He could tell at a single glance that extra lighting would have to be set up.

'Well, will it do?' a laconic, bored voice inquired lazily. Kier's roommate, Vivian Miles Tarquin Crane was the eldest son of the Earl of Dorminster. With his long legs hooked over the back of the seat in front of him he looked disreputable and hopelessly romantic, with dreaming looks and a wild streak. A bohemian at twenty, he was rich, precociously talented and had an aimless, directionless life that made Kier feel secretly sorry for him. They'd hit it off the moment Kier had walked into his room and found Viv already in residence, hung-over and begging for an aspirin.

'It'll have to, I suppose. It isn't exactly the Old Vic, though, is it?' Kier responded, thinking of Olivier, but also of the crop of English budding talent – Courtenay,

Finlay, and O'Toole. He longed to see *Look Back in Anger* by the new playwright, Osborne. The era of the 'angry young man' was upon them, and Oxford seemed a million miles away from it all.

'Bloody Yank,' Viv said affectionately. 'Why do I get the feeling this is going to be the best bloody play OU Drama has seen for years?'

'Because it probably will be,' Kier said, folding his arms and leaning back in the uncomfortable seat, a mock-arrogant scowl on his face.

'Bloody Yank,' Viv said again, then with a lazy grin charmingly changed tactics. 'Decided who's going to play the lead yet? What are you calling this shindig again?'

'Kate versus Pete,' Kier said, knowing Viv hadn't forgotten, but was merely trying to wind him up. After two years in England, he was beginning to learn a whole new concept in humour. He was even starting to grasp the intricacies of irony. Perhaps in his next play
. . .

'Ah, yes. Modernizing Shakespeare. You don't want to take on much, do you?' Viv said, his eyes twinkling.

'I'm a barbarian, remember? A marauding invader to these hallowed halls.'

'Bloody Yank.'

'Precisely. Why do you suppose all you drama cretins voted me as director, huh? A pipsqueak up-start Rhodes scholar whose only credentials were the annual Burmanville hoe-down.'

'Because we were mad,' Viv said, his beautiful face wearing a look of pitiful dejection. 'We were all half-drunk, and when you came up with the idea of butchering *The Taming of the Shrew*, we all thought it was hilarious. Especially since it put old Flakey's nose totally out of joint.'

'Malcolm Flakestone,' Kier said, deadpan, 'is a total moron. I may not have been here last year to see his production of *Faust*, but I'm still hearing about the reviews, most of which seem to have been written on the john walls.'

Viv began to laugh. 'My oh my, you should have been there to see it. Mass audience participation. They all threw up at the same time, right on cue.'

'Sounds great.'

'Oh it was. But I think you might top it. You're not really going to rename the play 'Kate versus Pete', are you?'

'I am.'

'Bloody Yank.'

'First, though, I need scenery painters, lighting technicians – you can pilfer them from the Engineering department – prompters, some dress designers and . . . what else?'

'Actors?' Viv asked archly, elongating the word and affecting it with a painfully upper-crust British accent that would have done Olivier proud. 'How now, good Kate. What goes on 'ere? Isn't that how it'll go?'

'Not quite. Mind you . . .' Kier scratched his ear, his face thoughtful. 'I could work it in.' For a second or two Viv stared at him, half-aghast, half-dumbfounded, and then caught the glitter in the American's eye.

Slowly he relaxed back against the chair. 'Bloody Yank.'

Two days later in Broad Street (known to everyone local as The Broad), the sun was shining on a cool October morning. Blackwell's, the biggest and most famous of all bookshops, presented its black and white, half-timbered façade to the street, looking misleadingly small and 'quaint'. Betty tucked her hand through Oriel's arm, and took a deep breath. 'Hummm. Oxford in Autumn. Nothing like it.' The beech trees still clung modestly to several golden copper leaves, and the creepers that clung to Trinity and Balliol college walls were a deep golden-veined red. Above them the sky was that curious deep blue of autumn, that in the summer would be alive with swifts and swallows, who made their cupped nests under the ancient eaves of Oxford's thirty plus colleges.

'I never realized till I got here, that there wasn't actually any place, any building I mean, that you could point to and say "There – that's Oxford University," Oriel looked at her friend, who grinned widely. 'It's just a collection of colleges.'

'That's us British for you. Never do anything the easy way.' Betty grinned. She was delighted to have her old friend back again. Oriel would make Oxford fun, somehow, Betty just knew it.

'When are the Matriculation photos' going to be ready?' Oriel asked, for about the fifth time in as many days.

'I already told you. Not till November. What's the matter – you got a fetish for subfusc or something?' Betty asked archly.

'Sub what?'

Betty grinned. 'Subfusc, dear. You know, that charming little uniform we had to wear for the photo? Black skirt, white blouse, bum-freezer and cap?'

Oriel laughed. 'I love it. I love all of this,' she looked around the ancient city, the mellow sandstone quads, the gothic towers, the domed majesty of the Sheldonian theatre, the ornate clock-faces and the quiet, academic ambiance that proliferated, even in the town centre. 'I'm so glad I came. Wait till Daddy gets the postcards I sent him.'

'Humph,' Betty said, hiding her pride in the beautiful city with typical modesty. 'Wait until you see the Bull pit.'

'That's even older than New College, isn't it?' When she'd first discovered that New College had been around for over 800 years, she'd nearly flipped.

'Yeah – with plumbing to match,' Betty predicted gloomily. 'We're going to freeze our cute little . . . things . . . off,' she mused delicately. 'Always providing we get hired of course. I hear the director's one of your lot.'

'We'll get hired,' Oriel said, her blue eyes sparkling with anticipation. 'You're the best scenery painter in the whole world.' Betty looked across at her friend, the usual, unmalicious envy filling her at the sight of Oriel's carefree beauty. Today she was dressed in lilac coloured velvet trousers and a fluffy pink cash-mere sweater. Her blonde hair was loose and gleamed like golden silver. If only I looked like that, Betty thought with a wistful pang, then shrugged. 'Here it is,' she said, leading her friend into an ancient quad. 'Can you see any arrows?'

'Nope.'

'Great. They said the theatre would be marked.'

Inside the unmarked theatre it was in chaos. Kier sat at the back, well out of the way, watching the engineering boffins set up an intricate display of lights. Hammer-ing, followed by mixed curses, came from the boys nailing canvas over the wooden frames that would soon be painted for the outdoor scenes. 'It'll never be done for Christmas,' Kier muttered angrily to himself. 'Never in a million years. Hell, what have I gotten myself into?'

'We've got a queue of girls auditioning for Kate,' Charlie Griffin, the co-director and top Classics scholar, yelled from down front. 'Shall we start?'

'Why not?' Kier yelled back, picking up his copy of the play that he'd re-written, its pages now forlornly dog-eared and coffee-stained. 'Cut out the hammering for a minute, will ya?' he called over to two Experi-mental Psychology students, who were only too happy to oblige. They left, muttering dire comments about Freud and masochism. For weeks the production team had been immersed in the technicalities of the play – the widening of the stage, the runners on which the scenery would be wheeled in, hopefully without a squeak. They'd discussed paint, light, cues, make-up, costume and everything but the fun part. The actual acting. Now the seats began to fill up with interested spectators as Kier walked to the stage and cleared a spot in the centre. He was dressed in disreputable jeans with tears at the knees, and his shirt was stained with sweat and covered with sawdust. He pushed the hair wearily off his forehead as several girls came through the door and stood nervously but with chattering bravado by the wall. Kier looked them over with a jaundiced eye, his gaze widening incredulously on one girl who looked like an overweight electrified poodle. Before he'd had time to think about what he was doing, he was walking over to her. 'Gal, I love your spirit,' Kier said to the startled Betty, 'but despite what you heard, this isn't gonna be a farce.'

'Huh?' Betty said, her eyes as wide as saucers.

'Look, we might be doing a Molière comedy next year. Why don't you come back then?'

'Huh?' Betty said again, totally numb in the face of so much masculine gorgeousness. He looked like a disreputable thug, and he had the brooding, sod-em-all air of Marlon Brando. Betty was wild about Brando.

'He means,' an icy voice said beside her, 'that he thinks you are not fit to play his precious Kate.' The voice, as well as dripping venom, was so mellow, so outlandishly southern-belle in accent, that Kier turned startled eyes to the girl by the electrified poodle's side, his mouth dropping open at the sight of her. He felt the barrage of antagonism coming from the blue eyes and quickly ran his eyes over her, taking in her small, slender frame, the heart-shaped face and peaches-and-cream complexion. She looked like a pink and lilac fairy, with spun silver hair and china blue eyes.

Betty went red. 'Oh no. I . . . huh . . . I'm not here to audition.'

'As you'd have known,' Oriel snapped out, 'if you'd taken the time to ask, instead of just jumping to conclusions.'

Kier heard a ripple of laughter wind its way around the theatre, and flushed dully. 'Oh, great,' he muttered, turning away to salvage what was left of his battered dignity. 'Just what we needed.' He stalked a few yards away, then turned back. 'We're not doing *Gone with the Wind*, sweetheart,' he mocked, gratified to hear the laughter come more loudly this time.

Oriel dragged in her breath swiftly. 'I'm not surprised, suh,' she said, exaggerating her accent to farcical extremes. 'To do such an epic would require a director with some modicum of skill.'

Betty looked from one to the other like a spectator at a tennis match. Both had colour high on their cheeks, both were breathing hard and both looked ready to kill.

'To direct *Gone with the Wind*, Scarlett,' Kier snapped back with savage mockery, 'you'd need a director without a brain. That would be the only way to make use of such utter trash.'

'Here here,' a very British voice applauded from the sidelines, and Oriel glanced briefly to where an out-

94

rageously handsome man was lounging over some seats. 'And you can shut up too,' Oriel spat at Viv, who blinked and began to grin widely.

'Kier, old sport,' he said, straightening out his long, lean form and walking over to where the two antagonists stood, very much the centre of attention now. 'I do believe we have our Kate right here. Have you ever seen such fire,' Viv took Oriel's chin, which she angrily shook off. 'Have you ever seen such shrewishness?' he continued like a bored Noël Coward, the bit well and truly between his teeth. Viv loved trouble like some of his contemporaries loved sex.

'Oh shit,' Kier said helplessly, rubbing his hand wearily across his forehead. 'Alright,' he called out, deliberately turning his back on Oriel and his troublemaking friend. He'd have a word with Viv later. 'Let's get this show on the road.' Kier clapped his hands, attempting to restore some order out of the chaos, and reaffirm his own leadership.

'Oh my gawd, just listen to him,' that voice again, that soft as maple syrup, Scarlett O'Hara voice. 'The king of clichés,' Oriel jibed. 'Somebody tell me he didn't write the script for this little ol' production.'

Kier jerked around, looking ready to flatten her, and the snickering laughter suddenly stopped. Oriel's pert little chin jutted up, ready to do battle. Kier took a long, deep breath, and then sighed ostentatiously. 'Do you mind, Scarlett, if we begin the auditions?' He asked it with such lavish humility, that Oriel felt her lips twitch. Her heart was hammering. Underneath her sweater, she could feel her nipples tingling,

95

burgeoning into hardened nubs. She was aware of fine sweat, creeping all over her, as she began to radiate heat.

He was the most handsome man she'd ever seen. And she hated him with such a passion it was exquisite.

Aware that he was watching her like a hawk, just waiting for her response, she quickly pulled herself together.

'Not at all, suh,' she responded in kind, and, just as an afterthought, gave a brief but perfectly executed, perfectly elegant curtsy.

Looking at Betty, who was doing her best to hide a wide grin, she stalked off to the front row and sat down, crossing her arms across her breasts with vicious strength, flattening them and making her wince. Kier stood a few yards away, watching her performance, and then half-bowed himself. 'So kind,' he said, getting in the last word.

He wanted to throttle her at the same time as he wanted to throw her onto her back in the middle of the stage and make love to her. He'd soon wipe that wide-eyed look off her face then, alright. He could just imagine his hands curling around her breasts, his tongue licking those nipples he could see straining against the pink fluffy wool of her sweater into ever harder points of pleasure/pain. Then they'd see who could keep up the wisecracks!

The whole theatre seemed to breathe a sigh of relief, and it snapped his mind back to the task at hand. He felt like spitting. Never had a woman, any woman, managed to distract him so much when he was trying to work. He'd always known directing was in his blood. Now, it seemed, this spitfire was trying to worm her way into it, as well.

'Now,' Kier took a deep breath, and reached for several copies of a scene and handed one out to each of the girls still stood by the door. 'I want you to read this scene, take five minutes, then we'll begin. Uh, Scarlett, would you like a copy, or are you a mind-reader as well as theatre critic?'

Oriel's lips thinned ominously as she all but catapulted herself out of her seat. She stalked to him like a tigress, yanked a copy out of his hand, then stalked back. Kier's eyes were glued to the exaggerated swaying of her hips, and the angry jerking movement of her limbs. His throat went dry.

Viv began a slow handclap.

'Shut up, you,' Kier rounded on him viciously, jabbing a finger in his direction. 'I can always cast Mark Jennings as Pete.'

Viv paled, then fell to his knees. 'Oh no, boss,' he said, his mimicry of Al Jolson perfect. He held up his hands, palm forwards. 'I begs yah, boss, don' do that tuh me.'

The makeshift audience began to clap uproariously, and Kier began to laugh. 'Get up, you clown.'

A few yards away, Oriel began to simmer as she listened to Kier giving out the orders. 'What a big-headed, no-good, show-off, no-talent . . .'

'Prat?' Betty, who'd followed her over, offered helpfully.

'Moron,' Oriel preferred, her heart hammering in her chest like a trip-hammer. She felt like committing murder as she watched him. But he looked so tall and capable up there, so powerful and dangerous, that she quickly lowered her eyes to read the script, hoping against hope that it was utter drivel. There was something so magnetic about him. She could actually feel her eyes straining to look up from the paper, but she valiantly fought the need to feast her eyes on him.

She took a deep breath, and noticed how badly her hands were shaking. She made a small, angry sound in the back of her throat.

This would never do!

She'd heard on the grapevine that the new director of the OU play, had also adapted it, and she scanned the lines quickly. It was *The Taming of the Shrew* she thought incredulously, and before she could stop herself, her eyes flew back to him on the stage.

'He's only re-written Shakespeare!' she said, her voice so shocked it was almost a whisper. Betty craned her neck to read the page for herself, and smiled.

'So he has. You've got to admire his guts.'

Oriel didn't have to do any such thing. And just at that moment, Kier turned and looked at her, and their eyes clashed. Oriel almost expected to hear the sound of sparking steel, the moment was so physical. For a second, time seemed to stand still. Her eyes widened, her breath caught. Her whole body seemed to leap, even as it froze.

Kier felt the power of her gaze, and knew he would never be able to look away from her. She was so damned beautiful. No woman had a right to look that perfect. He wanted . . .

Kier just wanted.

Then somebody coughed, and the theatre came flooding back. Kier turned once more to check on something in the middle of the stage, that didn't need checking, but allowed him to turn his back on her. His face was flushed.

Oriel let out her breath at last in a wonderful sense of release. If he hadn't turned away, she was sure, she'd have gone on gawping at him like some damned lovesick teenager.

Angrily, she turned her attention back to his so-called play. But although the scene was set in modern times, and used modern language, she saw immediately that it was as pithy, funny, aggravating and every bit as clever as the original. 'Well, at least he can write,' Betty said, having finished reading the script over her shoulder, then jerked away as Oriel turned her head savagely. 'OK, OK. It's awful,' she placated, but still her lips began to wobble.

'It is awful,' Oriel insisted. 'Messin' about with Shakespeare indeed,' she said loudly enough to be heard. 'Just who does he think he is?'

Sat three rows behind her now, Kier stared daggers at her silver head. She's going to be lousy, he thought hopefully. She was probably – no, almost certainly – going to stink. She thought she was such a bigshot. No doubt she came from some mansion someplace down south, and had all the men falling at her feet. Her doting mama had probably sent her to one of those fancy finishing schools. Kier knew her kind. For all her spoilt and pampered life she'd had everything she ever wanted, handed to her on a plate. And now she thought she could just waltz into *his* play, and secure herself the lead, just because she thought she could twist him around her little finger, with her big blue eyes and lovely . . . lovely . . . breasts.

Hah!

He'd soon put her right.

The first girl to read the lines was a tall brunette who looked perfect, but couldn't act to save her life. The second had a saucy teasing quality that would have been great in a *femme fatale* role, but was all wrong for man-hating Kate. Oriel watched them, her blood still boiling, all the time aware of his glowering presence behind her, burning two holes in her back. She shifted uncomfortably in her seat, ready to explode. The mean-mannered, arrogant, insensitive, handsome sonofabitch! She'd show him. Just wait and see.

Viv played opposite the girls with a swaggering bravado that was perfect, and Kier felt relieved. No one could accuse him of playing favourites after this performance. Viv might be his best friend, but anyone with an eye could see he was a born actor. If worse came to worst, he'd be able to carry the play alone. Viv, naturally, took the opportunity to flirt with all the girls outrageously, and the third try-out began to giggle helplessly.

Kier slapped his hand to his face and ran his fingers down his eyes, nose, and off the end of his chin. Let this last one be good, he prayed. Please, Lord, don't let Scarlett get a look in.

The last girl *was* good. She was competent, she had already memorized her lines, and she looked right. Kier felt a sigh of relief ripple over him. Below, Oriel could almost feel the waves of his relief washing over her, and she felt her backbone stiffen.

She had planned to go up there and play Kate like Scarlett O'Hara, just to show him. But now, as she heard his hateful cowboy drawl asking her if she'd care to participate, she suddenly felt her world dip dangerously around her. Because, suddenly, unbelievably, she wanted that part. She wanted it more than anything in the world. And she knew why, of course. It would mean being around him. It would mean seeing him every day. It would mean listening to his voice, and sneering at him, and feeling that wonderful heat that seemed to flood over her whenever he was near.

She was getting hooked on him. And it felt wonderful!

Slowly, trying to gather her thoughts and calm herself down, she walked onto the stage, her eyes blue fire. She had not been voted best drama student at both her Atlanta and Switzerland colleges for nothing!

Viv watched her approach, aware of the waves of empathy coming from her and whistled under his breath, instinctively sensitive to the lovely lady's mood. Suddenly the theatre became still as Oriel took several deep breaths. Kier's eyes widened as her face slowly relaxed, then transformed itself into

101

that of another woman. With her left eyebrow pushed up higher and her lips twisted into a parody of a smile she looked just like he would have expected Kate to look when meeting Pete for the first time.

'So – you're the whizz-kid from Birmingham, are you?' she said her first line with a sneer that was perfect, and not a trace of her Scarlett O'Hara accent. He could hear the contempt vibrating in her voice. Viv caught on in a flash. Walking closer he allowed himself a smug smile, falling into the character of the swaggering Pete with hearty gusto. 'And you must be Kate. I've heard a lot about you from your *lovely*,' he stressed the word, 'sister.'

Oriel strutted around him, and slowly ran her eyes up and down Viv. For the first time, she realized what a very handsome man he was. Not in Kier Harcourt's class of course, but . . .

Suddenly, she flicked a look across the theatre, her eyes instantly zeroing in on him. A strange smile flashed across her face and was gone.

Kier tensed. He was sure that smile was not a part of her performance. His lips twisted. What was she up to now?

On the stage, Oriel turned back to Viv, and looked him up and down, as Kate would have done. 'You're so *lovely* too, kiddo,' she read the line with cringe-making sarcasm, but at the same time, a husky breathiness that caught Viv unawares. His eyes sharpened on her. And what a sexy piece she was.

Kier felt his body shiver under the sexy double-whammy of her voice, and gritted his teeth. 'If you'll read the script, Scarlett,' he gritted, 'you'll see I've asked for contempt, mixed with a touch of fear. If I'd wanted a vamp, I'd have said so.'

Oriel smiled. Good. She was getting to him.

Viv caught the smile and almost laughed out loud. He glanced across at his friend, and envied him. What fun these two were going to have. 'Why, thank you, Kate,' Viv said. 'I'm so glad you noticed.'

Oriel, for a second, couldn't remember her next line, she was so busy trying to gauge Kier's reaction to her. She dragged her eyes back to Viv.

'Oh, I notice a lot of things, kiddo,' she drawled. 'I even notice flies on the wall, and snakes in the grass,' the last line she said, with her head turned and looking straight at Kier. His eyes narrowed.

Oriel turned back to Viv, who was helplessly wondering what she'd do next. It was like acting with a stick of dynamite. A *lit* stick of dynamite!

'A 12-stone man presents no problems for *me*,' she finished the line. She'd been meant, she knew, to say it with bravado and dismissal, but instead she had deliberately leaned her body towards Viv, slightly turning one shoulder his way, and again bringing a huskiness to her voice.

Viv felt his loins harden, even though he knew she had not played the scene for his benefit. But he just couldn't help it. It was the most sexy thing he'd ever seen.

Every male in the audience thought so too. You could cut the atmosphere with a knife.

Oriel smiled in satisfaction, and turned to the director.

Kier was now on the edge of his seat. His hands were curled into fists. He wanted to go across and shake her and tell her to stop coming on to Viv, dammit! But, of course, that was just what she wanted.

He'd be damned if he'd play it her way.

'Not quite what I'm after, sweetheart,' Kier said dismissively, and watched her eyes widen in alarm. 'You started off well, but I think we'll have to go with Janice,' he named the last girl, the girl who'd been so good.

Viv did a double-take. Was he mad? This girl was Kate, with a capital 'K'.

'Perhaps, if you'd made your directions clearer, I could do it again,' Oriel gritted, but there was a touch of very real fear in her voice. Kier heard it and grinned wolfishly.

Oriel's lips tightened. The bastard! She turned to Viv. 'Let's start again, shall we?' she said.

Kier reared up in his chair. 'Hey, Scarlett!' he yelled, his voice cutting through the now mouse-quiet theatre like a scythe. 'Remember me?'

'As if I could forget,' Oriel snarled back.

Kier ignored her. 'I'm the director, get it? I'm the one,' he ostentatiously pointed at his own chest with his own thumb. 'I'm the one who gets to say whether you should start again. That's my job, see?'

Oriel ground her teeth so loudly, that Viv could actually hear her. He coughed. 'Er, I think, old man, we really should try it, just one more time.' He looked at his friend, all his stirring and muck-racking instincts leaping to the fore. 'I do have to play Pete, you

104

know,' he added. 'And I would like *some* say in my partner.'

He gave Oriel an outrageous wink.

Kier fumed. He needed Viv badly, and Viv knew it, damn him. 'Alright,' he snapped. 'We'll do it one more time,' he agreed. 'But,' he jabbed a finger in Oriel's direction. 'Play it like it says.'

Oriel saw the savagery in his eyes and her heart leapt. He was jealous of Viv! Hah! Not so high-and-mighty now, are you, Mr Director?

She nodded graciously. 'I shall do my best,' she drawled, and did.

From the first word she uttered, with Viv's willing help, they became the Shrew and her determined lover.

Kier watched the rest of the scene with a sense of fatality. When they'd finished, the people around him erupted into spontaneous applause. They'd been great! A smash, and everyone knew it.

On the stage, Viv looked up and found Kier with his eyes, shrugging helplessly. 'What can I say, old sport?' He was once again the archetypal English gentleman. 'She's simply brilliant, what?'

Everyone looked at Kier, wondering what he was going to do.

What he did was rest his face in his hands and say with a heartrending groan, 'Oh, *hell*.'

CHAPTER 9

Two weeks later, Betty stood in baggy blue overalls, her forearms splashed with green paint. The scenery was almost finished, and behind her she listened to the rehearsals with half an ear. They were not going well, and yet they were going brilliantly. About on a par with the previous ones she thought, grinning as she daubed.

After their first explosive meeting, the cast and crew had expected things to die down between their director and leading lady. After all, everybody reasoned, that kind of grating, repressed sexual tension and electricity could not be kept up for long without burning itself out. But, boy, were they wrong, Betty thought with a wide grin, as she outlined the leaves of her canvas tree with precise artistic skill.

Oriel and Kier's first rehearsal had set the scene for the weeks that had followed.

'OK,' Kier said now, standing on stage with his two principal actors. 'This is where Pete is looking you over,' he glanced reluctantly at Oriel, 'and telling you that it's no wonder you've never had a boyfriend because you're always trying to wear the pants. That shouldn't be any trouble for you, I think?'

Kier hated looking at her, just because he loved it so much. All his concentration went out the window with the merest lift of one of her fair eyebrows, or a twitch of her eminently kissable mouth.

Oriel smiled sweetly, her eminently kissable mouth pouting now, and driving him secretly wild. 'Not for me,' she'd agreed through gritted teeth, then looked Kier over in such obvious and minute detail that everybody held their breath. 'Of course, I'm trusting your instincts on this,' she added. 'Because it's obvious you don't feel comfortable in pants.'

Viv yelped with laughter, then clamped a hand over his wide and mobile mouth as his friend shot daggers in his direction.

'Let's get one thing straight,' Kier began, sighing wearily, and Oriel smiled even more sweetly and interrupted him.

'That would be a nice change for you, I imagine.'

By now, everybody, naturally, had stopped to watch the spectacle. It was not often you got this calibre of entertainment for free. 'I'm the director of this production,' Kier carried on, ignoring her needling dig. His voice was low and dangerous as he walked closer to her, step by menacing step.

In spite of herself she felt her heart begin to pick up a beat, but she held her ground. It was like facing off a tiger. She could almost feel his claws on her, stroking, his nails raking gently across her breasts, and . . . She firmly clamped the thought off, and forced herself to concentrate on what he was saying.

'I wrote these lines,' Kier tapped his copy of the script ferociously, 'and if you want to play the part, you do what I say, when I say, how I say.' He'd been steadily bearing down on her throughout these hissed ultimatums, and now he leaned over her, so close, that their faces were barely inches away. 'Got it?' He snarled.

Oriel could feel the raw power of him and swore she could feel the heat from his skin scorching her bare face. Nervously she flicked out her tongue to moisten her lips, and then wished she hadn't. His incredibly soft orange-brown eyes wavered and then dipped to watch the movement. Oriel gasped, but so softly that only Viv and Kier heard it.

'Got it,' she managed to grate out with a good facsimile of her usual venom. Viv watched them in silence, then rubbed his hands together. This was going to be a very interesting season. Very interesting indeed.

Oriel decided to change tactics, and for the rest of the session she kept a wary distance. Icy politeness and exaggerated co-operation became the order of the day, allowing the rehearsal to speed along satisfactorily. But since the opening night was fast approaching, everybody was getting tense.

Behind her, the play carried on.

'NO!' Even Betty jumped as Kier's roar suddenly echoed throughout the confined interior of the room. 'I told you before,' he stalked on stage to where Oriel waited, fidgeting nervously.

This was the biggest play she'd ever been in, and she was beginning to feel unsure of herself. Although she wouldn't have admitted it to anybody, she was scared that she'd let her temper get her into a situation that she simply couldn't handle, and Kier's antagonism didn't help. Neither did the way her stomach flipped whenever he was near. 'You don't think it's funny when he tells you to shut up and kiss his ass. It enrages you, it doesn't make you grin, goddamit.'

Oriel finally snapped. For weeks she had put up with his bullying and his re-writing and his nit-picking criticisms. She'd just about had enough. Her anxiety and sexual tension was at fever pitch.

'I can't help it,' she yelled back. 'It's the way you wrote it. It is funny, dammit. Isn't it?' she appealed to the usual oddjob men and part-time audience, who began to nod. Her beauty, her talent, her good humour and her lack of prima donna vanity had long since endeared her to everyone but Kier over the last few weeks. But Kier's sole facial expression around her was that of a perpetual scowl.

'Don't ask them,' he yelped now, goaded beyond endurance. 'What the hell do they know?'

Oriel slammed down her script onto the stage floor, then stood staring at him, her breasts rising and falling so agitatedly behind her sweater that Kier couldn't keep his eyes off them.

'Why don't you,' she said softly, 'douse yourself in petrol, and go straight to hell?'

'Because, Scarlett,' Kier snarled back, 'with you as my leading lady, I'm already there.'

'Why, you . . . you . . .' Oriel felt the rage that had been on the backboiler since the moment she'd set eyes on him, suddenly erupt. With a yowl of pure, goaded fury, she swung her hand and hit him, full on the face.

It was not any kind of screen slap, but a clench-fisted effort that bore the brunt of her whole weight and fury. Kier staggered back, his face on fire. Viv covered his eyes and sorrowfully shook his head. As the slap echoed throughout the theatre with a sharp 'crack' the room fell totally silent. Everyone held their breath as they waited for Kier's reaction. Oriel felt an appalled fear wash over her, vying for first place with a self-satisfied desire to nod her head, brush her hands and add, 'So there,' just for good measure.

Kier slowly straightened and looked her. For a second, their eyes met in electrified silence. 'That,' he said clearly, 'is just what you should do to Pete, when he asks you to kiss his ass. Get it right this time. Viv, your mark.'

Oriel blinked, as did Viv, and then suddenly the room was filled with laughter and applause. 'Thatt-away, Director,' someone yelled from the back. 'You tell 'em.'

Kier rubbed his throbbing cheek ruefully and headed past her for the steps at stage right. Oriel was torn between the need to laugh along with every-one else and stamp her feet in temper. 'I hate you,' Oriel whispered as he went past her and she could smell the scent of his cologne, sweat, and the odour that was totally Kier. She wanted to kiss him so

110

viciously, so much, she felt herself actually swaying towards him.

'Naturally,' he whispered back, his tiger-eyes flashing like amber fire. 'You want me.'

And with that heart-stopping statement he left the stage, leaving Oriel open-mouthed and staring after him, her heart in her throat.

'Right, from the top again,' Kier called, sitting in his usual chair in the middle of the front row and leaning back, stretching his arms across the backs of the adjoining chairs, for all the world as if nothing had happened. He felt good. He felt so good he wanted to sing. He'd been dying to say that to her for weeks. And the shattered look in her eyes was so sweet, he could still feel the honey of it on his tongue.

On the stage, he watched her begin to shake with a mixture of rage, frustration and something else, much more potent that he doubted even she could name it. It was a relief to know that he was not the only one so totally head-over-heels in love.

'Huh . . . Kate darling,' Viv prompted, and Oriel turned to look at him, her eyes confused and tear-bright. 'Don't deliver the slap with quite as much wallop this time, hmm? I have a date tonight, and I don't want my beloved to be offered damaged goods. OK?' Viv wore a hang-dog puppy look of such dramatic proportions that she began to laugh helplessly.

From his seat Kier watched, scowling.

It was five-thirty, and Viv had to go for a class. The rehearsals broke up, the troops filed out. There were student meets to go to, politics to be discussed and grass to be passed round and smoked into the early hours whilst they listened to the radio or piled into a common room. This was Oxford, after all – radical, forever young Oxford. As usual Kier was left to last, making notes in the margins of his copy, taking pleasure in the way he could make vague and nebulous thoughts take solid shape up on the stage.

'It's going to be a good play.'

His head jerked up at the soft words, his eyes focusing lovingly on the woman on the stage. Without her audience and the persona of Kate to hide behind, she suddenly looked vulnerable and lost. He felt his heart lurch, painfully.

'Thanks,' he said briefly, folding his notes back into place and shoving them into the battered briefcase that he'd bought second-hand at a flea market.

'Look . . . I . . . I want to apologize for hitting you. I shouldn't have lost my temper like that.'

Kier, his body leaning forward as he shoved papers into the case on the floor, looked up at her through the fall of hair on his forehead, and then shrugged. 'Forget it,' he said shortly.

Oriel nodded glumly, and began to walk across stage. He was not making it easy for her, but then why should he? For a moment she felt a sharp stab of regret wash over her that they should be such bitter enemies. Kier straightened and saw the slouch of her shoulders, her head hung low, and felt like a prize bastard. 'Hey, look. Why don't we bounce over to

Browns and have something to eat, huh? After all this hard labour, I'm starved.'

Oriel turned hopefully at the sound of his suddenly softer and cajoling voice, and found an instantly answering smile leaping onto her face. Was she so starved for some kind words from him? It appeared so, she thought ruefully. 'OK. I'd like that. And since I'm the one throwing the punches, I'm even hungrier than you are,' she couldn't resist adding.

Kier laughed. 'You're a saucy minx, I'll say that for you'

'Sexist pig,' Oriel shot back, not totally joking, and Kier grinned.

'It's the play,' Kier explained. 'It gets into my blood, too. I always take on the character of whatever production I'm doing. I once did a *Tale of Two Cities* in Kansas, and turned nearly suicidal for the whole summer.'

'Kansas. Is that where you're from?' Oriel asked eagerly, hungry for any scrap of information about him.

'Yep.' Kier left her briefly in the quad to deposit the bag in his room and grab some change, then quickly rejoined her. Walking briskly in the cold November air, they passed the St Giles war memorial, crossing over to where the white corinthian columns of the Ashmolean museum reminded Oriel of home. Glancing up at it, she sighed with a touch of homesickness, then shrugged it off. Passing St Cross college, they made their way slowly up Woodstock Road. 'Betty says this street is beautiful in spring,'

113

she babbled, suddenly nervous now that they were not at loggerheads. 'She says all the cherry trees are out and in flower then.'

'Oh?' Kier looked at her oddly.

'Yeah, but Five Mile Drive is even prettier. She says.'

'Oh,' he said again.

Oriel rubbed her sweating palms on her jeans as they passed Little Clarendon Street. 'You ever been down there?' she nodded her head in the street's direction. 'It's got this great shop that sells all kind of junk.'

'Junk, huh?'

'Oh, will you stop it?' She gave an aggrieved sigh. 'I'm trying to be nice.'

'I know,' Kier said, deadpan. 'That's what's making me so nervous.'

They were still laughing when they entered Browns. It instantly reminded Kier of Casablanca. The chairs were wicker, the arched backs gleaming with black walnut. Rattan screens separated the tables, and living greenery climbed throughout from big terracotta tubs. Overhead, big old-fashioned rotary fans hung from the ceiling. They selected a padded window seat, ordering tea whilst they perused the menu.

'When in Rome, and all that,' Oriel said. 'I'll have the steak and kidney pie.'

Kier breathed a sigh of relief at her choice, half-terrified she'd order lobster. He didn't fancy washing up for the rest of the night because he couldn't afford to pay the bill. 'I'll have the same. So, tell me about

yourself, Scarlett,' he urged as the waiter left with
their order. 'Is that accent for real?'

Oriel laughed and apologized. ''Fraid so. Born and
raised in Georgia.'

'Ah, an Atlanta belle. I thought as much.'

'And you're a Kansas hick.'

'Touché.'

They began to talk, tentatively at first, and then
with growing honesty and detail about their homes,
their parents, their schools, their lives. It was as if,
now that the barriers were down, they couldn't talk
fast enough. For weeks they'd starved themselves of
information about one another, denying the real
reason for their antagonism. Now the floodgates
burst and they began to explore one another with
eager, youthful zeal. He could picture her life like a
movie playing before his eyes as she talked – the loving
hypocrisy of her mother, the weak-willed nature of her
father. He could see why she had needed to run away
from that kind of life, and why she found Betty so very
good for her. Kier, too, had come to like and respect
Betty enormously.

And Oriel, in turn, felt tears burn her eyes when he
described the hard life that had been his father's, and
the even harder death of his mother. And the reason
for the death of his eldest sister appalled her. Being
rich all her life, she had never realized that such things
could and did happen all the time to those who had no
money.

They drank a bottle of red wine between them, the
restaurant crowded by the time they left. Walking

115

back to the college, they passed two boys, dressed in shorts that came to just below the knee and grey, v-necked jumpers, who were carting a scarecrow about in a wheelbarrow. 'Penny for Guy, sir?' the eldest one, about eleven, asked hopefully, holding out a white tin cup.

'The what?'

'The guy.'

Kier glanced at Oriel, who shrugged.

'They're Yanks,' the littler one said scornfully as Oriel asked what a guy was. 'It's supposed to be Guy Fawkes,' he went on to explain, pointing his head to the straw-stuffed effigy in the barrow. 'The fifth is Guy Fawkes night.'

'What are you collecting the money for?' Oriel asked, reaching into her jeans' pocket and coming out with a shilling.

'For fireworks, of course,' the urchin said scornfully.

'Of course,' Kier repeated drolly, adding a penny of his own. 'What did this Guy Fawkes do anyway?' he asked, expecting a long-winded tale of heroic exploits.

'He tried to blow up the Houses of Parliament,' the younger one said, with ghoulish relish. 'And King James the First . . . or Second. One of them anyway.'

'My dad says it's a pity he didn't succeed,' the elder one said solemnly and Oriel bit her lip. But her grin broke loose and then she was laughing.

'Thanks,' the older boy said, grinning like a Cheshire cat when Kier put another penny in the mug.

'The British,' Kier said, 'Don't you just love 'em?'

They were almost at the college now, which was poorly lit at night. 'Do you want to risk coming in for a cup of tea or something?' Kier asked awkwardly, glad that the darkness hid the rising colour in his cheeks, but even more glad that Viv wouldn't be staggering back in until the early hours. It was, of course, against the rules for boys to enter the girls' rooms, or vice versa, but plenty of travelling went on at night, and any student stupid enough to report breaches of this law to the Dean were soon debagged and consigned to Coventry for the rest of the term. And Oxford – forever young and liberal Oxford – chose to turn a blind eye, unless of course, students were actually caught *in flagrante delicto*, so to speak. Oriel's breath fluttered nervously in her throat. She looked around guiltily, but seeing only moonlight and deserted quads she nodded quickly. 'OK.'

The room turned out to be quite like hers – small, square, with one window, flaking walls, two single beds, one large desk, and bookshelves overflowing with ponderous tomes. 'What are you reading anyway?' she asked, pushing a dirty shirt off the bed and sitting down, watching Kier carefully lock the door without comment, although her heart-beat picked up in a mixture of fear, excitement and longing.

'English. You?'

'Languages. When I read the prospectus I realized it was the only thing I could do.'

'French and German?'

'Uh-huh.'

He heaped two spoons of tea-leaves into the teapot and waited for the kettle to boil. 'This place is a mess,' he muttered, picking up dirty laundry by the armful and shoving it under a bed. 'Living with Viv is like living with a ferret.'

Oriel blinked at this analogy, then nodded towards the kettle. 'It's boiling.'

Kier made the tea, handed her hers, then sat down on the opposite bed, leaning against the white plaster walls, and looking at her closely.

'Now, isn't this better than screaming at each other?' she asked, sipping her cup, screwing up her face and demanding sugar. Kier spooned her in two, then retreated back to the far side of the room. He was aware of the dangers, and meant to keep them minimal. Already his body was thinking thoughts it shouldn't. 'It's certainly less painful,' he agreed, rubbing his jaw experimentally.

'Oh, Kier, I am sorry about that,' she said softly, putting down her mug and kneeling beside him on the bed. 'Does it hurt?' she asked, gently fingering his jaw. She could feel the stubble, deeply embedded in his skin, under her fingertips which began to tingle. Kier shrugged, shifting awkwardly back against the wall. 'Not really. It's fine.' He looked at his watch ostentatiously, but it was only 8.30. He almost groaned.

'Kier,' Oriel said softly, chidingly. He glanced at her reluctantly, then shrugged. 'Sorry. For one mad moment I thought I might actually escape.'

'No chance,' she said softly, then leaned forward and bit his ear – hard. He moaned, cursed, and then

118

grabbed a handful of her hair, twisting her around and onto the bed, in the same moment lowering his head. He kissed her hungrily, his whole body beginning to oil itself in passion's sweet sweat. His hands roamed over her breasts beneath the heavy wool of her jumper, brushing the iron-hard nub of her nipples with his thumbs.

Oriel whimpered, her vagina melting into a hot mess as she stretched out her legs, arching her back and pushing up her breasts into his palms in instinctive reaction. A pounding started up in his brain, and he dimly realized that it was his own hot blood, raging in torrents through his veins.

'For weeks I've been telling myself you're nothing but a spoilt brat,' he muttered, his hands tugging her sweater free of her waistband and then pulling it over her head. Child-like, she raised her arms to help him, and the static electricity in the wool made her hair feather out across the pillow like strands of gossamer. For the first time a man's hand unfastened her bra, and Oriel closed her eyes, an exquisite, pained expression on her face as he lowered his head to suck on her bare breasts. Her fingers ran over his scalp as she jerked in reaction, and Kier felt his body begin to burn.

He rose to his knees and impatiently yanked off his shirt. Oriel watched him with wide, observant eyes. His chest was muscular and darkly matted with hair, but his shoulders and arms were smooth. He looked like well-oiled teak, and her fingers went to his nipples, pulling playfully on the hairs that ringed them. Kier winced. 'You knew this was going to happen,' he accused her, his chest rising and falling rapidly as her tormenting caress robbed him of breath, and she laughed, a slow, southern chuckle.

'Of course I did, you bloody Yank,' she drawled, borrowing Viv's favourite phrase. 'I knew soon as I set eyes on you,' she confirmed, her hands on his belt buckle.

Kier gave a rueful grin then moaned as she slipped her hand inside his jeans and caressed his shaft through the white cotton of his underpants. Slowly he lowered the zip, satisfied to see all the humour leave her face as he stripped first himself, and then her, totally naked, revealing the virgin triangle of silver hair at the conjunction of her thighs. Slowly he lifted her ankle, his fingers closing around it as he drew her foot to his mouth. He licked her instep, then suckled on her toes, both things never having entered her head as having anything to do with an erotic seduction before. Then her eyes widened into saucers as delicious tingles shot straight up her leg and lodged in her womb. She began to moan softly.

'You picked on the wrong guy to play games with, Scarlett,' Kier said sadly, and kissed the back of her knees. Oriel jerked, and began to tremble. 'You see – ' he carried on kissing his way up her thighs '– I had this teacher, back home. Her name was Mrs Smith.'

'Smith?' Oriel repeated, her brain turning to jelly.

'Uh-huh.' Kier confirmed, gently holding her thighs apart. 'She was a good teacher too,' he told her, and slowly lowered his head. Oriel moaned, biting

120

down hard on her lower lip as his tongue flickered between the folds of flesh at the centre of her being and then found the taut, throbbing nub of her clitoris. She thrashed so hard she almost came off the bed as Kier sucked her to her first orgasm.

When it was over, and she lay throbbing and shaking in the aftermath, he slowly kissed his way past her navel, to her breasts, up her sternum to her throat, and then took tiny, supping kisses from her lips. She could feel his manhood against her thigh, and then felt its head, hot and persistent, nudge against her opening. 'Kier,' she gasped urgently, suddenly nervous, opening her eyes to meet his burning brown gaze head on. 'There's something I gotta tell you.'

Kier smiled a tender, gentle smile, that made her heart flip in her breast beneath his caressing hand. 'Sshhh,' he soothed her. 'I know, Scarlett.'

'You do?' she asked, her eyes widening as he began to slowly, gently push into her, entering her so tenderly, making her thighs tremble helplessly. His face was tight with concentration as he began to withdraw, then slowly surge forward again, gently taking her virginity. 'I've done nothing but watch you, breathe you, *live* you for weeks now,' he gritted, his body coiled tight as she began to moan and undulate her hips in time to his slow, thoughtful rhythm.

Oriel moaned and then thrashed as he began to slip in and out of her more forcefully, now that she had become used to accommodating him. The pain was gone and was replaced by a finer, more exquiste torture. His stroking shaft was now tormenting her, pushing her higher and higher, his hands on her breasts, his lips on her temples, her neck, her ears, all merging to have her screaming out her orgasm as he played her body like a virtuoso. When she had shuddered into a second shattering climax, she clutched his shoulders as he moaned, then lay still and quiet, Kier's head cushioned on her breast as their ragged breathing returned to normal.

It was chilly in the room, and Kier pulled the blankets around them.

'I'll let you have that round,' Oriel finally said, a secretive smile on her face. 'But from now on in, I'm gonna be learning fast.'

Kier grinned against her nipple and gave it a half-hearted nip, making her jump and clamp her legs warningly against his thigh.

'Scarlett,' he assured her drowsily, 'I wouldn't have it any other way.'

CHAPTER 10

Paris

The Jardin Luxembourg was sandwiched between the Boulevard Raspail, and the more famous Boulevards Saint Michel and Saint Germaine, and was Wayne's favourite spot for sunbathing. Through the trees behind him he could see the Gothic edifice of the Pantheon, and his own University, the Sorbonne, but he had long since become immune to the architectural beauties of Paris. Walking across the grass, he took off his shirt and crumpled the silk Armani creation for a pillow, then lay back on the newly mown grass. The scent of the lime trees around him wafted gently on the breeze, and in the distance he could hear the rumble of traffic that constantly clogged the famous Champs-Elysées.

Term would soon be over, and he'd be back in Monte Carlo. Since the drowning of Hans, he'd been only too glad to leave the gloom and almost frantic despair of the villa and escape to Paris, where he enjoyed a rather ironic kudos attached to the loss of his younger brother. Fellow students treated him with a touching sympathy that Wayne both enjoyed and found painfully repulsive. Guilt ate at his innards, filling his nights with nightmares. He enjoyed the pain like a masochist enjoys biting down on a bad tooth, and the pity of his professors, who gave him the extra assignments he asked for with sad shakes of their Gallic heads, gave him a perverse sense of pride.

It was twelve-thirty, and his few minutes of unusual relaxation made him feel oddly uneasy. The sun through the dappled shade of the trees warmed him; the drone of bees in the lime trees almost lulled him to sleep. But he couldn't afford to fall asleep – it was one thing to wake up screaming and sweating in the middle of the night when no one else could see him, and quite another to do so in the middle of Paris on a busy day.

On a bench nearby two teenage girls, no more than sixteen, watched him get to his feet, their eyes widening at his height. They had been watching him for some time now, making giggling whispered comments behind their hands. They fell into an awed silence as Wayne passed them, and he gave them a smile, glorying in their flushes and giggles. He left the Jardin by the south gate, ignoring the small boats that sailed in the Bassin, and crossed the Saint Michel heading towards the Sorbonne.

Wayne had 'done' all the usual things in his first term at the famous university where he was studying English and Economics. He had visited Versailles in a thunderstorm, and toured the Louvre, wondering what art treasures had been ransacked by his father's cronies. He had eaten real onion soup in the oddly named rue du Chat-Qui-Perche (Street of the Fishing Cat). He had eaten truffles and trout at the Bois de Boulogne, and seen the chandeliers hanging from the chestnut trees by the Seine at the Pont St-Michel. He'd watched the famous can-can dancers in the haunts of Toulouse-Lautrec. Not always alone, but never accompanied by the same woman twice. He had no intentions of limiting his sexual favours, and he already had the reputation of 'user.' He had never forgotten the incident with Urma, and although he was mature enough to understand that his father had only been embarrassed at getting caught in mid-coitus, he had never managed to shake off the feeling that sex was at best, unimportant, at worst, something obscene. All of which meant that he kept his sexual encounters both very passionate, and very brief. Nor was he always very tactful about his dismissals, as several of his fellow female students had come to realize. Not that it prevented the women from trying to change him, of course – each and every one sure that she would be able to tame the monster within.

Wayne mounted the ancient steps of the Sorbonne, and walked into the high-ceilinged hall, pausing by a notice board to peruse the music section. Jean-Paul Montage watched the tall copper-haired man from some arched shadows, his deep green eyes narrowed and angry. The son of the embassador to Turkey, Jean-Paul had been raised in seven different countries by his widowed father, learning the odd cosmopolitan trick or two en route. And from the Arab nation he had learned that a man who couldn't keep his own woman was less than a man. And to actually let your woman be seduced by another was the utmost in loss of face. And if that knowledge became public . . .

'They tell me the Rachmaninov concert is going to be superb,' Jean-Paul said softly, a feral smile on his lips as he moved forward, balancing his weight carefully and ready to lunge. Wayne turned abruptly. It took him only a second to register the anger in the other man's eyes and the tenseness with which he moved. 'Too bad you'll have to miss it.'

Wayne shifted, suddenly aware of something dangerous. But Jean-Paul was nothing, hardly worth his notice. Then his mind suddenly clicked. Jean-Paul was the boyfriend of his latest bedpartner, Jacqueline de Palin. She'd told Wayne she'd finished with Jean-Paul, but obviously the bitch had been lying. Very carefully, Wayne took the older man's measure, and let his lips curl back in a sneer.

'And why should I miss it?' he asked coolly, but was prepared for the answer. A man who was psyched up was a man to watch out for. And who should know that better than himself, who was permanently psyched and ready?

'Because you'll be in hospital, bastarde. *Cochon!*' Jean-Paul spat the insults, breathing deeply. His face was flushed, his rage so intense that it consumed him. Quick as a flash, Wayne's fist slammed square into his stomach, knuckles sinking deep into Jean-Paul's unprepared flesh with devastating force. The Frenchman doubled over and, with an agonized scream, fell to one knee. Wayne looked down on the bowed black head, thought briefly of giving him a good right hook in the face, and decided against it. The last thing he needed was to get expelled.

'Get out of Paris, you pathetic bastard,' he said softly, yanking Jean-Paul's head up by a fistful of black hair. The face was white and sweating, his eyes now black with pain. 'Because if you don't,' Wayne whispered, his voice almost cheerful, 'I'm going to kill you'. He shoved Jean-Paul away with the ease of a dog shaking off a rat and strode away, whistling an extract from Rachmaninov as he did so. He had an apartment near the Place de la Bastille, off the Avenue Daumesnil, and he was almost running by the time he reached it. The next morning his Maserati headed out of Paris in the early dawn sun.

As he drove along the Route Nationale, a Patek-Phillipe watch on his wrist ticked away the minutes from home. Home, where there was no Hans. Home, where his mother would be out at some art exhibition, coffee morning, charity bazaar or bridge meet. Home where Wolfgang would look like an old, bent man. Hans's death had seemed to halve his father, taking away half his strength, half his zest for life, half his arrogance. During those blissful two weeks after the funeral, when Wayne had been awash in guilt and euphoria, he had watched his father with hot, eager eyes, crowing silently over every meal he left uneaten, over every full glass of whisky he had guzzled down.

But if his father had changed, Monte Carlo looked no different. As he approached the perched village of La Turbie, Wayne slowed the purring car to negotiate the serpentine narrow streets that led to the Villa Mimosa and turned in. It was a huge, sprawling bungalow, painted such a brilliant white that it almost hurt the eyes. As its name suggested, mimosa grew in great profusion in the large, landscaped gardens. He pulled the car under the eaves of the two-level garage, and left his bags in the boot. A yucca grew in the middle of a perfect lawn, whilst in front of the house, two fountains sprayed water from stone lotus flowers. A pond full of flowering water lilies and golden koi carp were the highlights on the patio.

Juan, their Spanish major-domo, emerged from the house and took the bags from the car, greeting him subserviently.

'Where is everyone?' Wayne wondered idly.

Juan smiled briefly, more out of habit than out of any pleasure at seeing Wayne, and told him that his father was at the casino, his mother out lunching with friends. Wayne nodded curtly and abruptly went ahead, stripping as he walked into his bedroom, a vast expanse of white carpet, cream walls and hand-painted ceiling. His bed was a vast, king-sized four-poster, from which mosquito lace hung, giving the room an exotic flavour. Sliding doors of dark African wood revealed the locations of the built-in wardrobes, and green-painted shutters matched the green quilt of the bed and the cushions thrown onto a pair of dark leather armchairs. Orange orchids in a crystal vase

128

stood on a dresser, and out on the balcony a shell wind chime created impromptu music conducted by the sea breeze. Blinded by familiarity to all the luxury, he showered and changed, deciding to pass the rest of the afternoon away playing squash at a prestigious sports club by the harbour, of which he was, naturally, a member.

The dining-room was a round affair of cool white walls, highly polished naked floorboards and a pembroke table that could be extended to seat thirty comfortably. It was set for three at the moment, with a pink linen tablecloth, Royal Worcester plates and silver cutlery. As a centrepiece, pink and white carnations and fern-fronds added colour and life.

'Mother,' Wayne said emotionlessly, walking around to where she sat to give her proffered cheek a quick kiss. He nodded at his father, said 'Papa,' equally emotionlessly, and sat down. Wolfgang reached for his wine goblet, which Juan had just filled with the finest Bordeaux, and barked accusingly, 'You're back early.'

Wayne looked at his father steadily. 'I'm ahead with my studies.'

During the intervening months, some of the shock of his beloved son's death had begun to wear off. Wolfgang looked less grey and haggard, and as Wayne sipped his wine and waited for the first course to be served, he sensed something different, something new, in his father's gaze.

'The lessons are going well?'

'Very,' he replied without any pretence of warmth, sure that Wolfgang had a report of his grades on his desk somewhere in the casino.

'That's very good, Wayne,' Marlene said, speaking for the first time, and smiling at him absently. Wayne wondered if she was already drunk. She usually was, but was so adept at hiding it that it was often hard to tell.

'You'd better keep it up,' was all Wolfgang said, but to Wayne the words suddenly made sense. Of course! His father had been forced to look on him the way a man looks upon his heir. His lips twisted in a parody of a smile as Rosita Alvarez, Juan's daughter, walked in with the first course of deliciously chilled avocados. Wayne barely glanced at her, then did a swift double-take. Rosita had worked for them since she'd left school at sixteen, almost two years ago, and Wayne found himself noticing the luxuriant blackness of her long wavy hair, the deep depths of her black eyes that she cast his way and then lowered modestly. She flushed shyly as he smiled at her, and Wayne was pleased to see that she obviously had a crush on him. Her hand trembled as she placed the cut-crystal half-moon dish in front of him, and when she straightened, Wayne looked deep into her eyes.

'Thank you, Rosita,' he murmured softly.

'*De nada.*' She left quickly, amid more blushes. Used to dealing with hardened bitches, Wayne was surprised to realize that her innocence touched him, making him long to destroy it. He picked up his spoon, glancing across the table as he did so, and met his father's ironic gaze head on. Into his mind flashed the picture of Urma on top of his father, pumping away like a demented piston. His hand tightened on the spoon, then with deliberate precision, he cut a segment off the pear and raised it to his mouth. His eyes, which never left his father, were as hard as blue diamonds. Wolfgang sighed almost imperceptibly and, with a small shrug, set about his own meal. Marlene's glass was empty and she reached for the chilled decanter and refilled it, hoping no one noticed.

For a while Wayne was content just to watch Rosita, enjoying the way she shied away from him whenever he flirted with her. Her father occasionally cast harried and angry looks in Wayne's direction, but Wayne ignored him. He waited until Saturday night, when Juan was out chauffeuring his parents to a night-club opening being thrown in Cannes. He was sitting alone in the dining-room, the buzz of the air conditioner a low drone in the background. As soon as she served him the pâté de foie gras Strasbourg he could sense her fear mingled with little-girl excitement. Her breathing changed to agitated little gulps whenever she leant over him to serve, and he smiled like a shark.

'Why don't you join me, Rosita?'

'Join you?' she asked, puzzled, then shook her head, blushing furiously. 'Oh, no, *señor*, I am not permitted to sit at the same table as the *patron*.'

'How long have you worked here, Rosie?' he asked, shortening her name at the same time as he caught her hand and rubbed his thumb across her wrists.

'Over two years, *señor*.' Her voice trembled as she spoke, and her pulse fluttered wildly under his fingers as she looked around nervously.

'And you've never sat at this table for a meal?' Mutely she shook her head, and with one foot he hooked out the matching chair next to him. 'Then it's about time you did, hmm?' Slowly, reluctantly, she subsided into the chair, her hands nervously twisting over her white apron. 'Here – try this,' he urged, forking some of the pâté onto his fork, and then bringing it against her lips.

Obediently she opened her mouth and tasted it. Under the eagle eye of the French chef, Rosita had never been able to even sneak a taste of the gorgeous food she regularly served her employers, and her eyes widened as she sampled the delicacy of the flavourings. Her heart was pounding hard in her breast as they finished the course, and he insisted she try the roast pheasant, imported from England out of season, and then the lemon sorbet, which was so icy cold it made her cheeks numb. She said as much, laughing freely as she confessed to it, her eyes sparkling like black jet, amazed at how quickly the master's son had put her at her ease. He was, as she'd always suspected, wonderfully kind.

And this was easily the most exciting night of her life. She had secretly loved Wayne D'Arville for what seemed like all of her adult life. Whilst everyone else had fussed over poor little Henri, Rosita had looked longingly at the lonely and aloof figure of Wayne who always seemed to be on the outside looking in. She'd always felt the urge to love him, to hold him tenderly in her arms, her generous heart going out to one who was so clearly unhappy. But she had never, ever, expected him to actually notice her. Now she sipped the potent wine, feeling strangely light-headed. She demurred as he refilled her glass, but because he insisted so graciously, she sipped that too. She was a good Catholic, raised in the ways of her church, and knew that it was wrong for them to be alone in the villa. She prayed briefly for forgiveness, but could not summon up the strength to walk away from him. He was so beautiful, so interested in what she had to say. And surely, one night of shared food and wine and a few murmured secrets wasn't *that* sinful?

Wayne put on a slow Strauss walz, and asked her to dance. Immediately she was torn, feeling totally grown up and desirable, and yet at the same time, alarmed. But when he stood up, smiling that tender smile and opening his arms to her, she found herself unable to refuse him. As they danced, Wayne nuzzled her hair, which was silky against his cheek. She smelt of roses and soap, and he told her so, his seduction so practised it was almost mechanical.

'You're truly beautiful, Rosita,' he whispered, and as she thrilled to the words she'd never heard any man say to her before, he slowly danced his way to the patio, where the French doors to his bedroom stood open. As he led her protestingly into his bedroom, there was a heady excitement in his limbs, a sensation of heavy languorous desire bubbling just below the surface. Perhaps it was merely the eroticism of seducing a servant, as his father had seduced Urma all those years ago, but he suddenly found himself wanting Rosita with a savage intensity that was totally new.

'*Señor,*' she whispered, the protest barely audible above her tear-constricted throat as he began to undo her blouse. Despite her hands trying to slap his away, he quickly freed her breasts. They were full and uptilting, the nipples a very dark aureole. Gently he reached out and cupped them in his palms, their weight and the hot silky feel of them immediately arousing him. He ran a thumb over a nipple and Rosita moaned, half in fear, half in pleasure. Fuzzily, her brain told her that she must get away, that she must stop him. 'Please, *señor*. We . . . we musn't.'

Wayne demurred softly, enjoying the sensation of power he felt at such times almost as much as the sexual act itself. He picked her up as if she weighed no more than a cushion, and laid her on his huge bed, his lips sucking at one breast as her hands flew to his hair, her suntanned fingers dark and feverish in his copper hair as she tried to push him away.

Wayne, aware that the hardness in his trousers was becoming uncomfortable, reached down to the zipper. His hand brushed her thigh as he did so, and she suddenly tensed. With the cunning of a weasel sniffing out weaknesses, he curled his fingers around the hem of her skirt and lifted it higher, allowing him to run exploratory fingers up her long, smooth leg, curling around her inner thigh. Rosita closed her eyes. '*Por favor* . . . no, no,' she murmured, but

134

her legs fell treacherously open and he lost no time in pulling down her girlish, plain white knickers. For a moment he stared in surprise at the startlingly large bush of dark hair on her mound. Then he touched her there and Rosita clamped her legs together in instinctive, frightened rejection. Things were going too fast, and she couldn't think. Unused to alcohol, her head felt as if it were stuffed with cotton wool, preventing her from defending herself. Impatiently, he pushed her thighs apart, eager to tongue her red lips that were so different from his own anatomy, and when he brushed her clitoris with his tongue she moaned, a deep frown settling over her darkened brows. This was wrong . . . It felt so good, but it was wrong . . .

Wayne began to lave her in earnest and her moans turned to cries, her head thrashing from side to side on the pillow. With her skirt bunched up around her stomach and one of her nipples tweaked between the thumb and forefinger of his other hand, she became aware of a wave of crashing ecstasy building up between her legs, and her neck arched helplessly.

'*Por favor*,' she gasped, her body beginning to jerk under his hands, '*como se ilama.*'

Wayne smiled triumphantly as her features contorted in her first orgasm. Being unused and unprepared for such sensations, her untouched innocence cruelly aided him in his seduction, and he found it profoundly ironic. While she lay in a panting and moaning recovery, he stripped off his clothes with wordless efficiency, giving her no time to rally her

135

scattered defences, and when she next looked at him, her eyes widened in a mixture of fear and desire. Standing by the bed, he seemed to tower over her, his shoulders wide and tapering to a flat stomach. But it was to his manhood that her eyes flew, her gaze taking on the sheen of panic as she suddenly comprehended her dangerous position. She had never seen a naked man before, and the upright strength of his shaft made her womb suddenly contract. She murmured a denial, a plea for understanding, telling him she was still a virgin and appealing to his sense of honour and decency. Wayne, who with his knack for languages had picked up quite a bit of Spanish from various sources, understood her perfectly, but feigned ignorance, mocking her by making her believe he thought that she was egging him on. 'You really want it, don't you, little Rosita? You're really hungry. Yes?' He knelt quickly over her, his strong knees bent either side of her slender hips as she made a quick, abortive attempt to roll off the bed, but he quickly subdued her, his immense strength making it pitifully easy. Holding her confused, dazed eyes with his own, Wayne slowly released her, and took her hand. Gently but firmly he guided it to his shaft, curling her fingers around him. Rosita froze, her heart pounding. It's so hard, she thought incredulously, but also so soft. Like steel encased in velvet. Then she shook her head, shaking off the heady cloying temptations of sexual arousal. 'No, no!'

Wayne snarled impatiently, tiring of the game, and, pushing her thighs wide apart, he guided his organ between her legs and thrust forward deeply, with no regard for her innocence and uncaring whether he gave her pleasure or not.

Rosita screamed as her hymen broke and blood trickled onto the sheets, the pain chasing away the magic of the moonlit night, the heady drugging of the fine wine, the will-sapping lies of his murmured compliments and cajolings. She realized, too late, what had happened, understanding at last that because of her naïvety and weakness, she had been cheated and abused.

And then he began to thrust against her, withdrawing and them slamming into her time and time again, the nightmare escalating terrifyingly as she thrashed helplessly on the bed, unable to buck off his muscled weight. Tears cascaded from beneath her tightly closed lashes as Wayne began to moan, his face tight and ferocious as he chased his own pleasure. Rosita, whimpering under the onslaught, prayed that it would all soon be over.

Ten minutes later Wayne was in the shower. When he'd finished, he wrapped a towel around himself and walked back into the bedroom where Rosita still lay on her back, her undone blouse lying across her shoulders, her nipples wet with his saliva. The skirt was still bunched up under her buttocks and around her waist. The sheets were wet with sweat and blood and he felt disgust rise up in his throat, threatening to choke him. It was Urma all over again. Suddenly he felt unclean. 'Get out.'

Rosita's eyes snapped open at the harshness of his tone, but only one look at his tight and angry face had her scurrying off the bed and running through the door. She ran through the large, empty house to the servants' quarters, a hand clapped over her mouth. She flung herself onto the narrow bed in her tiny room where a wooden crucifix was the only ornamentation, and began to sob convulsively. She would surely go to hell for this thing she had done – the priests had warned her so. Just when she thought she could cry no more, she heard her father come home, and found that she could.

She dreaded facing him the next day, but he ignored her totally, acting as if nothing had happened. Better still, during the next two months she hardly ever saw him.

Wayne had gone back to work at the casino, amused at the change in Le Lepee, who was now sucking up to him like mad.

He went yachting with friends whom he'd deliberately cultivated, choosing only the richest and the most influential to invite back to the casino. He bought himself a small yacht with the money that Wolfgang had given him for his eighteenth birthday, and dined with the loveliest daughters of his mother's friends. He was hardly home, and when he was he couldn't bear to look at Rosita, whose hurt eyes constantly condemned him.

One day, at the beginning of September, Rosita went to his room very early, desperation making her bold. He would be leaving for Paris soon, and she had to tell him. She had waited for her period with fear and dread, all the tales of God punishing the wicked coming true when first one month, then two, and then three had gone by, and still no period. Three days ago she had been sick in the morning, and this morning she had been sick again. She could no longer fool herself or procrastinate. Now, as she stood looking down on his sleeping face, she felt a familiar sensation of shame and fear stir her, and she quickly crossed herself. Nevertheless, a baby was too important and too sacred to keep to herself, much as she might want to deny Wayne the joys of fatherhood.

Wayne began to moan then thrash around on the bed. Hans was swimming towards him, a grinning shark giving him a ride. No matter how fast Wayne swam, the shark and a grim-faced Hans gained on him. 'No!' he yelled, sitting up so fast that Rosita nearly screamed in shock. Slowly the nightmare faded and his eyes sharpened on her and a dull rage began to flush his blood. 'What the hell do you want?'

'I have to talk to you, *señor*. Please.'

Wayne swung his feet onto the floor and caught her greedy eyes on his groin. 'Please, I have to tell you . . . I . . . I . . .'

'Well? What is it? Will you just say it and get out before someone finds you here?' Anxious for her to be gone, he had a sudden premonition of history reversing itself, and could see in his mind's eye, his father

139

bursting in on him in an embarrassing situation. The thought had him leaping to his feet, his hands fastening hard around her shoulders as he dragged her to the door.

Frightened by the rough manhandling and scared he'd evict her before she had time to tell him what she knew she must, Rosita blurted out the truth.

Wayne stood stock still and stared at her, appalled. 'Pregnant?' he echoed, his voice little more than a stunned whisper. 'You're pregnant?'

'*Si*' Rosita saw his stunned face and smiled tentatively. 'It is wonderful news, no? A little bambino of your own?' The sweet, hopeful voice seemed to dig into him like bullets, and he staggered back and collapsed onto the bed, utterly dumbfounded. He'd got a serving girl pregnant? He could hear the gossip now, the sniggering laughter, the pointing fingers undoing all the hard work he'd done that summer, destroying all the groundwork he'd been laying to set himself up as one of Monte Carlo's elite. He could hear his mother's wailing and accusing voice – 'How could you? I am a laughing stock.'

But most of all he could see his father's ironical, smug smile and he felt sick. Sick to his stomach. His brain began to work feverishly. A way out – there had to be a way out. He had no doubts that the baby was his, but that was beside the point. He paced, realizing he had to get her out of the way – right out of the way – and fast. He stopped pacing and glanced at her. 'You're leaving this morning. I'll drive you to the airport. Where's your passport?'

The words snapped Rosita out of her subservience as nothing else could. The thought of going back to Spain, back to the poverty of the hills, the gruelling hard labour that was the lot of Spain's peasantry, was not even thinkable. Her mother had worked herself literally into the grave to give Rosita the chance to leave Spain and make a new life in glittering Monte Carlo. She would die rather than go back there.

'No,' she said, shaking her head, backing away and cringing against the corner as he menacingly walked towards her. But she was strong – stronger than even she had realized – and born of sturdy stock. As danger leapt to its highest point she felt a great shift of maternal strength flooding into her, and she straightened up, standing tall, all fear leaving her face. Even Wayne hesitated. Rosita put a protective hand on her stomach, and then thrust out her chin.

'I will not leave,' she stated, her voice clear and strong. 'This is your bambino and he will have all the things that I never had. He will live in this fancy house,' she waved her hands around her, 'and will call you Papa.' She might fear him, but for her baby she had the courage of a tigress.

Wayne saw at once there was no dissuading her. He recognized zeal when he saw it, and knew there was no reasoning with it. Immediately he abandoned the idea of giving her money, and instead held up his hands in a placating gesture. 'All right, have it your own way.' Seeing her suspicious look at his sudden about-face, he added grimly, 'But don't blame me if he's not accepted and is branded a bastard. Because I won't marry you,' he assured her, stabbing a viciously angry finger in her direction.

Rosita paled at the thought of the disgrace, and then forced herself to shrug, even though her heart was hammering painfully in her chest. She had no doubts left that he might actually care for her, but perhaps after the baby was born, when he held his son or daughter in his arms for the first time, surely then he would feel less resentful? Who knows, perhaps the baby might work some loving miracle and change his mind about marrying her and giving their child a legitimate name. She could but hope. More importantly, she could afford to wait.

She left to do the grocery shopping the next morning, happily searching the markets for the best buy, the freshest fish, the ripest fruit, feeling confident and much more at peace now that everything was settled. The sun was warm, reflecting her simple cotton dress of canary yellow, and as she walked back up the steep hill she felt young, strong, healthy and full of dreams. When she turned the corner and walked into the gardens, the police were waiting.

A search of her room revealed a pair of diamond and onyx cufflinks in a biscuit tin under her bed, along with Wayne's watch and silver cigarette lighter. She was given no chance to explain, no chance to call a lawyer, no chance even to pack her things or speak to her father, who was once again out chauffering Marlene.

She was numb with shock as they led her to the back of the police car, their hands hard and hurting as they shoved her onto the back seat. There she collapsed, hugging her slightly swollen stomach and sobbing uncontrollably.

From his bedroom window Wayne watched, his face expressionless. Looking around numbly, still too stunned to take it all in, Rosita saw him. Twisting around in the back seat as the car pulled away, she banged uselessly on the back of the window with her hands, her face agonized, tears streaming from her eyes, shouting in Spanish for mercy, beseeching him uselessly to save her.

The last he ever saw of her was when she was dragged away from the window and cuffed across the face by one of the policemen.

They took her not to the police station as she had expected, but to the airport, where they put her aboard the first flight back to Spain, after confiscating her passport. They told her that she must never come back. If she did, they assured her, she would be thrown into jail immediately.

Rosita believed it.

CHAPTER 11

Clarissa and Kyle's first glimpse of Oxford was a perfect one. Their plane had landed at Heathrow at 5 a.m., and as they approached Oxford in the hired, chauffeur-driven car, the sun was just rising. It was a clean December morning, with a lemony-yellow sun, a crisp frost turning everything silver, and low-lying mist in the valleys. The famous dreaming spires of Oxford were mellow in the sun and glittering with frost. Bells began to chime in St Ebbes; the streets were deserted.

'This place has even Charleston beat,' Kyle said, his eyes sweeping the vista with quick, appreciative eyes. The years had been more than kind to Kyle, turning him from a handsome, petulant boy, to a handsome, desperate man. The desperation lent him an air that made him irresistible to women, and Clarissa in particular. Without the haunted look in his eyes, he'd have been *too* handsome, turning him, perversely, into an unattractive man.

'It surely does,' Clarissa agreed with him, leaning back in the seat and pulling on soft, kid-leather gloves.

Perhaps she would take a few weeks and explore the old country in earnest once she had Oriel sorted out. She turned to glance at her lover of nearly fifteen years. She was the reason for his desperation, of course, and it both thrilled her, even as it slowly destroyed her. She found his name on her lips, and quickly bit it back. He would only turn to her, his pain in his eyes, and what did she say then? She couldn't let him go.

'Where are you booked?' Kyle asked, unaware of her thoughts, as they headed into the heart of the ancient university city, and Clarissa smiled.

'The Randolph, would you believe? Classiest hotel in Oxford, or so I'm told.' She hugged his arm close to hers. She'd never said the words 'I love you' to this man, but then, he had never said them to her, either.

Kyle felt his lips twist into a parody of a smile. 'I didn't doubt it.' Where else would his southern belle stay, but in the best place in town? As Clarissa raised a perfectly plucked and dyed eyebrow he added grimly, 'And where am I booked?'

'You're booked in the second-best, of course.' She reached forward to pat his smooth cheek with her hand, ignoring the way he gritted his teeth. 'Only the second best for you, lover,' she husked. She wanted to kiss him so badly, it hurt her. Kyle was not the only one to wear a mysterious aura of pain. But Clarissa kept hers much more cleverly disguised. Today she was wearing Chanel – clothes and perfume – and her smile was pure pussycat. Kyle didn't even suspect the power he had over her, and she intended to keep it that way. The passing years had been kind to her, too, but now in her fifties, she was even more inclined to panic than ever. If he should ever leave her now . . .

Kyle closed his eyes briefly, then snapped them open as the Bentley began to slow down. The classic black car, sharing the limelight with the famous Rolls-Royce as one of Britain's finest automobiles, had been something new for him. He now owned his own garage back home, and several others, but he still liked to keep his hands dirty, so to speak. Used to styleless, weighty American cars, the silent engine of this classic, with its walnut and mahogany interior and maroon leather seats had been an eye-opener for him. Perhaps he should think about going into foreign expensive cars back home? His love of classic cars had not diminished, and not even Clarissa had succeeded in driving the car mechanic from his soul completely.

'Nobody will be up yet at this godforsaken hour,' Clarissa pointed out as the chauffeur parked the car in front of the hotel, and began to take her bags from the back, 'so we'll have a shower, freshen up, and then you can meet me for breakfast here around eight o'clock.'

'Fine.'

Clarrisa walked across the parking lot, unaware of his hot and angry eyes following her. She was wearing a cape of cream velvet and a matching turban. Her figure was the same as ever – slender and elegant – and at her throat a huge antique cameo held the cape secure. Her handbag was black leather and Italian

146

with a gold glasp, and her makeup, although heavier now to hide the approaching march of time, was still classically understated.

Kyle watched her go, hating and wanting her. Nothing had changed in over a decade as her lover. No, that was not strictly true. Once, nearly five years ago, he'd been desperate enough to make a run for it. He'd got as far as Chicago when her private eyes had picked up his trail. Forced to leave out auto engineering from his list of jobs, (that would have been the first place they'd start looking,) he'd been working as a bus driver. He'd almost begun to think he was free, when, one day, he'd gone back to his bedsit after his 5 a.m. shift had ended. It had been a cramped one-room affair with damp walls and the suspicion of cockroaches, and found her waiting for him. He'd opened the door in his crumpled, grey uniform, and there she was, dressed in white satin. Her perfume had staved off the smell of boiled cabbage and garlic that always emanated from the bedsits below, and her lush pink lips were pulled into that mocking, depleting smile that immediately went to work on his nerves, sapping his will and stiffening his groin.

She had stripped slowly, giving him a chance to bolt through the door, but of course he hadn't. He hadn't been able to. The moment he'd seen her, he'd felt the chains, those delicious, dangerous, hated silken chains, wrap around him, pinning him to the spot. Oh, he'd had girls since he'd been on the run, two of them, in fact. He satisfied them, but not himself. And he'd known, then, that only Clarissa could send him to

147

the giddying heights. It had made him want to scream, and beat his fists against a wall until his hands bled.

And then, in that dirty, squalid room, she had slowly stripped, showing him silk undergarments, smooth pampered skin that was so much older than himself, and a truth that was now irrefutable – he would never be free of her . . . never.

He remembered leaning against the door and closing his eyes briefly in pain, but then she had been on him, bearing down on him with the merciless timing of a hunter. Her hands had been everywhere, her lips likewise, and within minutes he'd been naked, buried deep inside her, and straining to an orgasm that had him screaming. All night they'd made love, fighting, cursing, then loving some more. She'd left him in the morning, bitten, scratched, and unable to move. For a while he'd been surprised that she had gone. But then, after a day or two, he understood.

He could not run again. She'd not left him with the energy or the ability. Wearily he had packed up his pitiful belongings – two second-hand suits, a shaving kit and a book of antique cars – and went home. Home, where the garage was waiting for him, like some obscene consolation prize. Bought, signed, sealed and delivered. All his. With her as a silent partner, of course. Since then he'd opened two new garages – one in Savannah, and one in Dalton. He'd moved into a detached house in Atlanta, and now his hands were manicured, all traces of grease gone from the finger-nails. He wore suits and ties, talked properly and wittily, dined out at least once a week, and had a reputation as the Stud of Georgia. And every night he waited to see if she would come to his house. A house on the outskirts of town, that overlooked open fields and not nosy neighbours.

So things had not changed where it really mattered.

As the car pulled up in front of a modest building of red-brick and white paintwork, Kyle got out and lugged his own case from the boot, nodding the driver away. The hotel had lace curtains, a large well-kept garden, and was situated in a small cul-de-sac of private houses. Kyle gave a half-laugh of pure despair. Nobody was likely to see him here; or at least no one that mattered – none of the legion of matrons, politicians' wives, artists or charity organizers that seemed to come out of Clarissa's woodwork wherever she went. As he walked up the path toward the double-doors set with dark glass his lips were smiling, but his eyes were bleak.

Oriel awoke and discovered butterflies in her stomach. Of course – tonight was *it*. Opening night. Quickly she dressed and made her way to the dining hall. At High Table, dons drank tea and munched toast whilst discussing the theories of Plato and comparing the endeavours of Shakespeare and Langland. Oriel settled for coffee. Betty appeared beside her with a plate of bacon and eggs, and looked at her anxiously. 'How you doing?'

'I'm terrified.'

'Normal, then.'

Oriel watched her tuck into her food and smiled. 'You free this morning?'

'After a calculus lecture at Wadham. Why? Want to go through your lines again?'

Oriel shrugged. 'No point. I know I'll forget every one of them when I get on stage.'

'Rubbish. Hello, what does she want?' Oriel looked up just in time to see the Dean's secretary bear down on them.

'Miss Somerville?' At Oriel's nod, the woman informed her that her mother was here and would like to see her. Oriel found her mother waiting in her room. She got up, looking shockingly chic and exotic, and so totally out of place in the untidy room. Then Clarissa smiled, and held out her arms.

'Mama!' Oriel went to her for a kiss and a hug. 'Why didn't you tell me you were coming? Oh, I'm so nervous.' She led her mother to the bed. 'Sit down a minute. How's Daddy?'

Kier walked along the narrow corridor to her door, keeping a wary look-out for any monitors. He knew her nerves must be raw, but as he heard the feminine voices, he paused, wondering if he should interrupt.

'I didn't come just to watch the play, darling,' Clarissa said, and fiddled nervously with the ends of her cape.

'Oh? Nothing's wrong, is it, Mother?'

Outside Kier could hear the fear in Oriel's voice, and he moved closer, intending to knock and make his presence known.

'I'm not sure,' Clarissa said. 'I had a strange phone call about you and some young man. Margaret Swainton – you remember her? Her daughter Maybilene is studying at the Ruskin? She called me. She thought I should know.'

Oriel felt her heart suddenly trip, and a sick feeling settled in the pit of her stomach. She knew just what was coming next, and she didn't like it. Outside, Kier froze.

'Well, darling . . .' Clarissa looked miserably about her. She'd been dreading this confrontation, ever since Margaret's call. Through the open door Kier watched Oriel's face firm into stubborn lines. He let out a long, relieved breath, only then realizing how tense he had been. For an ugly moment, he'd wondered if Oriel would bow to the pressure her mother was certainly about to put on her, and he felt ashamed for ever doubting that she would come through for him.

'You see, she said there were rumours . . .' Clarissa began delicately, but Oriel was in no mood for games and came straight to the point.

'Rumours about what?'

Clarissa noticed the levelness of her daughter's gaze, the determined thrust of her chin, and recognized the signs. 'Now, darling . . . you know how things are,' she began worriedly. It would be just like her wayward daughter to let her hot head lead her into trouble. And Clarissa didn't think she could bear it, if Oriel should make a disaster of a marriage, the way she had. She had to stop her angel from making a mistake. 'I'm just concerned, that's all. There's been talk about you and

151

the young man directing the play. Some . . . cowboy from Kansas,' she finished, hoping to make her see how ridiculous this misalliance was.

Oriel almost laughed. The snobbery was so unnecessary! 'Kier Harcourt is not a cowboy,' she said. 'His father owned a ranch in Kansas, but he's dead now.'

'Yes,' Clarissa said grimly. 'I know all about it. A few hundred acres in a hick town called Burmanville. Really, darling, I hope things aren't serious with this boy. You're too young to . . .'

'Things are serious!' Oriel interrupted, just a small tug of doubt yanking on the back of her mind as she spoke. Since that first night, she and Kier had been lovers for over a month. They had talked, kissed, explored Oxford and its surrounding countryside, all the while laughing and holding hands, even making love behind a barn, shivering in the cold and then burning as they came together in an explosion of passion. They knew every minute detail of each other's lives. She had told him she loved him, whispering it in the night and in the mellow afternoons, and he had whispered back the same. But this was first love, and she wondered if Kier felt the same commitment that she did. It was the one raincloud on an otherwise brilliant horizon, and it worried her.

'Oh, darling,' Clarissa said, her heart drooping in dismay. How could she make her daughter see that marriage affected the rest of your life and, if you got it wrong . . . she thought of Kyle, and sighed deeply. If you got it wrong, you wrecked your own life and those of others.

Oriel looked at her mother helplessly, seeing the pain and the love in her eyes. But why couldn't she just leave them alone? 'You haven't even met Kier, Mama. You have no idea of the kind of man he really is, deep down, where it counts.'

Clarissa got up and walked to the window, looking down into the quad. 'What does this boy want to do when you've finished your studies here? Take you back to Kansas?'

'For pity's sake, Mother, Kier is a Rhodes Scholar – he's not some hick you can just dismiss like you do the bellboys back home. He wrote the play, he's directing it, and everybody says it's going to be good . . .'

'So he's going to take you to Broadway, or Hollywood, is he?' Clarissa asked wearily, turning back from the window and looking at her daughter with frustrated eyes. 'Darling, please wait. You're in a new country, you think you're in love for the first time, but things can change so quickly . . .'

'I am in love. And Kier is in love with me. And nothing you can say is going to change it, Mother, so you might as well face facts,' Oriel interrupted hastily.

'I couldn't have put it better myself,' Kier commented softly, making both women jump and look toward the door. Clarissa found herself startled by her first glimpse of the man who could so easily break her daughter's heart. She had convinced herself he was a raw hick who'd seduced her daughter with savage sex and charm. But now, as he met her challenging eyes head on, she could sense instinctively that Kier had something . . . an aura of power, perhaps, of something unnamed that very few men actually possessed. He reminded her – heartbreakingly – of Kyle. It rendered null and void his lack of background and breeding, and made him seem taller, greater than he was. Even dressed in dirty jeans and a black sweater with a hole at the elbows, he was a giant. Young, barely started out, yet still a giant. One of those men who were destined to take the world by the throat and shake it. All of this she could see, and it scared her. Oriel needed someone to look after her, not take her on a rollercoaster ride that would scare her half to death. Oriel had been raised in a genteel environment. This man . . . was a savage by comparison! She could feel desperation rise in her like a suffocating wave as, for the first time, it began to occur to her that she might not be able to nip the romance in the bud so easily.

'You're Kier, I assume,' Clarissa commented, forcing her voice into ice as she fought to regain her composure. 'Do you always lurk in doorways, spying on people's private conversations?'

Kier grinned. 'Whenever I can,' he said softly.

Oriel felt a wide smile pull on her mouth, feeling relieved that he couldn't be snowballed by her mother's icy disdain.

Clarissa looked steadily at Kier. 'I want to talk to you. Alone.'

'Mother, I'm not . . .' Oriel interrupted hotly, but it was Kier who held up his hand and said soothingly,

'It's alright. Don't worry.'

154

Reluctantly she got off the bed and walked past him, looking deep into his eyes. 'Be careful,' she whispered.

Kier cupped her face gently, and kissed her thoroughly, ignoring the hiss of outrage emanating from the other side of the room. 'It'll be OK,' he assured her softly. And, suddenly, Oriel knew it would be. Her mother was used to getting her way, but as she looked into the solid brown eyes of the man she had come to love with her heart and her soul, she realized that this time Clarissa would lose. She wondered what she'd done to be so lucky. To find a man like this, at first attempt, seemed almost greedy. She shot a triumphant look at her mother who stared stonily back at her, and then left, closing the door behind her.

Clarissa walked to her handbag and extracted a cigarette. 'She's obviously smitten with you,' Clarissa admitted shakily. 'But she's still young. Doubtless you are her first love.'

'And lover,' Kier clarified determinedly, but without spite. Much as he disliked her, he could admire Clarissa's control. Most mothers would have been ranting and raving.

'However,' she continued, as if he'd not spoken, 'these things are easily quashed. If I stop paying her tuition, she'll be forced to come home. We'll see what thousands of miles between you and months of separation can do.'

Kier smiled. 'I'll just quit college as well, and we'll both get a job.'

155

'A job?' Clarissa said incredulously. 'Oriel has never had to do a day's work in her life.'

Kier just looked at her, wondering how a girl's mother could know so little about her own daughter. 'She'll learn,' he said briefly. And the way he said it made Clarissa's heart lurch in fear. What did he intend to do? Live off Oriel?

'How much, you little Kansas hick?' she asked with soft but savage hatred. 'How much will it take for you to leave my daughter alone?'

Kier felt disbelief, then rage, then pity sweep over him in successive waves. 'Lady, you're pitiful,' he said, then turned and left her.

Oriel, who was waiting a little further down the corridor, straightened as he came out. 'What did she say.'

'The usual, I imagine.'

Oriel grimaced. 'What do we do now?'

'We find St John Courtenay. Better known as Jinksie. His father owns a private plane. He keeps it at Kidlington airport, a few miles away.'

'What do we want with a plane?'

'We're going to fly to Scotland.' They were outside, in the courtyard now, and Clarissa looked down on their heads, a vague sick feeling in the pit of her stomach. She would have to stay on in England for longer than she'd planned. Oriel needed protecting, whether she knew it or not. Clarissa would not let that one take advantage of her baby! She looked down on Kier's brown head with loathing.

'Scotland?' Oriel repeated, her voice barely above a whisper. 'Why should we want to go to Scotland? And what about the play tonight?'

'We'll be back in time for the play,' Kier assured her, hooking his arm around her shoulders. It felt heavy and warm and comforting, and Oriel fell into step beside him, suddenly so happy to be alive. 'What's in Scotland?' she asked after a few quiet moments, as they slowly walked towards the lodge gates, each filled with private thoughts.

'Gretna Green.'

'Who's that?'

'Where,' he corrected. 'It's a place where you can get married without parental consent.' They were past the lodge now, and Oriel stopped dead in her tracks to gape at him.

'Married?'

'Uh-huh. That woman back there – ' he nodded his head toward the college '– won't leave us alone.'

'And you're scared she'll break us up,' Oriel finished for him, a sensation of disappointment sinking in her stomach.

Kier shook his head. 'She couldn't break us up in a million years,' he stated bluntly. 'But until we're married, she's going to hang around here making a real pain of herself. And I, for one, don't need the hassle. Do you?'

Oriel stared at him and then found herself laughing helplessly. Passers-by stared at them, smiles forming on their lips as the young couple suddenly hugged each other, Kier swinging her around and around. Love on a Monday morning. What could be lovelier?

They found Roderick St John Courtenay in the dining room, wolfing down porridge. He was delighted at the romance of the proposition, and readily agreed to take them. He could be witness and best man, Kier told him, and on the private plane, St John actually found some champagne, with which they toasted themselves in advance. By midday they were in Scotland. St John loaned Oriel a tenner to buy a long, white dress and Kier used up the change in his pockets to buy her some flowers, some seasonal Michaelmas daisies in pink and purple, and a single red rose. The registry office was small and sparse, but what did it matter? It was a cathedral to them. St John's eyes were suspiciously bright as he listened to them take their vows, and afterwards insisted on flying them down to Edinburgh and treating them to a slap-up lunch, where they ordered beef Wellington and apple crumble. It was the best wedding feast Oriel could ever have imagined.

But the best moment of the day, as far as she was concerned, was just before the registrar called them in. St John had slapped a hand to his forehead, looking appalled. 'A ring,' he moaned. 'We haven't got a ring.'

And then Kier had smiled and pulled a simple plain band from his pocket. And looking at the golden ring in that dark hall as they waited to become man and wife, she suddenly knew that he had intended to marry her all along, and that the visit by her mother had only speeded things up. She had cried then, and laughed, and kissed him, and was still kissing him when the registrar had called them in.

The plane had been refuelled when they got back from their lunch, and they took off straight away, landing back at Kidlington airport at just after six. Rushing like mad, they dashed back to college, Oriel to change and Kier to go to the theatre, where everyone was in panic. Viv was the first to see him. 'Where the hell have you been?' he all but screamed, the rest of the cast and crew looking at Kier with mixed expressions of relief and annoyance.

'Sorry,' he apologized to the room in general. 'I had things to do.'

Viv stared at him, open-mouthed. 'Things to do,' he repeated incredulously, looking around at the others for support. Kier's best friend he might be, but even he had begun to wonder if his friend hadn't chickened out when the day had worn on, and curtain time drew ominously close, and still no bloody Yank. Now his voice was hard but also playful as he recited a list of grievances. 'You should have been here this morning. One of the stage props got broken, a set of lights has failed, and Midget called in sick.'

'Is it all fixed?' Kier asked, yanking off his coat and rolling up his shirtsleeves. Viv's mouth fell even further open. 'That's not the point. You're the director, you bloody Yank. Where've you been all day? You should have been here, holding our hands, protecting us from all this disaster. What have you been doing instead, that's what we'd all like to know?'

There was a general and still ill-humoured murmur of agreement and Kier glanced around at the hostile faces, and grinned, looking back at Viv before shrugging. 'I've been getting married,' he said simply. For a second there was total silence. 'In Gretna Green,' he added. More silence. 'To the Shrew,' he finished off, and suddenly everyone erupted into laughter, applause, ribald comments and wolf whistles as they realized he wasn't joking.

Viv walked up to him, then slowly shook his head. 'You bloody Yank,' he said softly, then thrust out his hand. Kier took it, a broad grin on his face. He was actually married. He actually had a wife. The world had a Mrs Kier Harcourt. Suddenly it began to sink in, and he sat down, feeling giddy, exultant, terrified.

'I've never had my leading lady snaffled right from under my nose with such panache before,' Viv wailed. 'How the hell did you get to Scotland and back in one day?'

Kier told them, the work grinding to a halt as he was forced to give them all the gory details. The only bit he left out was the arrival of Oriel's mother that morning. But no doubt that would soon get around. Especially since the lady herself would be present at curtain time in exactly . . . he glanced at his watch and yelped. 'We've got thirty minutes to go. Bloody hell!' At his horrified words and utter panic, everyone began to laugh.

'Welcome to the glorious world of showbiz, Yank,' Viv said heartily, and slapped him on the back.

* * *

By seven o'clock the lecture room was full. In the tiny room that had been set aside as 'backstage', Betty put the finishing touches of makeup on Oriel's face, because her own hands were shaking too much. She had just abjectly apologized for the seventh time for not taking Betty to Scotland with her, when the cue boy called for 'Curtain Up'.

'Oohhhhh nooooo!' Oriel stared at herself in the mirror. In the space of a day she'd probably lost a mother, gained a husband, and now she was due to step out on stage in front of a huge audience for the first time in her life. What a day!

In the front row, Clarissa sat between a physics don and a famous visiting conductor of the London Philharmonic. Behind her was the cream of Oxford society, all gathered together for the student drama of the year. If successful, the show would run until the last week before Christmas. The curtain went up to reveal the drawing-room of a suburban house. Clarissa frowned. Hadn't she heard that this was supposed to be the *Taming of the Shrew*? For the next two hours she sat and stared. On the stage her daughter was barely recognizable – the accent was gone, all the charm and class were gone and in her place was a man-hating shrew, intent on bringing down Peter, her male antagonist. Through the first scene Clarissa prayed that the play would fall flat on its face – that the audience would boo and hiss, and denigrate the upstart who had dared re-write Shakespeare so outlandishly and with such arrogant confidence. But by the interlude it was obvious the play was a smash. It was funny, aggravating, touching and almost unbelievably sexy. Viv, the leading man, was all potent power, and as she watched him with Oriel, Clarissa wondered if she couldn't ask Viv for help. Surely Oriel couldn't play opposite him like that without feeling some reaction to the man? She asked the don next to her who the male lead was, and was told he was the son of an Earl. Clarissa nodded, suddenly filled with hope. An English Earl was by far a better prospect for her daughter. Oriel was born to be a lady of a great house. And a title too . . .

As the curtain folded on a now meek and mild Kate, lovingly putting slippers over Peter's hole-filled socks, the audience rose as one to start clapping. The minor characters took their bows first, then Viv, then Oriel. The applause for the two leads was stunning. Oriel looked out over the clapping crowd, and felt breathless. She'd stepped out on stage a nervous wreck, her mind groping for her first line. Then she'd seen Viv and the look of encouragement in his eyes, and the next second her voice came out, loud and clear, just as she'd rehearsed it. Throughout the play Kier had watched closely from the sidelines, his presence a solid, comforting rock. By the third act she was enjoying herself immensely. The calls came now for author and director. When Kier hesitated, Oriel walked over to him and took his hand, leading him out onto the stage. The applause magnified as they all took their final bows.

* * *

Backstage, Kier sank down into a chair as Viv slapped him on the back. 'Well, you poor old married man you, you did it.'

Kier groaned. 'Never again. I'll never direct another play as long as I live.'

Everyone laughed, tension easing away in the aftermath of euphoria that came with a successful opening night.

'Did you see Flakey fuming in the back row?' somebody asked, to more helpless laughter. Then it went quiet as Viv suddenly raised his glass. It held cheap white wine, which was all the production could manage, but nobody minded.

'To Kate versus Pete,' he said. Unnoticed, Clarissa hesitated in the doorway, craning her neck to try and see Oriel. She intended to congratulate both her daughter and Kier Harcourt warmly. It *had* been a good play, after all.

'And to our leading lady and director. Congratulations on your marriage, good health, may all your troubles be little ones. And if you ever decide to go off and elope to Scotland again, don't do it on the opening night of your next play!' Viv raised his glass again, and there was another toast. Kier and Oriel grinned and kissed. There was a lot to be done. They'd have to find an apartment together, for one thing. Then tell the Dean, get their names altered on the college Registry . . . Kier held out his hand, and she took it, their eyes meeting and locking.

In the doorway Clarissa went white. Her eyes flew to the hand of her daughter and saw the glint of a golden ring. Wordlessly she turned and stumbled away. She walked like a robot up Broad Street and across St Giles, but by the time she had reached the hotel she was white-hot with pain-filled rage. Oh, Oriel, *what have you done?* Her mood swung wildly – she would disinherit her, leave her penniless. But of course, she couldn't do that. Oriel would never be able to cope. She'd force them to get divorced, somehow.

In her suite, Kyle stood beneath the shower. He heard the bathroom door open and through the frosted glass saw a shadowy figure walk to the bed and begin to undress. Suddenly the shower door opened, and he began to turn. He stumbled against the tiled wall as she launched herself at him, her hair darkening under the shower spray as she stepped beneath the spume. Her lips were hot and vicious on his, and he felt her sharp teeth nip his lower lip. Automatically his hands came out to her wet shoulders, his first thought being to shove her off. But, of course, the moment his fingers touched her skin he was lost, and he could only drag her closer. Her nipples were hard as iron against his chest, and his manhood leapt to attention, prodding impatiently against her thigh. Quickly her hand slipped down to clasp it, her fingers squeezing so tightly that he cried out, his whole body richocheting with the sexual punch of her savagery.

Clarissa stared at his tight, handsome face, Kier and Oriel momentarily forgotten. Kyle was her life. As she caressed him, her own body begin to tighten in sexual anticipation. Wordlessly she positioned herself in front of him, and holding on to his strong shoulders, leapt lithely off the ground. Kyle's arms automatically held her thighs as she hooked her legs behind his buttocks.

His eyes shot open as she took his shaft with her free hand and guided him into her. He moaned, then gasped as she began to slip up and down on him, his arms taking her weight easily. She worked hard and furiously, battering him against the wall, the shower water beating a warm and hard jet against her moving back. Her legs were locked like vicious scissors around his waist, making him gasp, opening his mouth to drag in air as she pumped frenziedly on his rock-hard shaft. She cried, shuddered, gasped for breath and then began all over again. Eventually even his great strength gave out, and he jerked hard, swinging around and pressing her against the wall. His face twisted and contorted in ecstasy, and he groaned as his seed burst forth in a red-hot torrent. Satisfied by the shattered look on his face, Clarrisa lovingly pushed him away. Slowly he slid down the tiles and onto the shower mat.

'That bastard married her today,' Clarissa said, her still pert breasts rising and falling with every tortured breath she took. 'He flew her to Scotland and married her. How could she be so . . . weak? And how could I have been so stupid?'

As Kyle learned the reason for his near-rape, he wanted to smile, but didn't have the energy.

Then Clarissa looked down on him and smiled gently. Reaching for the soap, she began to lather

her hands, intent on inflicting more sexual torment, her eyes pinning him to the floor. Kyle closed his eyes, glad that the shower spray hid the tears that squeezed past his tightly shut lids.

One day, she was going to push him too far.

CHAPTER 12

Paris

Opposite the Trocadero, with the definitive view of the Eiffel Tower, stood the Hotel D'Concordia, with three stories of mellow stone, arched and terraced windows, a centuries-old flag flapping in the Parisian breeze, and a clientele that could be read from a European book of *Who's Who*. It was towards this hotel that Wayne quickly walked, with a newly minted graduation document tucked in the inside of his jacket pocket. He had passed all the examinations in the top two per cent of the class, and only the formal ceremony was left, where parents could sip champagne, talk to lecturers and visiting dignitaries, and look on with satisfaction at the achievements of their embarrassed offspring.

But Wayne knew that neither Wolfgang nor Marlene would come to the official ceremony, and his steps were not as light or carefree as many of his fellow students who were now pouring into the Café Chat for a boisterous celebration. The Café Chat, with its smoky dark rooms, rustic red wine, sultry singer and dingy walls had never appealed to Wayne. But, in keeping with his decision to make it with the 'in' crowd, he frequently went there with a gang of five or more to discuss the French politics of the day, the latest new artist to make a splash, and, of course, the exploits of Alain Delon and Romy Schneider.

But this morning he had other fish to fry. Important fish.

The double arched-doors of the Hotel D'Concordia were made of solid English oak, inlaid with windows over two hundred years old. A doorman dressed in scarlet and gold livery opened the door for him, touching his cap respectfully as he did so. Royalty often visited the hotel and, in today's modern age, the doorman could not be sure that anyone passing between the hallowed portals, dressed in the most casual attire, was not actually a foreign prince or potentate. Wayne, dressed in a navy suit, walked like a prince. His eyes barely acknowledged the man who held open the door, and his advent into the loggia with the high domed hand-painted ceiling, where a walnut desk housed several receptionists, caused more than six female heads to turn his way.

A chandelier cast light in the circular hall, and beneath his feet the carpet was eighteenth-century Oriental. Tall yucca plants stood in corners, and from hanging baskets orchids and flowering stock cast a sweet perfume into the air. An antique clock chimed the hour behind him as he walked briskly towards the reception desk, where a pretty blonde straightened her back and thrust out her breasts behind the pale blue uniform jacket she wore. But a few yards from the desk Wayne paused, his eye caught by the glimpse of gold in a telephone kiosk, discreetly tucked away in one corner. It was an old-fashioned booth, made entirely of teak, with just a single window, at about face height, to reveal whether or not the booth was occupied. Wayne changed direction, his gaze fixed on the woman inside. Her long, golden hair gleamed in a stray beam of sunlight, and she was laughing as she spoke into the receiver. She had a high forehead, aristocratically straight nose, and wore an unmistakable panache of class along with her red lipstick and Balmain summer frock. Without hesitation, he slid open the door of the kiosk, and stepped inside. Before she could turn around he closed the door behind him, and took the telephone from her hand. A chattering female voice was suddenly cut off as he put down the telephone, and the blonde attempted to turn around. But the booth was too small and now infinitely too crowded with the two of them, and Wayne's hands on her arms forced her to face the wall before his hands slid down over her bare arms then curved over her shoulders, his fingers coming to rest momentarily on her curvaceous breasts before splaying over her flat stomach.

The blonde gasped, her head falling back onto his chest, her hair falling over the navy jacket fitting snugly across his shoulders. Slowly he reached forward and kissed her ear. 'Toinette. How do you know I'm not some randy bellboy?' he whispered, his hands sliding down to hike her skirt further up her thighs, which were bare of tights in the hot weather. Slowly his fingers caressed the soft skin of her inner thighs with circular, teasing movements.

Antoinette Montigny, the eldest daughter of the Duc d'Montigny, one of the oldest families from ancient Normandy stock, allowed herself a self-satisfied smile. 'I didn't,' she purred, her voice husky and breathless as his fingers found the elasticated band on her peach silk cami-knickers and began to caress her soft mound. 'The bellboys around here are all handsome, after all.'

Wayne smiled, but there was no humour in his eyes, and he bit her ear sharply. He had met Toinette at a party in Chateauvalliers, the residence of one of the richest couples in France. A murmured inquiry into a friend's ear had told him immediately the name of the gorgeous blonde flirting cruelly with the wine waiter. An heiress to millions, with a title and impeccable background, Toinette Montigny had been ideal material for a wife.

His approach had been to watch her, hold her gaze when their eyes met, smile ironically and then turn away. He had not even approached her by the time the party had begun to wind down, though she had obviously expected him to, her cool dove-grey eyes mocking and knowing as she watched him dance with the second most attractive girl there, a Parisian model with an Italian count for a father. But Wayne had surprised her, not to mention totally rocking her complacency, by leaving with the Italian model, and not even glancing her way. When they met for the second time, at the opening of an art gallery in Montelmarte, Toinette had taken matters in hand and aggressively attached herself to him, dragging him into her car at the end of the evening and driving into a narrow, deserted street, where they had made cramped but very vigorous love.

The French, Wayne had learned very early on, were not quite the romantics they would have the rest of the world believe. Though Toinette had had more lovers than Wayne cared to think about, when it came to marriage, there were other considerations to take into account. The first time he met her father, at a hunting weekend in the Noire Valley, the Duc had given him the third degree enough to make his head ache. He was left with the uneasy feeling that although he was presentable enough, and his family was rich enough, his pedigree left a lot to be desired. Of necessity the D'Arville family history was vague at best, and American immigrants, returned to Monte Carlo after the war, did not make for ideal in-laws. Which was why Wayne was working so hard to keep the insatiable Toinette happy. Hearing her gasp as his fingers found the sensitive nub they had been searching for, he began to stroke her hard. A man waiting to use the phone glanced in, his eyes widening, his mouth following suit. Smiling conspiratorially, he walked away to wait at another booth.

Rubbing her back against him as he caressed her into a noisy orgasm, Toinette closed her eyes. Her head reached just about to his shoulder, and that was in four-inch high heels. She loved tall men, she loved handsome men and she especially loved men who knew how to please her. Naturally astute and unclouded by the fog called love that affected some of her more intelligent friends, she'd recognized immediately what Wayne wanted. Her title, her respectability and the security of marrying a d'Montigny. At four years his senior, she knew full well that in order to keep getting the monthly cheques from her father, she would have to marry soon, and produce an heir. And Wayne, with his wonderful physique, his outlandish background and uncomplicated sexual expertise, was as good a proposition as any other. She enjoyed the novel and risqué idea of owning a casino and possessing a husband that any woman would want. And would probably get, once the marriage was safely secured. She was not foolish enough to expect fidelity, but there was a cold, calculating dangerous streak in Wayne that fascinated the rebel in Toinette and set him apart from the usual run-of-the-mill playboys that normally shared her bed and lifestyle.

Now, as her body shuddered convulsively in orgasm, she smiled, sighed, and straightened her clothing. Within a minute her breathing was normal, her body heat back to where it had been only a few minutes ago. 'That was nice,' she murmured, turning at last to look up at him, her grey eyes mocking but warm. As she reached up and kissed him, he felt a stab of resentment ripple through him, and wondered sourly how many other men had heard her say those words.

They made their way to the Chevallière restaurant, ordering Moët et Chandon to go with their choices of Turban of Chicken and Tongue, Roulade of Beef, and Baba au Rhum. Wayne drank and ate with little enthusiasm, but was content that all his plans were going so well.

Hundreds of miles away, on the treacherous roads of Monte Carlo, a car hurtled against a wall and was thrown over the barriers down a thirty-foot drop, to roll to a mangled stop on the corniche below. Inside, Gillian and Pierre Rissaud, the parents of Claude Rissaud, died instantly.

After lunch Toinette and Wayne went back to the hotel, where she stayed whenever she was in Paris, which was often. In England, she'd observed, living in the country was a way of life. But in France, living in the countryside was like living in exile. They had a boisterous afternoon testing the bedsprings of her Queen Anne bed, and afterwards she drove him to Orly airport, where he caught the plane for the brief flight to Nice.

It was nearly dark by the time he picked up his Maserati from the airport car terminal, and drove to the Villa Mimosa. The sun was going down as a ball of red fire behind him when he walked through the garden, the music of the fountains creating an atmosphere of tranquil peace in the velvet night.

Rosita's father had left their employ a few months after Rosita's disgrace, and now a new gardener, whose name escaped him, cut blooms from the flower-beds that would later grace the dining-table. Taking the key from his pocket, he opened the door, the smell of lavender polish and the lingering scent of his mother's Dior perfume giving him a rare sense of homecoming. The villa was in darkness, as he'd expected, and he walked briskly into the main salon, where a huge fireplace was laid with real logs. No fire burned during the hot summer nights, though, and he moved across to the open French windows, stopping at the mahogany bar *en route* to pour himself a snifter of Napoleon brandy.

His body felt pleasantly relaxed after today's session with the woman that he'd just become engaged to. He had popped the question when she was sucking on his hardened nipple, and she had lifted her head long enough to look up, take the expensive solitaire diamond ring he held out and slip it on her finger. Then her head dipped again, leaving Wayne to smile up at the ceiling, a pleasant picture of the château in Normandy flashing across his mind, with himself as the owner and occupier, once the old Duc finally did the decent thing and died.

Now Wayne glanced at his watch, and wondered what the reaction of his parents would be to the news of his marriage into one of the premier families in all of France. With his top Sorbonne qualifications, an eminently suitable wife, and heir to two fortunes, he was on top of the world. His first purchase after his marriage would be a bigger yacht. He could no longer live in Monte Carlo without a decent boat. A few thousand tonnes of two-storied boat, with every modern convenience, including a cinema room, a gym, several suites and games room, should do nicely for starters. Then, of course, to keep Toinette happy, a world cruise and a year off before taking up the reigns of his new office: President of the House of Montigny. His first act would be to tackle the American market. That was where the real money lay. Providing wine for the European elite was fine for prestige, but the serious money lay in middle-of-the-road wine for the American middle classes with their delusions of grandeur and enormous capacity to spend money. Marketing and promotion was the magic of the modern business world. The old Duc might scream and rave, but Wayne was confident that he'd be in a position of power that would be unbeatable after a few years. Of course, he'd have to take things carefully . . .

He turned from the window and poured himself a second glass. He felt oddly restless and on edge. He wanted to see his father's face when he heard the news – he wanted to feel his power grow and come to life right under Wolfgang's eyes. He wanted revenge. Still. Only. Always revenge.

As he walked through the hall to his bedroom, he noticed a light on in his father's study, the narrow wedge of light winking out from under the closed door. He frowned, surprised, and slowly walked toward the room that had been off-limits for as long as he could remember. His father's sanctuary, as he called it, it was his office at home, full of papers and files. Wayne wondered vaguely what could possibly have kept his father from the casino and, unable to resist giving him the news, he raised his hand and tapped briskly on the door, walking in without waiting for a reply. His father was sitting behind the desk, a single lamp illuminating his face. There were no papers set out in front of him, but his hands clutched the front of the walnut desk, his knuckles tensely white in the glow from the lamp. An expensive cut-crystal paperweight and a silver-handed stiletto-type paper knife glinted in the same light, but Wayne barely noticed the trappings of wealth that littered his father's desk.

Instead his eyes were on Wolfgang's face. As he slowly closed the door behind him, his father's blue eyes watched him with an expressionless, reptilian intensity, and he sat unnaturally still as Wayne slowly approached the massive desk. 'Father,' Wayne said, 'I have some news for you.'

Wolfgang said nothing.

'I became engaged this afternoon. To Antoinette D'Montigny.'

Wolfgang blinked, once, twice, and then slowly let go of the desk. He had been sitting there all afternoon, and only now became aware that he had put on the lamp, and that outside it was dark. His first instinct, on being told that afternoon by Jacques that there was a fisherman waiting to see him, had been to laugh and send the boy away with a flea in his ear. But curiosity had got the better of him, and Claude Rissaud had been admitted. Hours ago, it must have been, but

Wolfgang couldn't be sure. Time seemed to have no more meaning.

Wayne stood behind the black leather chair, resting his hands against the upholstery, watching his father with wary, puzzled eyes. Wolfgang looked at the elegant hands against the seat, then up into his murderous son's face and felt the numbness slowly begin to disperse. The fact that Wayne had killed meant nothing in itself, of course. But it was no Jew, or prisoner of war, or gypsy or other no-account rubbish that he had killed, but Hans, the best, the finest of them all. Hans. His Hans, his brightest, most beloved son.

'We thought we'd get married at Christmas time, and then take our honeymoon in St Moritz. Of course, the Duc will make me his vice-president, so I'll probably not be spending much time here.'

Wolfgang felt his fingers closed around the letter opener. What was he saying? He shook his head to clear it, and as he did so, Wayne's words fell like red-hot coals into his brain. Whilst Hans lay dead in his grave, his murderer was talking about marrying, about holidaying in the richest playground in the world. While Hans would never know the joys of a woman's bed, or feel the sun on his face again, his murderer . . .

Wayne was totally unprepared when his father launched himself from the chair, his startled brain barely having time to register the flash of silver in the lamplight as the wicked blade of the stiletto plunged toward him. Only instinct had him turning in time and raising his hand to deflect the accurately aimed blade from his heart. The razor-sharp tip skidded across his chest, ripping through the fine wool of his suit and lodging in his shoulder. Wayne screamed, but his left fist was already coming up automatically to slam into his father's jaw.

Wolfgang grunted, the impetus of his forward movement cannoning him first into Wayne's fist, and then knocking him back against the desk. It had all happened so quickly that for a second, as Wayne stared at the old man half-sprawled against the desk, he was unsure of what exactly had happened. He grabbed the stiletto handle in his shoulder, wincing as a vicious pain ran down his arm as he gingerly pulled it out and stared at it incredulously, the blade stained red with his blood.

Wolfgang straightened, calling him a murdering bastard in guttural, hate-filled German, his hand curling around the base of the lamp, and not for the first time did he curse his advancing years. He hated being old. Once he could have taken his son in a straight fight and killed him with his bare hands, as he now longed to do; instead, infirmity dictated that he use a weapon.

Wayne had barely a second to realize that somehow his father had found out about Hans, and then the lamp was being hurtled toward his face, its heavy steel frame glinting dully in his father's wrinkled hand. Ducking, he charged forward, his head burying itself in Wolfgang's belly as the lamp crashed down on his back, shattering and cutting into his skin as the bulb exploded. His own grunt of pain and that of his father's mixed as they crashed to the floor. Landing on top of him, Wayne began to punch his father with quick, vicious jabs to the face, chest and belly. Between the blows, Wolfgang managed to grab Wayne's throat, his old, bony fingers biting into his son's windpipe with remembered Gestapo skill. Wayne felt his eyes begin to bulge and black blotches flashed across his vision. His hands desperately circled his father's wrists, trying to prise them off, but Wolfgang was a man demented, and his fingers only dug deeper, threatening to shatter his son's larynx. Wayne's lungs were on fire now as he realized with mounting panic that he could not dislodge the throttling hands around his neck. Blindly, his hands groped toward his father's face, searching for a way to make him let loose. He could feel his senses beginning to fade, and just as he thought he was going to die, the soft orbs of Wolfgang's eyes rolled under his fingertips, and he dug in sharply, his fingers curving in and out with a ferocity born of panic. Wolfgang screamed, his hands losing their strength as the unbelievable pain penetrated even his hate-filled frenzy, allowing Wayne to pull away and stagger back, dragging painful breaths deep into his lungs as he stumbled to the leather chair and slumped down. There he dangled his hands limply between his legs as he leant forward, his head spinning, and his big body shaking all over. A few yards away, Wolfgang lay curled on the carpet, his hands clutching his eyes, moaning like an animal.

Slowly, Wayne became aware of a stickiness on his fingers. Looking down at them, he found them covered in blood, and a great wave of nausea engulfed him. Sprinting to the French windows, he opened them and was violently sick amongst the roses and hibiscus bushes. When he finally got up from his knees and walked back into the room he felt numb, his shoulder and back bleeding hard, staining his expensive suit beyond repair.

Wolfgang had crawled back behind his desk, his hands still covering his eyes. They felt on fire, and he could hardly breathe without moaning, but he daren't open his eyes, afraid of what he might see; or, more accurately, of what he might not see.

'I'll have you guillotined for this.' He had heard his son retching outside and heard him return, and his voice was a hiss of pure hatred. For a second, Wayne felt ice course through his veins as the spectre of capital punishment flittered horrifically across his brain. Then he laughed.

'No way, old man,' he said, his voice every bit as thick with hatred as Wolfgang's had been. 'You so much as call in the police and I'll notify the Nazi hunters as to your whereabouts. Remember the Heinzberg kidnapping, Papa?'

Wolfgang did. Vividly. Four years ago one of his contemporaries had been snatched from his home in Bolivia by the Israeli Secret Service, and had been tried and executed in the new state of Israel. It had made Wolfgang paranoid to a point where security at the casino and at the villa had made life unbearable for a few months. Marlene had finally been able to persuade him that such fanatical security would only make him look suspicious. Now, as Wolfgang realized just how powerless he actually was, he began to curse in German, his words so full of bile and filth that even Wayne blanched.

Through the fingers held over his eyes, Wayne could see blood trickling over Wolfgang's hand, and he turned away, suddenly feeling ill. He had to get out of there – he just couldn't stand the sight of the old man a moment longer.

As he heard the door open, Wolfgang's hand tightened over the ruined mess of his eyes. 'I'll kill you,' he whispered, thinking of hired assassins, of men who would do the job slowly and painfully . . .

'You do,' Wayne said, standing in the doorway, leaning back against the wall weakly, 'and copies of your life story will be released automatically to both the press and the Israeli Secret Service. You'll stand trial for the killer you really are – in Israel, in the sight of the whole world.' Then, because he thought his father might be beyond caring what happened to him, he played a trump card that he knew would assure his own safety. 'Your precious Hans will be dug up from out of that cemetery and put in unhallowed ground. You don't think the French will want the son of a Nazi contaminating their graveyard, do you, Father dearest?'

Wolfgang slumped back in his chair, utterly defeated, as Wayne staggered from the room, stained with their blood, knowing he would never have to fear

an assassin's bullet. He drove, with some difficulty, to
the home of their family doctor, knowing he could not
risk going to the hospital where one of the nurses
might tip off the press. The scandal magazines were
notorious for paying nurses well to spill the beans on
any 'celebrities' that might come their way.

Dr Hulot gave him ten stitches and a tetanus shot,
bandaging him up without asking a single question.
Wayne was halfway out the door when he hesitated, in
an agony of indecision. Then he sighed. 'You'd better
get up to Villa Mimosa,' he said curtly, then turned
and left.

He drove as far as St Jean de Luz, leaving Monte
Carlo behind with a sigh of relief. He stayed at the
Hotel Le Petit Trianon, close to the beach. He
needed to be somewhere clean and unpolluted. At
first he felt blissfully numb, but soon he began to
hurt, remembering back to his boyhood in Berlin and
praying for his mother to come to his room. He
wanted her now; he would have given anything to
have her hand on his forehead, her voice telling him
that everything would be all right. He felt ill, dis-
oriented, afraid and totally alone. For the first time in
his life, he knew that he actually needed someone, and
a fierce craving for human contact hit him. Not for
sex, but for something more lasting, more meaning-
ful. Suddenly he needed a friend, something that he
had never had. A man who understood him, who
liked him. A man that he could talk to, play cards
with, laugh with. A friend . . . The first acute wave of

longing slowly faded, but its core remained hidden, only awaiting the right moment to flare savagely into existence again.

He stayed for five days. His shoulder ached, and his nights were feverish. He awoke in the mornings drenched with sweat, feelings of euphoria, horror, regret and guilt warring for supremity. When he finally felt fit enough to drive, he motored north, to Normandy.

The Château Montigny was on the outskirts of a small provincial town, set in lush hay meadows, overlooking a fairytale river. The iron-gates were kept locked, but a camera set on one stone pillar monitored arrivals. He sounded the horn and looked at the camera, waiting for someone to open the gates. Five minutes passed and he thumped the horn again, but still there was no reaction. He cut the engine and got out, a nasty feeling slowly creeping into his innards as he walked to the gate. When he touched them, an electric charge shot through his arm, making him yelp and leap back. Rubbing his hand, he cursed graphically in French. A few moments later, he heard the crunch of footsteps on gravel and waited warily as the Duc walked towards him, a broken shotgun hung professionally over the crook of one arm.

He was a tall, thin man, with white hair and the enormous nose of a vintner. His eyes were steel grey and emotionless as he stopped on the other side of the gates and looked coolly at the man his daughter had chosen to marry.

Wayne looked back at him through the intricate ironwork of the seventeenth-century gates, his narrowed eyes following the movement of the Duc's hand as he wordlessly reached into the top pocket of his tweed jacket and withdrew a small object which he tossed through the ironwork. It fell onto the ground with a soft 'ting'. Looking down, Wayne saw a diamond ring. He glanced at it, but made no attempt to pick it up.

'I want to see Toinette.'

'She isn't here.'

Wayne met the unmoving eyes, his first instinct being to call him a liar. Then he realized that in all probability Toinette would have run away, her cowardice prompting her to avoid an embarrassing scene. It was just the kind of gutless reaction he'd come to expect from women and the world in general.

'Where is she?'

'America. She said to give you that.' The Duc nodded toward the ring, but Wayne didn't look down. Instead a helpless rage began to clog his brain, and his lips pulled back into a savage sneer.

'You never wanted me in your precious family in the first place, did you?'

'No,' the Duc admitted readily, without the least sign of unease.

'Don't think that this is over,' Wayne warned him, enraged by the man's careless dismissal. 'Toinette wants . . .'

'Toinette wants to live a life of luxury,' the Duc interrupted him. 'To indulge herself with everything

184

life has to offer. She can't do that with a man who has nothing.'

'Nothing?' The word sounded foreign on Wayne's tongue, and for the first time the Duc d'Montigny smiled.

'Your father phoned me yesterday to tell me he has disinherited you. He also tells me that you cannot go back to Monte Carlo . . . at least, not if you want to live. He assures me that nobody in Monte Carlo will give you the time of day. In fact,' the Duc said, with so much smug satisfaction that Wayne felt like reaching through the ironwork, electrified or not, and grabbing him by the throat, 'you're not wanted in France at all.'

Wayne stiffened, for the first time fully comprehending that he was practically penniless. His future which only days ago had been so promising, was now in ruins, and the enormity of his problems were suddenly overwhelming. He felt like shouting in rage and defiance, but none of his emotions showed on his face, except for a slight tightening of his jaw.

The Duc had taken an immediate dislike to the giant of a man Toinette had brought home just over three months ago, sensing that something dangerous lurked beneath his surface charm, manners and good looks; something that was dark and unstable. He had never been more relieved in his life when Marcus D'Arville had called, telling him the news, and he'd been even more satisfied when, with a few tears of regret, Toinette had agreed to let him go. Even she had seen the futility of trying to salvage the situation. Now, as he watched the man in front of him straighten and stiffen, the eyes turning opaque and expressionless, the Duc could not help but feel uneasy. Looking into his eyes was like looking into a diamond – there was nothing there that he could call human, and in his ears he could hear his own blood began to pound with a heavy, frightened beat.

Slowly Wayne stooped down and pocketed the ring, realizing that he'd need all the money he could get. The Duc watched, the look of contempt on his face quickly fleeing under the ice-cold, level stare of the younger man. Uneasily, the Duc took a step backwards, despite the electrified iron between them. Seeing it, Wayne felt his own power bite deep. It was something separate from money or position. It was in him, a vital and integral part of his very being. And suddenly he knew that he would be on the top again soon.

Somehow.

CHAPTER 13

San Francisco

The old lady had lived in San Francisco all her life, but for all the seventy-two years that she had trod the same hills, she'd never managed to tread them any flatter. It was nearly 90 degrees, and her shopping basket, weighted down with tins of cat food, seemed to pull her arms from her sockets.

'Hello, Mrs Dobson. Bit warm, isn't it?' The voice was soft and kind, and made her stop in her tracks. As she turned into the sun she saw the halo of a young man, the bright daylight behind him turning his hair a deep red. She blinked, and the boy moved, his face coming into focus.

'Oh, it's young Sebastien, isn't it? I'm a bit puffed, I'm afraid.'

'Here, let me take that. I'm going your way.'

He wasn't, but her old and lined face was bathed in perspiration, and her little wisps of white hair were plastered to her pink scalp in damp waves. He looked down in surprise at the weight of the wicker basket, and then saw all the tins of cat food, and a great wave of compassion had him mentally abandoning all his afternoon plans to visit the rehabilitation centre.

'How's school nowadays?' Enid Dobson asked, reaching out to the wall to give her extra support as they turned down Pitman Street, a residential street of quiet, slightly decayed elegance. When she had been a girl, it had been the height of fashion to live in this area. Of course, in those days everyone had been talking about the great quake as if it had only just happened. Everyone had seemed to lose someone to that giant earthquake and even now it was remembered with horror. Ah, those were the days, Enid thought, looking up at the tall, three-storey houses with their canary-yellow paintwork and Florentine lace curtains.

'I've just graduated,' Sebastien interrupted her thoughts, hoiking the basket onto another arm and taking her elbow in a courtly olde-worlde gesture that had the venerable Mrs Dobson blushing like a schoolgirl and looking at him coyly out of the corners of her rheumy blue eyes. Ah, young men nowadays! Sebastien was of medium height, but even so his five feet ten inches seemed to tower over the diminutive old woman, and she was briefly transported back to pre-war days, when they had danced walzes instead of the awful modern gyrations young people went through nowadays, and when more men looked and acted just like this one. In those days, it was easy to tell the sexes apart.

'Just graduated, eh?' she repeated, shaking her head. 'I would have liked to have gone to college. But . . . well, in my day, young ladies never seemed to go to college. And then there was the war, and we all went to the factories . . .' Her voice was cracked with age, but full of strength of character, nostalgia and wistfulness. Sebastien shook his head, his regret genuine at the thought of all that waste. To take her mind off bad days, and because he was genuinely interested, he prompted her with some gentle teasing. 'And what would you have liked to study, Mrs Dobson? Poetry, I bet. All those dashing exploits of the mad, bad and dangerous-to-know Lord Byron, for instance?'

Enid chuckled, her laughter surprisingly young and carefree, and several passers-by looked at them curiously. They made an odd couple – the small, bent old woman, and the young, handsome man, with hair the colour of English chestnuts, and liquid sherry-coloured eyes.

'Ahh, now wouldn't that have been nice. Poor Lady Caroline Lamb. She died of a broken heart, you know. I don't suppose anybody does that nowadays. And Tennyson, of course – 'The Lady of Shalott' was always my favourite. You majored in English?'

Sebastien grinned and shook his head, revealing a row of perfect white teeth in his square-jawed, boyishly handsome face.

'Uh-uh. Psychology. I'm due to start my psychiatry internship at the General this fall.'

'Oh,' Enid said. She wasn't at all sure she trusted this newfangled subject. It seemed to her that people should keep their problems to themselves, like they always did. Going around and revealing all your most intimate secrets to a perfect stranger filled her with horror. 'Oh. Well . . .' She struggled for something nice to say because she'd watched Sebastien Teale grow up from a kind-hearted and polite little boy, and she didn't want to be unkind to someone who had once rescued her Fluffy from beneath the wheels of a milk float. 'I'm sure you'll do very well indeed. I'll have to start calling you Doctor, then?'

Sebastien, reading her thoughts practically word for word, laughed. 'Not quite yet. I have five more years yet to do. At the same time I have to undergo three years' psychoanalysis myself.'

'You do? Aren't you the one who's going to be the doctor, then?'

'Uh-huh. But the medical board has got to be sure that I'm fit myself. After all, I can't go helping people if I'm a secret lunatic myself, now, can I?'

'Oh, you!' The little old woman tapped his arm playfully, then sighed. 'Ah, at last. Here we are. I'm quite worn out.' Her own house was at the end of the road, and she was forced to pause to catch her breath by the five stone steps that led up to the front door. A black and white cat of enormous proportions, most of it fluffy fur, sashayed down the steps and wound a tail seductively around his legs.

'Hello, Fluff. Still chasing milk floats, hmm?' The hand he ran over the cat was casual, but the cat went into immediately ecstasy. A loud, lawn-mower purr vibrated from his soft underbelly, and the green eyes narrowed into blissful slits. Thus encouraged, Sebastien began to rub the cat's belly, and the lawn-mower revved harder. 'Oh, that cat!' Enid said, her voice affectionately exasperated. 'He'll be the death of me.'

Sebastien had a way with animals that astonished many people. Vicious dogs, even some trained security animals, became putty in his hands the moment man and animal met. As a boy he had brought home almost weekly an injured or stray animal of almost every species known to his native California – including a big old bull frog whose hind leg had been mashed by a car. He'd called it Harry, and had kept it for six years, much to his mother's distress, before it had died of old age. He'd been the only boy in school who could catch bluebottles with his bare hands by the time Harry finally croaked.

But it was in his dealings with people that Sebastien's true talents lay. Always listening more than talking, he had been a keen observer of human nature from childhood. His own particularly sensitive nature had developed over the years into an uncanny, almost paranormal ability to see past the surface mask people habitually wore, and discover what lurked beneath. As a boy, instead of getting embroiled in the usual childhood squabbles and coming home with a bloody nose or bruised shin, he would come home instead with a note from the teacher, congratulating his parents on his behaviour in mediating between troublemakers, preventing fights, and even, more often than not, bringing antagonistic boys together to become the best of friends.

A good all-rounder, his main interest from an early age had leant towards the humanities, much to his father's dismay. His studies in sociology, at the age of fourteen, had totally fascinated him, unlike many of his friends, who found the subject boring. He had, with a special dispensation from a delighted psychology teacher, started studying the subject a year early, and by the age of sixteen had passed with flying colours exams that eighteen-year-olds struggled to get through. But it was not academic brilliance, or his good looks, or his ready and funny wit or sense of humour that attracted people to him by the droves, earning him more friends than he seemed able to count. There was something very human – not to mention *humane* – about Sebastien Teale that people reacted to both consciously and subconsciously. It drew wounded spirits to him like a magnet. His soft voice, soft eyes, listening ear, keen intelligence and total lack of judgemental superiority made him a perfect, if incongruous, father confessor.

At fifteen, Arthur Wight had confided to him that he was hooked on whisky, knowing that Sebastien would not squeal or condemn him. His belief in his friend was fully justified. Without talking to his parents or teachers, Sebastien read up on the subject of alcohol addiction and worked out a drying-out routine for his friend to follow, sticking with him through the withdrawal syptoms, spending weekend after weekend at his house, ostensibly to study, but in reality to make sure he didn't slip. Two years later, when Arthur was more able to face up to reality,

Sebastien had persuaded him to tell his parents and join an AA group. And there were many other incidents. Girls and boys came to him with any and every problem that agonized teenagers worldwide.

When she became pregnant, Sue Anne Haynes had turned to him, though in a higher year herself and hardly knowing him. He had gone with her to a family clinic, had held her hand as she talked with a doctor, had talked her through all the options, and went with her when she had told her parents.

In almost any other boy, such popularity would have inevitably led to jealousy, making for a painful backlash by some of the older boys. But not so with Sebastien. His level gaze, never judgemental but never weak, had seen him through several confrontations with older boys who were obviously insecure and afraid of him and his puzzling maturity, and bitterly envious of his status with girls, who found his good looks a delicious cherry on top of a very sweet cake.

Sometimes, as his mother had watched him grow, she wondered if he had ever really been a child. As a three-year-old, he'd watched her in the house with those warm sherry eyes, a ready smile always on his cherubic face, but the intelligence had been evident right from the start. An IQ test at twelve had placed him potentially in the Mensa bracket, and had opened the whole academic world to him. But he had stayed at home, studying at the local high and then college, doing in two years what others did in four, but without vanity.

Now, as the cat's soft paws clung to his hand in trusting adoration, he straightened, lifting the cat into his arms, and carrying the basket up the steps.

'You will have some lemonade, won't you?' Enid asked, hoping her voice did not sound as pitifully eager as she felt. Since her husband had died in the war, she had been so alone that sometimes she talked to her cat. She felt like a silly old woman, but Fluffy never seemed to mind.

Hearing the plea for company as if she had spoken it out loud, he smiled and nodded. 'I'd love to,' he said, and knowing the old woman wouldn't appreciate pity, added cleverly, 'This sun sure works up a giant thirst.'

Inside, the house was full of bric-à-brac, cheap crockery, chainstore pictures of autumns in New England, and faded chintz-covered sofas. She lived only on the first floor, the stairs being too much for her. Chattering happily, she led the way into the kitchen, a square room of yellow Formica and white furniture, where he began to unpack the groceries for her. As she poured icy lemonade into a glass, he sat down, looking around at the things that needed doing. He'd be here for at least three hours, he gauged, eyeing the flaking paint on the window-sills and the grime on the windows keeping out the sunlight and making the place look dim and dingy. He'd cook her a meal, too – something light and simple. Most old folk that lived alone didn't bother to eat properly – this he knew from his work with Age Concern.

'Why don't you rent out the top two floors, Mrs D.?' he asked, watching as she looked firstly startled, and then alarmed.

'Oh, no. No, I couldn't do that. I mean . . . well, it's such a mess up there.'

Sebastien took a sip, knowing he had to tread carefully now. She was picturing young couples having midnight parties, shuddering in humiliation at the notion of neighbours complaining, of dogs killing her Fluffy, of children making too much noise, and she was afraid. She'd lived alone so long, the thought of company all day, every day, scared her.

'I was thinking that you might want to rent out to retired couples. Take Mr and Mrs Pettit, for example. He worked for Growers Home and Garden for forty-six years in one of their company houses. The rent was only five dollars a month, but after having six children, who've all flown the nest now, they don't have any money left to buy a place of their own. Now that he's retired, they're living in a one-roomed bedsit at the shelter, just because landlords don't want to rent to old people.'

Enid, whose face had become more and more angry as he'd told the story, suddenly slammed down her glass. 'That's terrible. Really terrible. I don't know what this country is coming to. The Spanish . . . now they know how to look after their old folk. Poor dears. One room, you say?'

Sebastien nodded. 'All they want is a place of their own. They can pay twenty dollars a month at a stretch . . .'

'That's far too much!' Enid erupted, her flushed face indignant, her old eyes flashing sparks. 'Why, I don't even use those rooms upstairs.'

'And of course, Mrs Pettit, poor old thing, gets lonely with no one to talk to when her husband goes out during the day to work in the shelter. He's a proud man, and the Reverend needs all the help he can get. And you have such a big place here – plenty of room for poor old Mr Crocket. He's a widower, you know . . .'

Five hours later, he left the little house with its brown faded pictures of a handsome man in an Air Force uniform, its big black and white cat and its yellow kitchen, now freshly painted with sparkling windows, feeling pleasantly pleased with himself. The shelter would soon be minus four old people, leaving room for someone else. Mrs Dobson would have slightly younger hands to help her with her shopping and plenty of people to talk to.

The sun was getting low, sinking towards Fisherman's Wharf, the delight of every tourist that flocked to the city during the summer months. As he walked, Sebastien wondered if he felt like risking Ghirardelli Square, then decided he wasn't in the mood for a crowd. He felt tired and listless and was angry with himself because he knew why. He should do. He'd spent years getting to know himself, his every reaction subjected to intense scrutiny. If something annoyed him, he couldn't rest until he'd found out the exact root of it, and corrected it. He knew all his faults and kept a wary eye on them, being harder with himself than he would ever dream of being on anybody else. And so he knew that it was time, once and for all, to try and make his father understand that he was not going to change his mind about his career, no matter how much he was bribed, threatened or emotionally blackmailed. Nob Hill, in all its gleaming white, wealthy beauty spread out before him, but he didn't want to go home, just yet, to that sprawling bungalow, filled with the fine art that was currently all the rave in the executive set. He needed time before running the gauntlet of his father's disappointment and his mother's silent condemnation.

Chinatown was always distracting, but Sebastien was very much aware that he was as American as apple pie, and whilst the Oriental psyche was fascinating, he could only ever be on the outside looking in. He knew Lin Chun would welcome him if he went to his small restaurant, and would happily feed him on real Chinese food and not the kind he served to customers who expected chow mein and nothing else. It was ironic, in a sad way. He had friends everywhere – of every colour, race, religious belief and personality, and yet he knew that he didn't quite fit in with any of them.

Acknowledging this, he turned blind eyes to the oft-photographed Golden Gate Bridge, instead concentrating on the gloomy island that housed the famous Alcatraz prison, in a strange way the root of all his troubles. For he was determined to work in the field of criminal rehabilitation. Not for him a discreet clientele on Nob Hill of which his parents could approve and mention in polite company. He simply wasn't interested in petty problems that caused patients mere annoyance or social embarrassment. He wanted to *help* people. He wanted to tackle pain head on and defeat it. And as he looked on at Alcatraz, he knew that his goals were legitimate ones. Inside that grim fortress there lurked real pain and despair. And if there was one thing Sebastien truly hated, it was watching human beings suffer.

When he got home, about an hour of hard thinking later, he noticed that there were several lights on, and he glanced at his watch, puzzled. Usually his parents were out every night, ruthlessly climbing the social ladder. He shrugged, then dug into his jeans' pocket for the house key and let himself in, coming face to face with an ugly iron sculpture, his mother's most recent purchase. Throw rugs were currently all the rage, so the hall was littered with Mexican rugs of deep red, white and black. Next month it would be something else.

He walked into the living-room, which was redolent of pipe tobacco, and found both his parents sitting on the settee, dressed to go out. So, they had been waiting for him. He sighed slightly, then shut the door behind him, watching silently as his father uncrossed his legs and slowly got up. Sebastien sighed again. 'Tell me something, Dad. Do you actually like smoking a pipe, or did you only start because it . . .' he nodded at the expensive and showy pipe in his father's hand '. . . was a present from the company chairman?'

His father looked at him coolly for a few moments, then shrugged. 'It is politic, Sebastien, to be seen smoking Mr Helpmann's pipe, yes. He'll be retiring in two years' time, after all, and both Philip Swithen-

198

bank and Ralph Hines are in line for the job as well as myself. Do you want a drink?'

'No, thanks. I think I'll turn in.' His mother, who had been sitting in a high-backed, rattan chair imported from Japan, suddenly stood up, her movements uncharacteristically jerky and nervous. 'Can you wait a moment? Your father and I want to talk to you.'

Sebastien knew that tone well, and for a second felt a moment of pain, mixed with dread, snake down his back. Then he nodded and shrugged, knowing that this moment had been inevitable, and putting off an emotional scene was never a good idea. 'OK. I think I will have that drink after all.' He poured himself a small gin and tonic, more tonic than gin, and walked to the small settee, embroidered with Spanish sequins.

His father cleared his throat whilst Sebastien looked at him, feeling a great well of love and pity choke him. At forty-five, Donald Teale looked the epitome of the middle-aged, upper-class American. His hair was neat and grey, his moustache equally so. His body was just beginning to run to fat around the middle, but the extra weight, so far, suited him. He had a healthy tan, flat brown eyes, and on his hand was a single black signet ring. 'We wondered . . . that is . . . your mother and I . . . we had hoped – '

'Why don't you just spit it out, Pop? It's a lot easier that way,' Sebastien said gently.

'Very well. Do you still intend to – ' he coughed delicately '– work in the . . . er . . . penal community?'

For a moment he met his father's hopeful, dreadful look, and felt tempted to lie. Sebastien hated pain – he hated it with a ferocious vengeance that some people reserved for politics or religion. He hated it as if it were a personal enemy, and his instinct was to avoid inflicting it at any cost. Then common sense took over. Sometimes it was unavoidable, and the only option left was to keep it to an absolute minimum. So he took a deep breath and answered honestly. 'Yes, I am.'

'I see.' Donald looked at Jayne, his most satisfactory wife of twenty-one years, and shrugged helplessly.

'Sebastien,' Jayne said, elongating his name thoughtfully, a habit that indicated she was about to give an order, but trying to make it sound like a suggestion. 'Have you ever thought about Europe?'

Sebastien blinked. 'Europe?'

'Hmm. I mean, you're young, single, and you must want to travel, to see something of the world?' She stood up as she talked and paced restlessly about the room, her Italian shoes leaving tiny indentations in the carpet, her Chanel perfume battling against the aroma of her husband's expensive tobacco. Silk swished at her calves as she moved, but she carefully avoided eye contact with her only child.

'I would leave if I could,' Sebastien said, still not sure where all this was leading. 'But I have my training to do. And nothing, but nothing, is going to interfere with that,' he finished determinedly. And Sebastien, as his mother knew, was a very determined young man. Sometimes, surprisingly so.

Jayne turned to him, her eyes moist but resolute. He'd always been a good boy. Even as a baby he'd been obedient and hardly ever naughty. But still, this . . . this . . . obsession of his was just so, well . . . embarrassing!

'We understand that,' Douglas cut in tersely. 'But I've just been on the phone to Julius Remus. You remember, I told you about him? We met during the war, when I was in England.'

'I remember.'

'Sir Julius is the finest psychiatrist England has to offer. He studied with Jung in Switzerland, I believe. He and I became close during the war. Let me tell you, liaising with a man of that calibre . . . well, I need hardly point out what a fine career move it would be. He is a very fine man. Retired now, of course, but when I told him about you, about the way you've already got your doctorate . . . he said he'd be delighted to have you over there. He's still, technically, the chairman of St Edmunds in London.'

'*The* St Edmunds? The psychiatric home for the criminally insane?' Sebastien asked eagerly.

Douglas winced at the full title, but nodded coolly. 'The same. He says he can get you onto the staff there. In a junior capacity, of course. He also very kindly offered to be your . . . er . . . psychoanalyst.'

'I see. England is so wonderfully far away, isn't it?' Sebastien tried to laugh, but it did little to hide his hurt. 'And Sir Julius is a wonderful name to be able to drop when explaining away my absence to all your friends,' he added sadly.

Jayne gasped, tears coming to her eyes, excuses to her lips. 'Sebastien, please.'

She needn't have bothered with the latter. He was defeated the moment she began to cry.

'All right, Mother,' he said quickly, going to her side, and taking her gently in his arms. 'England sounds wonderful.'

The lake was cold but deserted, and Kyle began to strip eagerly, looking forward to its cold caress. Beside him, Clarissa laid out a large beach towel on the grass, and began to rub sun lotion onto her bare arms. She glanced up at her lover with gentle eyes, quickly looking away when he glanced down at her.

Kyle smiled wryly. Clarissa had no reason to be so coy. She still had the figure of a twenty-year-old and knew it. But then, he thought grimly, would it make any difference to him if she looked her age? He jerked his shirt over his head and flung it viciously onto the ground. Of course not. He'd be just as much her slave if she looked like a crone.

'Be careful, darlin',' Clarissa drawled, her sweet southern voice so slow and lazy it rippled over his skin like melted honey. 'The water's cold.'

Kyle stepped out of his pants, to reveal black swimming trunks that clung lovingly to his muscled body. He heeled his shoes off and dipped in a toe. He shuddered in pleasant, slightly masochistic anticipation.

Clarissa watched him wade into the lapping water and glanced around her. But there was no one in sight. Talman's Lake was set well away from the nearest town, and they'd discovered it quite by accident, a year or so ago. Now they came here often, to swim and make love.

'Are you coming in?' Kyle asked, turning to look at her. She was dressed in a one-piece peach-coloured costume that did wonders for her hair and skin.

'Not just yet, darlin'. You know I like to watch you.'

Kyle's lips twisted grimly. 'It's a pity your husband doesn't want to watch *you* more,' he muttered gruffly under his breath, but she heard him nevertheless.

Clarissa laughed gaily and wagged a finger at him. 'Now, now. You know Duncan doesn't mind about you. I told you – neither of us married for love. Duncan even has his own mistress over in Charleston. Did I tell you about her?'

Kyle sighed heavily. On the one hand, it was very nice to know he wasn't breaking up a marriage, or causing Duncan Somerville any pain. On the other hand, it was depressing to know that they had her husband's blessing.

'No, you didn't,' he said shortly, and neatly duckdived beneath the clear but startlingly cold water. He came up, the breath knocked out of him and gasping for air, a few yards further out, Clarissa's mocking laughter ringing in his ears.

Kyle began a slow lazy crawl. The coldness of the water brought out the goosebumps on his arms, but he ignored the draining effect it had on his limbs. Instead, he let his mind roam to other things.

And, as always, the 'other things' meant Clarissa. What malicious twist of fate had made their paths cross all those years ago? And why hadn't he outgrown his teenage fascination with her? He was in his thirties now, he thought angrily, turning over onto his back and staring up at the sky. And yet . . . he thought he would die if she should stop coming to him. Just curl up and wither away if she told him she was bored with him. He'd want to kill her if she told him she'd found another, younger lover to take his place. It was . . .

Love, he thought savagely. He might as well face it. He loved the manipulating, scathing, lying . . . wonderful . . . bitch.

Kyle felt a sudden sharp pain in his calf at the same instant that he felt himself begin to sink. He had time to give one startled yelp of surprise, before his head sunk under the cold water. The nasty taste of lake water filled his mouth. Cramp, he thought coolly, and without a hint of panic. Great. Just what he needed. He relaxed and let his body come vertical in the water, then, with his unaffected leg and arms, thrust back to the surface.

On the shore, Clarissa had been watching him with all her usual covetous longing, and had heard his sudden cry and seen him disappear. She'd realized what it was, even before he had, and without a thought she had plunged into the water. Now her heart raced with fear so sharp, it tasted like bile in her throat. Where was he? He hadn't come to the surface yet. Panic lent her slim body an amazing strength, and within moments she'd swum out to him.

As his dark head suddenly appeared on the surface, she gave a loud sob of relief, unaware that she'd been sobbing near-hysterically ever since hitting the water.

Kyle felt her presence beside him, and turned startled eyes towards her. Clarissa didn't give him a chance to speak. With surprisingly strong hands, she cupped his chin, and began to head for shore. Her legs kicked strongly, towing them both to the grassy bank. After a surprised instant, Kyle shrugged and let her get on with it. If she wanted to play lifeguard, why spoil her fun?

Once at the bank, Kyle managed to drag himself on to the grass, his chest heaving with the effort.

Clarissa, still half-sobbing, bent over him, her hands hard on his shoulders. 'Are you all right?' she all but screamed at him.

Kyle stared at her blankly. Her face was a mask of fear, pain and relief. Her hair hung in wet, lank strands on her shoulders, and her lips were washed free of all her expensive lipstick. She looked haggard, he realized incredulously. He'd never seen the elegant Clarissa Somerville look anything other than well-groomed and superior before.

Clarissa's hands were all over him – touching his face, his chest, his arms. But, for once, her touch was gentle, almost reverent. Her eyes were enormous, her face as pale as milk. She was trembling like an aspen.

Her eyes went to his calf, still twisted and contorted with cramp. Still unaware of it, she was sobbing as she breathed. 'Oh, Kyle. Oh, Kyle,' she said his name over and over again, like a talisman. 'I thought you were going to die.' Her hands went straight to his leg, her strong fingers kneading, taking away the sickening pain.

But Kyle barely noticed that the pain was receding.

Instead, he was staring at her, his own eyes wide and enormous, his mouth slack with shock at his astounding discovery.

Clarissa was terrified. She was sure he'd been about to drown. She –

'You love me,' he said, his voice accusing.

Clarissa's hands froze on his leg. Her shoulders stiffened as her heart leapt up into her throat. For a moment, she was unable to comprehend it. Then it crashed against her, like a hurricane. Her secret was out. He *knew*! Now . . . now she had no power over him. He'd laugh at her. The power that had kept him by her side for all these years was gone.

He'd leave her.

Slowly, inch by dreadful inch, she turned to look at him.

His face was pale with shock, his lovely navy blue eyes almost black with surprise. 'You love me,' he said again, his voice strong and furiously angry. 'All these years . . . *all these years* . . .' Kyle heard his voice crack.

Clarissa's eyes filled with tears. Before his astonished eyes, his beloved tormentor began to cry.

And not pretty little tears, either, but soul-wrenching, body-shuddering tears that tore at his heart as none of her cruel barbs had ever been able to do.

For a long moment, Kyle just stared at her. In the space of a second, his whole world had turned about-face on its axis.

He said again, for a third time, his voice wondering, husky, and full of disbelieving astonishment, 'You *love* me.'

CHAPTER 14

Hollywood

It was a golden spring in Hollywood, filled with golden stars, golden movies, golden screen goddesses and golden lives. James Dean had shocked the world a few years back by dying on the road to Salinas whilst driving the silver Porsche he fondly called 'little bastard'. He'd tasted the fame that *East of Eden* had given him, but had not lived to see *Rebel Without a Cause*, or his just-completed epic, *Giant*, hit the silver screens. America was in a fervour of thanks directed at Jonas Salk, who had cured the country of the terror of polio, and saved the public baths from extinction as children flocked back. Ike and Mamie were in the White House, and Oriel and Kier had left behind Antony Eden at Number 10 Downing Street.

'From Oxford to Hollywood,' Oriel said whimsically, sitting beside her husband of two years as he drove the second-hand Oldsmobile down Lexington, heading out of town to the less elitist part of Beverly Hills, that up-and-coming showplace attracting more and more of Hollywood's top stars. 'Can you imagine a greater culture shock than this?' she asked, looking around wide-eyed at the desert that was still the dominating factor of the fledgling city.

'Nope,' Kier admitted, coaxing the ancient car into third gear. They had left behind an Oxford of mellow buildings, dripping with centuries of history, and landed in Hollywood just two months ago, where the desert sun was fierce. Two months to become immunized to the gossip of Hedda Hopper, the glory of stars like Bogart and his baby, Victor Mature, Tony Curtis, the up-and-coming Kim Novak and, of course, Grace Kelly.

'It's like a dream,' Oriel whispered, still overawed with the city, and craned her neck as a Cadillac cruised by. 'Wasn't that Audrey Hepburn in the back of there? Did you see?' Her excited voice made him smile, and he looked in the mirror to see the tail lights of the luxury car fast disappearing.

'Could be.'

Oriel swatted him playfully. 'You don't fool me, Kier Harcourt,' she warned him. 'You're as gobsmacked as I am.'

'Gobsmacked? My, my, Scarlett, you do have such an interesting vocabulary.' He rendered up the voice of the much-loved W.C. Fields at the same time as he tweaked an imaginary cigar, making Oriel burst into delighted laughter.

The last two years at Oxford had been idyllic. They'd moved out of college and found a small apartment in Magpie Road, right in the centre of town. It was actually a converted attic in a tall narrow house, and had rickety plumbing, uncertain drains, and was definitely home to a fair number of mice. Kier had taken on a job as a waiter in one of the swankiest eateries in town, whilst Oriel completed her course. She'd also taken some small parts in the Oxford Playhouse, doing minor roles that nevertheless paid for half the rent. She liked it well enough, but had no desire to be an actress. She never enjoyed stage fright and found performing the same role night after night boring and repetitive. Besides, Kier gave her all the limelight she needed. They studied like maniacs, Kier working as much on making contacts with the English film industry as on his own postgraduate studies, and Oriel had graduated with a First Class degree. They had explored England in the holidays, and by visiting the homes of friends from college, sponging off them shamelessly, they had just about managed to keep body and soul together.

Now, the only cloud on Oriel's horizon was the break with her family. She missed her father pitifully, and had spoken to him several times on the telephone. She knew Duncan called her from his office so that Clarissa wouldn't be upset. At first, Oriel had been afraid that her father would be disappointed in her, but the first thing he had asked her was if she loved her husband.

Since Kier had been standing right beside her at the time, his hand splayed across her waist in silent love and support, her answer had been easy, and filled with a conviction that had satisfied Duncan

Somerville all those thousands of miles away. Now both Kier and Oriel had calls from him regularly, and she had gradually grown to accept the situation. Of her mother, they heard nothing. Oriel's allowance had been stopped immediately, of course, but they had expected it, and for the first few months Kier had been anxious, wondering how his new bride, used to every pampered luxury life had to offer, would take to a life of relative poverty. He need not have feared. She complained seldom, and only when she'd had a really bad day, and they laughed more than they cried. Their arguments had been few and far between, but had been humdingers, reminding them of the early days and the play when they had been so much at each other's throats. Vigorous and satisfying love-making followed every argument though, curled up in their creaky bed where they shivered in winter, because there was no proper heating, and sweltered in summer, because heat always rose to the top of the house. But they loved it, and the crooked, oddly named road where they lived.

They'd almost been reluctant to leave. Almost, but not quite. Hollywood was where Kier's dream was, and Oriel was fast learning that all that guff about a wife being by her husband's side through thick and thin was not guff at all.

'Do you suppose we got anywhere this morning?' Kier asked, interrupting her wonderful thoughts, and she frowned, thinking over the interview with Howard Shoesmith, the director of Cougar Studios.

'I'm not sure,' she said truthfully. 'I think he was interested, but . . .'

'But?' He took his eyes off the road for a scant second to look at her as they took a left into their street.

'Well. There are hundreds of guys in this damned town who want to direct. All of them probably have as much, or probably even more, experience as you do, honey. I think he liked you, but I wonder if anybody can be as hearty and friendly as he is, and still run a studio successfully? Know what I mean?'

Kier did. Howard Shoesmith was a small-town boy made good. Cougar Studios was small, but independent, and made small but solid profits every year. Howard Shoesmith couldn't have got as far as he had at the age of forty and actually be the good ol' boy that he tried so hard to appear. It had taken them twelve days to wangle an interview with the man, fighting through a barrage of secretaries, assistants, receptionists and a seemingly endless line of middlemen. Then, yesterday afternoon, when Kier had been out trying to sell a screenplay he had written, a secretary had phoned with the appointment. Hearing his wife answer, and knowing her employer very well, she had quickly informed her that the interview was for both of them, which had momentarily left Oriel speechless. Then she had quickly agreed. What did it matter, after all? A successful man in Hollywood was allowed his eccentricities.

Kier had worn his only suit, Oriel her best dress, one of the few she had packed to take to Oxford, so although it was years old, it was still a classic of hyacinth blue in pure silk. With her hair up in an elegant chignon, and a pair of pearl-drop earrings in her lobes, she looked like a movie star herself.

Kier had held open the door of the Olds for her, aware that the car wasn't fit for her. Then and there he vowed that one day he'd bring her a limousine to ride in, with a chauffeur to match.

One day.

The studios were on the outskirts of town to avoid the city noise, and they'd had to drive through false-fronted western towns where Ronald Reagan might have ridden up on a horse for a shoot-out with Gabby Hayes. The air of unreality and falsity made Oriel wince, but Kier was fascinated. He was so close now, discovering things that he had only read about, and to him the city was already home.

Determined to make a good impression, they arrived early and had to wait half an hour before being shown in to the hallowed office. It was a strange room, a mix of expensive imported furniture and the smell of cheap cigars. On the wall were posters of films that Cougar had made, mostly B-pictures, with B-stars. But most of those B-stars had gone on to become big box-office draws, and Cougar had a reputation that was not to be sneezed at.

Howard Shoesmith, like the room, was a mix of class and common man. His suit was expensive but rumpled, and cigar ash lay on his lapel. He was a small man with black hair and fierce black eyes and looked as if he came from Italian stock, but his voice, when he spoke, was straight out of Wyoming. He greeted Kier first, but his eyes were on Oriel. His first words set the tone for the meeting. 'I thought you were here to discuss being a director, son. But I see you have a star lined up already.'

Oriel, perversely, felt insulted and was not sure why; being told by a man who had created big-name stars that she herself was star material should have flattered her, but somehow it didn't. It was not even that his gaze was more open than it should have been, for she was used to men looking at her just as this one did now. There was just something about Howard Shoesmith that she didn't trust.

'My wife, Oriel,' Kier introduced her, his voice just a touch chilly.

'And I'm not an actress, I'm afraid. Nor do I want to be,' she added quickly, but with a smile to take the edge off her words.

Howard was surprised and looked it. He was used to beautiful women with the Hollywood bug conning their way into his office. He was used to making his conquests on the casting couch, and enjoyed his unique sense of power. Anywhere else in the world, a man like him would be a nothing and a nobody. But here he had some real power and a constant tap to the most beautiful women the country had to offer. It was not very often that he came across a beautiful woman who was not willing, and it intrigued him.

'Well now, sit yourselves down, and take the weight off. Cigar?'

Kier declined, not trusting the bonhomie. This man might talk like a cowboy, but he looked like a shark, and he had the sensation of treading through a mine-field as the interview progressed. For the next half-hour they talked about the three plays he had produced in Oxford, Shoesmith reading the excellent review clippings with obvious interest. He listened to Kier's ideas, nodding his head, smiling, agreeing, his eyes occasionally flicking to Oriel. Then he talked of Cougar, of the films they'd made in the past, finally finishing with a rough sketch of the latest studio idea for a film. 'You see, son,' Howard said in that aggravatingly condescending tone that Oriel was sure he used on purpose, 'I heard from a friend of mine in the know that all the big studios are making these new science-fiction things. They're cheap, give the audience a thrill, and are perfect for a studio like ours. They're effective in black and white and don't need big stars.'

Kier nodded, understanding immediately the budgeting advantages of this type of genre which would appeal to a man of Howard's money-pinching type. 'And if this new film *The Blob* makes it, your picture will have a ready-made audience.'

Howard nodded, obviously pleased with the answer, and acknowledging Kier's observation. In fact, he looked pleased about a lot of things, but not especially so. Kids like Kier Harcourt came to his office every day. They were a dime a dozen, and he did not have the sensitivity to realize that in Kier he had found a man who had greatness written all over him. All Howard could see was a mediocre man, bright, probably talented, but no more so than anyone else.

It was this sense of could-take-it-or-leave-it that Oriel tried to explain now, as Perez Padro came over the radio playing 'Cherry Pink and Apple Blossom White.'

But Kier understood just what she was saying. He'd gained the same impression himself, and knew all about vicious circles. No studio wanted to take a chance on a new director who hadn't made a film before. Until someone was willing to take a chance on a new boy, there was no way in. Although they didn't actually say it out loud, neither Kier nor Oriel thought that Howard Shoesmith was the man to give a guy a break. Since arriving in the fabulous city, both had heard the horror stories, meeting men who had been in the city for years and were still only second or third-string screenwriters, dogsbodies to established directors or little more than office clerks. He'd been here two months, had sold no play, had been offered no apprenticeship or way in, and their money was running low. Sometimes it seemed impossible.

They pulled up in front of their boarding house on Maple Road, and he turned off the noisy engine. The house was white clapboard, with a white picket fence that needed repainting, and a broken swing hung from an old oak in one corner. It looked like it belonged on the set of a thirties' movie, where cherry blossom fell in spring, and perfect children played in perfect gardens, and had perfect parents. The landlady was a Miss Tillson, a sprightly old thing, who had Hollywood fever. Her idol was Cary Grant, and she leased her rooms only to film people. Oriel's looks and Kier's tales of Oxford plays had been used to talk their way into the two rooms on the second floor that were all they could afford.

They were quiet now as they walked up the path, but the ever-alert Miss Tillson was waiting for them.

'Hi, there. How did you get on? Tell me about the studio!' She had a moon face, grey hair tucked into a tight bun, and always wore flowered aprons. Oriel and Kier's eyes met, a fond smile coming on to both their faces as they joined her on the old-fashioned porch swing, telling her outrageous tales of bumping into Cary Grant and watching them shoot a robbery scene.

In turn, Miss Tillson told them the latest gossip. It mattered not at all to her that Juan Peron was hiding out in Paraguay, or that the Reds-under-the-beds hysteria was affecting the country, stirring up para-noia about communism to extreme heights. Miss Tillson didn't care that people 'used Modess . . . because', and she had never heard of the revolution-ary roll-on deodorants and filter-tip cigarettes. Her talk was about important things. 'You know, of course, that the Yankie Clipper and Blonde Bombshell have decided to call it quits? You must have heard that, even in England?' England, to Mrs Tillson, might as well be another planet.

Oriel, blinking at the old lady's determined use of Hollywood jargon, translated in her mind that she was talking about the marriage of Marilyn Monroe and Joe DiMaggio being on the rocks, and shrugged, looking across at Kier, confident of her love and marriage. Especially now.

'That'll never happen to us,' she whispered, and Kier reached across and held her hand, much to the thrilled delight of Miss Tillson who loved romance in any shape or form. It would be just the kind of thing Cary Grant would do . . .

'Well, I must get on with the dinner,' Miss Tillson said, satisfied that she had gleaned the last drops of information about Cougar Studios from her favourite tenants, and picking up her copies of *Modern Screen*, *Movie Mirror* and *Photoplay*, she toddled off into the house, humming the theme tune from *From Here to Eternity*.

'I hear that everywhere,' Oriel commented idly, leaning back in the swing chair and closing her eyes, humming the tune softly, picking it up where their landlady had left off.

'Not surprising. That beach scene between Lancaster and Deborah Kerr is a classic. Believe me, that's going to be talked about for years to come.'

'You could have directed that picture,' she said seriously. It did not seem to her naïve to tell her young husband that, for she had no doubts at all that Kier would become one of the names in Hollywood; another Houston or Hughes. Even his surname began with the right letter.

Kier sat up, feeling depressed and discouraged, and began to pace the porch. 'I've got to make friends here. It's no good being the best damned director in the world if you don't know the right people in all the right places. I hate it – but it's a fact of life.'

'I know, honey. I really do.' She joined him at the wooden railing, warm from the sun's rays, and looped her arms around his waist, resting her chin against his back. Perhaps now was not the right time to tell him her own, very special, news. Then, again, perhaps it would cheer him up and give him the added motivation that he needed.

For two whole days she had hugged the knowledge to herself, and now she needed to share it. Now, when he was depressed, now before things took off and started to happen. Now, whilst she still had every bit of him all to herself. 'Kier . . .'

'That picture he was talking about. *Night of the Invaders*. It's just up my alley,' he interrupted her, the energy that was such a major part of him beginning to churn again, unable to be repressed for long. 'What is it that audiences want from that sort of film?' He turned to her, his face lit up with that look that she knew all too well. His whole face was animated, his eyes narrowed and excited, and she swallowed back her own news, forcing herself to think as he thought, to get into the mood, to play along.

'Excitement,' she said thoughtfully. 'They want to be scared by the monsters.'

'Yes, yes, that too. But they want to relate to the characters as well. Most of the people who watch movies are from small towns, girls who work in soda joints, boys who wait on tables. They want to believe that something extraordinary can actually happen in *their* town, that it can happen to them. Shoesmith was talking about setting the film in Los Angeles, but that's no good. Sure, it's got grandeur and it's local so it'll keep the budget down, but the layout's all wrong.'

Oriel felt a familiar excitement as she listened. It was when she heard him talk like this that she knew everything was going to work out.

'He's got the invaders coming in the opening scene,' Kier carried on, thinking out loud. 'That gives the audience all it wants right at the start. What it needs is a slower build up, to hint at things being wrong. We can use the girl, Sally, to show the audience that people in her town are changing, to make it dawn on them slowly that something's terribly wrong. It'll force the audience to the edge of their seats and get them wondering just *what* the hell *is* happening. Don't you see? The audience needs to guess about the invasion too, to experience it through the characters, and not just be saturated in gory monsters right from the start.'

Oriel caught his mood – she always did – and, like Kier, could now almost see the finished picture in her head. She could see what he was getting at, grasping immediately what he meant, and knew that he was right. 'That way, when the audience finally see the monster, they'll be all the more keyed up,' she finished for him, and he hugged her absently, kissing her for her cleverness.

'Right. Hell, I've got to write this all down.'

'Then send it by messenger to Shoesmith. I know it's expensive, but it'll get to him tonight while our interview is still fresh in his mind.'

Kier kissed her hard again. 'What would I do without you?' he murmured throatily, then ran into the house. A minute later she heard their battered old typewriter begin to rat-a-tat. Slowly she sat down on the swing, her euphoria evaporating now that Kier was no longer beside her.

She felt suddenly alone. Alone and missing something. Kier had a dream – he had fire in his belly and visions in his head, but what did she have? She placed a hand on her stomach, and smiled. She had a secret. She had another life in her body besides her own. And she had not told him. Whilst she understood and applauded his ambition, whilst she would stand by him and move any mountain she could to see him succeed, she had kept silent about the baby for the simple reason that when she told him about it she wanted it to be the most important thing in the world to him. For once, she didn't want to compete with a project, with the images in his head, with the fire in his eyes. For once, for just a moment, she wanted to be everything . . .

She felt a warm tickling on her cheeks, and raising her fingers to her skin, was surprised when they came away wet.

Suddenly, and without warning, she had a longing to speak to her mother. She was not sure why; she was still angry at her for trying to buy off Kier. He had let that slip only last week and it still rankled.

And yet . . . she'd never been pregnant before. When the doctor told her, she'd been thrilled, of course, but also just a little bit frightened. She felt vulnerable and nervous, and just now her mother's voice would be so welcome, bringing back memories of Georgia, of her old nanny, now dead, of afternoons in the nursery rocking on old Dobbin, of fried chicken cooked only the way Cook knew how, of mint juleps without the alcohol, of moss-draped trees . . .

She found Miss Tillson immersed in her magazines and walked through the hall to the payphone, digging in her purse for a few coins. She would have liked to make the call collect, but did not want her mother to know just how tight things really were financially. She might think she was calling for a handout and such a thought made her shudder. She dialled the numbers with a shaking finger and heard the phone ring all the way across the continent.

It was answered on the fifth ring by Willie, her mother's servant. 'Hello, Willie, it's me. Oriel.'

'Oh, Miss Oriel,' she heard the excited squeak and could almost see Willie's face split from ear to ear in a big, white-toothed grin. 'Oh, Miss Oriel, I ain't heard your voice in ages.'

'It's good to hear you, too, Willie,' Oriel said, meaning it, then bit her lip. 'Er . . . is my mother there?'

There was a small silence that spoke volumes, then Willie's voice again. 'Well, I don't know, Miss Oriel. Mrs Somerville . . . she was mighty hurt by your running off and gettin' married like that. She told me not to take no calls off'n you.'

'Please, Willie – just tell her I'm on the phone. Tell her it's important. Urgent, even.'

'OK, Miss Oriel – I'll do that. Hold on a minute.' A minute stretched to two, and she had to put in another coin. She felt her nerves begin to string out and was just about to hang up when she heard the phone being lifted, and then her mother's voice, crisp, clear and slightly anxious.

'Oriel? It's Clarissa. What's happened?' Her voice was sharp, but it was the kind of sharpness that came with anxiety and concern, and Oriel felt tears sting her eyes. In her heart of hearts she'd missed her mother and been hurt by the separation. Now, presented with evidence that her mother cared after all, she sniffed hard, wiping away the tears that were pouring down her face. 'Oriel. Oriel! Are you crying? What's wrong, baby? What has he done to you?' Clarissa's angry voice buzzed in her ear, making her smile.

'No, Mama, I'm not crying. That is, I am, but because I'm happy. Oh, Mama, I wanted you to know. I'm gonna have a baby!'

For a long, long second there was total silence. Oriel's fingers curled nervously around the wire, and then her breath exploded out of her as she heard Clarissa's voice, choked now with tears of her own.

'Oh, Oriel . . . oh, my baby . . . I'm . . . I'm . . .' Oriel waited, praying for the reaction she needed, then burst into more tears as Clarissa said, '. . . so happy. I'm crying like a silly schoolgirl. Hold on a minute while I get a hankie.'

Oriel leaned against the wall, grinning and crying like a mad woman. She was glad Kier was typing upstairs and that Miss Tillson was pouring over the latest gossip about Fernando Lamas and Arlene Dahl. She'd hate for anybody to see her like this!

'Honey, you still there?'

'I sure am, Mama. You are pleased, aren't you?' she asked, and over the miles Clarissa could hear the trace of the little girl that had so unexpectedly come back into her daughter's voice. In that instant, all of Clarissa's anger and sense of betrayal vanished as she groped for a chair, and gave a wavering smile at the hovering Willie, who was grinning from ear to ear, as she'd overheard the good news.

'Oh, baby, of course I am . . . but I'm too young to be a grandmother!' Even as she said it she glanced anxiously into a mirror, relieved that it told her that she was still a woman in her prime. She still had her period and could be a mother again if she wanted. And she still had Kyle.

Didn't she?

But she couldn't think of Kyle now. Or the terror that had been her constant companion since that day by the lake.

'Oh, darling, I'm so thrilled,' she said truthfully, forcing her mind back to Oriel and her startling, wonderful news. 'Just wait until I tell your father.'

'Where is Daddy?'

'In Germany. His committee are gathering evidence from that man Wolfgang Mueller's concentration camp. I tell you, that man has become obsessed by the Nazis,' Clarissa said, but without heat. To tell the truth, she was rather proud of Duncan's crusade, so much more so since Duncan had been personally unaffected by the war. But he knew evil when he saw it, and hated it, and was so gallantly determined to do something about it. If only more good men had his principles . . .

Oriel swallowed back more tears, and took a deep breath. 'Mama. Will you come over . . . for a visit? I . . . I want you to be here when the baby comes. I'm a little bit scared, Mama,' she finally admitted breathlessly, her lovely Scarlett O'Hara voice wobbling just a little.

Clarissa swallowed hard. 'Of course I'll come, honey. Nothing could keep me away . . .' She paused, then straightened in her chair, but only Willie could see the wariness creep over her face. 'What does Kier think of all this? Did he agree?'

Oriel bit her lip, then shrugged. 'He will. I haven't. . .' She was about to say that she hadn't told him about the baby, but something stopped her. It would sound disloyal, she realized, and give Clarissa a false impression of their marriage. Instead she said, 'I haven't any doubt at all that he'll be glad to have you visit. It wasn't his intention to split us up, Mama. That was all your doing. Kier loves me, and he'll do anything for me,' she stated confidently, sure that she spoke the truth.

Clarissa fiddled with a green jade ornament and swallowed her pride. 'I'll come over as soon as I can arrange it. Maybe next Monday. Is that all right?'

'Oh, yes. But . . . you'll have to book into a hotel, I'm afraid.'

There was a short silence then Clarissa said expressionlessly, 'I see.'

As they said tearful goodbyes, the rift at last and finally healed, Clarissa hung up thoughtfully. This changed everything, of course. She could not countenance her grandchildren growing up without her, and she simply refused to be strangers to her own kin. That meant accepting Kier as a son-in-law. There was no chance of a divorce now. And what if . . . what if Oriel really was happy? What if Kier Harcourt was the *man* for her? Such an outlandish thought had never crossed her mind before.

As she phoned her husband with the good news, Duncan agreeing to take time off to fly out with her, she was already thinking furiously. Clarissa had a practical streak that most people would have found surprising.

Clarissa wondered what kind of a dump Oriel was living in, if she felt too ashamed to have her mother stay with her. Probably in some squalid little backwater, filled with roaches and those dreadful film people. Well, if it must be Kier, then it must be Kier. She would have to do something to make him more acceptable. She simply couldn't have her daughter, or her grandchild, living in squalor.

She walked across the cool tiled hall of her mansion, ordering Willie to bring her tea. She reached for her address book, looking through the long list of names until she found the one she wanted. Lifting the phone she dialled the California code and number. 'Hello, Gloria? This is Clarissa. Yes, it's been simply ages, hasn't it. How are you?' Clarissa, like most women of her class and generation, kept in obsessively close contact with all her old schoolfriends. Even though Gloria Finchely-Gallerton had located to the other side of the country, when she married a Hollywood movie mogul.

After a few minutes of pleasantries, the two women got down to business. 'Look, Gloria, I had to call you and tell you the wonderful news. I'm about to become a grandmother. Can you believe it?' she squealed happily. 'Yes, me, can you imagine? Of course, my son-in-law lives in Hollywood as well, so you probably know him. Kier Harcourt? You'll have to invite him and Oriel over for dinner some time. Kier's a director I believe. I think your Frank must have heard of him. Frank is still on the board at Paramount, isn't he . . .?'

Gloria Finchely-Gallerton said of course they must have Oriel and her husband over. And Frank was still so very amenable . . .

Both women knew how the game was played. Gloria might need a favour of her own, one day.

Three days later, the rent was due, and Miss Tillson was listening enraptured to Oriel relating Kier's idea for the *Invaders*', carefully not mentioning the fact that they had not heard back from Howard Shoesmith.

She had at last told Kier about the baby. He'd been overjoyed, acting just like a typically expectant father, and treating her like precious china. Now, the two women talked baby talk, Miss Tillson, of course, bringing the conversation around to the stars who'd had children that year, and wondering what on earth had happened to Shirley Temple.

Suddenly the Olds screeched to a halt outside the gate, and Oriel stood up, her heart leaping as Kier jumped the gate without bothering to open it, his heroics making Miss Tillson's heart flutter. He'd acted just like Errol Flynn would have done.

Kier's face was alight as he leapt onto the porch, reached down and plucked her from her chair and then swung her around in his strong arms, ignoring Miss Tillson's warning about not doing that in her condition. 'I got the film!' he yelled, walzing her off her feet and onto the lawn. 'I got *Invaders*!'

Oriel squealed, and began to kiss his face all over, laughing with sheer delight.

'I just ran into the studio head at Cougar who told me to go down this afternoon and talk to Shoesmith. He loved the ideas I sent him about the film. He's willing to take the chance on me. Oh, baby, it's happening at last.'

'And so much quicker than we ever hoped,' she added, clasping his handsome, excited face between her hands. 'Ooohhhhheeeee!' she hollered, oblivious to neighbours, to passing cars, to children playing in the streets. Thus encouraged to abandon her ladylike ethics, Miss Tillson whooped louder than they did, and for a reward they took her out in the car to the drug store on Sunset Boulevard, where they had sodas and watched Miss Tillson's head swivelling in all directions as she counted the stars who came in for tubes of Ioana toothpaste and Tangee's Red Majesty lipstick.

The world was suddenly theirs. They had come, they had seen, and they had conquered. Kier's ideas, his brilliant ideas, his talent, his dream, his forceful character and personality, had won the day after all. They would soon have a baby, and he would soon have a career. Life was sweet, love was sweeter, and success was the sweetest of all.

'To us,' Kier toasted with strawberry soda, the three solemnly clinking glasses. Kier promised to take Miss Tillson to the studio one day to let her watch him making the movie. They talked about casting, about costume, about lighting, about everything, kissing openly, laughing at anything and everything, Kier even pulling the blushing Miss Tillson onto his lap and telling her he was going to introduce her to Bud Westmore, the famous make-up man to the stars who'd make her look thirty years younger again, and win her the heart of Cary Grant. That afternoon was the most golden of all their afternoons, knowing even then that *Invaders* was only the beginning – only the first step on the road to a sparkling career.

Over at Cougar Studios, Howard Shoesmith congratulated Clarissa Somerville warmly for investing so generously in the *Night of the Invaders*.

Clarissa inclined her head, and smiled. 'You must thank Mr Finchely-Gallerton for putting me in the know,' she dropped the name of the powerful man cleverly, and watched the ridiculous Mr Shoesmith preen. 'He's such a good friend,' she added, just to make sure he got the picture.

Howard Shoesmith gushed, and showed her out. Who'd have thought the Harcourt kid had such good contacts? Still, the world was his oyster now. And Howard Shoesmith would ride the rising Harcourt star for all it was worth.

Outside, Clarissa took her hired car back to the hotel. Time to let Oriel know she was in town.

Back at the first-class hotel, she walked tiredly to her bed, and pulled off her shoes. Then she glanced behind her at the empty bed, her lovely face slowly crumpling.

Kyle had refused to accompany her. And, for the first time ever, she'd been unable to force him.

CHAPTER 15

London

The Windsor Hotel, with four stories of mellow
sandstone, black wrought-iron terrace and good English cuisine had an ambiance that was priceless to its
usual and loyal clientele. It enjoyed a reputation for
English breakfasts, English maids, English conserva-
tism and, most of all, for English guests. Wayne chose
it over and above its more famous rivals such as the
Ritz, Connaught or the Savoy, for just this reason. At
the moment he had no use for more cosmopolitan
surroundings since the rest of Europe was, for the
moment, off limits.

He'd sold the Maserati in France, getting top money
from a collector. Such was the popularity of the car
that the waiting lists were huge, making second-hand
cars in prime condition sell for an even higher price
than the new models, simply because buyers had to
wait anything up to six months to a year for delivery.
Looking up a yachting acquaintance who was sailing
to England saved him an airfare and allowed him to

arrive in England with enough money to give the appearance of casual affluence.

The Windsor had been the next stop. Its fees were exorbitant, but Wayne fully expected it to be a wise investment. He was practising hard to rid himself of his French accent and was quickly succeeding, except for when ladies were present. French was still, after all, the language of love and he badly needed either a rich wife or a sponsor.

He had been at the Windsor a week. His arrival had caused something of a stir amongst the hotel's regulars and permanent residents for a variety of reasons. To the women, of course, the advent of the huge, handsome Frenchman had caused shockwaves, even affecting the chambermaids, who quarrelled amongst themselves for the privilege of cleaning his room. One maid had confessed to her friends that she'd seen him topless, shaving in his antiquated but efficient bathroom, and had assured everyone he was not at all hairy and had muscles that you could see quite nicely, but not the horrible kind that bulged and looked ugly.

Matrons, with unattached daughters, bristled visibly whenever he came down to the high-ceilinged, darkly decorated dining room, but Wayne was too clever to isolate himself by flirting. Instead, after almost a week, his quiet good manners, his lack of adventurousness and his gentlemanly conversation had done much to rub the stiff English bristles back the right way. His Savile Row suit, Turnbull & Asser shirts and Bull Brothers shoes helped. A Frenchman who dressed like an Englishman was marginally more acceptable than some foreigner who *looked* like a foreigner. Luckily for Wayne, his skin was naturally fair and his suntan was fast fading. That didn't hurt either.

Amongst the men, also, his presence had been immediately felt. A man of his size was an immediate rival to their own masculinity. The talk whenever he walked into the bar turned to boxing at Eton, or rowing at Cambridge, all the men present talking about some sporting triumph or other. Wayne, naturally, listened and complimented, decrying his own schooling at the Sorbonne where the emphasis had been on academic achievement, not sportsmanship. Thus, being able only to shoot (which was, Wayne knew, a must in English society) but not having any sporting tale to tell, manly pride had been quickly and expertly re-established.

Now Wayne was readily accepted into the little clique that gathered in the bar for pre-dinner drinks with good humour and just a little condescension. He was, after all, still a foreigner. This evening, Wayne joined Stanley Phipps-Wetherington at the bar, one of the Windsor's 'something-in-the-city' brigade.

'Good evening, Wetherington,' Wayne greeted him, having learned early on the English preference for surnames. He ordered drinks and asked for them to be put on his tab. As Wetherington murmured 'Jolly decent of you. I'll have a Scotch,' Wayne shook out a copy of *The Times* and turned to the business section. Wetherington, a part-time drunk, sipped his Scottish malt whisky with a true connoisseur's appreciation.

Dinner at the Windor was served at seven, never earlier, never later. It was not a restaurant and, if guests did not arrive on time, there was no second serving. Wayne found the English race both difficult to understand, and yet, in their own way, charming. The nation seemed to be cut in half; the aristocracy and the rest, and there was no intermingling, no overlapping, and definitely no room for manoeuvre. As a foreigner he avoided this particular trap, but it also precluded him from joining the aristocracy unless he could find a loophole. Turning to Wetherington he asked casually, 'Ever been to Bordeaux?'

'Bordeaux? No, but I've drunk enough of it,' Stanley's eyes, red-rimmed and a cheerful hazel, twinkled pleasantly, and Wayne laughed dutifully.

'My family has a vineyard there – several, in fact.'

'And you left? Are you crazy, man?'

Wayne shrugged – an English kind – and shook his head. 'I don't have the vintner's nose or feel for grapes. Besides, I have several younger siblings who do have, so I've managed to shake off the old man.'

'Ah. Spot of good luck, that. That's why you've moved over to jolly old Angleterre, hmm?'

The man's pretentiousness never ceased to amaze Wayne, but he managed a grin and nodded. 'Absolutely. The thing is' – he leaned forward in a confidential manner, immediately rousing Stanley's protectiveness – 'I'm not at all sure what I'm good at. Do you follow me?' Wayne was sure he would. For all his 'something-in-the-city' tag, Stanley was obviously one of life's drifters. As expected, his cowlike face took on a look of total sympathy.

'I know just what you mean, old bean. Bit of a bugger, isn't it?' Wayne agreed, and waited. Naturally, when a chap confided in you, you did your best to help him, especially when he was buying the drinks. Stanley ordered another whisky, and began to think. It was obviously a new and painful experience for him.

'Well, old chap . . . er . . . Darville,' he deliberately defrenchified Wayne's name and felt better for it. 'Well, Darville, the question is . . . what *can* you do?'

Wayne shrugged. 'Speak French and English. I studied economics at the Sorbonne. I'm pretty good with my own share portfolio, too. I can drive a sportscar, sail a yacht, and can be pretty useful in a casino. And that's about it.'

It wasn't, but Wayne had chosen the list carefully and it did its job. 'Hmm . . . just like the rest of us, then, in fact, old chap.' Stanley laughed at his own joke, then became thoughtful. 'Hold on . . . I wonder?' He turned on his stool and searched the small anteroom, his hazel eyes coming to rest on one old man, sitting in a corner, reading a heavy tome bound in ancient leather. 'Ahh, yes, he is. Come on. Follow me and let me do the talking.'

Wayne, curious but not especially hopeful, followed Wetherington to the old man's corner. Wayne had seen him before and knew him for a regular.

'Hello, Sir Mortimer. Head buried in the share index as per usual, eh?' The hearty greeting made Wayne wince, but the old man looked up without a hint of surprise, looked Stanley over quickly with all-seeing, disapproving eyes, and then looked over his shoulder to Wayne. There the bird-sharp green eyes remained.

Wayne felt a stirring of his instincts, his nose telling him that at last he might be on to something. The eyes were watery but full of intelligence, and Wayne felt his back stiffening automatically. He had to be careful here – very careful.

'Sir Mortimer, this is a friend of mine – Wayne Darville. He's a bit French, I'm afraid, but a good chap for all that.'

Wayne smiled, unable to help it, and found Sir Mortimer Platt doing the same. 'So, you're the chap who has my chambermaid in a tizz-wazz. She's always so damned anxious to get out of my room and into yours that she whizzes through it like a tornado.' The voice was crusty but humorous and Wayne shrugged, this time with exaggerated Frenchness.

'*Les femmes*,' he murmured, making Stanley look at him quickly, his eyes warning him not to go all foreign on them. Wayne apologized in a perfect English manner, and Sir Mortimer asked them to join him. He was drinking tea, Wayne saw at once, guessing accurately that he was probably teetotal. His suit was tweed, fifteen years old and perfect. His hair, white and wavy, had probably been cut in the same style all his life. He had false teeth, walked with a cane, and sported fierce, bushy eyebrows. Wayne understood him at once.

'Darville here is from France, just escaped from the family business.'

'Oh?'

'Wine,' Wayne said, sensing immediately the disapproval in the tone. 'In that business you have to have the nose. It is no good graduating from the Sorbonne with honours in economics and a way with shifting money about if you don't have the instinct for the vine. I don't. Nothing I can do about it, but strike out on my own in a totally different direction and make something of myself.'

Wayne had noticed the strange, almost staccato way many of his fellow guests talked, and had set about adopting every English habit he could unearth. As expected, the disapproval that had shuttered Sir Mortimer's face now turned to complete approval.

'Oh, well, there was nothing else for it, then,' Sir Mortimer conceded, understanding at once that a fellow couldn't bang his head against a brick wall indefinitely. He liked a man who could see straight, make firm decisions and then stick to them. Took guts, too, to leave your own country. Course, this Darville fellow showed taste and common sense in coming to England. If only Toby was cut from the same cloth . . .

'Thing is, Sir Mortimer,' Stanley chimed in, 'he needs a push in the right direction. And when he told me about studying economics, and being a whizz at shares and things, well . . . I immediately thought of Platt's.'

Something in Wayne's mind clicked. 'Platt's? The investment house?' he asked, genuine excitement in his tone.

Sir Mortimer nodded, flattered that a foreigner had heard of the English company. In England, of course, Platt's stood for tradition, centuries of trading and a reputation untouched by scandal, its very name synonymous with class and style. Platt's had provided financial advice to crowned heads, moguls and owners of diamond mines.

'Our people have access to the finest homes in England. Why, even the old King once consulted us about some . . . er . . . real estate purchases,' Sir Mortimer boasted with typical modesty.

Wayne nodded, not needing to feign his respect. 'At the Sorbonne library, practically every English book on modern economic policy devotes chapters to Platt's. Wasn't one of your founder members an ex-Chancellor of the Exchequer?'

'Dinner is served, ladies and gentlemen,' George, the head waiter for thirty years, dressed impeccably in royal navy serge, announced from the doorway, his voice not at all raised, yet somehow managing to carry to every corner of the room.

'I'm noshing with old Clinker Haycroft tonight,' Stanley apologized quickly. 'Sir Mortimer, could you take Darville here off my hands for this evening?'

'Of course?' He made it a question by raising one of those bushy eyebrows in the Frenchman's direction, and Wayne accepted readily.

George had an underling set another place at Sir Mortimer's table, and Wayne was left alone at last to begin a preliminary probe. The first course was game soup, brought down by train from Scotland where the Windsor had a sister hotel called the Highland. The soup, dark and rich, was pleasing to the palate, and Wayne found himself pleasantly surprised by the food. He had heard horrific tales of English cuisine from childhood, and was almost disappointed at finding them to be so untrue.

'So, you went to the Sorbonne. Who took you for economics?' Sir Mortimer opened the gambit, and Wayne launched into a tale of the university, racking his brains for amusing incidents, inventing them where necessary and making the most of his accomplishments without seeming to, and finishing up with a good dose of humility. 'So you see, I find myself in England, very well qualified, but actually, qualified for nothing, as it were.'

'Hmm. Well, that's not quite true. Platt's, of course, is always trying to expand. And why not into Europe? It might be interesting to take on a Johnny who knows how the French share market works. You have your own portfolio, you say?'

Wayne nodded. 'Oh, yes. Papa gave me a settlement when I finally persuaded him I had to leave the vineyards. Since then, with some careful buying, and watching blue-chip . . .'

For the next half an hour, Wayne talked competently about his non-existent portfolio.

'That sounds like some very careful dealing. Of course, at Platt's, you'd be doing much the same thing, only for select clients, and on a much grander scale. Fifty thousand pounds is the very least we take on. Most of our clients trust millions to us to invest, of course. If you had no objection to starting on the lesser commissions, would you be interested?'

The offer was made ultra-casually, but Wayne was not fooled, and he was too clever to snap at the bait like a novice.

'As an advisor? Well, that's very kind of you. And I'm sure it would be interesting . . . as a start. But I'm not looking for a job, *per se*. What I need is a . . . oh, I don't know. A career, of course, but also a . . . vocation, I suppose you could call it. I'd really be interested in seeing what your plans are to take Platt's into Europe. It might be useful to study more European law, also.'

Sir Mortimer nodded, his eyes narrowing on the handsome young man. What he meant, of course, was that he was not willing to be a paid clerk, not even one with a grandiose title. Sir Mortimer liked this man. Apart from his size and nationality, which were both unfortunate, he had intelligence, wit, tact, and charm. He was careful, too. Was he *too* careful? Sir Mortimer, tucking into roast duck with orange sauce, realized with a surprised start that he had spent over an hour in this man's company and knew practically nothing about him. Oh, he knew the background, he could see he dressed with under-stated style, which was excellent. There was nothing he despised more than a flashy dresser, and any outrageous flaunting of wealth was too vulgar to be endured. But what did he really know of the man's *character*?

Reading his mind, almost thought for thought, Wayne decided it was time to rectify the oversight. His instincts were now totally attuned and quivering, telling him that beyond doubt here was the mark, here was the sponsor he so desperately needed. But he had to secure his position fast.

'Of course, my younger brother will inherit the vineyards,' Wayne commented, sipping the wine, but not giving a run-down on its pedigree even though he could have ably done so. Showing off was definitely not on the agenda tonight. 'In France, the wine business is totally above the laws of common man.' He twisted his lips ruefully. 'And I don't envy Jean-Jacques the job. Wine tends to become the master of the man, instead of the other way around.'

Sir Mortimer nodded, his head movements as clear and precise as his speech. 'Hmm. A man who lets himself become a slave to anything is a fool.'

Wayne bit the inside of his cheek, knowing that pain always made him go pale. He looked down too quickly and deliberately took a bite out of his duck. Looking up at the alert eyes, he smiled bleakly. 'No. A man shouldn't. And especially not to a woman.'

'Ahh,' Sir Mortimer said, instantly relieved. There were worse things a man could be than a lady's man. As he knew only too well. If Toby had only . . . He cut his thoughts off abruptly. No good fretting about his son now. Instead, he glanced once more at the big

Frenchman. So he'd had a sour love affair, hmm? Well, a man who looked like this was almost certainly destined to get his fingers burnt by the fairer sex sooner or later. Best by far to get it over with when you're young. And, in Sir Mortimer's opinion, it did a man no harm at all to acquire a few knocks in life.

He himself had, in his earlier years, fallen completely under the spell of one Maud Fitzsimmons, a flighty little thing who had promised to wait for him until after the war. But she hadn't. He'd come home with a VC and found her married to Freddie Carstairs, a farmer who had avoided the draft on medical grounds. Now he grunted, half in laughter, half in self-mockery. 'Women!'

'You're married, of course?' Wayne prompted, his bland eyes showing no ulterior motive, and for once Sir Mortimer's usually accurate ability to read character let him down.

'Hmm, for the second time.'

Now that, thought Wayne, was interesting, but instinct warned him not to push it any further. When the duck was cleared, there was a choice of puddings, and Sir Mortimer plumped for the apple pie, whilst Wayne selected the gooseberry tart.

'So. You're at a loose end?' Sir Mortimer brought the subject back to the matter in hand, pleased that Wayne had not done so. He hated to be hurried, and the more time he spent in this man's company, the more he found himself admiring and liking the man.

'For the moment,' Wayne said, his voice firm but polite. Meeting the Frenchman's unwavering blue eyes head on, Sir Mortimer nodded, his mind made up.

'Of course. Well, the job of junior advisor is, of course, only the first step on the ladder. There are several departments in Platt's – insurance, brokerage, real estate, etc. – with heads who are, like me, getting on in life. Not that I plan to retire any time soon, of course,' Sir Mortimer added with such ferocity that Wayne blinked, then grinned.

'I don't blame you,' he said simply, the words more flattering and ingenious than fawning denials could ever have been.

'Humph,' Sir Mortimer grunted. 'You free tomorrow morning?'

'Yes.'

'Good – that's what I like to see in a man. No messing about. Can you find your way to my office, say . . . ten-thirty?'

'I'd be delighted.'

'Fine. That's settled, then. Ah, cheese and biscuits. I must confess to a weakness for water biscuits.'

Wayne leaned back and reached for a piece of Cheddar, his eyes on Sir Mortimer level and full of good will.

But the internal smile that lurked behind the bland façade belonged to that of a crocodile. A hunting crocodile . . .

Platt House had its main offices on the oddly named Tubb Street, a small, select area, where Wayne found himself surrounded by internationally famous names.

Platt House was five stories of red brick, with elegant cornerstones and a semi-circular, shallow flight of stone steps that led to two enormous double doors. Over the mantel there was a motto in Latin, that he translated to read 'Advisors to Kings' and the date of 1645. Inside, the hall was chilly, but Wayne was used to this by now. The English, for some obscure reason, liked to shiver. The tiles under his feet were a rich deep red, the panelling on the walls of a matching reddish wood that looked as if it might also be over four centuries old. Antiquated glass lamps were set in the walls, and the hall seemed to smell of bookdust and ink, confidence and wealth.

He approached the reception desk, glad of his English clothes and the English haircut he had taken a chance on having the second day he was in England. 'I have an appointment with Sir Mortimer at ten-thirty,' he told the desk clerk, who didn't bother to check the old-fashioned ledger in front of him.

'Of course, sir. This way.' He lead him to a lift, an old-fashioned concoction of sliding iron doors and pull-out buttons, and tugged on the one labelled '5'. Slowly the machine crawled to the top floor, the lift opening out on to a corridor that was carpeted with an ancient but hardy red weave. On the wall were prints of past famous clients and notable successes. Bridges that were built with investors from Platt's. A brand new marina. Works of art, sold to museums, with the aid of a Platt's Fine Art expert. It was all comfortingly traditionally and staidly impressive.

But everywhere he looked, Wayne could see only the potential for modernization, for profit, for different kinds of investments that appealed to a wider, less rarefied, market.

'Mr Darville, Sir Mortimer,' the clerk announced him, leaving his secretary (a middle-aged woman with a pair of fiercely pointed glasses and a mannish haircut) to remain in her seat, industriously typing on an antiquated Imperial typewriter.

'Ah, Darville,' Sir Mortimer's hearty greeting didn't go unnoticed by the clerk, who had it all over the building by the end of the morning that some foreigner had invaded the establishment.

Sir Mortimer's office was like a study from a country house. Wood panelling gave way to flocked velvet walls, whilst a huge aspidistra plant stood in one corner and African violets and spider plants lined the window-sills. The desk was a huge Sheraton, intricately patterned and an obvious antique.

Wayne shook Sir Mortimer's hand in a firm and warm greeting. 'This place is overwhelming,' he said, making no attempt to stint the childish delight in his voice. 'It's like walking back in time. Outside, the city seems to be changing, with buildings going up like mushrooms, and then I stepped in here and it was like nothing I'd ever felt before. I half-expected to meet Dickens himself.'

Sir Mortimer beamed. He had fiercely resisted modernizing the office, only allowing the installation of the lift to save his workers' feet. Every other modern encroachment, though, had been determinedly resisted. And since Platt's was now privately owned, with Sir Mortimer holding 90 per cent of the shares, it had been easy enough for him to get his own way. He firmly believed that when people handed you their money to invest, they wanted to do so to a favourite uncle figure, not a modern, jumped-up spiv.

And after Toby's continual whingeing about how old-fashioned and out of date he was, it did his old heart good to find a young man who shared his belief that the firm shouldn't be ransacked by modern ways. 'Well, I'm glad you came. Sit down. Tea?'

Wayne took tea. He drank tea. He hated tea, but he never mentioned it, instead letting his eyes feast on the room. Two of the walls were taken up with manuals, folders, brochures and portfolios from floor to ceiling, and he gravitated to these with an ease that looked natural, his eyes scanning the titles. For an hour, with Sir Mortimer at his side, they worked their way around the shelves. Wayne's obvious enthusiasm for handling other people's money did him no harm at all, and his seduction of Sir Mortimer became complete.

Retiring back to the desk and yet more tea, Sir Mortimer's lined face was flushed with pleasure. 'You obviously have the feel for the way money works, m'boy, if not for wine.'

Wayne smiled. 'It may be called "filthy lucre" but I like it!'

Sir Mortimer guffawed. 'Me too, old man. Me too. If only Toby – ' He broke off suddenly and shook his head. Wayne didn't bother to ask, because his weasel-like cunning had already enabled him to guess. Toby, who must be a son, was patently unsatisfactory. Sir Mortimer was obviously in need of a surrogate son who *did* measure up . . . Silently he sipped his tea, almost enjoying it this time.

'Why don't we stop off at the Windsor for some lunch, and then, if you're free this afternoon, I'll show you round the London Stock Exchange? A bit of a madhouse, but it has a kind of frantic energy that you wouldn't believe. We'll have to get you licensed and all fixed up, of course, but I know a man, who knows a man, as they say.'

Wayne laughed. 'I'd love to see it.'

'Splendid. I've got to see a man about a horse first. Why don't I meet you at the hotel later?'

Wayne rose and shook hands. 'The Windsor, then.'

Sir Mortimer walked him to the door, Wayne nodding pleasantly to his secretary on the way out. Only then did he permit himself a wolfish smile. The lift came and he entered, surprised when it stopped at the fourth floor and a huddle of staff crammed themselves inside.

Suddenly he realized it was probably their lunch hour, and he sighed, glancing at his watch impatiently. As he did so, his eyes met those of a young woman, crammed up in the front corner right beside him. She was of average height, with short black hair and chocolate eyes. Her skin, though, was magnolia-pale, her cheekbones high and exquisitely moulded, and as their eyes met Wayne felt jolt of electricity shoot through him. Vaguely, one part of his brain saw her eyes widen and her lips part on a small gasp, whilst another part of his brain began to sound delighted alarm bells.

She was wearing an ugly heavy skirt and a white blouse and clutched in front of her a huge black folder. She was obviously a secretary, Wayne realized, since Platt's would hardly employ women advisors, but the idea flashed only briefly across his mind.

The lift began its snail's-pace descent, and he half-turned so that his back was presented to the rest of the crowd. They were jammed so tight that her elbow was in his stomach, her hip against his thigh, and he felt his body stir.

Her eyes, trapped helplessly in the blue magnetic pull of his, never left his face. Time seemed to hang still, the noise of the lift and the chattering of secretaries and clerks diminishing to an indistinct hum, like bees on a midsummer's day. They were both simultaneously aware that there was something primitive and basic weaving a web around them, something that went beyond civilization, whipping past normal words or explanations.

In fact, Wayne didn't think he could speak at that moment if his life depended on it.

Veronica Coltrane could hear only the hammering of her heart, which was deafening her. Where the stranger touched her, her skin burned, and in his eyes she could feel herself drowning.

Nothing, but nothing, in her mundane, uneventful middle-class upbringing had prepared her for a moment like this. She had, up until the moment she'd first looked into the stranger's eyes, thought herself to be an ordinary girl, with good common sense and a fine head on her shoulders. Now, she knew herself to be nothing of the kind. Her bones felt liquefied, and as he continued to stare at her, hooked by the same magic that had her own mouth going as dry as a bone, she began to sway back against the lift wall.

She forced herself to drag in a ragged breath. What on earth was the matter with her?

Wayne moved an inch closer. Unbidden, he watched his hands reach up in front of him, reaching under the folder she clutched with white-knuckled intensity, and closing around her breast.

Veronica gasped, the tiny sound lost in the noise of the cramped lift. Oblivious to the fact that they might be seen, uncaring that she was letting a stranger touch her in a way that not even her steady boyfriend was permitted to do, her eyes widened, then half-closed. Her mouth, with the barest touch of lipstick, fell open.

Her mind put up the faintest murmur of warning, which was quickly drowned out by the thump-thump of her heart. Here was a dream come true. She had stepped into a lift, to find the most handsome man in the world staring at her as if he loved her more than the breath in his body. He was bold, like a knight from a fairy tale, touching her as if he had a right. She was mad. Utterly mad. But she couldn't seem to find the key to her usual sanity. Where was Veronica, the level-headed, Veronica, the school blue-stocking?

Wayne saw her lovely chocolate eyes feather close, and for the first time in his life, literally felt himself becoming ensnared by a woman. He felt almost giddily relieved, and yet, at the same time, horrified.

Yet he couldn't pull away. Under his thumbs, he felt her nipple harden, and as she arched her back in helpless instinctive reaction, her eyes came wide open again.

Veronica had meant to tell him to stop. That he mustn't . . . touch her so. But instead, when she opened her eyes, it was to see a strange, almost pleading look on his face that made her want to reach out and hold him instead.

So she was not the only one bowled over by a thunderclap? She felt her whole body tingling, as if she'd been struck by an invisible lightning strike.

Her vagina contracted, her knees weakened, and Wayne straightened stiffly as the lift doors slid open and the tiny cubicle began to empty. A hot wave of embarrassed colour belatedly flooded her cheeks, and Veronica dashed forward, hugging the folder to her chest as if her life depended on it.

She looked over her shoulder only once, to see the stranger all alone in the lift and watching her with those compelling blue eyes, then she dashed into the Ladies', her breasts heaving as she took deep, shuddering breaths. Shakily, she leant her burning forehead against the cool, white tiles, wondering what on earth had just happened to her.

Wayne took a taxi back to the hotel, his mind a curiously shocked blank whilst he changed and awaited Sir Mortimer. He kept his mind diligently off the girl, telling himself it was nothing, nothing at all. Just a little risqué touch-up in a lift, that was all. Nothing to get so . . . unsettled about.

Sir Mortimer unwittingly helped him dismiss the incident from his mind as he proudly showed him around the London Stock Exchange an hour later. When Wayne finally left, it was with his ears still buzzing from the raucous male shouts and the strident ringing of telephones, and with a weekend invitation to visit Sir Mortimer's country residence in Berkshire.

Being without transport, he rode down on Friday afternoon with Sir Mortimer himself in a 1930s Bentley, an overnight case slung in the back boot.

The Platt residence turned out to be an eighteenth-century manor house of solid stone with neat rows of windows set in a squarish building. It had a yew-lined gravel drive, formal lawns, two fountains, clipped box-hedging in formal rose gardens, and acres of landscaped grounds by Capability Brown. He was shown to the east wing by a blank-faced servant, where a four-poster bed and antique wooden wardrobes awaited him. He unpacked in record time, and stood outside his room, looking up and down the portrait-lined corridor with interested eyes. The place was a rabbit warren; as he hesitated, a young woman turned the corner. She was dressed in jodphurs and a green velvet riding jacket with matching hat, and was obviously on her way to the stables.

'Hullo, you're a new face.'

Wayne introduced himself, noticing how the hazel eyes looked him over with brief, almost impersonal appreciation. 'I'm Amanda Platt, Morty's daughter-in-law.' They shook hands. 'You're here for the weekend bash, I take it? I suppose I'd better take you in hand, then, seeing as you're new,' Amanda Platt offered without preamble. 'First of all' – she set off down the corridor at a brisk pace – 'you'll have to avoid my husband, Toby,' she warned him, pausing long enough to eye him over, 'especially looking like you do. He goes for big boys – know what I mean?'

Wayne went cold, then hot, then smiled charmingly. 'I assure you, I shall avoid him as if he were leprous.'

Amanda shrugged uninterestedly. 'Next, don't eat the rhubarb. It'll have you on the loo for weeks. Then there's her ladyship, of course – the second Lady Platt. First gal died when she went over Old Man's Dyke but her horse didn't. Our Beatrice, a younger filly, was brought in by the old man to try and get another son or two, but it hasn't worked out. Poor old Morty's past it, you know, so she consoles herself with the groom.'

They had reached the grand staircase by now and were rapidly descending the curved marble steps, and still Amanda was in full swing. 'Toby's sister, Cynthia, has three children, all of them terrors, I'm afraid. Oh, yes, and mind out for the Labrador. The bugger bites. Right-i-ho, I think that'll do you. Welcome to England, Mr Darville.'

Wayne watched her go, not sure whether to laugh or not. Didn't she care a fig for what she said?

'Ahh, Darville.'

Wayne turned quickly at the sound of Sir Mortimer's voice. By his side was a handsome woman of well-preserved years, with short blonde hair, interesting grey eyes and a wide mouth. She was dressed in burgundy silk. 'Let me introduce you to my wife, Beatrice. Beatrice, this is the young man I was telling you about, and our latest acquisition to Platt's.'

As she approached, Wayne felt her eyes coolly assess him and felt an instant reaction of dislike tinged with desire. 'Mr Darville.' She inclined her head.

'Lady Platt,' he said, and took her hand, capturing it with a steely grip and then bringing it to his lips to kiss it with deliberate skill. Beatrice stiffened, her eyes beginning to spit flames even as she dragged a hissing breath between her perfectly painted, peach-tinted lips. It was during this moment of mutual antipathy, unspoken challenge and heady sexual one-upmanship, that Sir Mortimer said, 'I don't think you've met one of our junior advisors from the Jewellery Acquisition Department, have you?'

Wayne turned, still holding on to the simmering Beatrice's hand, and found himself looking into the lovely face of the woman from the lift.

CHAPTER 16

The woman sitting by the window looked dead. Her hair was kept short by the nurses, and her lips had not moved in five years. Sebastien kept checking that her chest was rising and falling just to reassure himself that she was actually still breathing. Her eyes never blinked, not even when a blackbird landed in a bush near the open window and began to sing.

'Sarah. Sarah, are you listening to me?'

The woman frowned fiercely and the sudden expression made Sebastien jump.

'Sarah. Can you hear that bird singing?'

The eyes, a neutral grey, not blue, not hazel, but a colour in limbo, began to flicker. That voice again – she'd heard it before, coming from the clouds. Was it God? It sounded nice, sort of warm and loving, like she thought God's voice would be. What was it asking?

'Sarah, listen to the bird singing.'

Bird? What was a bird? She seemed to remember something . . . Sarah Cashman couldn't remember a bird, but sounds, like a flute, began to roll in on the smoke that surrounded her. She could hear it . . . 'God's flute,' she said, then wondered if she'd said it right. Sometimes she only thought things, and assumed she'd said them. But the angels in white frocks never listened to her, so perhaps she never said it at all.

Sebastien turned to Harry Chamberlain, the chief of the psychiatric staff at St Edmunds, who was a tall, florid-faced man, a father of nine children and Winchester-educated, and asked, 'When was the last time she spoke?'

'Five years ago – after she murdered her daughter.'

Sebastien nodded, and turned back to the woman, whose skin was so pale it was almost translucent.

'Sarah, can you hear the bird?'

'Yes, God.'

The words came out in a croaking, rasping breath that was nevertheless the sweetest thing either man had ever heard. 'You've got through to her, Seb. By hell, you have!' Harry crowed as Sebastien moved closer. But not too close – Sarah had a habit of suddenly launching herself at people who came too close.

'Do you like the bird singing, Sarah?' Seb asked, praying that the blackbird would not move on just yet. Again a ferocious frown crouched on her face, which was pitifully thin and old before its time. Sarah was tired – she thought she hadn't slept in a hundred years.

'Tell me what you're thinking, Sarah,' the voice demanded, making her rub her ear against her shoulder as she thought. He had a lovely voice, this bird.

'Sing for Janey, bird,' she said, but the ugly sound that was her own voice made her clamp her teeth shut tight.

'She's biting on her tongue,' Sebastien said urgently and Harry moved forward to help him prise open her mouth and free her badly bleeding tongue. Summoning an orderly, one of the many large men with rubber-soled shoes, well-muscled bodies and discreet mouths that proliferated in the asylum, he ordered her to be taken to surgery where one of the medics would see to her. Sebastien watched her go, noting that her face was dead again.

Seeing his expression and understanding how tough the first few months always were, Harry clapped a hand on his shoulder. 'Congratulations, Teale. You're the only one who's been able to get through to her since she became catatonic.'

Sebastien nodded, but felt no self-congratulatory smugness. There was still so far to go. So much pain and struggle ahead, and even then . . . 'Lord, I'm tired,' he said, unknowingly echoing his patient's very sentiments. He had been working at the asylum for over five months now, so far just learning his way around and getting to know his colleagues. Sarah Cashman was only one of his patients, but hers was the first sign of progress he'd seen.

'You know, Sir Julius was telling me that he thought you had a flair for this kind of thing,' Harry Chamberlain said, his offhand language taking Sebastien by surprise for a moment, before he remembered that he was in England. The English had a way of bringing everything down to a proper size. When it was cold enough to make brass monkeys run for cover, the janitor in his apartment building would comment that it was 'a touch nippy;' when a ferocious pair of pint-size dogs yapped constantly in an empty flat below, the general complaint to the dog's owners was that the 'little chaps did tend to make something of a racket.' This determination by the whole country to make everything sound manageable and reasonable took some getting used to. Even when they were talking about mental disease and human suffering, it was all couched in terms of mild understatement.

'Sir Julius, I'm fast learning, is a very capable judge of character, so I hope he's right,' Sebastien laughed, thinking back to his first meeting with Sir Julius Remus, the second day after his arrival at Heathrow.

It had been Sir Julius's secretary who had met him at the airport and showed him to the flat her employer had selected for him. Located just out of town, it was housed at the top of a three-storied Victorian house in a quiet residential street. His landlady had once been a patient of Sir Julius, was now completely cured of her mild para-noia, and was only too thrilled to have one of his 'young men' living in her house. She showed him to a bay-windowed room, pleasantly light and airy, that over-looked a flower-bedecked back garden. It had the added bonus of being very reasonably priced.

The following morning, he unashamedly played the tourist. From the elegant dome of St Pauls to the grandiose size of Buckingham Palace, from the chilly ancient rooms of the Tower of London with its ravens and Crown Jewels, to the Father of Parliaments, where Big Ben chimed the hour and where Tower Bridge raised its massive hinges to let through tall-masted vessels on the River Thames, Sebastien snapped away with his camera. Photography was his only hobby, and he was good at it.

But in spite of giving himself a good talking-to, he'd felt nervous when he finally took a taxi to Mayfair to dine with his tutor. He was shown in immediately by the cheerful, slender housekeeper Vivienne, and barely had time to draw breath before finding himself face to face with the famous man himself.

Sir Julius was a commanding figure. Six feet tall with thick white hair, he was dressed in a maroon smoking-jacket and black creased trousers. He looked so English and venerable that for a second Sebastien felt totally out of place. Then his hand was taken in a firm grip, and he found himself meeting head-on a pair of penetrating, all-seeing electric-blue eyes. It was an odd sensation; he could feel a probe going right through him, ferreting out every weakness, every dream, every secret he ever had.

'Sebastien – you don't look much like your father,' were the great man's first words to him.

'Thank you,' Sebastien had instantly replied, meaning it, and then blinked. Sir Julius had roared with laughter. It had broken whatever ice there was instantly and, despite the differences in age and culture, the two men quickly established themselves as equals.

'I wanted to thank you for smoothing the way to St Edmunds, Sir Julius,' Sebastien said the first opportunity he got, uncomfortably aware that he didn't feel happy about receiving any privileged treatment. Sir

Julius told him to drop the 'Sir' and assured him that with his examination results, references, and experience with the shelter and his many other community projects, St Edmunds had been only too pleased to have him.

Over dinner, and at Sir Julius's request, Sebastien gave a clinical account of his own mental condition, Julius listening intently. He liked this boy immensely, and could well imagine that everyone else did too. Years of experience told him that this boy had an indefinable but definite 'something extra' that would draw people to him, freeing them to confide, to trust him and believe in him. And that, as any good psychiatrist knew, was more than half the battle fought and won.

Now, following Harry Chamberlain into the staff canteen, Sebastien selected apple and cheese for a light lunch, knowing he would be having a good dinner tonight with Julius. Every Monday, Wednesday and Friday night he ate regularly at the Mayfair house where they would talk for hours, Sir Julius keeping notes for the obligatory records that would have to be approved by the medical commission before Sebastien was finally and legally qualified as a practising and licensed psychiatrist.

Sir Julius rang Sebastien's office a few days later to tell him that there was a small cocktail party being given by one of his friends that evening, and did he want to come? 'It's an anniversary party really, for a big financial advice firm. One of my oldest friends, the chairman, invited me. There'll be free champers and finger sandwiches, the whole kit and caboodle. It'll give you a chance to see the English upper classes in full swing, complete with snobs, the compulsory company drunk and nymphettes.'

Sebastien laughed. 'It sounds like just the sort of hotchpotch of neurosis and paranoia that a budding shrink shouldn't miss. What time?'

The party was being held in a private residence in Belgravia and, forewarned by Sir Julius, he rented a tuxedo, much to Mrs Glynn's approval. His landlady was not so old that she couldn't see immediately the startling and handsome effect the black and white outfit had on his auburn hair and amber eyes. He took a taxi to the address given him by Sir Julius, and introduced himself at the door. In the foyer, festooned with enormous arrays of gladioli and roses, a butler took his handwritten, silver-edged invitation. He half-expected an official announcer to boom his name into the hall that was already crammed with a dazzling array of people, and was mightily relieved when he didn't.

Sensing his unease, Julius bore down on him immediately. 'Bloody hell,' Sebastien practised the English phrase experimentally, 'there are more couture dresses here than in a Paris boutique.'

Julius laughed delightedly. He approved of the boy's no-nonsense sense of humour, and Sir Julius noted that the American's easy-going grin earned him several approving glances from many of the bejewelled women.

'Ah, there's a young lady I'd like you to meet,' Julius said, unashamedly matchmaking, and led Sebastien through the throng to a woman who reached up to kiss Julius's cheek in obvious and genuine affection.

'Veronica, I want you to meet Sebastien Teale, a visitor from overseas, currently working out his slavery notice at St Edmunds. Sebastien, Veronica Coltrane.'

Sebastien immediately liked the young woman who laughed up at him, with her exotic black hair and chocolate eyes, and her simple, pale blue velvet evening gown.

'Sebastien, nice to meet you. This is Wayne . . . Wayne . . . oh, there you are.' As she spoke, half-turning to bring forward a man who had been waylaid by a white-haired patron of the arts, Sebastien found himself looking up into the most handsomely arresting face he'd ever seen. Heavy-lidded blue eyes sat widely spaced in a squarish, powerful face. But whilst the man's size was the first thing that struck most people about him, Sebastien found his breath being taken away by the aura of pain and anger that emanated from the giant stranger like a toxic cloud. There was such a feeling of silent suffering about the man, that for a moment Sebastien found it hard to breathe.

'Dr Teale, nice to meet you. Sir Julius.'

During his few moments of shock, Veronica had introduced Julius as well, and the French accent took all but Veronica by surprise.

'Monsieur D'Arville has just joined Platt's to help us break into the European money markets,' Veronica explained, looking from Julius to Sebastien. She loved Julius like a second father, and she sensed his strong interest in the young man who was obviously something of a protégé. She turned sharp eyes on the American again, but it took her only a second to be reassured, immediately soothed by the kind, sherry-coloured eyes. Trust canny old Julius to pick a winner.

'So Platt's is trying out the waters in Europe?' Sir Julius said, eyeing the Frenchman with a wary eye. 'That's interesting.' He, too, was fond of Veronica, and there was something about the big Frenchman that made him uneasy.

Wayne hardly heard him, and found it hard to respond to Sir Julius's intelligent questions with his usual care. Instead, he found his eyes again and again wandering to the young American, a strange feeling, almost of peace, coming over him whenever he met the steady, reassuring gaze. Yet at the same time, he felt uncomfortably exposed, and in the back of his head he felt a throbbing pressure begin to build.

'Sir Julius is a top man in his field, Wayne,' Veronica told him softly. 'He practically revolutionized psychiatric care in this country. We're all so proud of him. Don't say I never introduce you to anyone interesting.' She laughed up at him, her eyes caressive and unknowingly expressive as she gazed up at him.

'Really? And are you too a . . . psychiatrist?' Wayne turned to Sebastien, already knowing and dreading the answer. Something screamed at him that this man was dangerous and to keep away, but something else, something deeper and stronger, urged him to get closer, to learn more, to find out what mysterious power lay behind those sherry-coloured eyes. There was a power about this man, and Wayne knew all about power. But there was something more . . .

'I'm only a beginner,' Sebastien said, his voice quiet and thoughtful.

'Don't you believe it,' Sir Julius snorted. 'He might not have the paperwork yet, but this boy's a genius with people. Only today, I heard he got through to a catatonic patient that nobody else had been able to reach in five years. Take my word for it – Sebastien is a healer,' he finished with typical theatricality.

Wayne stiffened, almost imperceptibly, at this news, but Sebastien noticed it instantly. And Wayne knew that he had. His jaw clenched and an expression of panic, pain, anger and, finally, of forced cynical amusement crossed his face, all of which Sebastien read accurately.

At that moment, Veronica saw a friend of hers, and Wayne made no objection to being led away. Sebastien watched them go, noting the Frenchman's stiff and tense shoulders and the way the blue eyes constantly flickered over the room.

'I think my little Veronica has fallen in love,' Sir Julius said, a trifle anxiously. 'I used to live next door to the Coltranes, years back. Used to dandle Veronica on my knee . . .'

Sebastien beckoned a waiter and took two glasses, but his eyes remained fixed on Wayne's broad back. At that moment Sir Julius looked up at him, noticing his intense expression, and nodded, somewhat relieved. Perhaps Sebastien would be able to save the big Frenchman from whatever demons were destroying his soul. He hoped so. For Veronica's sake.

★ ★ ★

The party wore on. Sir Julius introduced him to an old Cambridge chum, but Seb found himself again and again seeking out Wayne, who was currently dancing with Veronica. He held her too tightly, and his eyes were fixed on the floor. A casual observer might have been inclined to put the display down to passion, but Sebastien knew that there was something else, something tormented that lurked deeper down in the Frenchman's psyche that had nothing to do with desire.

Sir Julius introduced him to his host, the oddly named Sir Mortimer Platt, a fierce seventy-year-old who was the personification of Old England. And still he watched the tall Frenchman, watching him drink and then eat without even a scmblance of enjoyment. In a flash of intuitive realization, he wondered if Wayne D'Arville had ever actually enjoyed anything at all in his entire life.

Wayne nodded when Veronica breathlessly excused herself to go the ladies' room. 'Don't be too long,' he told her, his words a command but also a plea. He felt ridiculously alone and vulnerable since meeting Sebastien Teale. Oddly, he felt himself to be in some kind of danger.

Veronica nodded quickly, her eyes as bright as coals that had been set alight, and promised huskily, 'I'll only be a moment.'

Since the weekend at Sir Mortimer's, Veronica spent as much time with Wayne as he'd allow. She knew he was wary of her, and suspected a bad love affair in his past, but she was determined to break down his barriers. She was already halfway in love with him.

264

Wayne watched her go, unaware that every nuance of expression on his face had been seen and noted. He looked around, wincing as a woman's diamond necklace caught the light and dazzled him. Suddenly the sound of music, the 'Blue Danube' by Strauss, sounded nauseatingly trite, and the smell of cucumber and celery made him want to heave. He turned and bumped into Sir Mortimer, who was looking for an old friend. 'Wayne. You haven't seen Henry, have you?'

For just a moment Wayne went white as he heard his dead brother's name for the first time since watching him drown, and he stared blankly at the old man's face. From a few yards away, Sebastien almost made a dash towards him, sure he was going to keel over. As it was, he had moved close enough to be able to hear Wayne's weak reply.

'Er . . . n-no. Can't s-say as I have,' the hated old stutter was back but, in Sir Mortimer's inebriated state, it went unnoticed. But Sebastien heard, and understood. Almost shouldering his way outside, Wayne stepped out onto the balcony, dragging in lungfuls of air, his whole body shaking. It had been raining, and the breeze was cool and heavy. Automatically he plucked a flower from the tree that grew by the side of the stone balustrade, and began to twirl it absently in his fingers. The terrace was lit only with candles, and in the cool darkness Wayne slowly felt his heart beat returning to normal.

'Damn,' he said, his voice tormented. He'd thought he'd seen the last of those ugly moments, when the world felt as if it were about to crash in on him. He'd had these attacks regularly after Hans had drowned, but over the last year they had diminished to nothing. Why tonight, of all nights, did they have to return?

In the doorway, Sebastien watched him, listening, waiting.

Wayne's head hung low, as if it were too heavy for his head. In his treacherous mind, he could see again a picture of that young, hurtling body splashing into the sea. He rubbed a hand across his eyes, feeling the unexpected brush of flower petals against his face. It was a stem of lilac – Hans's favourite flower. Looking down at the bloom in his hand, Wayne hissed in a breath that was clearly audible to the man who stood watching him. Then, slowly and deliberately, Wayne held the flower over a candle flame and watched the simple flowers curl up, go brown and wither.

Wayne stared for a moment at the pathetic burnt corpse in his hand, then gave a strangled yelp that barely sounded human. Quickly, as if it was he and not the flower that had been burned, he dropped the mangled stem over the balustrade where it disappeared into the darkness of the lawn. He felt suddenly lost and totally without hope, almost wishing for death and the precious oblivion that meant the end of all pain. He didn't think it was possible to endure so much agony and confusion and just keep going. But he must. He had to.

Then he turned and found sherry-coloured eyes silently, steadily, offering him an alternative.

Thousands of miles away, Kyle snatched up the telephone, his head full of facts and figures. 'Yes?' he said absently. He was reading the specs for a new chain of garages he was thinking of opening in the Carolinas.

'Darling,' Clarissa's soft tone snaked into his ear, making him catch his breath. Carefully, he put down the papers and moved to the bed.

'Clarissa,' he said softly. 'How's Hollywood?'

'About like you'd expect.' Clarissa, from the other side of the country, gave a slightly nervous-sounding laugh. 'I wish you were here. We could do all those trashy things people are supposed to do. You know, walk down that sidewalk where all the stars have their own plaque on the ground. Visit the Chinese theatre. Picnic under the big Hollywood sign . . .' Her voice sounded wistful.

And scared.

For the first time, Kyle heard the fear in her voice as plain as day, and wondered how he'd ever missed it before. 'I told you, I had work to do that just couldn't wait,' he said truthfully, his voice becoming gentler now. 'It really couldn't, Clarry,' he tried to explain to her, for what seemed like the hundredth time. 'I have managers, money-men, bankers to see. This new garage chain is really going to happen. I can't just take time off in the middle of it to take you to Hollywood.'

Clarissa sighed. 'I see,' she said, her voice tremulous. What he really meant was he had a good excuse, and now he could use it. Before that day at the lake, he wouldn't have dared. Now . . . now, she thought miserably, she no longer had a hold on him. And he was slipping away, just as she'd always known he would.

Kyle sighed heavily. 'I don't think you do, sweetheart,' he said gently. 'I think you're like I was once. Blind.'

Now, Kyle could look back over all their years together and see it in a totally different light. He no longer saw himself as the helpless victim, a man trapped by his own inexplicable longings and sexual desire. And Clarissa was no longer the Queen Bitch. The spider in his web.

In Hollywood, Clarissa tensed like an animal waiting for a rifle-shot, and noticed how her fingers had curled around the telephone cord. Her knuckles were white. When she glanced up and saw her reflection in the mirror, she was not surprised to see that her face was even whiter. For she knew what was coming. Kyle was going to dump her. At last, the nightmare that had plagued her ever since meeting him, was upon her. The only man she'd ever loved was going to tell her goodbye . . .

'Clarissa? Are you still there?' Kyle asked sharply and, over the miles separating them, heard her catch her breath.

'Of course I am, darling, where would I be going?' she asked with her usual waspish sarcasm, and heard him drag his breath in sharply.

'Don't!' Kyle said harshly.

Clarissa closed her eyes. Have pity, my darling, she thought silently, a tear trickling down her cheek. Didn't he realize she needed to build up all the pitiful defences she had?

'Don't what, sugar?' she purred.

Kyle picked up the phone and paced the room. He ran a hand across his forehead, his throat feeling suddenly dry. So much depended on what happened next, and he was unprepared for it. Ever since his startling discovery at the lake, he knew that this moment was coming. But he'd not expected to be doing it over the telephone, of all things. 'Don't come the southern bitch with me, Clarissa,' Kyle warned her, his voice harsher than he meant it to be. 'I won't fall for it. Not again. Not ever again. Do you hear me?' he demanded.

In her luxurious hotel room, Clarissa disguised her sob as a laugh. 'Why, darling, what else could I ever be?' she asked, and felt her heart crack in her chest. She actually had to double over, to put her hand out on the bed, to keep herself upright. This was just too hard. She couldn't listen to her world collapse around her and not perish.

'You could be whatever you wanted to be,' Kyle's voice said in her ear, and Clarissa blinked, not trusting her own senses. Whatever she'd expected him to say, it had not been that.

'I don't . . .' she began, then stopped. Oh, what did it all matter? It was over and she just couldn't stand it. 'Kyle . . .' she said, 'don't leave me. Oh, Kyle, please,' she begged unashamedly and began to cry, her lovely waspish southern voice breaking into ragged sobs. 'I'll die if you leave me.'

Kyle closed his eyes. A huge weight seemed to lift from his shoulders. He felt as if he could actually float around the room. 'I know,' he said softly. 'I know.'

He returned to the bed and sank down, his dark head lowering. 'Oh, Clarry,' he said. 'All those years wasted . . .'

In Hollywood, Clarissa drew in a deep ragged breath. He was not saying goodbye. Unbelievably, he wasn't. Or was he playing some game of his own? Did he want revenge now? 'I don't understand,' she said at last.

Kyle gave a derisive bark of laughter. 'Neither of us understood,' he said grimly. 'That was the problem. We played a game, we set the rules, and it nearly destroyed both of us. But the game's over now. You love me. I love you. And we're going to do something about it,' he promised grimly.

For a second, Clarissa was positive she hadn't heard what she thought she'd heard. She had wanted him to say those words for so long, she was half-convinced her disintegrating mind had conjured them up. Then, she swallowed hard.

'You love me?' she said numbly.

'Yes,' Kyle confirmed, almost aggressively. 'And I know you love me, so don't try to deny it,' he warned, his back straightening, his head lifting. 'And if you don't leave your husband, divorce him, and marry me . . . we're through.'

CHAPTER 17

Hollywood

The stars were out tonight. Limousines pulled up in front of the première cinema like taxi cabs pulled up on Rodeo Drive, and the gathering crowd jostled and shoved as every new car disgorged its glamorous occupant.

Gina Lollobrigida, with her famous waist the same size as that of her husband's neck, was dressed in black silk, so crisp it looked like layers of fine metal, rising to stand in a high collar around her carefully coiffed head where diamonds sparked at her earlobes and around her throat. The Shah of Iran was in town, having sailed his yacht halfway around the world to visit the American West Coast, and Earl Williams, the famous newspaper columnist, kept mental notes in his computer-like brain.

All of Hollywood's 'A' list had turned out for the première of *Night of the Invaders*, since the gossip concerning its stars and director had begun almost from the first week of shooting. Kirk Douglas was there, just to see if Cougar Studios, that veteran producer of B movies, actually could pull a first-class box office smash out of its hat, as rumour insisted it had. Certainly the budget for *Invaders* had been astronomical, increasing the speculation tenfold. Not noted for such generosity, Howard Shoesmith's behaviour had been noted avidly. Louella Parsons teased him constantly in her column, hinting at a mid-life crisis. First he takes on a brand new director, from Kansas no less, that nobody had ever heard of, and fresh from producing plays at Oxford University! Then he allots a budget that would not have looked miserly at giants like Paramount, MGM and Universal. And how, Louella asked daily, had Howard Shoesmith and the most talked-about director, Kier Harcourt, managed to persuade Bud Westmore to do the intricate makeup? How had they managed to get Bette Daniels, the rising star contracted to Universal, for the leading lady? Or Warren Wainwright, the hottest up-and-coming sex symbol in town, for the lead role? And as for importing English technicians for the special effects . . . Louella had a field day. Somebody, somewhere, was pulling some very special strings for Kier Harcourt.

The hype had been astronomical. Newspaper reporters had been wined and dined as they never had been before, and even television chat-show hosts had been dragged into the circus, calling a cease-fire between the film studios and their hated rivals, the TV networks. Yes, *Night of the Invaders* was breaking all the rules, and pulling in all the stars. The crowds jostled for Kim Novak, oohing at her daring low-cut lemon yellow dress, the exact shade of her hair. They jostled even more for Robert Mitchum and Ava Gardner, and women practically swooned over the debonair good looks of James Mason.

A mile from the cinema, Kier sat in the back of the limousine, feeling uncomfortable in his tux. The collar felt as if it were strangling him, he had iron butterflies in his stomach, and he was sweating all over.

'Honey, leave your collar alone. See, you've messed up your bow tie.' Oriel leaned over to fix it, her eyes teasing and wry, making Kier grin.

'OK, OK. I admit it. I'm nervous.'

'Nervous?'

'OK. Scared witless. Does that make you feel better?'

'Of course not, darlin'. It's just nice to be reminded that you are only human after all, and not superman.'

Kier looked across at her, his eyes taking in every detail, from the elegant chignon of her hair, interwoven with the family pearls her mother had brought from Georgia, to the peach satin dress's full skirt and V-shaped neck, where a single topaz hung from a slender gold chain. She didn't look as if she'd given birth to a daughter just eight months ago. 'Did I tell you you look ravishing?'

'No. You told me the projector hadn't better break down, and that the seating had better be right, and that the red carpet had better have arrived, and that the usherette uniforms had better be the ones you wanted and not the flash ones Howard wanted, and you told me . . .'

'Don't,' he groaned. 'I'm a monster. I know. But I'll make it up to you and Bethany now that the film's finally finished.'

'Bethany isn't yet a year old,' Oriel smiled, rubbing the back of her hand down his smooth cheek. 'She's clever as a button, though, and she loves her daddy no matter when she sees him, whether it's the middle of the night or in broad daylight.'

'I haven't been coming home that late!'

Oriel cocked one eyebrow up at him, saying nothing.

Kier gave her a sheepish look, then shrugged. 'OK. But you do look ravishing,' he added irreverently, then suddenly grabbed her. Oriel squealed. 'So I suppose it would be downright insulting of me not to ravish the lady,' Kier growled, and bent down to nibble on her ear, his hand slipping inside the V-shaped neckline to cup her left breast.

Oriel moaned, oblivious to the chauffeur who might or might not have been watching. 'Oh, darlin', you do pick the damndest times!' Oriel sighed, thinking of the many nights she had spent over the last year, her body aching for him. There had been times when she had cursed the film, swearing over the perfection he demanded, bemoaning the constant re-writes he did to keep *Invaders* up to date and, most of all, different.

'I want to make a *different* kind of film,' he'd said to her a thousand times. 'A new kind, one that will change the way this damned town sees films. It's still in the thirties, in the days of Bette Davis and Ronald Colman! America's changed and changing every day. Jimmy Dean practically invented teen-agers, and more and more . . .' On that occasion she'd managed to shut him up with a kiss on his throat and a well-placed hand on his thigh.

Now she moaned, her body reacting as it always did to the expertise of his touch.

'Kier, for pity's sake,' she gasped as he bent down, nuzzling aside the peach satin of her bodice to suckle on her pert nipple. Since Bethany had been born, her breasts had become bigger and sometimes, like now, he felt a trickle of sweet milk spill into his mouth. Urgently his fingers tightened on her waist. He'd been neglecting her this past year, he knew that. But by the time production had finally started she'd been eight and a half months pregnant, and he'd been in the middle of the space-craft landing scene when the call came from the hospital. And since that magical moment when he'd held his newborn daughter in his hands, looking so tiny, so red and wrinkled, and so incredibly beautiful, things had been pure chaos.

As director and screenwriter, he never stopped, and even after shooting had finished, he'd spent ten weeks with the editor, learning so much about that side of things that his name would appear on the screen three times – as director, screenwriter and assistant editor. Sometimes, watching his daughter become a toddler seemingly overnight, he wondered if it had all been worth it.

Oriel struggled to sit up. 'Kier, oh hell, we're there.' She struggled to tug her bodice back into place, her cheeks flushed with desire, her eyes sparkling gems. Kier took several deep breaths, willing the embarrassing hardness between his legs to subside. Glancing out of the smoke-glassed windows at the cinema lit up with rows of coloured lights, his eyes blinked at the dazzle of flashing camera bulbs. The media cameras and paparazzi were everywhere. And when he took in the sheer size of the avid crowd, Kier found the iron butterflies had come back with a vengeance.

'Hell, the zoo is out in force tonight,' he commented, making Oriel grin. The phenomena of 'film watchers' had been something new to him. For parts of the film he had actually shot on location in a small town in Ohio, taking the cameras out into the streets. It had been daring, practically unheard of, and the whole town had been out in force to watch, which was, of course, the last thing he'd needed. Great crowds didn't usually congregate in small towns, and he'd been forced to make a barrier to keep them back so that the actors could work. But for the scene where the space ship landed, he'd had the chief cameraman take shots of the crowd during the filming of a minor stunt, and the awed, avid faces of genuine people had been worth a whole cart-load of extras.

'Would you rather have the place deserted, darlin'?' Oriel asked mildly, and Kier shot her a quick look, then smiled.

'Did I ever tell you how glad I am that you married me?'

'Nope.'

'Aren't I a stinker?'

'Yep.'

The crowd surged forward again as their limo drew to a halt, and as they alighted there was a ripple of disappointment. No famous faces there. Then the whispers began – this was the director, the one they were all talking about. And wasn't he young, and handsome? Was that his wife, or a mistress, or what? And wasn't she beautiful? Kier felt the uncomfortable weight of hundreds of eyes boring into his back as they walked along the red carpet, shaking hands with the cinema manager to a sudden spurt of flashing of camera bulbs. Finally, after what seemed like an eternity, they walked inside, meeting Howard Shoesmith in the lobby.

'We got a good turnout, boy,' Howard said, a fat cigar in his mouth, a smug grin firmly in place on his face.

'And to think my stars actually enjoy that,' Kier laughed, and nodded to the crowd outside, just as a white stretch limo pulled up to disgorge the leading lady and man. That had been Kier's idea. Usually the leads showed up separately with separate dates, but Kier had thought it prudent to give the crowd something more to gossip about. Were they lovers in real life? He could almost read Hedda's or Louella's column tomorrow, word for word, alive with their usual innuendo and bitchy wit.

'Well, here we go,' Howard said, looking over Kier with an amused eye. 'Now we get to see if all the ballyhoo has been worth it.'

Kier smiled coldly, wondering if Howard wasn't actually hoping for the film to flop just for the satisfaction of seeing Kier fall flat on his face. Then he shrugged the thought off as unworthy. Dislike him though he might, Howard had given him the job and had lavished an amazing amount of money on the budget. He had given in to every demand Kier had made, from experimental lighting to the English special-effects crew, and revolutionary camera angles.

Kier had stuck his neck out, and he knew it. Inside, the critics would be already seated, along with the big brass. If the film flopped . . .

He felt a small hand slip into his, and squeeze. Looking down into blue eyes, still hot from remembered passion, he felt himself relax, even smile.

'Come on,' Oriel said softly, and together they walked into the dimly lit auditorium.

They were seated, at Kier's request, midway in the front section. He wanted to sit behind the critics and newspaper columnists, the better to watch their reactions. And he had no desire to sit with the 'stars.'

As they took their seats, they found themselves amongst the lucky Joe public, who'd queued for hours to buy the 100 tickets available.

The lights went down, and the opening credits rolled, presenting the audience straight away with something new. Usually, films began with music and a straight roll of credits. Not so with *Night of the Invaders*. Kier had asked an old friend of Betty's from the Ruskin School of Art in Oxford to do the graphics for the opening credits, and one of Viv's musical friends had composed a score that was a weird mix of classical musical with a creepy undertone, overlaid by a haunting melody. With the arty, startling graphics that used animation to turn flying saucers, planets and robots into the leading names, the audience was hooked from the start.

Kier leaned back, beyond nerves now, feeling utterly calm. The film was either going to flop or take off like one of the flying saucers that was as far away from Flash Gordon's smoking rockets as it was possible to get. Kier had gone to NASA for ideas, and had let the set designer run wild. And it showed. What also showed was the on-location shooting in Ohio. Instead of being presented with the mock-up studio idea of a town, the audience was presented with the real thing and he felt immediately a sense of rapport from the people around him, a rapport that was transferred to the actors as the leading man and lady got into their roles.

Every girl there knew what Sally was going through as she prepared for her date, the audience actually seeing the curlers come off, the tangles in her hair being brushed out and the makeup being applied, instead of just being presented with another Hollywood glamour model that was light-years away from their own, mundane lives.

The camera angles were stunning, too. Kier shot from second-story windows, looking down on the actors. He shot from the floor, looking up at them in the confrontation scene between Joe, the hero, and the local bully boys. Sound effects, too, had been changed. Out were the wild, overstated punches, crunches and explosions. In were more realistic sounds, and under his direction, the acting had the gritty bite of realism. When forty-five minutes had passed, the tension was high. The characters were real flesh-and-blood good ol' boys, and the sense of something being seriously wrong had transferred itself to the audience. Kier could feel the tension all around him when Sally finally stumbled onto the underground landing sight. There she turned slowly, her eyes finding the creature that stood behind her. But Kier forced the audience to guess at what she saw, giving out clues only sparingly in the shape of its shadow, in the shuffling of its feet. As he'd always known it would, the ambiguity added to the terror.

Sally did not scream. Sally did not faint. *The Night of the Invaders* was not playing by the set rules, and every critic there knew it. The hero Joe was also fallible, and his mistakes were all very human and very plausible. By the time the climax of the film had come around, the audience wasn't at all convinced that he'd actually arrive on time to save the girl, and the safety of the usual foregone conclusion that there would be a happy ending had been long since snatched away from the spellbound audience.

For long, long minutes, the audience warred with differing opinions – Sally was doomed. Then Joe was getting nearer, Sally would be saved. Then, and only then, was the monster at last revealed, full-faced, and here Bud Westmore had earned his exorbitant fee.

This was no Hollywood monster, a mere man dressed up in green gunge, his very human eyes clearly visible through the slits in the mask. This was a combination of makeup, animal, man, and other-worldly ugliness. Several girls in the audience screamed as, on screen, everything went silent. Joe and the monster faced off, the camera swivelling from one to the other, slowly at first, and then faster, until the audience could hardly tell what was happening.

And then the *coup de grâce*. Joe took the home-made flame thrower that the alien had already seen, but instead of just firing it off, he dove under the monster, firing up, the camera angle going with him. High-pitched, eerie squeals, which his dubbing editor had gleaned from dolphins and speeded up, filled the cinema, making the audience jump and then look around in surprise. Kier had had the wiring men place the speakers all around the room, so that the noise seemed to come from everywhere.

And then Sally crawled over to Joe and helped him up. Together, battered, human, shaking, crying, they stumbled out into the cool night air. A mile away, the small town was lit up and the audience could hear a barn hoe-down tune fill the air. As he'd expected, the return to normality was startling.

Then the final credits – this time the night stars forming the words, the sun and moon shimmering into the name of the stars and the director. The lights went up and there was total silence. All around him people were blinking, dumbfounded, looking at their partners to see what they made of it.

A boy a few seats away from Kier said loud enough for everywhere to hear, 'Gee-whizz! I think I'll cancel the visit to Uncle Elmer's farm.'

And then everyone was laughing, the kind of laughter that came after tension, and Oriel started to clap. In a moment the room was awash with applause, whistles and stomping feet.

Kier got up, every head turning his way and for once ignoring the leading actors who also stood up. Slowly, Kier walked on stiff legs to the bottom of the screen to where his leading lady was beaming – as well she might. She'd just been made into a superstar, and she stretched up on tiptoe to kiss him. Kier turned to look at the critics, his eyes level. Now they could write what they damned well liked. He knew he'd done it. He knew he was there.

Clarissa looked across at Howard Shoesmith, then away again, her face blank. Howard stood up, but suddenly there was a crowd around his director, other leading men from the big studios and gossip columnists, all eager now to talk to the boy-genius, as Hedda Hopper would call him the next day, which would be his nickname for the next twenty years.

Alone in her seat, Oriel watched him, tears running down her cheeks.

'Darling, are you all right?'

Hearing the soft southern drawl, she turned to her mother and nodded speechlessly, her eyes travelling on to those of her father. Duncan looked almost as proud as the day he'd first held his little granddaughter.

Finally Oriel said, 'Isn't he wonderful? Didn't I tell you?'

Duncan's face split into a wide grin. 'You sure did, honey. I think I've just gone and gotten myself a famous son-in-law.'

Oriel laughed and cried and hugged her mother and kissed her father and watched her husband being mobbed. After a while the whole circus decamped to the Beverly Hills Hotel. The Polo Lounge was ready for them, the elegant *porte-cochère* at the front of the hotel entrance quickly becoming blocked with stars, producers, directors, newspaper men, agents and models. With great aplomb, the *maître d'* moved them along, seating the most prominent in the curved banquette tables, the priority seating being quickly taken up with the film world's elite. Pride of place was left for Kier Harcourt and his lovely wife.

Clarissa looked around, satisfied that everything had been prepared correctly. Huge floral displays were everywhere and the menu she'd discussed with the hotel's French chefs had been strictly adhered to. Pâté de foie gras Strasbourg littered silver trays, along with Beluga caviar with chopped boiled eggs and raw onion, served on Melba toast with wedges of lemon. Lobster souffle competed with Dover sole and shallots, turtle soup with sherry rubbed shoulders with salmon and capers. Roast lamb with mint, roulade of beef, turban of chicken and tongue, and quenelles of pheasant tempted the appetites of the most ardent carnivores. Dessert trolleys overflowed, with baba au rhum, parfait, apricot snow, fruit soaked in Kirsch and jellied consommés the order of the day. As well as the pink champagnes of Pommery and Grende, there was a selection of harder liquor, not to mention the more exotic, feminine concoctions of white mint over ice, Kirsch-wasser, a cherry-flavoured liqueur Clarissa herself favoured, and of course, Mouton Rothschild and Pouilly Fuissé by the crateload.

There had never been an *après*-film party like it. But then, Clarissa Somerville had never sojourned in Hollywood territory before.

A ten-piece, world-famous band serenaded the guests with thirties' Glenn Miller classics and mod-ern jive.

'Well, how are you feeling?' Oriel asked when the last of the emptied plates had been cleared away, and it seemed the endless hours of congratulations were at last winding down. Kier leaned back in his chair, his bow tie long since having been discarded.

'I don't know . . .' He met her mocking eyes and began to laugh. 'Yes, I do,' he said softly, then shouted, 'I feel bloody great!'

Several heads turned and teeth flashed in grins, the ambiance one of high good humour. Success was all that counted in this town, and when you made it, people were magnanimous. Stars who'd never spoken to him before congratulated him heartily, angling for roles.

Oriel licked her lips slowly, her hand gently going to her throat, where she began to trail a finger down her sternum. Abruptly Kier stopped laughing. 'You feel so great you're gonna stay here all night?' she asked huskily.

'Uh-uh.' Kier shook his head, rising to his feet as Oriel excused herself to go to the Ladies' room and collect her coat. Watching her daughter leave, Clarissa slipped a little nervously into the chair her daughter had just vacated. With a sinking heart, she watched Kier's eyes become shuttered. Although she had stayed for two weeks when Bethany had been born, Clarissa had lacked the courage to try and reach out to her son-in-law. Now, the neutral state of their relationship was beginning to wear her down.

'Clarissa,' Kier said, his voice carefully bland, 'I hope you've enjoyed this evening?'

Since Clarissa's advent back into their lives, Kier had been determinedly polite. He had not failed to see that having her there for the birth of Bethany had meant a lot to Oriel, and he had to admit that, so far, Clarissa had kept her pretty nose out of their marriage and had graciously met Kier halfway, always polite and never descending on them without prior warning. And Kier was not a man to hold grudges.

'Indeed I have,' Clarissa agreed. How best to offer the olive branch? 'I'm really glad I was able to help,' she said, and smiled hopefully.

Kier stiffened. 'Help?'

Clarissa put a tentative hand on his arm. 'It was after Oriel rang me for the first time – to tell me she was going to have a baby. I . . . so wanted to do something . . . positive for you both.'

Kier felt a cold hard knot forming in his stomach. 'Oh?'

Clarissa looked at him warily. 'Didn't it occur to you that the budget for the movie was much higher than Howard usually allowed?' she began, trying to feel her way into it. She had always thought that, when she told him, he'd be grateful for all her help. So why was she beginning to feel so tense? 'I thought I should invest in your career. After all, I so wanted you to be successful.'

Kier paled but said only, 'You're a backer?'

'That's right,' she agreed, relieved at last that they were beginning to speak the same language. 'And I must say, you used my money so well. All those wonderful little gadgets you used, and things. It really made the film *shine*. And, of course, I arranged this little shindig,' she added offhandedly, and looked vaguely around the room.

Kier took a deep, shaken breath. 'Clarissa, as long as I live, I'll never ask you for one damned thing. And neither shall Oriel.'

Clarissa smile faltered. 'But! . . . I thought it made things easier for you. I so wanted the film to be a success . . .' she began, dismayed.

'So that you could rub my nose in it?' Kier gritted. 'So that you could say I'd never have made it without my mother-in-law's money?'

Clarissa felt her jaw drop open. 'No! No, I swear. I . . . well, I will admit, when I came over, I was worried about Oriel living in such a poky little place. But I could see she was happy. I only wanted to *help*.'

Clarissa's fingers tightened on his arm. 'We got off to such a bad start, and then all those years we didn't even talk . . .' She felt her voice begin to wobble, and her eyes to water, and cursed softly. She reached into her handbag for a hanky, and so missed the astonished expression that crossed Kier's face.

'You really mean that, don't you?' he said, so surprised he couldn't think of anything else to say.

Clarissa glanced, saw his astonishment, and smiled ruefully. 'I'm not *that* much of a bitch,' she said wryly. 'Can't we start all over again, you and I? And if you don't want me to back any more of your films, I won't.'

Kier laughed and reached across to her. 'It's a deal,' he said, and kissed her cheek. Oriel, watching them from the other side of the room, felt a lump rise in her throat and went to collect him. She noted her mother's happy eyes, and smiled. 'See you tomorrow, Mama,' she said happily, and Clarissa nodded.

Then her eyes picked out those of her husband, and a troubled expression crept into them. Oriel was about to ask her what was wrong, but Kier was already tugging anxiously on her elbow. He was anxious to finish what he'd started in the back of their limo!

On the way to the hall, Frank Lockwood from Paramount waylaid him. 'Well, m'boy, you certainly scored a hit tonight. Look, not to beat about the bush, I'd like to offer you a three-film contract, right now. You can choose the genre, you can even do the screenplay. *Carte blanche*, and a budget even better than this one. What do you say?'

Kier grinned. 'I say yes please, Frank!'

In the car, Oriel leaned her head on his shoulder, and sighed tiredly. 'I'm glad it's all over,' she admitted softly, turning to run a finger over his nose, across his chin, and then tracing his lips. 'And I'm so glad you and Mama have finally patched things up.'

Kier grinned. 'She's not such a dragon after all.'

Oriel thumped him playfully. 'I think tonight has been the third best night of my life,' she sighed.

Their house, once owned by Bogart, was only a short drive away; as they alighted from the limo, Kier nodded a curt goodnight to the driver and took her possessively by the elbow. Inside were twenty-five rooms, an indoor and outdoor pool, a conservatory, a gym, a games room, en-suite bathrooms and marble flooring. And now, with *Invaders* an unqualified success, he was going to be able to pay off the mortgage in one fell swoop. Wearily they trudged up the stairs, Kier shrugging off his jacket and shirt as he did so. In the bedroom the circular bed awaited, with its over-the-top white satin head-board, sheets and canopy. Quickly, Kier stripped himself of his clothes.

Standing in front of the vanity mirror, Oriel had just taken off her jewellery when his arms slipped around her, his hands slipping flat inside her gown and covering her breasts. Oriel sighed, leaning back against his naked body, her gown cool and soft against his skin. In the mirror she watched him free her hair, kiss the nape of her neck and then sweep hot avid kisses across her naked shoulders, making her spine tingle deliciously.

'Kier,' Oriel whispered his name softly as he drew down the zip at her back and the dress rustled to the floor in a silken whisper. She was wearing no bra, and he picked her up, laying her in the middle of the round bed, and staring down into her eyes as he took off her silken stockings and panties. He kissed the instep of her foot, then the backs of her knees, working up her thighs, holding them apart with hard, firm hands as he thrust his tongue deep inside her. Oriel jerked and cried out, her peach-painted nails digging into the pillows either side of her head. Above them their reflection was mirrored in a pink-tinted mirror. Her breasts were white, her nipples stiff and red, and she could see the top of his silky head between her thighs, his arms dark and hairy across her stomach as they held her still.

'Kier!' she moaned his name urgently, pulling him up, watching as his head hovered first over one breast and then the other as he tugged passionately on her nipples.

Finally, when his lips were against hers, he whispered, 'I love you, Mrs Harcourt.'

Oriel's eyes widened as he plunged into her, big and strong, deep and sure, her eyes fixed on the mirror above her. She looked small and white and almost crushed underneath the muscular frame of her husband, whose buttocks rose and fell as he plunged into her, over and over again. The erotic image began to waver as she felt the first sweet wave of ecstasy begin to build inside her with tense, unbearable pleasure.

'Oriel!' Kier shouted her name, his voice hoarse and breathless. And then, as her legs locked around him, her vagina contracting and caressing him into a frenzy, he added gruffly, 'Don't ever leave me. I'll die!' And they both moaned their ecstasy into each other's mouths as their bodies sweetly exploded.

In their room, Clarissa slowly slipped off her tight shoes and sighed in relief. By the dresser, taking off his cufflinks, Duncan smiled at her. 'Happy, m'dear?' he asked vaguely. Clarissa hesitated, then took a deep, deep breath.

'Not really, no.'

Duncan paused, one cufflink still in his hand, and turned to look at her thoughtfully. For a long moment, man and wife stared at one another, and then Duncan smiled slowly. It was a sad but oddly relieved sort of a smile.

'You want to be free, don't you, Clarry?' he asked softly, and watched her nod miserably. She ducked her head, her eyes suspiciously bright. 'Am I the only one, Duncan?' she asked softly, and heard her husband sigh.

'No. Perhaps not. We both did what was expected of us, old thing.' Duncan wearily put down the cufflink and glanced at his reflection in the mirror. He looked old, suddenly. 'It just wasn't enough, that's all. You're going to marry him, aren't you?' he added quietly, and Clarissa's head shot up.

'Yes,' she said at last. 'Yes, I am. When Kyle first gave me the ultimatum, I thought I'd never be able to go through with it. Divorce you, turn my back on the old way of life. Ride the gauntlet of cruel gossip to marry a man so much younger than myself. But . . . the more I thought about it, the more I knew . . . Duncan, darling, I just can't live without him. I'm so sorry. I never meant to hurt you.'

'I'll see to the lawyers as soon as we get back.'

Clarissa nodded numbly. So that was that. The safety of her old life was gone. But . . . a new life with Kyle awaited her.

CHAPTER 18

Veronica Coltrane dove neatly into the pool, resurfaced and pushed the hair from her eyes. It was six-thirty in the morning, and she doubted if even Sir Mortimer was up yet. She was once again spending a weekend in the country, and she loved staying at the big house. There was something deliciously hedonistic about swimming in an indoor heated swimming pool on a Sunday morning.

Especially on a Sunday morning when you awoke to find yourself in love. Ridiculous, she knew, to fall in love so quickly, but there it was.

She touched the side of the pool, flipped neatly and began the return journey, her muscles stretching nicely. The tiles beneath her were patterned into a peacock's tail, whilst above her a glass dome helped the greenhouse-plants littering the side of the pool to thrive. As she swam, however, her mind remained on Wayne D'Arville.

When he had caressed her in the lift at Platt's, she'd felt thrilled and afraid, like a rabbit caught in headlights. She hadn't objected to his outrageous behaviour, simply because she hadn't been able to. She'd only been able to look up into his eyes and fall prey to a shattering excitement that gnawed at her still whenever she thought about him.

And just when she'd made up her mind to try and forget him, she'd found him again – here at Sir Mortimer's. The heart-stopping stranger would actually be a work-mate. It was like a miracle, and she could only wonder why she had been so lucky. She was, after all, just plain Veronica Coltrane, who had lived in Canterbury with her parents for most of her life. She was averagely pretty, and had an average job. But suddenly, without warning, something extraordinary had happened to her in the guise of a tall Frenchman, with heavy-lidded azure eyes who had caressed her outrageously in a lift, turning her brain to mush and her body to quivering, responsive jelly.

She closed her eyes, a slight smile on her lips as she swam mechanically, remembering the dancing last night. She had felt dwarfed in his arms, the scent of his expensive aftershave tantalizing her nostrils. She was fascinated by his voice, by its timbre and tone, making the simplest and most ordinary of words something special.

He had not asked her, as an Englishman might, 'Would you care to dance?' but instead had walked straight up to her, taken her hand and said instead, 'You will dance with me. Now . . .'

And she had. The way he never took his eyes off her all night, looking at her openly and without shame or pretence, made her feel at first flustered, but then so painfully needy that, by the time the night was over, she craved the feel of his eyes on her like a drunk craved his bottle.

Veronica was not totally naïve. Although twenty-one and still a virgin, she knew enough to understand what the smouldering looks in his eyes meant, and what the corresponding melting feeling deep inside her own body signified.

A loud splash had her thoughts jerking back to the present, and she looked around, the wake at the other end of the pool warning her she was no longer alone. Her mouth went dry as he resurfaced a few feet away, his copper head darkened by the water. As Wayne stood and waded towards her, water ran in rivulets off his deep, hairless chest. He was wearing short, black trunks that did little to disguise his aroused condition, and she turned towards the steps, instinct urging her to run.

She wasn't ready for this, she knew that. She was far too unsure of the game of love to play it like a professional.

Wayne reached her as she had her foot on the first step, his hand around her waist pulling her back firmly but gently. As her back pressed against his chest, she felt her heart flip in her breast. 'Wayne, I . . .'

His lips on her neck drained the energy right out of her, and she felt her legs buckle beneath her. Wayne lifted her slightly, turning her around and holding her against the tiles that surrounded the pool, her head falling back against the black rubber surround that circled the pool.

'Wayne,' she whispered again, not sure of what she wanted any more, now that his eyes were burning into hers and his body heat was doing strange things to her skin. She felt her nipples tingle and harden against the clammy cloth of her one-piece swimsuit, and then gasped as she felt his fingers caress her there, tweaking her between his thumb and forefinger, making her jerk in helpless reaction. She drew in a harsh breath, the sound of it shocking her.

Wayne slowly pulled the straps past her shivering shoulders, freeing her breasts that were covered with gooseflesh, rosy nipples burgeoned and uptilting.

'Wayne, please . . . I can't.'

He bent his head to her right breast and pulled on the rosy bud that trembled there, aware of her knees jerking either side of his thighs. She raised her hands to his chest, her feeble strength barely making any impression as she tried half-heartedly to push him away. He responded by taking her hands and spreading her arms out along the poolside, the action lifting her body even further from the pool, allowing him even easier access to her body.

'Someone might see!' she implored, her voice sounding thick and strange to her own ears.

In reply, Wayne left her breasts and moved up her throat, kissing and nibbling his way to her ears, where the sound of his hot amplified breath made her heart pound even harder.

'No one's up yet,' he muttered, nipping her lobe and smiling at her small moan. Over the weeks he'd found his growing fascination with Veronica Coltrane startling. He'd watched her, listened to her, asked about her, but only when his mental file on her was complete did he feel safe enough to decide that he had to have her.

Even though she was a little nobody – a little Miss Average.

He pulled down his trunks, unable to stand the pressure on his groin any longer, but was careful to turn slightly to one side so that he didn't press directly against her and frighten her away.

Gently and so subtly she was hardly aware of it at first, he pulled her swimsuit down her stomach and past her thighs.

He kissed her hard and deeply, his tongue pushing past hers in an erotic sword-dance. She thrashed in the water, the sensation so overpowering that she found it sparking off other, clamouring needs deep inside her. Dimly she was aware that she was being seduced, but his hands were on her legs now, pulling the swimsuit free and running his hands over her well-shaped, naked buttocks. She gasped, her eyes widening ever further as his clever fingers parted her thighs, dipping in between to find her clitoris.

'We sh-shouldn't,' she gulped, her voice hopelessly cracked. But his hands were between her thighs now, and no matter how hard she clasped them together, his fingers still rubbed her, spreading heat and flame throughout her entire body. After a few minutes she was delirious with pleasure, uncaring about anything as the water splashed around them in time to her undulating rhythm, which was in turn dictated by his diabolical rubbing. Just when she thought she would die of it, he suddenly stopped. She whimpered, looking up at him with wide, bruised eyes.

He was only inches away now, and she could see his pupils dilate. 'Open your legs for me, Veronica,' he demanded, and she found her legs falling open magically. Before she could even think, he was between them, his hands lifting her buttocks, forcing her to grab his shoulders for support and balance. It was then that she felt the heat and strength of his throbbing shaft between her legs. Her eyes opened wide in a fleeting moment of recognition, and then Wayne thrust deep inside her, filling her.

At first there was only sudden pain, but his lips on hers quickly cut off her cry of surprise. But then, slowly, the pain began to fade, and she felt a quivering surge of relief. Then her eyes flooded with total surprise and disbelief as the relief gave way to a mounting sensation of pleasure that strove ever higher, quickly becoming a gasp-inducing ecstasy.

She found her body responding to his invasion with eagerness, as if it had been pre-programmed in some primeval lesson that her consciousness had all but forgotten. A delicious tight tension began to build in her womb, her vagina and stomach. Her mouth fell open as she began to convulse, caught totally offguard by the violence of her first orgasm. Wayne hung on to her grimly, thrusting ever more quickly, ever more deeply into her tight, hot, sweet body as he fought past the peak of his own pleasure. He kept his lips on hers as her cries of pain became cries of pleasure and he shuddered against her as his seed exploded from him, jetting deeply into her body as he, too, cried out in the final moments.

He pulled out and away from her, and swam sluggishly to the side, climbing out on limbs that felt leaden. He walked, naked and silent, to the changing rooms, and never looked back.

Veronica lay gasping in the pool, her mind slowly collecting together its shattered fragments.

In his room Wayne began to pack, the urge to leave totally overwhelming. He didn't trust women – and he didn't trust his own reaction to Veronica Coltrane. Love was a foreign thing – a disease to be avoided. Besides, he couldn't afford to be distracted when he had other things to do.

Determinedly, he shrugged her from him, like a man shrugging off an unwanted coat, and reached for the telephone by his bedside, dialling a number in Soho he'd paid twenty pounds for. It rang five times, then a sharp, openly aggressive and suspicious voice barked, 'Yeah?'

'I want to speak to Ryan. Vince gave me this number.'

'Hold on a mo'.' A few seconds later another voice came on the line, and Wayne got quickly to the point. He wanted a man by the name of Toby Platt to be set up with a call boy. It wouldn't be difficult, he told the anonymous voice, his lips twisted into a sneer. Toby Platt was a known homosexual. Once that was arranged, the dirtiest, sleaziest rag in London was to send over a photographer to catch them in the act.

Ryan, as expected, agreed at once, and when Wayne promised an extra hundred pounds for quick action, was told it could be arranged for that very night.

Wayne hung up and fastened his suitcase.

At breakfast the next morning, he barely glanced at Veronica, but she didn't mind. The breakfast table was too crowded anyway, and she wanted to avoid any potentially knowing, smirking eyes. Although Sir Mortimer liked to entertain his staff and friends at these cosy little weekends, Veronica had no desire to become the unofficial entertainment.

As the meal wore on, however, Veronica realized Lady Beatrice had taken a dislike to Wayne for some reason, and it was only Sir Mortimer himself who seemed unaware of the tenseness around the table.

'I hope you enjoyed your second weekend with us, Mr Darville,' Beatrice gritted, 'now that you've had a chance to settle down at Platt's.'

Wayne smiled at her pleasantly. 'Very much so. I look forward to coming again.'

Beatrice's eyes flashed, but she didn't speak fast enough to forestall her husband.

'Of course you will, m'boy,' he said pleasantly, smashing down his spoon on a boiled egg. 'You'll be needing a lift back to London, I suppose? I'll get Higgins to drive you.'

'Oh, that won't be necessary, Sir Mortimer,' Veronica said quickly, with what she hoped was a bland smile. 'I have to get back too. I can give Mr Darville a lift.'

Sir Mortimer looked from one to the other with a twinkle in his eye. 'Course. You'll stay to lunch, though?'

'We'd love to,' Wayne said, angry at her for leaving him no way out. His glance slewed from Veronica's openly happy smile to Beatrice's smirking one, and his hand tightened ominously on his fork.

Veronica ate little. She was still too euphoric to have an appetite. She'd never before guessed how wonderful intimacy could be. And not just the physical side of it, either. As she looked at Wayne, she felt so close to him she wanted to cry. She knew that beneath his pristine shirt was a mole on his left shoulder, and she longed to kiss it. She could still feel the memory of him inside her, and she wanted to reach across and hold his hand. Simply that. Just hold his hand. She'd had no idea how wonderful love could be.

With breakfast at an end, Beatrice suggested Veronica show Wayne the garden, since he hadn't had a chance to see it when he'd first come down, stirring up trouble with real finesse and gloating openly as Wayne reluctantly followed her out into the sunshine.

Once outside, Wayne remained so strangely quiet, however, that Veronica began to feel uncertain of herself. She led him silently to the boxed rose-garden, glancing at him anxiously. 'I feel . . . awkward somehow,' she eventually said, her voice coming out in a nervous laugh. 'I feel like I know everything about you. We've been working at the same office for a while, and yet, at the same time, it's as if I don't know anything at all, really. Do you feel the same about me?'

He looked at her – at her wide innocent eyes, full now with anxiety, and remembered the feel of her silken limbs around him.

He frowned. So far in his life he'd been able to fit everyone into a category – they were either his enemies, like Hans and Wolfgang, or they were to be used, like Sir Mortimer. A brief vision of kind, sherry-coloured eyes flitted across his mind, but he quickly squashed it. The last time he'd seen Sebastien Teale, he'd all but shoved past the psychiatrist with the dangerously kind, knowing eyes to run back into the safety of the crowded room. Once there, he'd kept a safe distance, never letting the American shrink get near him again. Even now, weeks later, Sebastien Teale had the ability to terrify him.

Still getting no response from the stranger who was her lover, Veronica launched nervously into the story of her life – her home, her father and her job. Her voice was innocent, her motives honest as she laughed at herself a lot, further confusing him. It was only when she mentioned her book that he found his mind sharpening.

'What sort of book?'

Veronica shrugged embarrassedly. 'It's a theory, really. An economic forecast for the coming years. I see computers as really taking off . . .' Glad at last to have some kind of response from him, she gave him a blow-by-blow account of her work to date. And as she talked, Wayne's interest sharpened even more. Having studied economics, he knew genius when he heard it. Some of the points she made were naïve, and would need work, and, of course, could be phrased in much more academic terms, but even he could see that Veronica had one of those brains to which money, and the way it worked, held no mysteries. More, Veronica had an original concept that sounded, to Wayne, little short of brilliant.

'And what does Sir Mortimer think of it?' he asked curiously. He knew Sir Mortimer was already ahead of the times in his thinking, having employed a woman in the first place. Obviously, Veronica more than earned her pay.

Veronica laughed. 'He doesn't know. I haven't told a soul. Practically everyone who works at Platt's is writing a book. We're all convinced we have the secret to economic fame and fortune.'

Wayne's eyes narrowed thoughtfully. 'So no one knows about it?' he asked, his voice strangely tense. 'What about your parents? A friend? You must have told somebody?'

Veronica shook her head. 'No. Only you,' she added, her heart in her eyes. 'I wanted you to know.'

Wayne looked down into her soft, trusting eyes, then smiled and kissed her tenderly.

He needn't have worried after all, he thought, relieved. Veronica Coltrane had just slotted herself neatly into her own pigeon hole. Victim. If this book of hers was as good as he thought, of course.

Gently he took her hand in his and held it as they walked around the grounds, stopping every now and then to kiss and smell the roses.

The scandal broke on Monday morning. Buying a scandal sheet for the first time in his life, Wayne read of Toby's disgrace over a glass of orange juice and a slice of toast.

The caption read: 'Platt Boy in Homosexual Love Tangle Shock.'

Wayne ate heartily and went to work, where the company was abuzz. Office boys whispered together in huddles and executives went around as if there was a bad smell under their noses. His own immediate superior, Alfred Hawkes, spent the entire morning shaking his head, wondering what was to become of Platt's.

Wayne, of course, knew exactly what was to become of Platt's. He worked through his lunch-hour, making sure Alfred was aware that he did so. Consequently, it was mid-afternoon before he saw Veronica again. She was working at her desk and looked up, love shining in her eyes as he whispered softly '*Bonjour*.'

'Hello. How about this for a rotten day! Poor Toby!'

Wayne shrugged a very Gallic shrug. 'I came to ask if I could read your book. You know I did a degree in economics at the Sorbonne? I could give it a proof-reading for you and give you an honest opinion on it before you try to submit it to a publishing company.'

'Would you?' Veronica half-smiled, half-frowned, and forced back a nagging feeling of unease that was suddenly and unaccountably eating away at the back of her mind. 'OK.' She glanced around a little self-consciously, unlocked the bottom drawer of her desk and took out a thick, padded envelope, and handed it over.

Wayne took it, but didn't even so much as glance inside. 'Don't worry – ' he leaned over and kissed her quickly, '– I shall be honest but gentle, hmm?'

Veronica smiled. 'OK.'

'Dinner tonight? Yes?'

Veronica nodded, so happy she thought she'd burst. 'Yes.'

Wayne nodded and left. If the book was good, it would be easy enough to convince her it was not. And if she proved bothersome . . . well, he could always have a discreet word with Sir Mortimer. He planned to have many discreet words with the old man, now that his son had turned out to be such a disappointing embarrassment . . .

Wayne left the office at six, and went straight to the Windsor, where he bathed and changed before settling down to give the book a quick speed-read. She didn't have a title yet, he noticed, and wondered if that was a bad omen. The first page gave him his answer. It was not.

The book was a winner, he could tell that five minutes into his reading. Her theories were well-rounded and sweeping, but different enough to be exciting. Her predictions on computers had his heart pounding. If she was right . . . there were fortunes to be made. And a book like this meant instant kudos and fame for its author. Her money-management schemes were revolutionary and foolproof. He'd even re-invest his own pitiful pool of money, based on her ideas.

A few hours later he was on the last chapter when a knock came at the door. An angry glance at the clock told him it was still too early for Veronica, so he carefully put the book away out of sight, and walked to the door, yanking it open.

Sebastien watched the look of panic flood his eyes before the barriers came down and a cold smile gave way to carefully blank eyes.

'Hi,' Sebastien said softly. 'You remember me?' It was not a question, for they both knew that Wayne remembered.

Silently, without knowing really why, Wayne stood aside, and Sebastien entered, looking around curiously. He saw a hotel room – neat and impersonal. There was nothing of the man in here. No pictures on the dresser. No ornaments on the shelves. Sebastien knew from Sir Mortimer Platt that Wayne had lived at the hotel for over three months now. Time enough to add some individuality to the room. But there was nothing.

Wayne stood looking at the psychiatrist, feeling curiously numb. He knew this man was dangerous – he knew it with every fibre of his being, and yet another instinct, equally as strong, was urging him to keep the American near. There was something so wonderfully . . . warm . . . about him. He could feel ice, deep in his soul, threatening

305

to melt. The urge to talk to the man, to bare his soul, to cry and rant and rave, was almost overwhelming. The floodgates that kept the secrets of his darkened soul wanted to crumble at his feet. But why? Why this man? His own father hadn't been strong enough to bring him to his knees. Why did this man, with just his mere presence, make him feel so vulnerable? Curiosity, not something he felt very often, began to nibble at him like vicious piranhas.

He felt giddy, and curiously light-headed.

'What can I do for you?' Wayne finally asked, aware that the psychiatrist was not going to be the first to speak. His own voice sounded dry and nervous. The man's power angered him slightly, even as it intrigued him.

Deep down, he knew this man, Sebastien Teale, was his match – his equal. Younger he might be. Softer he most definitely was. But still, in some odd, terrifying way that was oddly not terrifying at all, Sebastien had the power to destroy him.

Why then was he not already busily planning how to destroy him first?

Sebastien looked at Wayne, who was staring determinedly out the window, and said nothing. Waiting patiently until Wayne finally met his gaze head on, then, and only then did he say softly, 'I think it's more a question of what I can do for you. Isn't it . . . Wayne?'

CHAPTER 19

Spain

Andalucía lies in the deep south, an area of Spain where tourists seldom venture, and where electricity, gas and such twentieth-century conveniences as cars and radio have yet to leave any notable mark. The extraordinarily high and crumpled mountains cluster around sun-baked, half-green valleys, where tiny villages huddle up steep slopes with houses piled high around narrow alleys. Clothes flutter on washing lines strung between houses, and everybody seems to be somebody else's relative.

And everyone was equally poor.

Buzzards wheel high overhead, their sharp cries the only birdsong the bleak mountains can tolerate. Here Spanish flows in harsh, guttural, regional dialects, and women still congregate around the village wells whilst men still play an ancient form of checkers around the village taverns in the morning sun.

The region invariably struck its few visitors as desolate and remote. Few trees can grow in the poor soil and those that do are twisted by the harsh mountain winds. Only a few crippled olive groves and the occasional orange orchard defies the bleak landscape by frothing forth beautiful blossom and fruit.

The village of Guajar Frontera, a humble collection of stone and earth-baked dwellings, with a pitiful square complete with defunct fountain and one grandiose residence, lay high in the hills, unchanged since its beginnings centuries ago.

No cars came to the village, except the Don's, and even that car, hardy as it was, found the mountainous tracks strenuous and the narrow alleys hazardous to its pristine paintwork.

It wound its way through the village now, its windows glinting in the sun. Sitting in the back of the Italian model, imported only last year, was Don Luis de Silva Cortez.

Don Cortez was a man extremely proud of his name, never letting any of his intermittent visitors forget that his ancestry could be traced back to *the* Cortez of Mexican fame and notoriety. He even had a family tree, hung up in pride of place in his palatial villa's main salon, showing the tortuous route by which he could claim his illustrious ancestor. It was a beautiful piece of workmanship, the calligraphy written in natural-dyed black ink, the capitals enscrolled with real gold and silver, the parchment hundreds of years old, cracked and creamy now with age.

Only Don Luis knew it to be a fake. But what did it matter? None of the peons in the village were going to argue, and his occasional guests, picked for their fame or wealth, were too polite to mention it.

The car slowed down as it approached the village square, where two donkeys with loaded panniers of potatoes and turnips, was slowly ambling up the village's one main street.

'Frederico, get him out of the way,' Don Luis imperiously ordered his driver, impatient as always with the locals who lived in his village all year round.

The Cortezes had owned Guajar Frontera for centuries, the peasants paying him a pitiful rent for the houses, whilst in return he paid them a pitiful wage for working in his olive groves, orchards, farms and quarries. He had been educated in Madrid, had seen the world, had courted Italian princesses and married a Spanish countess. His home in the hills did not please him, but it was his home.

His wife had provided him with two sons, and then very decently died, leaving him free to pursue his own pleasures. He had just returned from visiting his eldest son in Barcelona, but bouncing his grandson on his knee had not improved his temper or patience and the sudden blast of the car horn frightened the donkeys, who brayed loudly, kicking out filthy back legs in panic, upsetting the panniers, and dumping vegetables into the street.

The young boy leading the donkeys began to sniffle, knowing his papa was certain to beat him when he got home for bruising the vegetables. Not only would he be late, but already young children were filing into the streets and stealing the produce, and he could not run, his stick held up and shouting threats, in four different directions at once.

Balefully, he stared at the car as it crawled by. Catching a brief glimpse of the silver-haired Don, with neatly trimmed moustache, grandee beard, and small black eyes, like vicious jets, the boy shuddered and crossed himself.

Once the car was out of sight, he set about beating off the tenacious thieves, quietening the donkeys, and reloading the cart. Perhaps, if he told his papa it was Don Luis's car, he would be spared the beating. For, of one accord, all the villagers hated Don Luis de Silva Cortez.

There were rumours and tales about him that curdled the blood of even the village priest. The sudden and odd disappearance of one of the Don's serving maids (brought back from Seville) was still not forgotten, fifteen years after the fact, and Carlos Montoya swore he heard someone screaming up at his villa late at night.

The Villa Cortez was situated on the very outskirts of the village, its grand architecture and opulence set apart from the ramshackle, ugly group of houses, much to Don Luis's delight. It overlooked the valley, and had fruit orchards to its right, and a formal garden spread on the north, east and west borders. Here the fountains worked perfectly and modern technology thrived in the form of sprinklers, carefully timed, to give the Villa Cortez lush lawns and exotic blooms. Here a generator provided the villa with as much electricity as was needed to power the heated pool, the sauna, the private cinema-screen, the kitchen with its vast ovens and the electric chandeliers hung in practically every room.

Don Luis alighted from the car and stepped onto the paved driveway, his white suit a little crumpled. He was a small man, no more than five feet five, and thin as a whippet. He walked with a silver-topped ebony cane, and as he approached the portico, the tap-tap of his stick could be heard echoing inside the villa where doors were left constantly open to catch the cooling mountain breeze. The heat, high in the unprotected mountains, was phenomenal.

Rosita Alvarez, one-time maid to the D'Arvilles of Monte Carlo, heard the cane and went as cold as ice. She was in the kitchen, preparing the prosciutto with figs for the first course for his midday meal. His leanness was misleading, as she had soon found out. He ate like a horse, and demanded the best. Quickly she wiped her hands on the voluminous white apron she wore and glanced nervously at her little daughter, now nearly six years old, playing with a straw doll the gardener's boy had made for her. Thankfully, she looked nothing like her father, the devil called Wayne.

'Maria, *por favor*, go play outside,' Rosita said quickly.

Sometimes Rosita remembered to speak English to the little girl, sometimes not. Vaguely she had a half-formed idea, more of a hope than a plan, that her child would one day somehow escape from the village of her birth, with its rigid social strata that had placed her, as a hated bastard Americano, at the bottom of the heap.

311

Some way, Rosita and her daughter would make their way back to civilization.

Of Wayne D'Arville she had forced herself not think at all. The harsh, ugly years had not been kind to Rosita.

Now, as Maria Alvarez glanced up from her straw doll, she saw not the beautiful woman Rosita had once been, but only her mama, with a streak of premature grey at her temples, and worried eyes surrounded by creases, her face tired and defeated.

'*Madre*, I don't want to play on the garden,' she wheedled in her imperfect English, jutting out her bottom lip and looking mutinous.

The tap-tapping of the cane came closer, and Rosita glanced fearfully across her shoulder, her anxiety rising to fever-pitch.

'Maria, *rapidamente*. If you go, I will take you to the supermercado in Arcos de la Frontera tomorrow. *Si*?' she begged, near to tears now.

The promise of a trip to the nearest town, with its brand new supermarket, was enough to make Maria's eyes glow. 'You promises? And can we buy some *pasta de dientes*?'

'Yes, yes, you can have some toothpaste,' Rosita promised, not bothering to scold her daughter for her vanity.

Although she was still only a child, Maria nevertheless seemed aware of her extraordinarily delicate beauty that, even at such a tender age, set her apart from the rest of the earthy peasant children of the village.

Almost beside herself now that she heard the outer door to the kitchen swing open, Rosita hissed urgently, 'But only if you go now. Right this moment!'

Maria quickly scampered up, her long legs allowing her to run through the open door and out into the vegetable garden by the orchard just as Don Luis entered the kitchen, bringing with him the scent of Havana cigars and terror.

Briefly Maria heard his voice say in purring Spanish, 'Ah, there you are, my little harlot. I have been away too long from my house and my comforts, I think . . .'

Maria realized she'd left her doll behind, but she did not go back to the kitchen. She did not like Don Luis, although she always curtsied when he spoke to her, as her mother had told her to, and he sometimes gave her a sweet.

But she never felt safe around him, which was strange. All the other servants pinched her and tripped her up and called her horrid names. The Don never did such things, and yet she felt she would rather be with the spiteful village women who pulled her hair, than sit on the Don's lap as he sometimes insisted she did.

She sighed now, a heavy sigh that shook her little body, making Juan, the gardener's boy busy tending radishes, glance her way and grin. 'Hey, *chiquita*. Why the long face, hmm?' he asked her, his voice thick with an accent that was missing from the cultured, smooth voice of Don Luis.

'Nothing, Juan,' Maria lied, coming closer to watch him wield the hoe in the dusty earth.

Juan, only fourteen, watched her approach with appreciative, male eyes. Although not yet seven, Juan could tell this little bastard of the kitchen maid was going to turn out to be a stunning beauty. Her hair was raven black, but her skin, no doubt a legacy from her father, was not the dusky, olive tone of the rest of the villagers, but a smooth, camellia white. And not even the hot sun could rid her of this all-too-obvious evidence of her mother's disgrace. Her eyes were dark brown, but not black, and not so perfectly round like those of the other girls; rather they tilted mysteriously upwards at the ends, and were widely spaced either side of a slender nose. Her body, too, was going to stretch taller than the other girls, who tended to be squat and square, and she already moved with the grace of a gazelle.

Juan looked forward happily to the time, when she'd grown another eight years older or so, that he could have her. Oh, not to marry her, of course, he hastily and silently qualified with a shiver of repugnance that Maria noticed but didn't understand. His *madre* would have a fit if he brought home such a tainted bride, and he'd be bound to be ostracized by the rest of the village.

But as a mistress, she would be perfect. She would be glad to have him, too. In the village, where dogs were perpetually on the scrounge for food, the glass-less windows were always shuttered against her. Neither she nor her mother were allowed in the whitewashed church, and when Rosita Alvarez died, she would not be buried in hallowed ground.

No, the little Maria would be glad enough to have Juan Rodriguez in her bed, to protect and feed her.

'Why is *Madre* afraid of Don Luis, Juan?' Maria asked, her childishly high voice interrupting his pleasant thoughts, and she noticed immediately the way the candid brown eyes suddenly slewed nervously away.

Maria noticed many things. She was brighter than the other children, even though they went to school where the *padre* taught them the rudiments of reading and writing. They did not realize that Rosita taught her daughter privately, late at night, after stealing books from the Don's library, forcing the little girl to learn English as well. With a determination that bordered on obsession, Rosita taught her daughter not only the rudiments of a basic education, but much more.

As much as she was able, Rosita taught her daughter about the modern world, about cars, huge cities, people as different from the suspicious, hardened villagers as it was possible to be. Maria's eyes would widen as she listened to the stories of Monte Carlo, her imagination allowing her to see the palm trees, the lush gardens of hotels bigger than all of the village put together.

Maria hated the servants at the villa who called her *bastarda* and never let her play with their own precious sons and daughters. She cried herself to sleep every night, but the next day she stuck out her proud little chin at the villagers, who treated every stranger with suspicion and distrust, and threw stones at her whenever she walked down the streets.

But most of all, Maria hated Don Luis, who hurt her mother and looked at her, Maria, so strangely.

'Nobody likes the patron,' Juan whispered now, looking around to make sure that not even his whisper could be overheard. 'But you must never say so. Without the Don, we would all starve,' he repeated the words hammered into him by his own parents since he was old enough to understand. The Don was all-powerful, and without him they would all perish. The Don owned the land, so he owned everything. Including the villagers.

Maria scowled, the answer insulting her simplistic, childish logic. If people could live in cities as big as the mountains, then people could live without Don Luis, surely? Maria sighed and shrugged, and looked back at the villa. The Don would have left the kitchen by now, wouldn't he?

Saying *adios* to the only friend she had at the villa, she walked back on tiptoe, peering cautiously into the kitchen which was now empty. Good. She sneaked in and picked up her doll, then suddenly jumped, her eyes widening, her heart hammering at the sound of her mother's muffled scream.

It came from their room – a small, box-like room, with a single mattress on the floor, which they both shared, a crucifix on the wall, a single rickety chair and a chipped washstand.

Maria licked her lips nervously, but curiosity goaded her on. With typical childish craftiness, she took off her shoes and left them by the door, then walked silently down the cool passage, dodging the cook and one of the other maids to pause outside the door of their cell-like room.

Slowly and carefully, her little heart thumping, she turned the handle very slowly, barely a quarter of an inch at a time. She could hear muffled sounds coming from within; her mother's voice, begging for something, and Don Luis, laughing.

But she couldn't make out what her mother was asking for because she was sobbing so hard, the noise making Maria's own eyes fill with tears of sympathy and a nasty kind of creeping fear.

She pushed the door open a crack, her eyes widening at what she saw. Her mother was lying flat on her stomach on the mattress, her face buried in a pillow. She was stark naked, and kneeling above her, Don Luis was also naked. He was sweating like a pig, and his lips were pulled back over his teeth in a feral smile. But Maria's eyes barely glanced at his face, for she was too fascinated by the thing between his legs. It was long and thin and red, and he kept touching it. Then his hands parted Rosita's buttocks and the red thing was pushing down into her.

Rosita's body convulsed and she moaned in pain. Briefly Maria felt the urge to run into the room, to launch herself at the Don, to punch him and bite him and scratch him like she did the cook's daughters, who were always picking on her. Even though she was

317

always punished for fighting back, Maria felt her hands clench into fists.

The pig was hurting her mummy. She wanted to kill him. If she had Juan's knife now, she would kill him! She would, would, *would*!

But even as she put one foot forward, she suddenly felt a strange sense of shame steal over her, and could almost taste the disgust that her mother must be feeling. Without really knowing why, Maria was suddenly sure that her mother would hate it if she knew that Maria was there, that she had seen what was happening to her.

So instead of launching herself in fury at the Don, Maria silently closed the door on the ugly scene and ran out into the orchard, passing a startled Juan, who watched her hurtling body with interested eyes and then glanced back at the beautiful villa basking in the sun. All the servants knew how the Don used Maria Alvarez, of course. But what could she expect? Coming back to the village of her birth in disgrace, with a bastard child, after her father had worked so hard to work passage to France? What chance had any of them had to escape?

Juan shrugged and got back to his hoeing.

Deep in the orchard, Maria leant against an orange tree, her arms around the trunk, her face pressed against the rough bark. She cried savagely, great howls of anguish that shuddered her whole frame, making her throat ache and her eyes and nose run.

Young though she was, she knew she had witnessed a forbidden scene, one that she must never, ever repeat

318

to anyone. They would only blame her *madre*, anyway. Nobody ever blamed the Don for anything.

But she hated the Don more than ever now. The Don with his red thing and his ugly words, calling her mother a whore. She would never forget, or forgive. Never.

Never!

By one o'clock, the Don's five-course lunch was ready. Maria, dry-eyed now, went back to the kitchens where the cook had prepared the last tray, and was ordering her mother to scrub out the ovens. Maria hid until the cook had gone, her ample girth making her waddle like a duck, and then slowly walked into the room.

Rosita glanced up at her, and smiled wanly. 'Hello, baby. Are you hungry?'

Maria nodded, although she could not look at her mother without remembering what she had just seen, and feeling sick. Quickly Rosita cut open a crusty roll, adding to it a runny goat's cheese and sliced tomato. She handed it over, looking behind her to make sure no one was looking, and then cut a huge slice of banana cake and gave it to her daughter.

She was beyond caring that the cook would notice it missing and heap yet more abuse on her head.

'*Madre*, why have we to stay here?' Maria asked plaintively. Rosita corrected her grammar automatically, before shrugging. Once, a long time ago, she had promised herself that her job at the villa would only be until her baby was born, and then she would leave. Once, she had still believed she could make a decent

319

life for herself and her daughter. But no more. Spain was not Monte Carlo.

'We have nowhere else to go, Maria. In this life it is money that matters. Only money. Not goodness, or being right, or being clever. If you have money, you can do anything, be anything you like and no one will stop you.'

Her eyes became harder than ever, her mouth thinning into such a bitter line that her lips almost disappeared. Maria hung her head, shuffling in her chair and then taking a desultory bite out of her roll.

Her mother had told her all this before, but she didn't understand the vehemence and hatred that crept into Rosita's usually kind and gentle voice whenever she mentioned leaving.

'*Madre*,' she said slowly, thinking that now was as good a time as any to ask a question that had been burning in her brain ever since Anita de Avalonso had told her that her father was an Americano dog, '*Madre*, won't my *padre* help us to leave?'

Rosita glanced at her daughter sharply, her lips twisting into an ugly sneer, the hatred so obvious on her once-pretty face that Maria took a quick, instinctive step backwards. 'Your *padre*,' Rosita spat, 'was the reason we were left to rot in this stinking hole in the first place. He doesn't care whether we live or die. He . . .'

They heard the cook returning, Maria already backing out of the room as Rosita fell to her knees to ferociously scrub the oven, her hands red and chapped and soon beginning to bleed against the wire wool and wood.

Maria took her booty out into the orchard where she ate the banana cake, but left the roll. In her mind she linked Don Luis with her *padre*. Her *madre* hated them both the same and she would too.

She left the orchard after feeding her roll to the sparrows, and walked towards the tropical house, where Don Luis grew his orchids. Some were rare, so the cook said, and worth thousands of pesos.

Maria could hardly imagine such a thing. Who would pay so much just for flowers? You couldn't eat them.

The greenhouse was off limits, but today Maria didn't care. Walking to the glasshouse, she peered in, then gave a muffled scream as she came face to face with Don Luis, who had been bending down to water some seedlings.

Maria backed away slowly, not understanding, but instinctively shivering under the speculative gaze from the small black eyes as they ran over her body dressed in a faded pink smock.

As she turned and fled, she prayed piteously for somebody, anybody, to help her and her *madre* to escape the village. To escape the Don.

But deep inside, she already knew that nobody would.

CHAPTER 20

After three months, the scandal at Platt's was old news. Other events had taken place to fill in the countless hours of gossip, and clubs and restaurants now rang to hushed conversations on newer, juicier disasters. Only Toby and his long-suffering wife still suffered from the backlash. Sent to a family estate in the highlands of Scotland with strict instructions to lie low and keep their heads down, Toby's presence was now hardly missed in the London offices or the Kent mansion.

Wayne D'Arville pulled up to the front of the now-familiar mansion in his second-hand Bentley, old enough to look a classic, new enough to be within his budget, and cut the engine. Since Toby's disgrace, he had motored down to the house practically every other weekend, much to Beatrice's distress. Sir Mortimer's wife was in a quandary about the man she both desired and feared, and had decided today was the day to do something about it.

Looking out of the library window, Beatrice watched him alight, her eyes narrowing as two distinct emotions assailed her – anger and pleasure. She had never seen a man more masculinely pleasing. Neither had she met one who rivalled herself in cunning, deceit, manipulation and downright ruthlessness. At first the game had been fun, the barbed comments, the sexual punch whenever their eyes met, the rivalry of cat and mouse. But that had been in the beginning, when she had thought herself the cat. Now things had changed. Alfred Hawkes, her husband's right-hand man at Platt's, had retired, and in his place Wayne D'Arville had somehow managed to reign supreme.

The scandal with Toby couldn't have come at a worse time; as she watched Wayne jog lightly up the steps, she was convinced he was behind the whole thing. And Mortimer, the idiot, was playing right into his hands. Long into the night, the two of them would sit in his study talking about this marvellous new book of Wayne's Mortimer was so keen on. She could picture them clearly: Mortimer sniffing into his brandy and bemoaning his son while the Frenchman, damn him, comforted, wheedled, and oh-so-carefully ingratiated himself. It was enough to make Beatrice want to spit.

Now Wayne was such a regular visitor that Mortimer would comment on it late on a Friday night if he hadn't appeared. His talk was full of the Frenchman – the good job he had done on the French connection, the new European department he was setting up, the damned book that was going to change the face of current economic thinking.

Beatrice let the lace curtain swing back into place, her eyes thoughtful. She had to do something. Fast. Wayne bloody D'Arville was making himself too indispensable, setting himself up too well as the ideal surrogate son. With Toby and Amanda languishing already forgotten in Scotland, there was no one but herself to tackle the interloper. And tackle him she would. She opened the french windows, her eyes scanning the stables for John. She was feeling in the mood for the groom, admitting to herself that it was the Frenchman's arrival that had prompted the desire to light up her body. Catching the groom's eye, she nodded to the upper floors and John, who knew the route to her room via the servants' back stairs as well as he knew the back of his own hand, nodded and held up both hands, indicating ten minutes.

From the study Wayne watched the by-play, and smiled slowly.

'Hmm . . . good opening, I must admit,' Sir Mortimer said, making Wayne turn to look at him questioningly. The old man looked older than ever, his fingers gnarled and trembling as he turned over the pages of the manuscript. He had totally rewritten Veronica's manuscript, of course, making it sound more academically significant, and carefully writing, in his own hand, notes in the margin. He'd made sure it also sounded as if it had been written by a Frenchman. No one would now believe Veronica, if she should be foolish enough to try and tell anyone the book was really her work.

'I'm glad you think so,' he smiled modestly.

'Language needs a bit of tightening up, though,' Sir Mortimer said. 'Make it less . . . foreign-sounding. Hope you don't mind if I put a good editor onto it?'

Wayne almost laughed out loud. 'Of course not.'

Sir Mortimer grunted. 'Always knew you had a good head on your shoulders. Nothing of the prima donna about you either, praise be!'

'Look, I'll leave you in peace to make any notes on it you want. Then, after dinner, perhaps you can give me a good idea of which publisher to approach?'

'I'll do that. And if this – ' he tapped the manuscript '– has as much impact as I think it will, you might as well have a seat on the board while we're at it. Platt's could always use the kudos of having an economic genius at its board table.'

Wayne turned at the door, an astonished, then sheepishly gratified look on his face. 'I don't know what to say, Si – Mortimer. I certainly never expected it.'

'Well, well, it hasn't happened yet,' Sir Mortimer said gruffly, waving him away, but his old face was smiling and well pleased.

Wayne left, closing the door softly behind him, then beckoned the butler and told him to ask the groom, when he'd finished with his other duties, to give his car a wash and waxing. That done, he walked quickly up the stairs to the room where Lady Beatrice slept alone at nights. How she had managed to wangle the separate sleeping arrangements he wasn't sure, and didn't care. It was time he dealt with Lady Beatrice once and for all. He opened the door, his eyes making a quick inventory of the room. The deep maroon velvet curtains were drawn, throwing the room into semi-darkness. Lady Beatrice lay in the middle of a four-poster bed, completely naked, wearing only a black velvet sleeping mask. Wayne slowly smiled and walked across the Savonière carpet, past the Venetian mirrors, the Louis XIV bergères, the Sheraton tables and beautiful matching armchairs, his eyes fixed on the woman on the bed. She had kept herself well, he saw at once, for her body was still slender and appealing.

She sighed, twisting on the bed, her mouth curling up into a smile. 'Hurry, John,' she whispered, patting the bed with her hands invitingly, and Wayne glanced at the bed, then at the door behind him, and then smiled, reaching for the buttons of his Savile Row jacket.

Beatrice heard the rustle of clothes being removed and smiled like a cat, stretching luxuriously, her body pleasantly a-tingle and trembling in anticipation. Wayne, naked now, sat on the side of the bed and reached for her calf, trailing a hand across the smooth expanse of shaved skin. He stared at the black mask across her eyes, his hardening body already burning with desire. He knew damned well she would never have slept with him willingly, knowing that withholding her body was practically the only weapon she had at her disposal. She had no real power over Sir Mortimer since failing to produce another heir, and they both knew it.

'Hmm . . . yes,' Beatrice murmured, her legs falling open as he knelt either side of them, his free hand coming to her other calf, slowly moving to the back of her knees and then further up her thighs. She was wet already, her triangle of corn-coloured hair moist and waiting. Watching her closely, he slipped two fingers between the moist red lips and began to move them tantalizingly. Beatrice moaned and licked her lips, her heels digging into the hundred-year-old white satin quilt as she shuddered in brief climax.

Quickly, Wayne delved his tongue into her navel and then travelled higher. He kissed every part of her breasts in slowly decreasing circles until his lips fastened over her nipples. When her hands lifted to caress his back he caught them quickly and pinned them either side of her head, so that she could not feel the lack of hair on his back, or the size of his shoulders. John was smaller and certainly more hirsute than himself.

'Hurry, hurry,' she urged him, her voice thick with desire and Wayne smiled, opening her thighs with his own and pressing the tip of his penis again her. 'Yes, yes, hurry!' she moaned again, and Wayne grinned savagely.

'Anything you say, *chérie*,' he whispered in French. Beatrice stiffened, and behind the black velvet her eyes struggled to open. Her hands began to twist in his grip as she struggled to free herself.

'You French bast – ' she began, but then his lips were on hers and he plunged deep inside her. Beatrice felt her body convulse at the invasion. Never had she felt a penis that big inside her before. Beatrice moaned under his lips, in frustration at first and then in

327

helplessly growing passion. She could feel the muscles of her vagina stretching to accommodate him, could feel him pushing up, up, up all the way into her womb. She wanted to scream, to curse him, to kill him for doing this to her, but already a shattering climax was upon her. She bucked and shuddered, and still Wayne kept up the erotic rhythm, watching her sweating face only an inch away with savage satisfaction. But it was not enough. Quickly he yanked off the mask. He wanted her to see who was mounting her, so that she would never forget. Her eyes snapped open, spitting hate, fire and passion in equal proportions.

'I'll kill you for this,' she panted, and Wayne laughed, increasing the rhythm to even faster, deeper thrusts, watching her face contort helplessly as she once again began to climax. Quickly he released his seed into her, his collapsing weight pinioning her to the bed.

Beatrice dragged in deep gulps of air, ripples of pleasure still seeping through her body minutes later. His breath back to normal, Wayne quickly got off her and pulled on his clothes.

'Thank you, Lady Platt. That was very nice,' he said, his voice painstakingly English now, even down to the upper-crust accent.

Beatrice watched him walk to the door, and gave a yowl of hatred, picking up a delicate Meissen vase worth easily a thousand pounds, and lobbing it at his head. But Wayne was already out of the door, listening to the china shatter harmlessly on the other side. All he had to do now was wait until she was entertaining the real John again, and then find an excuse to send Sir Mortimer into the room. That would put paid to any poison she might try to whisper into the old man's ear about him. As he walked back to his room, he began to whistle.

In London, Veronica was dining with Sebastien and Sir Julius.

'Hmm, this is delicious,' Veronica complimented Sir Julius's cook on the beef Wellington, her mouth pleasantly full.

'Well, when I knew you were coming, I made enough for six,' Sir Julius teased her, watching her eyes widen at the insult, before she began to laugh, putting a hand to her mouth as she attempted to swallow the tender beef.

'You pig. Isn't he a pig, Sebastien?' Veronica appealed for support.

'He oinks when he walks,' Sebastien agreed, his face deadpan as he reached for his glass that held a fruity red Bordeaux. Opposite him, Veronica began to choke on her food.

Sir Julius slapped her back heartily, then turned to Sebastien. 'You see? I can't take her anywhere,' he complained. 'Even as a little girl no higher than my kneecap, she ate like a gannet. Tell her something interesting – it's the only thing that stops her wolfing down her food.'

Veronica threw her napkin at Sir Julius, who fielded it neatly with his fork.

Sebastien grinned. 'We certainly can't let her choke, can we? That's not at all gallant. Let me see . . . Well, there have been some interesting psychological experiments done recently.'

'Oh, goodie,' Veronica enthused, batting her eyelashes extravagantly. 'Do tell!'

Sebastien blinked under the battery of eyes suddenly watching him and grinned. 'Well, one done in America last year had to do with measuring conformity.' Veronica stared at him blankly. 'What happens is that a volunteer is put into a room with three or four stooges,' Sebastien explained.

'Stooges?' Veronica looked puzzled.

'Hmm, assistants of the doctors – not genuine guinea pigs. The tester gives the stooges and the genuine testee a simple sum – say 15 + 34 + 58. Something like that.'

'A hundred and seven,' Sir Julius said promptly.

'I'll take your word for it,' Sebastien grinned. 'Anyway, the plants each give the answer as 106, say. Now the testee may have got the right answer, and he probably tallied it up again, and still came up with the right answer. But more often than not, he'll say 106 as well.'

'So that he doesn't stand out in the crowd,' Veronica said, understanding the reasons why most people would do the same.

'Huh,' Sir Julius snorted. 'I'd say 107, no matter what.'

'You would,' Sebastien said fondly, then leaned back as the housekeeper brought in the plates and a fresh walnut and mandarin gâteau.

'I hate you,' Veronicia said, staring at the luscious dessert. 'You want me to get fat – admit it.'

'You don't want any, then?' Sir Julius asked, winking at Sebastien as he cut a fair-sized wedge and handed it over to him.

'Not fair!' Veronica wailed. 'I want a bigger piece.'

'Didn't I say she was gannet?' Sir Julius groaned, cutting the cake in half and lumping it onto a dish, setting it before his startled guest. Veronica shot Sir Julius a killer look, then reached for her spoon.

'How are things at Platt's nowadays?' Sebastien asked Veronica later, when they were all sitting on the settee, sipping coffee and trying to digest their huge meal.

'Oh, not so bad. Toby never really did much work anyway, and now that Wayne . . . well, he and Sir Mortimer are getting on really well. Wayne's set up a European department that's doing killer business. Everyone is going around with a big grin on their faces. Especially the accounts department. The initial expenditure Sir Mortimer forked out is already showing signs of paying off.'

'So, it's back to normal, then,' Sebastien said softly, then added very casually, 'Are you and Wayne still seeing each other?'

Veronica flushed, then smiled, her face so open and happy that Sebastien felt a trickle of unease drip down his spine and land in the pit of his stomach. Beside him, he felt Sir Julius stiffen.

'Hmm,' Veronica murmured, thinking of the nights they spent together making love. Her world couldn't be better. And yet . . . 'He's wonderful,' she said softly, and Sir Julius glanced at Seb.

For months now, ever since Sebastien had gone to Wayne's hotel room to ask him to let him help, he'd been seeing Wayne on a strictly casual basis.

Whenever he and Wayne met for lunch or the occasional trip to the theatre or musical concert, Sebastien would write up his meticulous and detailed notes, then pace about restlessly. But even though Sir Julius knew that he regarded Wayne as a patient, the old man was worried. Sebastien, of course, never discussed what the Frenchman's problems were, but Sir Julius was deeply concerned that Wayne D'Arville was much more seriously disturbed than Sebastien knew. For all his natural potential, Sebastien was still very young and inexperienced.

Now Sebastien said carefully to Veronica. 'Things are moving very fast between you two. That isn't always good for a man, you know.'

'Oh, but Wayne's different,' Veronica said quickly. *Too* quickly. Her defence of him lacked conviction, and Sir Julius could hear the stress in her voice. 'He's a wonderful man, he really is. I . . .' She met Sebastien's devastatingly kind sherry-coloured eyes, so lacking in judgement and so knowing, and faltered to a halt. 'Sometimes,' she said, her voice less strident, more afraid, 'I get the feeling . . .'

'Yes?'

'I don't know how to explain it. I get the feeling he isn't always . . . well . . . aware of things. It's as if life is just something he gets through . . . He seems to see things in black and white, with no shades of grey . . . Oh, hell, I can't seem to put it into words.'

'It's all right,' Sebastien said soothingly. 'I understand. And I think he sees a lot more black than white.' He wondered, in fact, if Wayne saw any white at all. From what little he'd said about his childhood, Sebastien knew that he suffered from maternal deprivation for a start. A long time ago, S. Levine had raised rats, half of which he petted and stroked daily, half of which he left totally alone. The petted ones opened their eyes sooner, showed less fear in strange situations and were less emotional. From such humble beginnings came the theory that maternal deprivation lead to 'affectionless psychopathy.' And the more he saw of Wayne, the more convinced he became that the Frenchman felt nothing for people, but saw them only in distinct categories, as either threats, victims or allies. And that, Sebastien knew, was only the beginning of his problems. Sebastien had watched him carefully, noting how deeply he felt insults, always reacting way over what could safely be termed 'normal' to emotional stimuli. But how could he explain any of this to Veronica, who was so in love with the man it scared him? Nevertheless, he felt the need to warn her. But before he could speak, she turned to look at him intently.

'You know that Wayne is always talking about you, don't you? I don't think he has any other friends. He never talks about them, anyway, and I've never seen him with anyone. Even when he left the Windsor and moved into his new flat, he never invited anyone over for a housewarming party.'

Sebastien nodded, well aware of how Wayne regarded him – as a cross between a father-confessor and a possible victim. After visiting him at the Windsor that night, Seb had been constantly aware of how dangerous the game was that he was playing with the Frenchman. It would have been all too easy for Wayne to have pigeon-holed him as yet another threat, and the fact that he hadn't – that over the months he had gradually allowed Sebastien to become his confidant and even his friend – was due solely to Sebastien's skill.

Of course, Wayne lied to him. He was sure that the family background Wayne had given him about the wine business back in France was totally false, but that, in itself, was irrelevant. Wayne, fascinated by Sebastien and their growing friendship, talked much more than he realized. Sebastien already knew that his mother had rarely shown him physical affection, that from an early age his parents had expected little from him, and there was strong evidence of psychopathic sibling rivalry. In particular, though, Sebastien was very worried about the way Wayne saw his father. Concerned with protecting Veronica and touched by her innocence and warmth, he found himself, very uncharacteristically, abandoning his usual tact. 'I think Wayne is deeply disturbed, Veronica,' he said gently. 'I think he is capable of doing almost anything . . .'

Veronica blinked, totally unprepared for Sebastien – kind, gentle Sebastien – to say something so cruel, and she reacted instinctively, quashing down a small voice in her brain that was already telling her that she was not surprised at all. 'That's not true,' she denied hotly. 'You just don't like Wayne, do you?' she accused them. 'Neither of you do. Did you think I was too blind to see that?'

Sebastien reached for her quickly. 'No, it's not that. You don't understand . . .'

Veronica stood up stiffly. 'I understand that Wayne needs you. I think he needs a friend, and I had hoped you'd be good for him. But if you're going to put him down behind his back . . .'

She was halfway to the door and openly crying, with Sebastien close behind her when Sir Julius held him back. 'Let her go,' he advised softly. 'She's not in the mood to listen. I'll ring her up tomorrow and talk to her. Tell her, for what it's worth, that I agree with your diagnosis.'

Outside, Veronica felt ashamed of herself for the scene she'd just created. She sniffled and hailed a taxi, knowing full well the real reason behind her emotionalism.

She was pregnant.

The following Monday she waited nervously for Wayne in his office, pushing Sebastien's warning to the back of her mind. She was sure Wayne would marry her, and was equally sure he would be thrilled about the baby. After all, Frenchmen were notorious for delighting in big families, weren't they?

335

Five minutes later Wayne opened the door to his new office, his eyes narrowing on her for a moment before he smiled. 'Hello.' He shrugged off his coat, glad in a way to find her there. He had to tell her about the book some time.

'Wayne, I have something to . . .' she began nervously, licked her lips, fidgeted, then said in one quick breath, 'I'm pregnant. Isn't that marvellous?'

Wayne stared at her for a moment, then slowly sat down, visibly shocked. This was no Spanish maid about to produce a bastard offspring, but a respectable English girl. The thought of a son and heir was appealing for one brief moment, but then he shook his head. He could produce an heir any time, that was obvious, but the book and the chance of making some real money, was different. He had to seize *that* opportunity now.

'I see,' he said, his cool, thoughtful words giving her a premonition of what was to come. Slowly she sank down onto a chair, and swallowed hard. 'I have something to tell you as well. I took your manuscript to Kent with me. I've spent the last few weeks totally rewriting it. Tidying it up. It was rather naïve in places.' He lifted his head and looked her straight in the eye. 'I told Sir Mortimer that I had written it.'

Veronica blinked. She'd been so concentrated on the baby, that at first she couldn't take in what he'd said. 'What did he think of it?'

'He loved it. I'm going to publish it. Under my name, of course,' he added the last words with quiet finality, watching as the excitement faded from her face. He'd been getting far too fond of Veronica Coltrane recently. This was the perfect opportunity of cutting her out of his life once and for all. The thought should have pleased him, but he was suddenly assailed by a feeling of bereft despair. He clenched his hands together tightly.

'Under your name. But . . . Wayne, you can't be serious. Having a book published is like a dream come true. I'm glad, really grateful to you for taking it to Sir Mortimer, but you can't really mean to publish it with your name on it!' Her voice trailed off, her mind refusing to believe what her heart already knew. 'You think it will sell better under a man's name, is that it? You're right of course. I could always use yours as a pseudonym.' She was babbling now, and knew it. But her heart was breaking, her head was whirling, and she needed something, some single sane thought, to hold on to. He couldn't be betraying her like this. *He just couldn't*!

Wayne needed to be angry with her now. Very angry. No doubt she wanted to believe the best of his motives, and it was touching in a way. She probably even thought he was going to marry her because of the child she was carrying. But how could she have been so careless as to get pregnant in the first place? Didn't she realize she was trying to ruin everything for him? She never loved him. If she did, she'd stand by him, damn her.

'I told Sir Mortimer I wrote it, and as far as he's concerned, that's that,' he said flatly, his hands clenching and unclenching on the desk. 'I've already signed the deal with the publishers. Quite simply, I need the royalties, Veronica. The flat and the car and living at the Windsor all those months left me practically broke.'

Veronica slowly shook her head, her face pale, her eyes bruised dark pools in her face. 'Wayne, you can't . . .' she began, but suddenly Sebastien's words came flitting back into her mind. *He's capable of anything* . . . And he was right.

Suddenly, her pain fled, and with it the numbness. In its place was a growing, healthy surge of anger.

'You won't get away with this,' she warned him, her voice hardening as she got up and slowly backed away. 'I won't let you.'

'Oh?' Wayne slowly raised an eyebrow, looking nonchalant and amused. 'And why not? Who knows you were even writing a book, *chérie*?' he asked, almost feeling sorry for her. It must be terrible to be so stupid. 'I already have the manuscript with my name on it' – he nodded towards the safe set in his new office wall – 'along with your pathetic original.'

Veronica's eyes followed the direction of his, and froze. Suddenly she realized how vulnerable she was. There was only one copy of her original manuscript, and surely Wayne would destroy that now? At the same time, she suddenly remembered that, as an executive officer, she too had keys to her own office safe. And all the safes might open with the same key. They were designed to store company papers safe from burglars, not to keep out other executives. If she came back tonight, and took back her manuscript

. . . Possession was nine-tenths of the law. She could take it to Sir Mortimer and explain. He'd listen to her. She'd worked at Platt's for over three years, after all.

'Sebastien was right about you,' she said at last, her voice full of contempt. She was also bitterly aware of the way he had suddenly come alive at the mention of the American's name. It hurt even now to realize that her love and her belief in him meant nothing.

'What did he say?' Wayne demanded sharply, always eager for news about Sebastien. Sebastien, the greatest danger in his life. Sebastien, his obsession.

But Veronica shook her head, too sick at heart to bear it another moment. She stumbled through the door, wounded to her soul. She felt sick and ill, but fought the urge to crawl into some dark corner and die. She would fight back. She was not her father's daughter for nothing.

Wayne leaned back in the chair and glanced at the safe. Slowly he shook his head in a mixture of pity and contempt. She was so transparent, she might as well have broadcast her thoughts aloud.

That night when she came back to sneak into his offices and open the safe, the police were waiting for her.

Two weeks later, Sebastien and Sir Julius left a top criminal lawyer's office, having secured his services for Veronica's defence. Sir Julius had tried to talk Sir Mortimer out of prosecuting, but the old man had been adamant.

It was the principle of the thing, he had insisted. The betrayal of trust. And to accuse Wayne of the things she had ... No, Sir Mortimer had been vindictive in his determination that Veronica Coltrane should stand trial.

Sebastien understood why, of course. Having been so disappointed in Toby, Sir Mortimer simply *couldn't* and *wouldn't* face the possibility that Wayne, too, might let him down. And, to be fair to him, the evidence in favour of Wayne, and against Veronica, was overwhelming.

Outside the lawyer's office, Sir Julius sighed deeply. 'Sir Mortimer needs his golden boy. If only Veronica had told somebody, *anybody*, about the book ...'

Sebastien sighed deeply. He had been allowed to visit Veronica only briefly. She had still been in shock then, uncommunicative, dull-voiced and without hope. She told him about the baby and the book in flat tones, as if she was reciting a recipe. She seemed unaware of the grimness of her surroundings, unaware of the possibility of being found guilty of attempted burglary, and serving time.

Listening to her, watching her, Sebastien felt more and more guilty. He should have foreseen it somehow. He should have followed her that night she'd left Sir Julius's flat, and explained ... But how? He could not break Wayne's trust. To do so would be totally irresponsible and against all his training. Besides, he was well aware that one false move on his part could send Wayne plummeting into insanity. And he had seen too many drowning souls at

St Edmunds to do that to anybody, regardless of what they had done.

He told the investigating officer about Veronica's claim to the book, but nobody believed Veronica's version. Literary experts called in by Platt's were unanimous in their verdict that the writer had been male, foreign – probably French – with a distinctly academic background, and nobody was going to go against Sir Mortimer's favourite.

'He didn't sound very optimistic,' Sir Julius said now as they left the offices of Jackson, Smythe and Cruickshank in Tate Square, thinking back over the interview with the sharp-eyed, no-nonsense barrister who had laid the cards straight on the table.

'No, he didn't,' Sebastien agreed, unaware that other eyes watched him as they got into Sir Julius's car and drove away. A few cars back in the line of traffic, Wayne followed them, feeling cold and empty.

He'd seen Sebastien only once since the arrest, and although he couldn't admit it, even to himself, he felt scared. The soft sherry-coloured eyes had been harder than he'd ever known them, the voice not quite so soothing. And now his hands trembled on the wheel.

'You think she's telling the truth, don't you?' Sir Julius said in the back of his Bentley as his driver stopped at a red light.

Sebastien nodded grimly. 'I'm sure of it.'

'What did Wayne say when you confronted him?'

Sebastien was silent for a long while, then said tiredly, 'He denied it, of course. What else?'

'And?'

341

He shook his head. 'I said I believed him, but that I'd also try and help Veronica at her trial.'

'And how did that go down?'

'Once he was reassured that I wasn't going to fight *him*, it didn't seem to matter to him whether I helped Veronica or not. It was amazing. I think he'd already forgotten her. She was dealt with. Gone. I think . . . I think he was becoming too involved with her. He's terrified of women, you know. Of falling in love. And Veronica came so close to . . . touching him.'

Sir Julius grunted angrily. 'Didn't he care about the possibility of his baby being born behind bars?'

'No,' Sebastien said tiredly. 'I tried to get him to see what he was doing, but I honestly don't think he's capable of seeing his own offspring as another human being. It's just an inconvenience to him and definitely Veronica's problem.'

At his home, Sir Julius opened the door, unaware that his voice carried across the quiet street to where another Bentley had just pulled in opposite.

'Sebastien, I want you to seriously consider the possibility of not seeing him any more. He's dangerous – I know he is.'

Wayne's eyes narrowed, his fingers on the wheel tightening. His eyes shot to Sebastien, scrambling to read his expression, relieved beyond measure to see him shake his head. 'You know I can't do that, Sir Julius,' Sebastien said quietly, and Wayne almost wept with relief.

If Sebastien had agreed to drop him back into the bleak black hole where Sebastien had first found him

. . . The thought made him shudder. He'd have to kill him. And to kill Sebastien would be like killing himself.

Inside the house, Sir Julius was still trying to convince Sebastien to stop seeing Wayne. 'It's Veronica who really needs you, not that bloody Frenchman.'

'You're wrong,' Sebastien said quietly. 'We've got the best lawyer for her, we'll testify for her, and we'll visit her as often as visiting times permit. We're doing all we can for Veronica, and in the end, even if the worst happens and she's found guilty, her jail sentence won't be too stiff and in the end she'll be free. She's strong and whole. But Wayne . . .' He shook his head, his expression pained. 'Wayne's been given a life sentence, and he's already served thirty years of it. And he's so brittle, one knock will shatter him like a cracked vase.'

'That doesn't change the fact that he set her up,' Sir Julius pointed out. For the first time in his life, he felt helpless, and he didn't like it.

'No, it doesn't,' Sebastien agreed quietly. 'And because of Veronica, I quite understand why it doesn't matter to you why he did it. But it matters to me. He's damaged, Julius. You, of all people, have to acknowledge that.' He took a sip of his drink and frowned down into his glass, unaware that his every expression was being monitored as Wayne watched them through the open window, eyes blazing dangerously as his acute hearing listened in to every word. 'He's in constant pain, I'm sure of that. He has a guilt complex, maybe more than one. Oh, hell . . . Let me worry about Wayne.' He sounded so dejected and weary, that Sir Julius immediately felt guilty for pushing him.

'All right, m'boy. If you really want to take him on . . .'

Sebastien smiled grimly. 'Julius, when I think of what he must have gone through to make him like he is I could . . . I could just damned well cry.'

Sir Julius nodded. His compassion was what made him so good. But, he thought with a shiver, it was his compassion that made him so damned vulnerable.

Outside, Wayne took deep, shaky breaths. For a moment he wanted to kill them both, but the thought of life without Sebastien made him want to cry out loud. Slowly he leaned back in his seat and shook his head. He could do nothing about Sebastien. Sebastien was the drug he needed to get through the day. His own human painkiller. He could only pray that Sebastien would never let him down. Because if he did . . .

CHAPTER 21

Hollywood

Oriel stepped carefully from the back of the chauffeur-driven limousine, gratefully taking the hand of her driver as he helped her out. She was seven months pregnant with twins, and she looked, even to her own eyes, huge.

She had chosen Chasen's over Ciro's to have lunch with Theresa Schwartz, whom she sometimes thought was the only true friend she had in this crazy town. Since *Invaders* had smashed previous box-office records, things had become so hectic, and she saw Kier so seldom, she often found herself wishing she were back in Oxford when she had Kier all to herself. Lovely Oxford, where there were no would-be agents, studio lackeys and the ever-present fans ready to mob them. And no would-be actresses on the make!

The sun bounced off the paving stones and onto her face as she left the car behind, and even with the dark glasses, the glare made her wince. She felt sweaty and sticky just from walking the short distance into the restaurant's cool interior, and found herself looking forward longingly to the birth, just for the sheer relief afterwards of not having to carry around so much weight.

'Ah, Madame Harcourt. We are delighted to see you again so soon.' André, the *maître d'*, was famous for using the royal 'we' and for being the greatest snob in all of Beverly Hills. And that was some feat. 'Your usual table, madame?'

Oriel shook her head, taking off her glasses and looking around. 'No, I'm meeting Mrs Schwartz . . . ah, there she is.' She nodded towards a very tall woman with short curly hair, who had just stood up and was waving frantically. André's eyes swivelled to the table in a definitely second-rate area, tucked into one corner on the side nearest the kitchen. He sniffed disdainfully. If only he'd known the dreadful English woman was dining with Oriel Harcourt, he would have placed her in the priority-seating section. Still, the damage was done now. 'Very good, madame,' he murmured, escorting her himself to the humble table.

Oriel, in her Christine Manning maternity dress of purest cotton, so pale a blue it was almost white, bit back the smile of amusement she felt at the great honour, and nodded to several people who turned to look at her. It was mid-week, and the place was quiet, boasting only a few television stars, the odd chat-show host, and an Italian producer who was causing a bit of a stir because of his wealth and honest-to-betsy title of 'Prince' something-or-other.

'Hi, Tease,' Oriel greeted Theresa with her pet

name, and collapsed into the chair André held out with more relief than grace. André magnanimously decided to let it pass. The woman after all was very *enceinte*, and could be excused the social gaffe. 'Boy, I tell you,' Oriel said, 'I feel like I'm carrying a sack of coal around with me!' She poured some iced mineral water that was kept on every table into a long fluted glass and gulped thirstily.

'Just think of all the muscles you're building up in your back and legs,' Tease advised her, her round amber-flecked eyes sympathetic.

Oriel was glad she had found Tease. The English wife of an American television producer, Tease had only recently come to Hollywood and was, consequently, still free from the Hollywood disease that she called the 'get-ahead syndrome.' It could, she had grumpily told Kier one morning (when he had not left for the studio at the usual crack of dawn), mean either the obvious, or refer to Tinseltown's distressing habit of taking scalps in order to push your own personal star higher into the ascendant. She had known women sell their best friend's secret to the gossip magazines in order to discredit her if they were up for the same bit-part in a movie. She had known agents lie, steal and cheat their own clients to accommodate one of the studios who were having casting difficulties. Nothing but nothing was sacred in a town where betrayal was a way of life.

'What are you having?' Tease asked, perusing the menu with a jaundiced eye. She was not totally convinced, yet, that she liked American food.

'Just a salad,' Oriel said quickly. 'I can't face much else these days.'

Tease joined her in a Caesar salad, followed by fresh fruit, Tease selecting a dry white wine to wash it down whilst Oriel stuck it out with water.

'So, how's the new film coming? Rumour has it that it's nearly in the can, as you lot say, and that Wiseman is walking around on razor blades.' Tease got characteristically straight to the point, her curiosity open and in no way the furtive, ugly kind that Oriel was getting used to.

She shrugged, speared a piece of pineapple, chewed and said thoughtfully, 'I think Kier has just begun the editing. You know him – he isn't happy with just directing – he's got to do it all. I'm surprised he doesn't work the cameras and set up the lights as well.'

Tease gave a sympathetic grunt. 'Men,' she said succinctly.

'I suppose you've been pumped over *Sacred Hearts* more than anyone else?'

Oriel smiled grimly. 'You got that right. Everyone's waiting to see what Kier will do with his own picture. He wanted to do a completely independent film first, just to see how hard it was. I ask you! But he was right. He's had much more creative freedom than he ever did on *Invaders*. He wrote the script for *Sacred Hearts*, he got Wiseman to back it, and he's rented out part of Finegal Studios in order to shoot it. I swear, the fuss that caused, you'd think this town had just been dealt an earthquake warning.'

Tease laughed, throwing back her head and making no effort to disguise the volume or pitch of her raucous hoot of derision. Several heads turned their way, failed to recognize Tease, lingered on Oriel, and then got back to their steaks and French chablis. 'I'll bet,' Tease said. 'An upstart director actually having the gall to lease a studio. I'll bet the bigwigs at Paramount and MGM had seven different kinds of fits all at once.'

'They did. They all tried to talk Jason Finegal out of it. Kier even thinks someone at Colombia tried to sue him. But Jase knew a good thing when he was on to it. When *Hearts* comes out, it'll have the Finegal trademark.'

'Do you think it's going to be a hit?' Tease asked, more thoughtful than avid. She had the English openness and not messing-about attitude that Oriel sorely missed in the town of tinsel, make-believe and perpetual gossip.

'I think everyone will go to see it just to see what all the fuss is about,' Oriel said, her lips ruefully twisted as she added, 'Rumours can have a great effect on the public pocket.'

'Hmm. Old Hedda's certainly straining a gasket. How did that blow about Grace Kelly affect Kier?'

'Not at all. He asked Grace if she wanted the part of Maureen, she said no. That was that. She's too busy with her Monaco prince anyway.'

'Hmm . . . Is it really as risqué as the gossip has it? Come on, give me all the hot and readies.'

'Hot and readies?' Oriel echoed, and began to grin. 'Don't ask me. Kier's the genius. Now that some of the

349

censorship's been lifted, I know he's taking advantages of it. But that's all. Besides, hints of sexy scenes never hurt a movie that I know of.'

'And he actually shot some of the footage in Ireland?'

'Yep.'

'That must have cost Wiseman a pretty penny.'

'Yep. He didn't like it none, but Kier won't be stopped. Honestly, Tease, you should see him. He's like a . . . a . . .'

'Steamroller?' Tease offered helpfully, and Oriel nodded, chasing a cherry around her dish with a silver-handled spoon.

'Ever since Mama stuck her oar in over *Invaders*, he's got this bee in his bonnet about being his own boss on *Hearts*. And that's only the beginning. He's got feelers out already about his next film, and this one's not even in the bag.'

Tease grunted, her long thin nose quivering at the vehemence with which she sniffed. 'It's this damned town. I tell you, it's nothing like I expected. To start with, LA airport is so damned pot-bellied-pig ugly.'

Oriel loved the way Tease talked. The second daughter of a minor baronet, her voice was that of a perfect lady, but her words were more like those of a weird and wonderful eccentric the English race habitually threw out. Tease was like a juicy bone tossed from a nation of dog-lovers.

Kier had been responsible for the two of them meeting over five months ago at a small party that was strictly non-prestigious. No 'A' list for Herman Schwartz. Just a barbecue, a small pool, a few real friends in informal clothes, and a wife who said exactly what she pleased. And from the moment Oriel had looked into the six-foot-tall woman's open amber eyes, she'd felt better. She had been lonely, high up in her Beverly Hills mansion whilst Kier worked all the hours God sent and then some. Her mother was an infrequent visitor now that the divorce from Daddy was going through, and she didn't count her hairdresser, manicurist, masseuse, chauffeur or pool man as bosom buddies. Occasionally Betty came over, with her slimmed-down figure and her racehorse owner fiancé, but when her old finishing school buddy and Oxford cohort left, her loneliness was only that much more acute.

Naturally, the unexpected news of her pregnancy had been greeted with total joy by the Harcourt household, even little Bethany becoming affected by the excitement in the air. Oriel had insisted that Bethany have a tutor at the age of two, and she'd been right. Already her daughter was reading anything and everything given to her, and had grasped the basics of mathematics.

'We've got a little genius here,' Kier would say, lifting his flaxen-haired, placid daughter onto his lap, watching her build toy houses with her building bricks, the structures square on all sides, with windows and doors catered for. But the pregnancy was hardly enough to keep Oriel occupied, nor was playing with Bethany, although their afternoons together were the highlight of her day.

Yes, there was no doubt about it, Tease had been a godsend.

The very first thing she'd ever said to her was, 'You look as bored as I feel. Is this rinky-dink town real?' From then on their friendship was inevitable, and they spent at least every other day together. 'No use going to that Rodeo Dive place,' Tease would dismiss Rodeo Drive with its glamorous boutiques and 'in' salons with a wave of her blunt-fingered hands. 'Nothing would fit me there. Don't you have any jumble sales in this place?'

Oriel was hard-pressed to find jumble sales, but they did tour flea-markets, venturing deep into LA where the Hollywood bug didn't bite quite so hard, and where Tease remarked that at least there were some 'real people' around.

'So, what did you expect from Hollywood?' Oriel asked now, watching her friend with a lifted eyebrow. Tease wasn't wearing makeup, but didn't consider that as particularly brave. She had confided to Oriel long ago that she hated putting 'gunge' on her face.

'I don't know. I suppose I expected it to be Bette Davis transferred to brick and stone. You know – elegance, glamour, quirky fun. I thought Katherine Hepburn would have given the place some sort of *savoir-faire.*'

'You poor, misguided, naïve child,' Oriel commiserated, fluttering her eyelashes and drawling in her best Scarlett O'Hara voice. 'And what did you find?'

Tease grimaced, her face contorting into a marvellous mask. 'Ugh. Where do I begin? First of all, everything's instant. Instant food, instant sex. Did I tell you when I called for a pool man, this six-foot-two gorgeous hunk arrived, expecting a roll in the hay?'

Oriel gagged on her mineral water. 'Oh dear.'

'Oh dear's right. I told him to get clearing the bloody pool before I tossed him in and held him under with the rake. Bloody cheek. Then there's the lack of class! I mean, I don't care being ignored as a humble wife of a humble producer, but the first thing everyone wanted to know was how much money we had! I mean, hell's bells and buckets of blood, in England we do our best to hide our wealth. Out here, if you don't have money, then . . .' She waved her square, mannish hand in the air, and sneered off to a speechless halt.

'Ain't Hollywood grand?' Oriel piped in, her voice as sweet as maple syrup, and again that loud, messy laugh of her friend's filled the restaurant.

'Thank cotton-picking bluebells I've got you, miss wife of the hot-shot tightrope-walking director. Otherwise I think I might just pack my bags and swan off back to Kent and let poor old Herman sink or swim on his own.'

'Yeah, sure,' Oriel said, knowing that wild horses wouldn't drag Tease away from her five-foot-seven, easygoing husband.

'You know, I had no idea when I married him that he was so rich? He said he inherited the family business from his father. How was I to know that it was a bloody great steelworks in Lucerne? Or that he'd get stars in his eyes and yearn for Hollywood? Men!' she snorted again, mashing an innocent grape against her dish.

'Don't worry,' Oriel said, deadpan, 'Herm's only worth a million or so. In this town, if you tell them you're down on your luck, they think you're down to your last million or so.'

Tease grunted, then ordered a second fruit salad from the scandalized André, who secretly complied whilst thinking dire thoughts about women with appetites like horses. 'I think if I hear one more person say "Have you heard the latest gossip this week?" I'll stop doing whatever it is I am doing, and scream my bloody head off. Honest, I mean it,' Tease threatened, attacking her replenished dish of fruit, picking out all the strawberries first.

'Well, just give me a bell and I'll come over and join you,' Oriel promised, pushing her plate away and ordering coffee. 'I get the feeling everyone's just waiting around to watch my marriage disintegrate.'

Tease looked at her shrewdly, then shook her head. 'You and Kier haven't got any worries there. Kier's a class act. If anyone's going to lure him away from you, it would have to be a *femme fatale* in Garbo's class. Nowadays there are so many young girls just giving it away, sex has become boring. 'Sides, your husband loves you. Even if he hasn't been around much just lately.'

'I know it,' Oriel said with smug satisfaction. 'And I don't mind him slogging away so hard. He's got a point to prove at the moment, that's all. Once he's done it, things will bottom out.'

'Then you can go around chanting "yah-yah yah-yah-yah" and thumb your noses up at all this lot,' Tease nodded her head vigorously, giving the general inhabitants of the restaurant a ferocious scowl.

Oriel grinned, then glanced at her watch. 'Look, I can't stay long. Bethany's having her first piano lesson today, and I want to be there.'

'Oh, don't mind me,' Tease said, chewing a pert raspberry. 'Just bugger off any time you like.' A passing waiter, who was the epitome of servile elegance, heard the remark, paused in mid-stride, then carried on, his face expressionless. Oriel watched him, laughing helplessly, and then struggled to her feet.

'Take it easy. And don't go taking any chances,' Tease warned, noticing the difficulty with which her friend moved. She really was *very* pregnant.

'Huh, tell that to Kier,' Oriel commented. 'He's already got the cinema's booked for the previews, and he has to have the film cut by Friday if he's gonna keep to the schedule.'

'Rather him than me,' Tease said with feeling, and watched her friend go with warm, speculative eyes. She hoped *Hearts* made it. If not, Kier Harcourt was washed up in this town. The old guard wouldn't allow a youngster who took so many risks and sailed so close to the wind to survive if the film fell flat. Then Tease wondered if perhaps being exiled from this ugly, backstabbing town would be such a bad thing after all.

★　★　★

Nearly a month later, *Sacred Hearts* opened at the Wilshire Palladium cinema. After Grace had turned him down, Kier had cast an unknown for Maureen, the heroine of his turn-of-the-century love story set in Ireland, choosing an Irish immigrant actress for the part. He'd had to fight the American union of actors all the way, and that was only the beginning of his troubles. It was common knowledge that the film had gone way over budget, and that Wiseman had consulted his lawyers. No papers had been served yet, but every critic, guest and paying member of the public knew, as they sat in their seats, that they would be if the film flopped.

Oriel, dressed in raw Singapore silk the colour of jade, had a weird feeling of *déjà vu* as they sat in their chairs, the lights dimming around them, Kier's hand holding hers tightly as the hum of conversation slowly died. But this time there was no Howard Shoesmith and no Clarissa Somerville. Her mother was too busy happily planning her wedding to Kyle.

The opening credits began to roll across a colour scene of Irish moors, purple with heather and yellow with gorse. There was a grey stormy sky, and no music played as the credits rolled. Instead, a howling wind and a lone curlew were the only sounds, together with the roaring of the sea as below the craggy cliffs, white water broke over the cruel black rocks. As 'Directed by Kier Harcourt' disappeared from the screen, the camera picked out a seagull, then the scene suddenly swept up into the air, the camera angle lifting high above the hills. The audience gasped.

For this shot, Kier had hired a glider (silence being a necessity) and the audience strained forward as a small figure, at first no more than a white speck between the rolling hills of gorse and heather came into view, the figure getting bigger and bigger as the camera swooped lower. Kier had used a crane for the next shot, swinging the camera around and around Colleen McGyver, the unknown actress he'd discovered working in a laundry in downtown LA. The shot almost made the audience feel giddy.

Maureen was dressed in a rough black woollen dress and wide white apron. A white cloth cap covered her tumble of auburn curls, but her face was flushed and pretty, her green eyes sparkling with the joy of life, and Oriel felt every man in the audience react to her screen presence.

She let loose a long, low breath, and turned to Kier, who was watching her. He looked tired, but already jubilant, and slowly she began to smile.

The story was a love story, beautiful in its simplicity. Maureen, a simple Irish girl who worked in a big Irish house, falls in love with an English soldier, stationed in Ireland during the peace talks. She has to weather the hatred of her own family as they slowly turn against her, whilst Aubrey, the English hero, played by the current flavour-of-the-month actor, faced the scorn of his own regiment and the disapproval of his commanding officer.

But *Sacred Hearts* did not run as the audience expected it to. There was no tragic ending, with Maureen dying, or Aubrey getting killed in the uprising of the Irish peasants. Nor was there a happy ending, with Maureen sailing off into the sunset with her lover. Throughout, the film firmly kept hold of gritty reality. There were no mock-ups of cosy Irish cottages, but interior shots of the real thing – dark, damp, small. Maureen hardly wore any makeup, relying on Colleen's own pure skin and natural beauty to give the illusion of a simple country lass. The love scenes were long, tender, but passionate, a chemical reaction between the two leading players so obvious that rumours about a real-life romance were now inevitable.

But it was the dialogue, more than anything else, that lifted the film from the usual run-of-the-mill Hollywood glamour into a classic. The accents were right, the mood was one of hopelessness, and the situation was fraught. The film had only one possible ending under the circumstances, with the two lovers being forced to bow to the peer pressure of their differing class and status, and agreeing to part. Aubrey went back home to his fiancée, the daughter of a rich farmer and landowner, and Maureen married her simple Irish crofter, who had stood by her through thick and thin.

When the lights went up the audience was forced reluctantly back to modern-day America, left with the feeling of a real tragedy – of two people, so right for each other, being forced apart by prejudice. Women were openly crying, and some of the men looked suspiciously bright-eyed, too. As the applause started, Kier and Oriel had one last quiet moment together, Kier raising her hand to his lips for a gentle kiss, before the circus began all over again.

Outside in the foyer, the pressmen had first pickings.

'Mr Harcourt, the audience reaction to this first showing of *Sacred Hearts* has been phenomenal.' A big radio-mike was stuck under Kier's nose, bearing the logo of a network TV station. 'How do you feel right at this moment?'

Kier looked the youngish, eager-faced reporter straight in the face and smiled grimly. 'Wonderful. And I'm sure Mr Wiseman also feels wonderful, even if his lawyers don't share the joyousness of this occasion.' Not after losing their prospects of a big fat fee, he thought, the same thought obviously shared by the others as a ripple of genuine laughter spread amongst the spectators. Next came the woman who was Hedda Hopper's main rival in the gossip stakes, nudging her way closer, ruthlessly elbowing out younger novices.

'Mr Harcourt, do you think the rest of the country's cinemas are going to take to heart *Sacred Hearts* as readily as our Hollywood audiences have done?'

Kier glanced across the sea of eager faces and found Oriel's loving, proud eyes. 'I hope so,' he said smoothly, 'but if not, I feel confident we'll have better luck at Cannes.'

The bombshell exploded quietly, then there was a great torrent of noise. Kier held up his hands, eventually the hubbub dying down. 'I've been invited to show my film at Cannes next week when the film festival opens. And yes, I'm definitely showing it there.'

'Mr Harcourt, that's quite an honour. And only your second film, too. Do you expect to win an award?' He couldn't see the face behind the voice, but it hardly mattered.

'Yes, I do.'

The answer, so candid and so without the usual show of false modesty, momentarily stunned the crowd. Kier took advantage of it to make an announcement of his own. 'My wife and I will be flying to Paris tomorrow for a short holiday before going on to Cannes. I think she deserves it, and I know I do.' He grinned feelingly into the television cameras, and all across the county feminine hearts melted at the handsome, boyish grin.

The interview went on for ten more minutes, then Kier wrapped it up. Oriel, in deference to her condition, had long since been escorted to the limo, and she looked up as Kier opened the door and climbed in amid a sea of flashlights. The car quickly moved away. Kier muttered a heartfelt 'Never again,' and closed his eyes, letting rip with a deep, heavy sigh.

'Thanks for letting me know about Paris in such good time,' she said drily, then patted her rounded stomach. 'We appreciate it no end.'

Kier grinned at her, then yanked off his bow tie. This year his tuxedo was white, and just one of a whole wardrobe of expensive clothes. This year, his face was tanned after three years of Hollywood sun. This year, there was nobody to take the limelight away from him. This year, there was Cannes.

He felt like singing and shouting and sleeping for a whole week. Oriel ankled off one sensible flat shoe and then slowly ran her foot up his calf. He looked across at her, his lids lazily half-closing as her toes nudged the bend in his knee and then moved even higher, her dress riding up her thighs and showing off her still exquisitely shaped, long legs. 'If you weren't so pregnant, Scarlett, I would come across there and make the chauffeur blush.'

'If I weren't pregnant, you wouldn't get the chance. I'd already be ravishing *you*!' Oriel shot back, her stockinged foot slipping higher up his white-clad thigh. 'But there's more than one way to skin a cat, as Tease told me only the other day.'

Wriggling into a more comfortable position and ignoring the niggling pain in her back, Oriel slipped her foot between his thighs, which obliging fell open, her big toe nudging the hardening bulge it found there, then slowly beginning to rub it. A red tide of colour began to ebb high on his cheekbones, and he leaned back, his breathing becoming ragged.

'If you don't stop,' he warned, 'my tux is going to be ruined.'

'So? It's not a rented one this time,' she said, grinning widely as he began to gnaw on his bottom lip.

'This is your revenge, isn't it?' he accused her, swallowing hard. 'You're getting back at me for all these weeks of neglect.'

'True,' Oriel said, wriggling her other foot between his thighs, her feet massaging him now in earnest. His hands dug into the cream leather of the upholstery, the material squeaking under his clawing fingers. He stared at her, his nostrils flaring as she stared openly back at him, her eyes dancing with mischief.

'Have you ever been to Paris?' he gritted, and Oriel shook her head, her eyes wide and innocent.

'Nope. I think I'll like it though.'

'Hmm, I hope so. It s-supposed to be quite r-r-romantic . . . oh, hell!' He shuddered briefly, letting out a long, harsh gasp, and then slowly opened his eyes. 'Just you wait until those kids are born,' he warned, his mouth soft and vulnerable now as he smiled, making Oriel laugh. 'I'll make you regret your feet were ever out of their shoes.'

Oriel raised one eyebrow, trying to look scared. 'Oh? Well now, I have four weeks until they are born. If I'm lucky you'll have gotten over your pique by then.'

They flew to Paris the next day, booking into the Paris Plaza where they occupied the whole of the top floor. They ate in their room, the flight having exhausted her, but strangely enough she couldn't sleep. A niggling pain in her back was beginning to make her wonder if coming to Paris had been such a good idea after all.

Nevertheless, the next morning she kept quiet and packed him off to a business lunch with some of Cannes' representatives, and settled down to a couple of boiled eggs and forty winks.

When Kier came back two hours later, an overwrought desk clerk pounced on him, telling him his wife had called down for an ambulance to take her to hospital just an hour ago. It was hard to tell which of the two men panicked more, but eventually the desk clerk managed to hail him a taxi and explain to the driver in rapid and excited French what was going on.

Inside the battered Citroën, Kier was rolled about in the back seat like a football as the driver careered around the streets of Paris, paying scant heed to the policemen directing traffic, and paying even less heed to his fellow drivers. Watching his pale passenger intently in his mirror, gesturing and gabbling on in unintelligible French, the taxi driver delivered the expectant father to the maternity hospital in record time. Kier stumbled out, surprised to still be alive, and handed over a huge bundle of money, not bothering to wait for change, and running up the stone steps with the Frenchman's words of good luck and congratulations still ringing in his ears.

Inside, he found a receptionist who spoke broken English, and after five nerve-wracking minutes was shown into a small, whitewashed room. He expected Oriel to still be in labour, and he skidded comically to a halt at the sight of his wife, pale and sweating, but beaming happily, with a tiny baby in each arm.

'That was quick,' Kier said the first thing that came into his head, and Oriel grinned, then shrugged.

'Well, why hang about, that's what I always say,' she shot back. The nurse, looking slightly puzzled, backed out, wondering sadly about the strange behaviour of Americans. Now a Frenchman presented with new-born twins would already be kissing his wife and babies, and blubbing his eyes out.

'Well, what have we got?' Kier asked after a short, emotional silence, walking nervously to the bed, as if afraid any of its three occupants might jump up and bite him.

'Well, this one –' Oriel nodded to her left '– is a boy. And this one is a girl.'

'One of each, then?' His mouth was dry as he stared at his babies, both dark-haired, both red and wrinkled and so tiny. 'Well, that's handy, at any rate. They're . . . a little early, aren't they?'

Oriel nodded. 'A little. But they're both all right. The doctors said so. We always have strong, healthy babies. You know that,' she said softly.

'We wouldn't dare do otherwise,' Kier swallowed hard, and sounded jaunty.

Oriel wasn't fooled for a minute. There were tears in her eyes as she said, 'I thought I'd name this one . . .' she nudged her son's forehead tenderly with her lips '. . . and leave you to do the honours for this one.'

'Sound's fair to me,' Kier agreed, taking a deep shaky breath. Then he reached down and gingerly picked up his minutes-old daughter, holding her in his hands as if he were holding the crown jewels.

He glanced down at Oriel, then back at the tiny scrap of life in his hands. 'What are you calling yours?' he asked suspiciously.

Oriel looked a little shamefaced for a moment and then blurted out defiantly, 'I'm calling him Paris – after the city where he was born. And because he's going to be handsome enough to win his own Helen of Troy one day.'

Kier grinned, then looked down at his daughter as Oriel countered softly, 'What are you calling yours?'

Kier watched as his daughter opened her deep brown eyes and frowned, punching a tiny fist in the air. 'Oh-oh,' he said softly. 'We're going to have trouble with this one.'

After a thoughtful few moments he said quietly, 'Gemma,' then looked down at his wife with eyes that were bright with tears.

'Why Gemma?' Oriel asked curiously, swallowing hard, feeling impossibly full.

Kier laughed. 'Because she's going to be a little gem, of course.'

Oriel smiled. 'Of course. And we're going to be so happy.'

Kier glanced at her, a little surprised. 'Did you ever doubt it?'

'What? That we'd be married, have three precious babies, and that you'd be the best and most famous director and filmmaker in Hollywood?' she asked.

Kier nodded.

Oriel threw her head back and laughed. 'I never doubted it for a second. Not from the moment I first set eyes on you, and you called me "Scarlett" in that damned sarcastic way of yours and tried to have me thrown out of your precious play.'

Kier bent and kissed his daughter's head. She responded by yowling at him angrily.

'I never had a single doubt either . . . Scarlett.'

CHAPTER 22

Veronica had not been granted bail after the preliminary hearing. Sir Mortimer's old school tie was one of the best, and although her father had been prepared to sell his house and everything else of value to free his daughter until the trial began, he was never given the opportunity. Sir Mortimer was dedicated in his defence of Wayne – his new, unofficial son and heir.

Consequently, Veronica arrived at the Nottinghamshire Open Prison for Women on a bleak November morning, with one small suitcase and the judge's words still echoing in her brain.

The prison itself was – oddly – pleasant enough, with tall brick buildings full of windows, square courtyards and car parks, but the place had an institutional flavour that curtained windows and flowerboxes couldn't quite dispel.

She was now four months' pregnant, still prone to morning sickness, and had at last shaken off the shock that had been a constant companion. But she was paying the price. Her palms sweated and her heart hammered as she was escorted to the Warden's office by a tall but pleasant-faced woman guard.

The Warden was a middle-aged woman with bobbed blonde hair, kind hazel eyes and a firm voice. The name plate on her office door proclaimed her to be Mrs H.A. Gardner, Governor. Veronica was shown quickly into the office, which was small, whitewashed and full of pot plants. Old green filing cabinets lined the walls, whilst under her feet a dusty beige carpet softened the sound of her footsteps. Faded curtains hung at the windows, keeping out a cold draught.

Mrs Gardner looked up from behind her desk, eyes quickly taking inventory of her latest acquisition. Her file recorded that Miss Coltrane was pregnant, but as yet the slender, dark-haired woman showed no signs of it. She had wide, nervous eyes, a pale pinched face, and looked too vulnerable to survive the prison system for long. Honor Gardner sighed, then stood up, forcing a smile onto her round, pleasant face. 'Miss Coltrane. Welcome to Nottingham.'

Veronica blinked, then quickly took the out-stretched hand and shook it. During the journey to this place, sitting in the back of a swaying security van, she had not quite known what to expect. Scenes from old movies kept coming back to haunt her, bringing nightmare visions of damp, dark cells and vicious, mentally unbalanced bullying guards. To come to this inconspicuous office and meet this totally normal woman of the same type that she saw in the shops and on the streets every day of her life, made Veronica feel oddly off-balance.

'Please, sit down, Veronica. I always like to have a little talk to all my new girls, especially the ones still awaiting trial.'

Veronica sank down gratefully onto a firmly padded wooden-backed chair, and took several deep, calming breaths.

'It is important that you understand the rules, of course,' Honor Gardner said, promptly reciting a bewildering list of statutory prison rules. 'If you can't remember them all, don't worry. There's a set of them taped up in every room.'

'I see.' They were the first words Veronica had spoken since arriving, and she was glad (but a little surprised) to find that her voice came out both firm and polite. Mrs Gardner nodded and, looking deeper into the brown eyes, was relieved to find a good deal of steady strength growing in them. Honor was glad. This beautiful young girl was going to need all the strength she had for some time to come.

'It's important that you understand the difference in status between yourself, who has yet to stand trial, and the prisoners here who are actually serving out their sentences. In effect, and to put it simply, you are not yet guilty of anything. That is to say, you are not a convicted criminal. As such, you have much more liberty than most of the women here.'

Veronica nodded grimly. She was not guilty, but she was still locked up. She glanced down at her hands twisting in her lap, and quickly unfolded them.

'Mrs Gardner – ' She took a deep breath, needing an answer to the question that had been gnawing at her innards like a cancer. 'Can you tell me . . . I was wondering . . . is it possible for me to . . . have my b-baby here, instead of . . . in a real prison?' She now had no doubts about Wayne's ruthlessness or his thoroughness. Although she told herself she was being stupidly pessimistic, in her heart, she didn't believe she would be found innocent at her trial.

'You're four months' pregnant?'

'Yes.'

'Then I think it's highly probable that the judge will order a delay until after the birth.'

'Oh, thank God for that.'

Honor opened her mouth and then quickly shut it again. It would serve no purpose to tell this naïve young girl that judges knew that juries, when faced with pregnant women, were often inclined to bring in a not-guilty verdict. In all probability, Sir Mortimer's prosecuting lawyer himself had already argued that Veronica should have her child before standing trial.

'Well, I think that's all for the moment,' Mrs Gardner stood up slowly. Veronica did the same and was led to the door. 'I think you'll find the food here is passable, and the prison doctor will monitor your pregnancy as closely and as professionally as any other doctor. Ah, Adams. Escort Miss Coltrane to room 113, will you?'

Adams, a tall, smiling-faced woman wearing a navy blue prison officer's uniform, nodded and then smiled at Veronica, making no attempt to take her arm or touch her in any way. Again Veronica felt foolish for her dire imaginings about the hellish quality of prison life. The woman called Adams even chattered amicably as they walked down stairs and corridors, where the sound of music came from individual rooms, and chattering voices made the place seem more like a girls' school than a prison. They passed several common rooms, where women sat reading, drinking coffee, playing board games and even watching television.

'Here we are.' Adams opened the door marked 113 on the second floor. A young girl, no more than sixteen, with long lanky yellow hair, a spotty face and big blue eyes, lay sprawled on a single bed. She sat up as Veronica walked in and put her case by the second bed, which had two folded sheets and several blankets placed on the mattress, ready to be made up.

'Well, I'll leave you to unpack. Lunch is from twelve-thirty to one-fifteen, in the dining-room. Mary will show you around.' Adams nodded and left. Veronica looked at the younger girl awkwardly, and then wandered to the window. It overlooked a lawn and flower border where two women were busy weeding.

'That's the gardening brigade,' Mary said, coming to stand beside her, her voice childishly clear and shockingly young. 'Old Gardy – that's the big chief – works out gardening details every month. We do all the other stuff as well. Laundry, ironing, even cooking. She says it saves money on auxiliary staff, stops us getting idle and gives us exercise too. Ginny Fuller, she's the dumps mole, says that the rest of the open prison lot might follow suit. She's a real trendsetter, is Gardy.'

'Dump mole?'

'Hmm – this place is the dump and Ginny works in the office – she can type, you see, so she sneaks a look at the memos and stuff. She's a whizz at reading upside down.'

'Oh.' Veronica felt an absurd desire to laugh. This morning she had left the holding cells convinced she was heading for some Dickensian horror prison, and here she was, in a pleasant if small room, listening to a little cockney sparrow of a girl chatter on about dump moles.

''Ere, why don't you unpack your stuff? This half of the wardrobe's yours, and I moved my clobber from the bottom two drawers.' She pointed to the cheap but functional furniture against one wall and then bounced back onto her bed, watching with avid, all-seeing eyes as Veronica unpacked her few clothes. Shaking out the maternity dresses, she saw the girl's eyes widen, and prepared herself for what was coming.

'You up the duff, then?'

'Yes.' She managed a shaky smile. Now that she was here, she felt a deep and dangerous desire to just collapse on her unmade bed and cry her eyes out.

'Married? Nah, course you ain't. Some man got you in here, didn't he? What did he do? Leave some stolen stuff in your flat?'

Veronica shook her head, but didn't volunteer any information. She couldn't even think about Wayne without a whole wave of emotional bitterness bogging her down. And somewhere in the back of her mind she already knew that she was going to have to fight it fiercely if she didn't want to end up a nervous, twisted wreck of a human being.

Mary shrugged, not concerned about her new room-mate's lack of chatter. She'd start talking soon enough. They always did, once they settled down.

'I'm in here for shoplifting,' she said, studying her nails, which were chewed to the quick. 'I knew this little girl in the home where I used to live who was wild about this new pop music stuff. Crazy about it. So I thought I'd get her this little radio from Woolies and, well . . . got nicked. Damned store detectives. Thought I knew all about their tricks. Oh well, just goes to show – ' the girl gave a huge grin that bore no grudge '– you live and learn. That's what my old matron used to say.'

Veronica nodded grimly. 'You certainly do.'

'When you go to court, then?'

'I'm not sure. After the baby's born, I hope.'

'Sure to,' Mary nodded sagely, knowing the ropes as well as Honor Gardner. 'Who you got to take care of the sprog?'

'My father. He said he'll hire a nurse.'

'Oh, la-de-dah,' Mary said, then jumped up as a bell buzzed loudly outside, making Veronica jump. 'Don't panic,' Mary grinned, tucking a wad of greasy hair behind one ear. 'The dump ain't on fire. That's the dinner bell. Coming?'

Veronica wasn't hungry but she forced herself to go, following her chirpy little room-mate down a flight of stairs and into a long, warm room where about eight or nine long tables were set with plastic place mats and cutlery.

Veronica found herself running the gauntlet of what seemed like a thousand eyes, and unknowingly moved closer to her room-mate as they stood in line by a long, heated counter, where other women, with equally interested eyes, dished out steak and kidney pudding and string beans.

'Don't worry about this lot,' Mary said loudly, looking around her. 'You won't be new for long, then they won't even know you're here.'

And strangely, out of all the words that had been thrown at her over the past month, from solicitors, doctors, prison guards, Sebastien Teale, friends and fellow inmates, those simple words were the ones that would stick with her for the rest of her life. She found them echoing in her head, even as she sat down on a long bench, and picked at her food. 'You won't be new for long, then they won't even know you're here.' Did Wayne, she wondered, prodding her cooling dinner, even remember that she was here?

Wayne didn't. Sir Mortimer Platt had had a slight stroke, throwing everyone into a panic, and especially Beatrice, who had been the cause of it. Sir Mortimer had found his wife in bed with his groom, and had not been amused. He had done nothing so dramatic as collapse on the spot, but instead had walked stiff-legged from the room where a red-faced John was yanking on his trousers, and made his way into the study. A pain in his chest and a trembling weakness in his left arm had been enough to make Wayne send for his doctor, who had then diagnosed the stroke.

Sir Mortimer, pale-faced and looking a hundred years old, now met the Frenchman's concerned blue eyes over the head of the doctor knelt by his chair, a stethoscope placed on Sir Mortimer's withered chest, and said grimly, 'See to that damned woman, will you, dear boy?' His words were slurred and tired, and he looked more defeated than disgusted.

Wayne dealt with Beatrice with extreme pleasure. She was forced to bear the humiliation of watching the servants pack all her bags, and then as added insult to injury, had to ask their chauffeur to drive her to the train station in his own little jalopy, as Wayne gave orders for all the family cars to be locked in the garage.

The stroke, the doctor told them, was a mild one, but should be treated as a warning. 'You must take things easy, Sir Mortimer. No more working, no more board meetings. And no more cigars. You can keep off the brandy, too.'

Sir Mortimer grunted, then listened gravely to the doctor as he prescribed pills and gentle exercise. Wayne saw the man out, then went back to the study. The first thing Sir Mortimer said was, 'Pass me the cigar box, will you, m'boy?'

Wayne smiled and handed over the teak and mahogany box. Sir Mortimer's hands shook as he took one out but his gnarled fingers were unable to hold it. Wayne gently took it from him, clipped and lighted it, then handed it back.

'Thanks,' he said, taking a deep puff, then glancing at Wayne sharply. 'You knew about Beatrice, didn't you?' he said, both his words and knowing eyes catching Wayne by surprise. 'Don't look so surprised,' Sir Mortimer grunted, his voice almost fond. 'I don't think there's much your eyes miss. Not like mine.'

'I'm sorry,' Wayne said. 'I suppose I should have told you.'

Sir Mortimer shrugged his painfully thin shoulders, took a deep drag on his cigar, coughed, and then licked his lips. Wordlessly, Wayne poured him a brandy. 'I don't suppose I shall last long now,' Sir Mortimer mused meditatively. 'People don't, you know, when the old ticker starts to grumble.'

Wayne opened his mouth, then closed it again. He had to be careful now. Very careful. One wrong word, one missed opportunity, and he could ruin it all. 'That's not always the case,' he said, helping himself to a brandy, suddenly needing it. He had not expected to feel so . . . sorry, for the old man. Briefly the absurd thought flashed across his brain with deep and soul-cutting clarity. *If only you had been my father.* Then, when he found the old man staring at him, he went white, looking genuinely appalled when he realized he'd blurted it out loud.

'Forget I said that,' Wayne said quickly, then took a deep gulp of brandy, the liquid settling his stomach. 'I think your damned stroke has addled MY brain.'

Sir Mortimer laughed, then stared into the fire in the grate. 'What am I going to do about Platt's,

Wayne?' he asked, the question more rhetorical than anything else, but it gave Wayne the opening he needed.

'Leave it to your grandchildren, of course,' he said, sounding surprised that there could be any doubt.

Mortimer snorted. 'How the hell do I do that? The kids have years yet until they come of age. And Toby will have control, to all intents and purposes. He'll run the company into the ground.'

'So appoint a trustee.'

'You?' Sir Mortimer said, looking at him closely.

Wayne jerked his eyes away from his own contemplation of the fire and looked at the old man with rounded eyes. 'Me? Why me? Surely you have people on the board you can trust? The very first thing that struck me about Platt's was its family atmosphere. I kept bumping into people who told me what the firm was like before the war. The first one, I mean!'

Sir Mortimer smiled crookedly. 'Just my point. They're all as old as I am. I need a younger man to take over the reins. The world is changing . . . yes, it is,' Sir Mortimer said quickly as Wayne looked about to argue. 'I'm glad I shan't live to see it, but if Platt's is to survive, then I need a man not only with a feeling for tradition, but also able to compete in a modern market. A man like you. You know your book is due out in four months, don't you?'

Wayne shook his head. 'As soon as that?'

'Yes. And it'll sell. That's what we need at Platt's. A man who knows how to rewrite economic history. A man who knows how money works. That's what Platt's needs.'

'Toby is bound to contest the will if you indicate me as trustee. I'm a foreigner, don't forget, and still relatively new to the firm. And I don't see how an English court would ever go against him.' Wayne watched him closely as he spoke, and only when he saw the anger gradually creep over Sir Mortimer's face did he relax. If there was one thing the old man hated, it was being defied. He had become used to having his own way, and the thought of his last wishes being denied when he was dead and unable to do anything about it made him as mad as Wayne had guessed and hoped it would.

'I won't have my will contested,' Sir Mortimer said, banging his hand against the armrest of his chair like a spoiled, petulant child. 'I won't!'

'There might be a way . . .' Wayne began gingerly, then shook his head. 'No. No, that isn't – '

'What?' Sir Mortimer said testily. 'Out with it, boy.'

'Well . . . I was thinking . . . you could write out a new will, naming me as the sole beneficiary. Then I go to Toby, telling him what you've done, and asking him to come down and make you change your mind. After all, I'm rich enough in my own right, I don't need your money. Naturally, Toby will come down to talk you out of it.'

Sir Mortimer snorted. 'You bet your sweet Fanny Adams he will. That boy was always a sponger . . .'

'Yes, but the point is, if he thinks he's going to lose everything, then you're in a good bargaining position.

You can tell him you'll change the will so that the grandchildren inherit, but only on condition that I'm appointed as the trustee. Surely your lawyers can draft an agreement whereby he agrees not to contest the will under such circumstances? That way I can steer the firm and teach the children how to run Platt's at the same time.'

He held his breath, letting it out only when the old man began to grin mischievously. Sir Mortimer began to cackle as he thought about the look on his son's face when he heard the shattering news. 'I'll do it! And while I'm at it, I'll cut Beatrice off without a damned penny to boot.' He began to cackle again, and Wayne sat back in his chair, laughing with him, swirling the Napoleon brandy in his glass, his eyes glittering like blue diamonds.

Two months later Sir Mortimer's will was rewritten, in the presence of three lawyers, and signed by five servants as witnesses. Sir Mortimer lay in bed, the victim of a second stroke that had paralyzed the whole of his left side. The side of his mouth was pulled down, as was his left eyelid, but he'd had several doctors confirm that his mind was still as sound as a bell.

As he signed the document, he looked up at Wayne dressed sombrely in black, then gave a gasping chuckle as Wayne winked at him. It was a good idea of Wayne's to have the doctors sign official documents testifying to his solid state of mind. He was quite right in saying that his weasel of a son might contest the will on the grounds of mental incompetency.

As the servants left with the two other lawyers, Wayne watched Sir Mortimer's official solicitor fold away the will. Graham Hines had been Sir Mortimer's oldest and closest friend for years. He was a small man, bent and white-haired, but button-sharp. He glanced now at the tall Frenchman, then at his friend, lying like a pitiful wreck of his former self in the big four-poster bed. 'Mortimer, are you sure you want to do this? I know Toby made a damned mess of things a while back, but . . .'

'Don't w-worry, Graham. I know ex-exactly what I'm doing.'

Graham didn't like it. And he most definitely didn't like the giant of a Frenchman, who was never far away. He had tried and failed on numerous occasions to get Sir Mortimer on his own, but always the Frenchman showed up. Every instinct in his body cried out against this new will, but Mortimer was adamant. So Graham decided to try a different tack. Turning to Wayne, he folded the airtight legal will into his briefcase, and said coldly, 'I hear from friends at Platt's that there are big changes afoot?'

Wayne, who knew just what the interfering old bastard was up to, nodded and smiled easily. 'Yes, I suppose most people would think so. Having a new man in Mortimer's office sent cold shivers running down many spines. Mine included!' Both men turned as a dry wheezy laugh came from the direction of the bed.

'Get that will f-filed or r-registered, or whatever you do with it,' Sir Mortimer said, nodding to the briefcase. 'I know I've been r-riding you to have it w-watertight, and I've seen the suspicious looks you've been c-casting our f-friend over there.' Sir Mortimer nodded to Wayne, who smiled briefly. 'B-but we have our r-reasons. Don't we, boy?'

Wayne nodded again, and said softly, 'Yes, we do.'

Graham, who knew when he was beaten, left a few minutes later, a very unhappy man. 'W-well, that's part "A" over with,' Sir Mortimer said, closing his eyes for a few moments as a fresh wave of weakness washed over him. Lord, he felt tired.

'Don't worry about part "B",' Wayne reassured him. 'I've already booked a ticket to Edinburgh from Paddington. I'm travelling up to see Toby this weekend. I shall be suitably distressed and assure him that I had no idea what you were up to.'

Sir Mortimer wheezed another laugh. 'G-good. Oh – by the way, I have s-something for you. Here, in the top drawer.' He pointed awkwardly to his bedside nightstand. Wayne walked over and opened the drawer. Lying inside was a hardback book in pale blue. On the cover was a picture of a stock-market, in full, hectic swing. The title read, *Computers and the New Economic Wave* by Wayne D'Arville.

'The first copy. The rest come out in two months' time. I thought you might like the very first one off the presses,' the dry-as-old-leaves voice informed him.

Wayne picked up the book, stroked it, turned the first page and read the first line that Veronica had written. Then he turned away from the man lying as still as death on the bed and walked to the window, so that he couldn't see the satisfied smile on his face.

On the same day that the first of the books were finally delivered to the London shops, Veronica Coltrane gave birth to a six-pounds, ten-ounce baby boy in the Nottinghamshire prison. She named her son Travis, and a few hours after the birth she had her first visitor.

Geoffrey Coltrane held his grandson in his hands, unspeakably relieved that his hair at least was dark, like that of his mother. Yet the baby face was already square-shaped and lantern-jawed, with his father's nose and mouth, but Geoffrey cuddled him lovingly as he looked down at his pale, hollow-eyed daughter, feeling totally useless and frustrated.

'Daddy, I want you to tell . . . *him* . . . that the baby died. That it was stillborn. He won't bother to check up on it. He won't care.' Her voice was dull and lifeless.

Geoffrey nodded. He wasn't sure that he could face the Frenchman without killing him, though, so he compromised. 'I'll telephone him.'

Veronica nodded, then turned her head away as Geoffrey went to hand the baby back. 'No,' she cried wretchedly. 'I daren't hold him.' Her eyes screwed tightly closed. 'Tell the nurse to take him away now.'

'But, darling, he needs to be fed.'

'I can't. Don't you understand, I can't?' she screamed. 'How can I nurse him, feed him and then . . . watch him being taken away? For pity's sake, do it now.'

The nurse, who'd been sitting in one corner, rose at the first sign of Veronica's distress and took the baby wordlessly from Geoffrey, who then walked out of his daughter's room on unsteady legs, unable to bear the sound of her sobs.

'When can I collect him?' he asked the nurse when they were safely outside, watching the chubby, sympathetic woman cradle the sleeping baby in her arms.

'In about ten days, when we're sure there are no problems with the little mite.'

'Ten days?' Geoffrey echoed. 'My daughter's trial starts in ten days.'

True to his word, Geoffrey called the Frenchman at his office the next day. He kept it very brief, saying only that Veronica had given birth to a dead baby boy, before hanging up. Wayne put down the phone and slowly leaned back in a black leather swivel armchair. For a few moments he stared blindly around his big new office, with all the wealth and power it represented, his eyes finally resting on the copper nameplate that sat squarely on his desk: 'Wayne D'Arville – President.'

He reached for a decanter of expensive brandy and poured a full glass. His limbs felt stiff and disjointed, and he emptied the glass in one swift toss of his head. So – the baby was dead. It was probably just as well. And since he could do nothing about it, why think about it? It was not as if he didn't have other things to do.

He left the office quickly and drove his brand new Italian Ferrari downtown, toward his new Belgravia apartment. He wound the window down, letting the cold air attack his face. He didn't fancy going back to the office that afternoon, so instead he headed north to Charrington Private Hospital, where Sir Mortimer had lain for the past four days in the intensive care unit.

Wayne hated the smell of the antiseptic and the uniform whiteness of the rooms, but he visited the old man every day, giving the nursing staff strict instructions that no one else was to visit. And since he was paying the medical bills, no one argued with him. Sir Mortimer's last and certainly fatal attack had arrived just in time. The old man had begun to ask questions about Toby's conspicuous and continuing absence. Why wasn't the boy battering down the doors, demanding that the will be torn up, like they'd always planned?

Of course, Wayne had never informed Toby Mortimer about the new will. He had never intended to.

As he stood at the foot of the old man's bed, machines bleeping out the frail heartbeat, the old man's eyes fluttered open. A question that he could no longer physically speak was obvious in his eyes.

Wayne smiled gently. 'Don't worry, Sir Mortimer.' He took the old man's hand and squeezed it. 'It's all sorted out. It's all gone just as I planned . . .'

Three days later, Sir Mortimer Platt died, his last will and testament unaltered. The day after that, Veronica Coltrane was found guilty of attempted burglary, and sentenced to three years' imprisonment. As she had served six months already, and as it was a first offence, the judge abbreviated the sentence to one year, with the possibility of parole in six months.

Wayne hadn't needed to testify, and now only her father sat in the public gallery to hear her being sentenced.

As she felt a firm hand on her elbow pulling her away from the dock and down into the holding cells, she wondered where Wayne was, and what he was doing. Then she made a vow.

She would never think about Wayne again. She would never allow even the image of him to cross her mind.

She gave a final glance around the courtroom, and smiled bravely at Sebastien Teale, who'd always been there for her, helping her through it. He'd been her lifeline after Travis was born, getting her to talk, helping her to control and understand the guilt she felt at being forced to abandon her baby, listening sympathetically as she offloaded much of her anger and bitterness. His kindness, constancy and warmth had been the only things that had kept her sane the last few months.

But she knew that she wouldn't be seeing Sebastien again. Sebastien was on a crusade to help Wayne. And Wayne . . . Wayne no longer existed.

As she climbed into the police van and heard the cell door slam shut behind her, she told herself that, in future, she wouldn't trust anybody.

She would certainly never trust a man again as long as she lived.

EPILOGUE

One fine day in June, so many things were happening to so many people.

In Atlanta, the 'ageing belle' Clarissa married her 'dirty, low-born' Kyle, amid much gossip and malicious glee. All her friends cattily agreed that the marriage wouldn't last.

Only Clarissa and Kyle knew better.

As she walked down the aisle with her young, handsome new husband on her arm, Clarissa smiled at her daughter, her daughter's husband, and their beautiful children.

Life was wonderful.

A few miles away, Duncan Somerville was reading a startling new document on Wolfgang Mueller, the hated commandant of a notorious concentration camp.

If the evidence was true, then Wolfgang Mueller was alive and well and living in Monte Carlo.

And Duncan Somerville was going to get him.

Life was exciting.

* * *

In Spain, a little girl played in a garden, careful to keep out of sight of the Don, who was beginning to watch her with such an odd, greedy look in his eyes.

But Maria had a secret. She and her mother were running away to a big city that very night.

And much later, when she was all grown up, Maria was going to find her papa and make him pay for what he had done to them. Maria Alvarez would not cry herself to sleep at night like her poor mama did.

Maria had a mission in life now.

Life was full of possibilities.

In Holloway prison, Veronica Coltrane began to plan her future. She didn't want to stay in England – she wanted to take her son and just go. Somewhere, anywhere, far away from where she was.

Life was dark.

In his little semi-detached home in Reading, Geoffrey Coltrane nursed his grandson. Travis was a handsome, loving baby, and Geoff had no doubts that he'd grow to be a fine young man. A man that any father would be proud to call his own . . .

Walking down the ward of a psychiatric hospital, Sebastien Teale thought about his patient, Wayne D'Arville. As he soothed a woman convinced she was being eaten alive by snails, only he knew how close Wayne was to a similar insanity.

And he also knew, deep in his heart, that it was up to him to save him.

Life was frightening.

In his office, Wayne D'Arville signed some papers that would make him another eighty-eight thousand pounds. His personal fortune was now massive. His career as head of Platt's was unchallenged.

He was riding high.

But that only meant he had a long way to fall . . .

We hope you've enjoyed DESTINIES. You'll no doubt be delighted to hear that Maxine Barry has written a sequel to this novel. On the following pages, you'll find a short introduction to RESOLUTIONS, part two of the 'All His Prey' duet, which we know will leave you wanting to read on!

Look out for RESOLUTIONS next month . . .

New York, 1975

Veronica Coltrane paused outside Ohrbach's to study the fascinating window display before hurrying on to Nibbits Department Store on 68th and West.

It was a freezing January morning, and as she waited by the crossing for the 'Walk' sign, she blew into her hands to try and warm them, without much success. She had thought her native home of England could get cold in winter, but this was something new to her.

Not that she regretted coming to America, of course. No, she would never, *never* do that. She had needed to escape from England and all the hideous memories it still held for her with a passion that she knew was not healthy. The knowledge of her own vulnerability, even after all this time, still lurked uneasily at the back of her mind.

She still had so much to do. And keeping her job was, at the moment, top of her list. Travis was relying on her. But on a cold January morning, her responsibilities seemed to lie all the more heavily on her shoulders. It sometimes felt as if she was carrying around her own personal iceberg. It made life so cold.

And so many people, kind, good people, had had to pull so many strings just to get her an entry visa and work permit to this new country, that she simply had to make a go of it. She couldn't let them down. Not when they'd taken such chances for her. And she knew, more than anyone, how hard it must have been for them to trust her. Considering . . .

The 'Walk' sign flashed on, and her unhappy thoughts were suddenly jostled out of her. She found herself abruptly carried along by a human tide as thirty people made a mad dash across the road. Once on the other side, she glanced at her inexpensive watch and gave a sigh of relief. She was not as late as she'd thought.

But Travis had had to start a new school today, and he'd been scared, poor mite. She'd had to walk him to school and introduce him to his teachers, just to settle him down. His English accent would no doubt let him in for a lot of teasing by his fellow classmates, but Veronica was confident he'd soon make friends. Her son was a very open and lovable five-year-old, even if she did say so herself. Everyone said he was full of fun and a charming kind of cheek. Everybody commented on his warm and generous nature.

If only they'd known who his father was . . .

THE EXCITING NEW NAME
IN WOMEN'S FICTION!

PLEASE HELP ME TO HELP YOU!

Dear *Scarlet* Reader,

As Editor of *Scarlet* Books I want to make sure that the
books I offer you every month are up to the high standards
Scarlet readers expect. And to do that I need to know a
little more about you and your reading likes and dislikes. So
please spare a few minutes to fill in the short questionnaire
on the following pages and send it to me. I'll send *you* a
surprise gift as a thank you!*

Looking forward to hearing from you,

Sally Cooper

Editor-in-Chief, *Scarlet*

*Offer applies only in the UK, only one offer per household.

Note: further offers which might be of interest may be sent to you by other,
carefully selected, companies. If you do not want to receive them, please write to
Robinson Publishing Ltd, 7 Kensington Church Court, London W8 4SP, UK.

QUESTIONNAIRE

Please tick the appropriate boxes to indicate your answers

1 Where did you get this Scarlet title?
Bought in supermarket ☐
Bought at my local bookstore ☐ Bought at chain bookstore ☐
Bought at book exchange or used bookstore ☐
Borrowed from a friend ☐
Other (please indicate) _____

2 Did you enjoy reading it?
A lot ☐   A little ☐   Not at all ☐

3 What did you particularly like about this book?
Believable characters ☐   Easy to read ☐
Good value for money ☐   Enjoyable locations ☐
Interesting story ☐   Modern setting ☐
Other _____

4 What did you particularly dislike about this book?
_____

5 Would you buy another Scarlet book?
Yes ☐   No ☐

6 What other kinds of book do you enjoy reading?
Horror ☐   Puzzle books ☐   Historical fiction ☐
General fiction ☐   Crime/Detective ☐   Cookery ☐
Other (please indicate) _____

7 Which magazines do you enjoy reading?
1. _____
2. _____
3. _____

And now a little about you –
8 How old are you?
Under 25 ☐   25–34 ☐   35–44 ☐
45–54 ☐   55–64 ☐   over 65 ☐

cont.

9 What is your marital status?
   Single ☐   Married/living with partner ☐
   Widowed ☐   Separated/divorced ☐

10 What is your current occupation?
   Employed full-time ☐   Employed part-time ☐
   Student ☐   Housewife full-time ☐
   Unemployed ☐   Retired ☐

11 Do you have children? If so, how many and how old are they?
   _____
   _____

12 What is your annual household income?
   under $15,000 ☐   or   £10,000   ☐
   $15–25,000   ☐   or   £10–20,000   ☐
   $25–35,000   ☐   or   £20–30,000   ☐
   $35–50,000   ☐   or   £30–40,000   ☐
   over $50,000 ☐   or   over £40,000 ☐

Miss/Mrs/Ms _____
Address _____
   _____
   _____

Thank you for completing this questionnaire. Now tear it out – put
it in an envelope and send it before 31 July 1997 to:

Sally Cooper, Editor-in-Chief

USA/Can. address   *UK address/No stamp required*
SCARLET c/o London Bridge   SCARLET
85 River Rock Drive   FREEPOST LON 3335
Suite 202   LONDON W8 4BR
Buffalo   *Please use block capitals for*
NY 14207   *address*
USA

DESTI/1/97

Scarlet titles coming next month:

AN IMPROPER PROPOSAL   Tiffany Bond
Carrie has always had a love/hate relationship with Alexis.
Now only Alexis can help her. But the repayment he
demands horrifies her: Alexis *will* help, if Carrie bears his
child and then disappears from his life . . .

THE MARRIAGE PLAN   Judy Jackson
After an unhappy marriage, Becky Hanson doesn't trust
men. Ryan McLeod has managed to avoid wedding bells so
far. Now he's been left with a child to care for and he needs
help! What he hasn't counted on is falling in love with his
hired help . . . Becky.

RESOLUTIONS   Maxine Barry
The story of 'All His Prey', which began last month with
Destinies, concludes now with an exciting story of mystery,
passion and revenge: Maria has been ignored for too many
years and now she's had enough. But love, so they say, is
stronger than vengeance, and Maria has just fallen in love . . .

A DARK AND DANGEROUS MAN   Patricia Wilson
We are delighted to announce the best-selling author
Patricia Wilson's first *Scarlet* novel:
Kathryn Holden is as anti-men as Jake Trelawny is against
women. But maybe she is right to avoid Jake – after all, isn't
this dark and dangerous man responsible for the disappearance of his first wife?